YURI VYNNYCHUK

THE FANTASTIC WORLDS OF YURI VYNNYCHUK

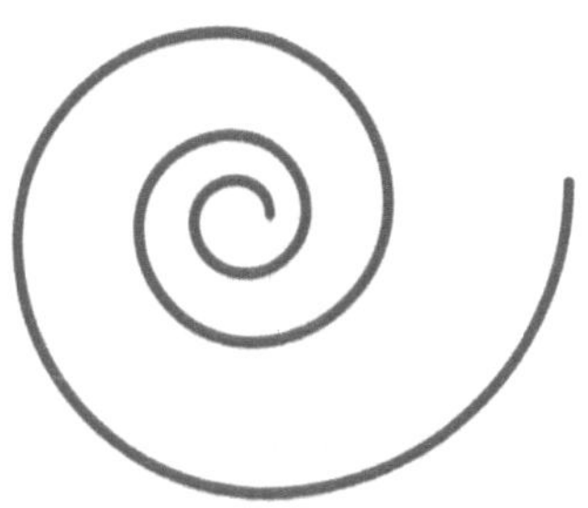

GLAGOSLAV PUBLICATIONS

THE FANTASTIC WORLDS
OF YURI VYNNYCHUK

by Yuri Vynnychuk

Translated from Ukrainian by Michael M. Naydan
(with one translation by Askold Melnyczuk
and two translations by Mark Andryczyk)

Translations edited by Oksana Tatsyak

Publishers: Maxim Hodak and Max Mendor

© 2016, Yuriy P. Vynnychuk
© 2016, Glagoslav Publications, United Kingdom

Glagoslav Publications Ltd
88-90 Hatton Garden
EC1N 8PN London
United Kingdom

www.glagoslav.com

ISBN: 978-1-911414-06-3

A catalogue record for this book is available from the British Library

YURI VYNNYCHUK

THE FANTASTIC WORLDS OF YURI VYNNYCHUK

ACKNOWLEDGMENTS

The story *An Embroidered World* first appeared in the summer 1996 issue of *Kenyon Review* and the story *Max and Me* has been published previously in the journal *Glas* as well as in the Zephyr Press anthology *From Three Worlds: New Ukrainian Writing* (1996, 2nd ed. 1997). Many thanks to Ed Hogan and Elizabeth Searle for their editorial comments on the translation of "Max and Me" that appeared in the Zephyr Press anthology. Askold Melnyczuk's translation of "The Island of Ziz" was published first in the journal *Index on Censorship*. Excerpts of *Tango of Death* appeared in issue #7 of Trafika Europe. The stories "Pea Soup" and "The Flowerbed in the Kilim" appeared in *The Contemporary Ukrainian Literature Series: An Anthology*, Vol. I with Academic Studies Press.

I want to express my gratitude to Susan Blanset Harkavy for inputting many of the texts of my translations for that volume onto disk and for repairing my English prose on the way. Thanks also to Irena Makaryk for her editorial suggestions that served to improve my introduction to the earlier paperback edition of translations of Vynnychuk under the title *The Windows of Time Frozen and Other Stories* (Klasyka Publishers, 2000). I am especially grateful for Fulbright Fellowships to Lviv, Ukraine in the spring of 1999 and the spring of 2007 that allowed me to hone my colloquial Ukrainian and to interact considerably with Yuri Vynnychuk on his home territory. I have the greatest debt of thanks to Oksana Tatsyak of the University of Toronto for doing such a meticulous job in checking the translations against the originals of the original edition. Thanks also to Svitlana Bednazh for her very helpful suggestions on the more recent translations that I made for this expanded edition. And special thanks to Olha Tytarenko for editing my translations of *Tango of Death*. I, of course, accept any responsibility for any errors or omissions.

INTRODUCTION:
THE ARTFUL WIZARD OF VYNNYKY

Ukrainian writer Yuri Vynnychuk was born in 1952 in Stanislav, Ukraine. The city is now called Ivano-Frankivsk (affectionately known as "Frankivsk" by the locals) and has been an epicenter of literary and artistic activity. A bevy of exciting new post-modernist writers have emerged there including Vynnychuk's postmodernist contemporaries Yuri Andrukhovych, Yuri Izdryk and Taras Prokhasko as well as extremely talented younger writers such as Tanya Malyarchuk. Ukrainian literati have dubbed this concentration of prominent writers from this provincial city "The Stanislav Phenomenon." While Vynnychuk does not belong anymore geographically to The Stanislav Phenomenon nor to Post-Modernism, his roots still lie there — a little less that three hours away by dingy, dusty, sluggish train. The charming city of Lviv with its cobblestone streets and endless cafes on every corner has been his physical and spiritual home for a considerable amount of time.

Vynnychuk's father was a doctor for the anti-Stalinist and anti-Nazi Ukrainian partisans during World War II, and his uncle on his mother's side Yuri Sapiha was killed by the Soviet secret police (the Cheka) in 1941.Vynnychuk was named in memory of his murdered uncle. In 1973 Vynnychuk completed the Stanislav Pedagogical Institute where he developed the reputation of a prankster. At that time he became involved in student publications as well as in the literary underground. In 1974 the KGB conducted a search of his house but found no materials that would have incriminated him in the eyes of the Soviet regime. In order to avoid inevitable arrest, he moved to the larger city of Lviv, where he hid at apartments of several friends, constantly covering his tracks from the all-seeing eye of the KGB.

Until 1980 Vynnychuk was blacklisted and not allowed to publish in official sources. Till then he published works under the names of various other writers and ghost wrote books on occasion. He eked out a living from the honoraria from his various pseudonymous publications, a practice which, by habit and by design, he continues to this day. During the 1980s he held readings of his works in the apartments of friends and became well-known for his satiric poetry and stories about a mythical country called Arcanumia – a land where the streets and, in fact, everything, are paved with fecal matter. Any association of Arcanumia with the Soviet Union or Soviet Ukraine, of course, would have been purely coincidental. "The Island of Ziz" ("Ostriv Ziz") is the best-known story from this cycle. From 1980 on, Vynnychuk was allowed to publish his articles and translations in the Ukrainian periodical press. He made a number of enemies among the Soviet literary establishment for his merciless attacks against hack writers. In 1987 Vynnychuk was instrumental in the creation of a stage singing and performance group "Ne zhurys'!" (Don't Worry!), which rose to swift popularity in Ukraine. After a tour to Canada and the United States in 1989, Vynnychuk decided to leave the group and devote his time exclusively to literature. Off and on he has continued to participate in concerts with the group. Under Mikhail Gorbachev's *perestroika-perebudova* and subsequent Ukrainian independence, Vynnychuk emerged from the underground (always keeping one foot there even to this very day) to occupy an eminent place in the new Ukrainian literature. His collection of fantastic stories *The Flashing Beacon* (Spalakh; 1990) sold out almost immediately. He also published a collection of poetry *Reflections* (Vidobrazhennia; 1990) and compiled and edited two anthologies of Ukrainian fantastic stories from the 19th century. His pulp fiction novellas *Maidens of the Night* (Divy nochi, 1992) and *Harem Life* (Zhytiie haremnoie, 1996) enjoyed extraordinary popularity. His love of storytelling and of his adopted hometown is combined in several volumes – *Legends of Lviv* (Lehendy Lvova, 1999), *Pubs of Lviv* (Knaipy Lvova, 2000), and *Mysteries of Lviv Coffee* (Taiemytsi lvivskoi kavy, 2001). His fantasy novel *Malva Landa* (the heroine's name) appeared in 2000 and a collection of fantastic tales *Windows of Time Frozen* (Vikna zastyhloho chasu) in 2001. And his novel *Spring Games in Autumn Gardens* (Vesniani ihry v osinnikh sadakh, 2005) won the 2005 BBC Ukrainian Book of the Year Award. His collection of autobiographical works, *Pears a la Crepe* (Hrushi v tisti, 2010) also was nominated for the BBC Prize. His book *Tango of Death* won the 2012 BBC Book of the Year Award for Ukraine and has been garnering an extraordinary amount of attention both in Ukraine and in European circles, particularly in German and Czech translations. His most recent novel *The Apothecary* appeared in 2015. Its plot harkens back to seventeenth-century Venice and Lviv.

Vynnychuk currently resides on the periphery of the Ukrainian literary establishment, appropriately just outside the city limits of Lviv in the village of Vynnyky (yes, the name of his home bears a close resemblance to his last name). He worked as a columnist and culture commentator for the anti-establishment newspaper *Postup* and *Post-Postup* for much of the 1990s, inviting the rancor and lawsuits of crusty scions of both neo-Soviet fascism and neo-nationalistic excesses and falsehoods, the warmed over leftovers from Soviet times. He became editor-in-chief of the new *Postup* newspaper in 1996, which he continues to edit. Just as virtually every satirist, Vynnychuk is a seeker of justice and truth with no holds barred. When I published my first book of translations of his works, the elusive Vynnychuk used to be difficult to locate in Lviv, but you could find him on occasion at the Femida Cafe on Sichovi Striltsi Street, devouring the exquisite potato pancakes (*deruny*) and sipping home-grown Ukrainian beer in a room that the local Kulturtragers in Lviv called "The Vynnychuk Room." Alas, that café closed down several years ago to become a store, and you're more likely now to find him at the café in the Dziga Art Gallery in the oldest part of the city at the end of Armenian Street.

Vynnychuk is an astoundingly versatile writer and an accomplished storyteller. He is a chameleon who can adapt his narrative voice in a variety of ways. He is also, perhaps, the most politically incorrect writer writing in Ukraine today. He often intends to shock with his prose. He has the uncanny ability to take his reader to the very edge of decorum (in the story "Max and Me" and in his novel *Malva Landa* in particular), but not go beyond it. He creates anticipation, and then artfully frustrates it (largely to the reader's relief). I have divided his writings in this edition into eight categories, which, under no circumstances, comprise all of his narrative voices. I added four of those categories in this expanded edition of translations of his works:

excerpts from his more recent novels. His lyrical and philosophical stories such as "An Embroidered World" and "The Windows of Time Frozen" are exquisitely crafted pieces that capture a fecund poeticality that is both powerful and sublime. "An Embroidered World" captures the essence of the tragedies of Ukrainian history and the Ukrainian soul in the style of magical realism with bittersweet charm. Vynnychuk, the psychologist of the human condition, appears in stories like "The Clover Was So Fragrant" and "The Doorbell," in which the characters, who go to great lengths not to be their brother's keeper, either implode or explode into their own psychological hells. Vynnychuk's fantastic tales and alternate worlds function both as social commentaries and satires; they as well often provide outstanding examples of the application of the literary device defined by Viktor Shklovsky as "making strange" (*ostranenie*), of jolting the expectations presented by the status quo of the narrative by creating strikingly new perceptions of reality. We find that at work in stories such as "Pea Soup" and "The Flowerbed on the Kilim." Many of Vynnychuk's stories suggest that some extraterrestrial force that imposed its will on humankind could only have created something as vile as communism. The snails of "The Snail Chronicles," for example, take over humans by means of thought control.

Vynnychuk is also the contemporary Ukrainian master of black humor and the grotesque — much in the tradition of his countryman Mykola Hohol (aka Nikolai Gogol). Pictures of Vynnychuk from the late 1970s and 1980s even have a marked resemblance to Hohol. This, of course, may only be pure coincidence... The story "Max and Me" (a smirking *Hy-hy-hy* in its original Ukrainian title) is a wicked satire of Ukrainian life circa 1979 through the depiction of a hillbilly-like family of demented cannibal capitalists. The mythical town of Ratburg (*Shchurohrad*) is another manifestation of an allegory of the old Soviet ways. Vynnychuk's works in the area of pulp fiction erotica are emblems of the newfound literary freedom in post-independence Ukraine, which allows for the publication of previously taboo subjects. His novel *Malva Landa* resides on the edge of taboo and black humor with an opening scene that stops short of realized pedophilia, but lyrically and artfully draws the reader into its chimerical world.

Vynnychuk and the characterization of women in his works from his unapologetically male perspective begs for extensive literary analysis, and often is the locus of his novel *Spring Games in Autumn Gardens* as well as his autobiographical novel *Pears a la Crepe*.

Vynnychuk is an incontrovertible iconoclast and satirist, who much like the Ancient Greek penner of iambiks Archilochus in ancient times, pummeled Soviet icons and demons with words that killed. Now he lambastes forces of stasis and backwardness, whatever their political or national ilk. A subtle and a sometimes less than subtle bitter irony infuses much of Vynnychuk's writing. But all writers are products of their times and experiences, and a writer must write what he sees. These stories represent some of the best short works and excerpts of novels of one of the finest prose stylists and storytellers from the first generation of Ukrainian writers able to write in complete freedom. It is my hope that these translations will provide an inkling of the author's narrative range and polyphony of voices, giving the reader glimpses into his many fantastic worlds of the imagination.

Michael M. Naydan
Woskob Family Professor of Ukrainian Studies
The Pennsylvania State University

I. THE LYRICAL AND PHILOSOPHICAL IMAGINATION

In as much as I remember my grandmother, she was always sewing. At first I didn't really pay attention to her embroidering, but one time I noticed that an old cherry tree that was growing near our window had disappeared after Granny had embroidered it. The cherry tree had completely dried up, and Gramps had planned on chopping it down several times, but for some reason his hands never seemed to get to it. But now it's gone.

At that time I began to try and recall whether anything else had disappeared, and suddenly I remembered that quite recently a wild dog that had settled in the wilderness had disappeared. He wailed so awfully during the night that the entire neighborhood cursed him to the depths of hell. No one could let their children out for a walk without someone keeping an eye on them, for fear that the dog was mad. It's true that several times they tried to hunt him down, but he was either too quick or just as crafty, because all those attempts at hunting him down were in vain. But no one had heard him for a week already. Of course, he could have died or moved on somewhere else. I began to look through Granny's embroideries, and on one of the pillows I saw him. Now I understood it all—everything that Granny embroiders disappears at that very moment she embroiders it. It's not for nothing that there weren't any people on a single one of her embroideries. The sun wasn't there; there wasn't anything you'd feel sorry about losing.

I couldn't restrain myself from sharing my discovery with my grandfather. Gramps just shrugged his shoulders:

"Well, what of it? I know about it."

"Then why didn't you ever tell me?"

"For some reason I always forgot. It's either this or that... I forgot."

Then he looked at me with a warm smile and added:

"Well, good. I'll tell you about what I know. Though this was right after the war... At that time they began arresting us. Every night they were carting off people to Siberia. The prisons were packed. They threw the young guys to the front without any preparation, without any training. They threw them right at the tanks... Lord, how many of them were killed then!... You know the way they looked at the Galicians… The tiniest suspicion—and you're in the slammer. That's how they arrested me. Your grandmother couldn't find herself a place to escape from her grief. She walked back and forth, poor thing, near that prison and tried to look through everything to see if she could see me. Then once out of sorrow she was sitting down in the evening and began to embroider. She just couldn't get the prison out of her head, so she began to embroider it. She embroidered the walls around it; she embroidered the guard and the dogs. She finished her sewing late in the middle of the night... And what kind of sleep does a prisoner get? We lie there and think about everything, we just can't sleep. When once, suddenly, it was as though everything had come tumbling down. There were no walls in the room, no stone walls of the prison—we were lying in the middle of the yard. Hey, we figured this out right away, and we made our way wherever we could... Well, the prison disappeared, but those who put us in prison were left. We had to hide. The younger ones went to the woods, and the older ones—to the villages and farms. At that time we moved to the village. That's the way it was... Although, we didn't figure out things with Granny right away, that this was a result of her embroidering. We thought all different kinds of things. And the people spoke about the Mother of God, that she showed pity on us and saved us from captivity with a miracle... But after some time, I looked— and our cat was gone. 'Hannusya,' I says, 'where did our Matsko get to, why can't we see him?' When I take a look—the embroidery is lying on the table and right there is our embroidered Matsko. Then something dawned in my head. 'Well,' I says, 'Hannusya, wouldn't it be nice if you'd unstitch the embroidery?' And she answers: 'What kind of silly thoughts are these? I was going blind working so hard over it, and you want to destroy it for me?' Yoy, ya think I'm gonna listen to the old bat? I took the scissors and unstitched it. Just as I plucked out the last thread I heard a meow, meow! And it's our Matsko! And he had a hungry look, because just as he saw the milk in the dish, he threw himself at it. 'Well,' I say, 'Hannusya, now you have some real *tsores*! It turns out if you don't embroider something, then it doesn't disappear.' And she doesn't believe it, she laughs at me. Well, good... Then I ask her to embroider the scarecrow that juts out in our garden. And what do you guess? She embroiders the scarecrow, looks, and it's gone in the blink of an eyelash! Well, now she's finally convinced of her ability. From that time on she took care not to embroider anything she'd regret losing or that might inadvertently disappear."

As it turned out later, not only Gramps and I had found out about this, but also the neighbors... umm... about my grandmother's curse. Everybody began to speculate whether they'd done anything nasty to Hannusya, what if she gets angry and embroiders it? And Dzunyo suddenly remembered that he once swiped a rooster from our chicken house. Gathering courage, he came to Granny and confessed it, and likewise brought a goose in place of that rooster. He apologized in such a manner that Granny charitably forgave him his sin. It's true that on the next day Mrs. Buslyk ran over for that goose because it was her goose, but junior's mood didn't worsen at all because of it. It was most interesting that once again that very same goose returned to us. Mrs. Buslyk brought it and said:

"Mrs. Hannusya, take the goose, but I really beg you, if you'd be so kind as to also embroider my husband. Cause that drunk will drive me to the grave."

And one has to say that Granny held that drunks were the worst and without even thinking it over much, took to embroidering Mr. Buslyk. And what do you guess? Not a week had passed and Mrs. Buslyk ran up with another goose to ask that her husband be returned.

"Why are you bugging me?" Granny gestured that she go away.

But my mother felt the goose and said:

"What kind of filling should I give it? Buckwheat groats or rice?"

"I'm not going to undo the embroidery," Granny replied harshly.

"With rice and mushrooms," Dad advised.

"Good Lord," Mrs. Buslyk began to sob. "What am I now? I'm neither a widow or a maiden!"

"It seems like you're a widow," my Gramps said.

"Well, who's going to wring its neck for me?" Momma asked, transferring her gaze from Dad to Gramps.

"And even if a goose'd kick me in the butt, I'm not going to unstitch the embroidery!" Granny vowed.

"Ehh, I'm gonna really fuss over it—I'll chop off it's head," Dad grimaced. "Here I'll take the ax—whack, whack, and it's kaput."

In the meanwhile Grandma had straightened out the cloth on the table.

"Well, take a gander—your husband turned out just like a painting. And, look, I even made his legs wobbly so it'd be obvious he's drunk. And now you want me to destroy it?"

"The ax is under the steps in the foyer," said Gramps. "I'd wanted to sharpen it, but I forgot."

"I'll sharpen it right now," Dad wiped his hands and started off toward the foyer.

"If you stuff that goose a la Chinese, it'll taste so good you'll swallow your fingers," Momma insisted.

"I don't like the Chinese," Gramps strained through his teeth.

After Gramps had been investigated and had been locked up in the slammer again, there was a certain man there in charge they called The Chinaman. He amused himself by calling in one of the political prisoners in the middle of the night and keeping him standing at attention till dawn. Because of it, Gramps, having learned something new about the Mao boys, often used to repeat:

"If there's going to be a war with the Chinese, then I'm going to be the first to volunteer. I have a special interest in them."

The Chinese, however, were unbelievably lucky, because my Gramps died before the border conflict.

"My husband wasn't so bad," Mrs. Buslyk whined. "There were times he'd go for water... to the store for milk..."

"Ehh," Granny waved her hands, "you do the job and don't get squat for it!"

And so she undid the embroidery.

On the next day Mr. Buslyk got drunk as a skunk, and he got under Mrs. Buslyk's skin for losing two geese for nothing.

My Granny stretched through the window and began to shout:

"You sweet good-for-nothing! If you don't stop, I'll embroider you again right away! And then two more geese will be gone!"

Buslyk opened his mouth to rasp out something, but, in spite of the fog in his head, he figured that it was better to keep quiet.

Then we had lunch. Momma stuffed the goose a la Chinese, and told Gramps that it was according to an old-fashioned recipe. Gramps was delighted and praised her:

"Eh, whatever you say, Ukrainian cuisine is the best in the world. And just for the fact that we thought up *kovbasa*, garlic ring sausage, we're worthy of eternal memory. But who knows about this now?.. Here, Yurko, learn so that you'll be wise and remind the world that it's in great debt to us for *kovbasa*."

Well, so I learned and now I'm reminding you.

This was the way my Granny was, may she rest in the Heavenly Kingdom, cause the last thing that she did was to embroider herself.

THE WINDOWS OF TIME FROZEN

I came here and stood amid the trickily winding streets, the multitudes of people, of trees, of buildings, to conjure her name.

I extend my hand, and proclaim three times:

"Ilayáli! Ilayáli! Ilayáli!" And people turn into woodworms, they begin to nibble trees, and the trees fall, and they don't know the reason why.

Something strange is happening to me: every morning, waking up from dreams, I feel I'm the dew. The way the dew with its beauty blinds your eyes from the flowers and grass, that's how I blind myself to all the living things and to this earth.

Weep, because when the sun stoops over your head, the dew will disappear.

I fear the sun. Sometimes I walk out at night into the garden and stare into the cold sky. The whole time it seems like it wants to remind me of something or to explain something. I listen ardently to the quiet of the night sky and catch separate words, sentences. Just recently I began to write them down. And suddenly I understood—it was telling me about me, telling me what I'd forgotten long ago.

And yesterday I stepped out into the garden, listened hard and heard nothing. I crawled up onto the tallest apple tree to hear better, but the sky was silent. I sat on the branches the entire night, without taking my eyes from the sky, and the sun rose, and its rays struck my face, and I saw that I am no longer the dew, but someone just like everyone else, and maybe even ten times worse, and when someone threw a stone at me, I picked up the stone and kissed it.

1

In the childhood of everyone there once was a garden—one's own or someone else's. We had a garden that was no-one's—no one besides us ever entered it, but we knew that if we should stop going there for a day, it would disappear, never to return again.

This was so long ago when we were pure as angels, when we knew nothing of love, but already leaned with our lips to one another and didn't really know what was going on, or if you happen to do it this way. And we believed that we'd come from a fairy tale and that we'd return to the fairy tale, and we took pledges of fidelity, and I said that I would always defend her, the little girl Ilayáli, from beasts of prey, from evil spirits and fierce dragons...

2

Ilayáli couldn't have died. More probably it was I who have died. Countless years ago I had dissolved in the wind and from time to time in tiny specks of dust I fall onto the earth with the rain and snow. And no one in the world knows that this rain and that snow are me. Young girls wash their hair in me, children make snowmen out of me, and a part of my despair appears on the face of every snowman.

3

I often dream of our street that I abandoned so long ago, but I particularly remember its trees, its buildings and its windows. It was a thoroughly small street with one- and two-storied brick houses. Everything that happened behind the wall of any of them immediately became known to the whole street in great detail.

In the summer the windows of my street turned green and bloomed in cyclamen, azaleas, primrose, asparagus, and in the winter they were stuffed with cotton and covered lightly with colored foil. On the upper part of the window puffy angels with white wings were attached, and for Christmas they put up a Christmas tree at the window. When it got dark, all the windows were shut with drapes, but the one where the Christmas tree stood was always lit and beckoned us little ones to it. The whole time we bounded along the street comparing trees to see who had the best. And the best was always at Mr. Mandryk's who, by some miracle unknown to anyone, had managed to hold on to some pre-war toys. No one else had that kind. On Mr. Mandryk's tree princes and princesses shone in exquisite clothes, birds of paradise with fluffy tails, sparkling round balls, and even fairy-tale candies that none of us had ever relished; we always argued whether they were real or just empty wrappers. And on the tree there were lots of elegant tiny angels and cherubim, and beneath the tree stood Saint Nicholas with a full bag of presents. He wore a blue *zhupán* sewn in gold, cut in half by a wide golden belt, and from beneath the *zhupán* jutted out red *sharováry*. With his long white mustache he resembled more of a Zaporozhian Cossack than a saint. We felt a boundless respect for the real Saint Nicholas, wrote him letters in which we swore to be good and listen to our parents, and at the end of the letter, as if matter-of-factly, listed the gifts we wanted to get. On the contrary, we completely ignored Father Frost, not for a moment believing in his existence. Once, when mother bought a Father Frost to put under the tree, my grandfather took off his beard, shortened his sheepskin coat, remade his felt shoes into boots and attached a red pointed beret onto his hat. Now Saint Nicholas had appeared even at our place. Having seen such a marvel, the entire street immediately rushed to learn how to do it. Even then our tree didn't become any nicer than Mandryk's. We continued to stand under his window anyway.

For a long time I resisted the inclination to see the sleepy old street. I feared finding it different than I remembered—the way it appeared in my dreams. I was afraid I wouldn't see the green plank fences because they were supposed to have been replaced with metal mesh. I was afraid that those trees on which the turtledoves always cooed were already gone. And most of all I was afraid of the asphalt that imprisoned it...

To the very last minute I figured it was crazy to show up at Holuba Street. The road that led there was unfamiliar, not a single one of those streets that led directly to mine remained the way I remembered it. This filled me with despair. I had no hope that Holuba Street had survived, that the continually advancing level of our civilization hadn't affected it.

That's why I didn't believe my eyes when I came upon Holuba Street. It seemed to me that this was just a continuation of a dream, for in life such things never happen. My street had changed very little in 20 whole years. I could say that it hadn't changed at all—things just grayed with age, maybe peeled off a little more, but still it remained just as quiet and daydreamy.

On a bench several old ladies by the plank fence were chewing soft warm words, caressing me with interested glances and then coughing... If I'd ask them about Ilayáli, then I'd see only surprised faces... Here no one can know anything about Ilayáli, for it is I who bestowed this name on her.

The coalman's little building retained its untidiness and its unfriendliness. Wild grapevines striving to cover up everything, but they manage to do so only partially. As long ago, in the thickets of the wild grapevines, sparrows nest and spill out onto the street with their loud warbling. What can I say when I go inside? Who am I? The ticket controller of my dreams? If I remind them of me and they recognize me, they won't utter anything. They won't want to talk to me, so as not to stir up old wounds.

But if a person comes here for the first time he should at least check for the building number before going in. I opportunely stop and cock up my head. The sign on the wall can't be seen, it's under the grapevines. If I don't want them to know my secret, then I should ask the old ladies where Number 7 is... Though... am I sure that it's really seven?.. It's better for me to ask about that building, and then I'll simply nod my head—that's the one I need...

Why are you looking for this building?.. What a silly question. Silly because I hadn't expected it. Now I have to explain that I'm from the gas company. Though, when I was little, there wasn't any gas here and we burned wood, but now it has to be... Has to?... They could have refused to hook up the gas... But it's too late. You are from the gas company?... Why question again... Oh that's good, 'cause my stove just broke and it's been three days... Good, good, definitely what's your building number, yes, last name, nationality, sorry, just a joke. But—Mrs. Mandryk! My Lord, is it you?! I wonder what your Christmas tree looks like now...

The wicket gate squeaks just the way it used to. Though not exactly: some kind of strange sound seemed to emanate from it. It reminded me of something that had nothing to do with this street or my childhood. Anyway I couldn't comprehend what and opened and closed the gate once more, without even thinking how silly it must have looked.

The leaves cautioned quietly, you shouldn't give yourself away, a gas company man should be filled with the joy of life, he has no nostalgia, he never remembers anything, that's why it's not right to listen to the music of the gate. Otherwise these old ladies will figure you out.

Good, good, I won't any more.

The chilled brass doorknob squeals sickly, the doors obstinately yield, and I end up in a dark vestibule where the scent of mustiness dominates, of pickled cabbage and old furniture puffed up with rags soaked with naphthalene.

"Anybody here?"

All around it's quiet and unfriendly, but I sense as though someone invisible is waiting cautiously, listening to my every word and step. A startled rustle slides along my ear and grows quiet so quickly that I'm no longer sure whether I've heard it at all.

"I'm from the gas company!"

Finally somebody's hoarse voice that could have been a man's or a woman's reverberated from above, from behind the open doors, and crawled along the stairs to me.

"He is from the gas company! Go and open the door!"

Heavy footsteps echo above my head, from the ceiling the plaster crumbles until the wooden steps, along which a dark heavy figure descends, begin to squeal.

"Good day. I've come to check the gas."

"The gas is fine."

The woman, hands gripping her waist from both sides, was big and heavy-set, her face in the dark. Could this really be Ilayáli's mother? She was grumbling about something.

"Anyway, I have to check. You understand—it's my job."

"We understand, follow me."

We recognize you, we recognize you, the steps whisper... You used to come here a long, long time ago and you were so small and light, in short-short crisscrossed overalls. Do you remember how you carved out three letters on us—ILA?... Don't be afraid, we won't turn you in, we've forgiven you for it, even though it hurt. Those letters are already gone, don't look for them here, when the little girl died, the lady of the house scratched them off. We asked her why she had done it, but she didn't answer.

"Come here."

The room was large and cluttered with all kinds of junk, filled with cobwebs and dust. In the corner an iron bed, on the bed a scraggly man was sitting with a face like crumpled paper, with mussed hair and veiny hands on his knees. It looks like this is Ilayáli's father... How do I ask about her?... There under the window on the floor was her doll.

"You have children?" I nod my head at the doll.

His wife wrinkled her face and stretched to her husband:

"He's asking if we have children... What should I answer him?"

Her husband draws away his head, looks at me with eyes white as milk and says:

"Tell him that it doesn't concern him."

And the wife: "There's the meter."

I am leafing through my notebook, conscientiously writing down the numbers and furtively following the two of them. They're silent and don't move. They're waiting anxiously for me to finally get out of here. They're looking like I caught them committing a horrible crime. Why are his eyes so white? He's dark, but his eyes...

"Your eyes... why do you have white eyes?"

But his wife interrupts: "He's really becoming annoying. Say something to him..."

She was sure that her husband would say something that would carry me away like the wind. Perhaps it's already been tried, because a satisfied smile contorted the corner of her mouth in the expectation of delight. She switched her gaze from me to her husband and back, she doesn't believe anymore that I'm from the gas company.

"I won't say anything," her husband wheezed, "I don't have anything to say. Anybody who doesn't like my eyes doesn't have to look at them."

"I'm not looking..."

"Do you hear?" His wife joins in. "He's looking at the meter."

"He's looking at the meter...," her husband repeats after her and grows quiet.

"Can I look at the oven?"

I try to hang around a little longer next to the oven.

How can I find out about Ilayáli from them?

I feel over the pipes, the doors, I even smudge some ashes on my finger and stupidly examine them. The ashes are hot, but the oven is barely warm. That is, they didn't fire the oven, but were burning something. Perhaps the letter I wrote to her?

Back then we used to write letters to each other. In the corner of the sheet in red pencil we used to draw large lips and kissed them, writing: "I've kissed this spot," and while re-reading them in the evening we would revel in joy.

"What kind of ashes are those? Were you burning paper?"

"These are the ashes of my old pants," his wife responds and breaks out in laughter. Between her teeth there is a lot of saliva, entirely in fine white bubbles; like dough steeped in yeast, her entire body chokes in spasms of laughter, and every fold of her gigantic stomach shakes, and the bundle of black hairs that sticks out of a wart on her chin also shakes and... Lord, how could it be that it's she who gave birth to Ilayáli?

Have to say something... something...

"One of my friends..."

They've become defensive and no longer hide their hostile glances.

"...is looking for an apartment..."

They're thinking: what does he want?

"...and I... could you have... ah... possibly..."

They exchange glances like a ball being tossed back and forth.

"...a room?"

With a hollow voice his wife utters, as though it were a prayer she has just learned:

"We don't... have... a free... room..."

"Too bad," I yawn, "'cause if..."

"No, we don't have a free room," her husband interrupts.

"...if there are only two of you..."

"There aren't just two of us."

"Then is she alive?" I nearly scream. And I want to rush to them with hugs... But have the stairs, does it turn out, have they lied? Why would they?

"...but even if there are three of you, then..."

Suddenly he cuts me off sharply as though with a saber:

"There aren't three of us!" And then he gets up from the bed, staggering. With all his strength he forces himself to stand up, even though it isn't easy for him. I involuntarily step back to the wall.

"And not four, or five, or ten!"

He spits in my face with those words, and they spread along me, splatter on the floor, and turn into white slime. I cast a glance at the mirror and don't see that man there, although the mirror's hanging behind his shoulders.

"What do you want from us? Are you from..."

"No, I'm not from the police... and not from... I'm from the gas company."

"Then why do you..."

"I'll tell you: my friend..."

"That's not true! What do you want?!"

His cracked voice breaks in his dry throat, he waves his arms, then grabs for his heart and painfully, greedily catches air with his mouth. His wife restrains his arms–"Calm down calm down calm down..."

"Let him tell us what he wants!"

"He'll tell us, he'll tell us..."

And I can't see her in the mirror. It's not reflecting anything. Maybe they don't really exist?

"Listen, maybe you aren't here? Maybe you never were?!"

At first his wife only stares at me silently, and then turns her head to her husband and, as though she had arranged it with him in advance, they begin to encircle me with frenzied laughter, stretching their arms. They do this unhurriedly, cutting me off from the doors, the way you'd get ready to catch a chicken. I feverishly gaze about the room in the hopes of grabbing something with a long reach, because I'm not afraid of these old people at all, I'm sure I can handle them easily... Though... though this man—dammit—has veiny hands...

"Ilayáli!" I suddenly scream. And this name, with which I honored the little girl, echoes like an oath, which, in fact, it is.

The old people jump back from me as though they have been pricked. His wife covers her mouth with her hand, and I now see that her eyes are dilating, dilating, and how her husband's hands are shaking, he's making extraordinary efforts to keep his balance.

My hands fall powerlessly, my pencil strikes the floor hollowly and rolls to the feet of his wife, she steps away, and the notebook flaps its page-wings like a pigeon and flies off...

"Ilayáli! I want Ilayáli!"

"Go with him down the stairs so he doesn't fall," her husband says.

"But I want Ilayáli!"'

"...'cause it's dark..."

His wife goes to the door, waiting guardedly.

"I won't go until you show her to me! Where have you hidden her? What have you done with her?"

With a pleading voice his wife says:

"Listen, tell him... tell him... let him go..."

"I won't go... I..."

"She...she's gone...she died...so many years ago...there's nothing left of her...her grave's beneath the elms...it's marked...there...Go!"

"It's marked 'Go'?"

"Don't you see—he's crazy!"

"Then she's dead?!"He starts back from me, flicks his hands at my shout, as though burning his face on a flame with long tongues.

"Then it's not she who's dead, but me! Me! Me! Don't you see? Before you is a corpse that decayed long ago! Don't you smell the odor? Come closer! Don't be afraid of the worms—they're tame, they don't bite their own kind!"

His wife hides her face in her hands.

"Go!"

"Ah, you want to get rid of me? I know you've burned her! And it's not the ashes of old pants, but the ashes of poor Ilayáli! Why have you burned her?"

"Have mercy on us! Have mercy on us!"

They both utter these words, not knowing to whom, but with such faith in their voice that I understand the words aren't directed to God."Who are you asking mercy from? The devil? No use! Ask it of me! Beg on your knees so that I'll have mercy! Sprinkle ashes on your heads!"

And here I once again gazed at the mirror and no longer could make out the room, already there was nothing there, just the thick gray fog curled inside, while below silver soap bubbles rose, bursting with a hollow crackle, and in the distance two barely visible figures disappeared, becoming smaller and smaller in my eyes. Suddenly someone's thin white arm appeared with fingers sticking out and shielded those two figures from me, and then dissolved in the fog, but just before the fog was about to lift, a pair of familiar greenish eyes winked, these were the eyes of Ilayáli, and when the fog disappeared in the mirror I could see an empty lot, I ushered my eyes away from the mirror, looked around and saw just an empty lot: gray mounds of stones, plaited with bind-weed, surrounded with thistle, and mosquitoes flew above them, and the wind overflowed playfully and quivered. High in the sky—the voice of a hawk.

Suddenly in my throat the coil of a desperate scream unreeled:

"It's true—she's alive!!!"

The thistles nodded their heads condemningly.

"Then she's gone?"

Whom did I turn to?

"And she'll never ever be back?"

The hawk screeches again, and I can see how it swiftly falls to the grass and in a moment flies upward, and in terror some kind of creature squeals in its claws, and that squeal reminds me of my own voice, and I no longer sense my legs beneath me and I am running through the empty lot, and coming toward me—a branchy walnut tree with a swing attached to the boughs. Once it used to grow in Ilayáli's yard, she loved to swing. (Swing—swing! Higher, higher! Swing!) The creature is squealing so shrilly, and it's as though someone is pulling a strong thread through my ears. (Swing—swing! Don't be afraid, I won't fall!) Suddenly I hear the voice of the hawk above me and the whistle of its body, that cuts the air, and with all my strength I run to the tree in hopes of hiding in its hollow, and fear squeezes my frightened heart in its pincers, and the hawk look-look is diving at my forehead, and I squeal just like that creature, because already I see that I can't save myself—the hollow of the tree is so narrow, and I will never squeeze into it, and my Ilayáli laughs: "Swing-swing-swing!"

BEATRICE: TWILIGHT, THE COLD

Aged Beatrice pulls the cover over her eyes and with her tepid breath warms herself.

Aged Beatrice tries to fall asleep and, with her sleep, to put a stop to her hunger.

She's also thinking about the river, whose shores are covered with green willow branches, and on the branches there are birds and flies of many colors. Beatrice floats along the river's current in a blue boat and delights in the morning sun. A light fog curls above the water, and her body is so light, so loved, so pampered, and every one of her movements is the flapping of a bird's wing...

Her imagination just stops at this point, she's incapable of more, her whole life she's been trying to figure out: what's next?–but she never succeeds. Whether she remains in that boat forever among the green willow branches, among the birds, like a bird...

And this still isn't sleep, it's ordinary drowsiness. Again she shivers from the cold, and her hungry stomach draws into itself the cover, the room, the entire building, together with the squeaking weather vane on the roof.

–ah how I so want to eat—

–ah how I so want warmth—

–ah why am I so old—so unwanted by anyone.

The moon peeps into the window, a lonely fox moans at the window

I shut the window: your finger once danced along the pane

here

at midnight I shut the window

a bee is dying on the sill

the grass is humming and the pond is croaking in this deserted place

I shut my heart with the translucent wing of a bee

I sense—A LONELY WOUNDED FOX IS CRAWLING TO ME THROUGH THE WALLS.

A garden with a head, filled with birds, deeply breathes in and exhales the night air. Above the trees and roofs rain floats and contemplates—whether it should descend or not...

Beatrice crawls out of her bed, shuffles to the dresser and rummages among her rags. She finds a cotton scarf with countless holes in it and ties it around her back. Again she lies down in bed. Beneath the cover she turns up her nightshirt and scratches her thigh, but it's already itching worse, and her fingers rub along her hot sweaty skin. Finally her thigh calms down.

Tomorrow I'll wash up tomorrow I'll wash up tomorrow I'll wash up tomorrow tomorrow

Many years ago she drove her lovers mad. Young J. M. breathed his last on her, on her body, becoming fatigued from the excess of love. At first Beatrice noticed in the corner of his mouth a thin stream of blood. The blood rolled down his chin and dripped onto her neck, but he was in such a frenzy that he completely stopped seeing a woman beneath him, and stopped hearing her scream. Suddenly he saw a race—they're catching up to him, he's rushing with all his might, the horse snorts, and bits of lather fly in every direction, I'm escaping, escaping, escaping...

Then from his mouth—an entire stream of blood. His mouth turned into a giant red rose... I'm escaping, escaping, escaping escaping, escaping, escaping... escaping?

I've closed and spread my legs, my whole life I've done nothing but that...

But then it all was snuffed out, and for twenty years already she's been living in memories, from time to time tracing her hand along her stomach, pressing her fingers there, here, not feeling anything, pressing harder there, here, not feeling anything, she cries quietly, fingers next to her nostrils—a pungent odor, her fingers above the cover—the scent of rain, fingers on the wall—the scent of spider webs.

She closed her legs, then spread them... Letting the moon into herself, releasing it...

The rain thought: I'm going to fall further down the road. The garden thought: fall asleep, or what? The pond croaked and croaked, the grass hummed and hummed...

tomorrowI'llwashuptomorrowI'llwashuptomorrowI'llwashuptom orrowI'll

washuptomorrow

Someone's bare feet stepped up to the door. The door went on alert, the alert was passed along to the walls, the ceiling bent.

Who's there? It's so late. Beatrice wants to sleep.

tomorrowI'llwashuptomorrowI'llwashup...morrow...

ash.........

I'll fall down not here, but somewhere far-far away, the rain thought, I can't fall there, where memories return.

"Beatrice, open up!"

Whose voice is it? Maybe it's the door? Maybe the floor?

"Beatrice, open up!"

She tore away from the bed, a certain magical power seized her, threw her to the door, the door—creaked.

"Who is it?"

Why is she asking—she knows who it is.

In front of her was a hunched over gray-haired man, he had just traversed a long road, and his clothing had rotted away, and his ribs stuck out like the top of a picket fence...

.... a whole row of fences..... a garden behind a picket fence...

...in the garden poppies and nightshade... tall hemp... and tiny

Beatrice... sits down on the ground, hides... someone's voice:

"Beatrice! Beatrice!"

"What?" She asks.

"Beatrice," the voice says, "I came to you." "Oh, I see, I see you came to me so exhausted, you came to me, and I am so exhausted... You found me after many years, the way they find long lost things, about which they had already begun to forget; but it's in vain, the stone will not float from the bottom to the surface, the stone becomes overgrown with moss, slippery, a man, crossing a river, steps onto a stone and slips, taking water into his mouth—he chokes, his body floats beyond the water, the stone begins to weep, the stone didn't want to joke around this way, the stone begins to weep... eepstonebeginstoweep...

"Beatrice, Beatrice, I've been walking to you for many years. Look—my clothes have rotted away, my feet have become callused, my mouth dried up, my eyes have sunken, blackened, my eyes are wretched...

"No, no, you died! You died so long ago, that I've already forgotten. You couldn't return. You're just a shadow that somehow moves by itself.

"Beatrice, light up a light and you'll see I'm not a shadow!"

Beatrice lights a candle.

"Yes, you're not a shadow. But you've died. You died a long time ago."

"Really?.. I already don't remember that. But you... you remember... my poems?"

"Yes."

"At least recite one..."

"Bend to me, my Beatrice..."

Her entire body swings, the candle swings, and the room swings.

"Bend to me, my Beatrice..."

Then he saves her:

"Where the poppies bloom and the birds sing..."

She feels embarrassed, it seems to her that it's not her, because that Beatrice, to whom so many sonnets were dedicated, died on the same day with their creator. She feels like telling him something so gentle and warm, but she can't find the words.

"So, you've returned?" She asks, because nothing else comes to mind.

"I've returned to you, just to you."

"Certainly I'm not the same one. You could return just to me, but not to poetry, for there is no more poetry in me. Look at me—I no longer conceal anything mysterious in me, I've become so ordinary and plain, like this armchair you've sat down in, like this table you placed your hand on. And moreover I feel hunger and I'm cold."

Then he pulls dried up bread out from beneath his arm and offers it to her:

"Take it. While I was walking to you, I was given charity. I didn't refuse, I didn't want to insult people."

Beatrice chews on the bread, or perhaps, on her old age, her infirmity...

And he breaks his walking stick, cracks his wooden shoes and starts up a fire. The flame crackles, licks its lips and blows out the warmth bit by bit.

"O Beatrice, there, in non-being, I thought about you. I searched for truth in my poems. You say that there's nothing mysterious in you anymore... But that's not so. For me you're just as mysterious as before. I certainly never saw you naked. I never kissed you. I loved you, but never touched you. You bared your body in front of so many... Just I, I alone didn't see you. I recalled my poems and saw that I had deceived myself. I sculpted your image from imagination. Everything is there in my poems about you except you. Then I understood that I must see all of you as you are, and put everything in its place. That's why I've returned. I've traversed the long road to gaze at your body...

Beatrice becomes terrified, bread crumbs scatter from her lips, her hands tremble, she covers her mouth so as not to scream.

SOMEWHERE FAR-FAR AWAY, WHERE MEMORIES ALREADY NO LONGER RETURN, RAIN FALLS...

"No-no, how could you dare!"

tomorrowI'llwashup tomorrow I'llwashup tomorrow I'llwashup tomorrow I'llwashup

Croak-croak the pond, hum-hum the grass.

tomorrow tomorrow tomorrow I'll chop up the table chop up the armchair

tomorrow tomorrow tomorrow I'll heat up some water I'll wash up

"Beatrice, I've crossed such a long road, I've completely decayed, I feel like a pile of dust. The wind puffs—I fly in different directions.

Again her thigh itches oh how it itches

her sweaty slippery thigh if you stand on it—

you'll slip water will drown your mouth—you'll choke

IN YOUR MOUTH A GLASS ROSE WILL BLOOM

A rose-colored boat on the water, and I am in the boat. Willow branches above the shore. Birds. LOOK AT ME HOW BEAUTIFUL I AM HOW NICE I AM! There where the poppies bloom, there, where the birds sing. MY BODY IS LIKE THE SUN—IT BLINDS THE EYES. Young J. from an excess of love such frenzied races—I'm escaping escaping escaping

"Beatrice, pity me!"

"Lord! How can you ask for that! How can you dare!"

"Beatrice, I didn't see your body, I didn't ever see it. Let me guide my hand along it and kiss it along the trail of my hand!"

"Have mercy! How can you? I won't allow you to ask me this way. So many years have passed. No one has seen my body in so long, not even a mirror."

Ah, how will I show myself to him? I'm old and so horrifying. My skin is wrinkled, all blistered. Where have the golden hairs disappeared that used to cover it? They've gone gray and become saddened... the color of my body became oh-so-white, like paper... such an unpleasant color... my legs got covered with ugly blue veins...

"Beatrice, you won't chase me away, you'll pity me."

"How do you know whether I'll take pity on you? Do you guess I cried when young J. was at the point of death? Or when my husband died? No, I didn't cry..."

"Don't slander yourself, Beatrice. All of this is untrue. I saw how young J. M. died. He was murdered!"

"Not true! He died in my arms!"

"And you were lamenting for your husband and biting your lips!"

"Not true! I hated him!"

"Ha-ha-ha-ha!" He laughed.

"Go away! I don't want to listen to you! Go away!"

"Beatrice, take heart!"

She waved her arms, rushed to the door, and suddenly her shirt got caught on something, and the worn cloth tore and slipped off her, and her body shone like a stiletto.

"A-a-a!" She began to scream in despair.

....and with eyes wide open from surprise he apprehended her body—a young orange body, yet to be tasted by anyone, so smooth, like alabaster, so sweet and so much aflame.

"It's not me! Not me!" She shouted with horror. "I'm old and vile! This isn't my body! Who substituted me?"

And he:

"O no, this is you, you—I know it! I saw you this way in my dreams! You're the way I wanted you!"

"Don't look at me! For the sake of all that is holy don't look! This isn't me! These are the devil's jokes! My body's crawling with fat, it's grown white and flabby all over! This is all the devil's doing!"

But he had already fallen on his knees, and was groping her with his hands, and he whispered a prayer or his poems, but she could not hear, suddenly turned her head around and fell down, without understanding how her old and shabby body suddenly had become young.

. . . . . . no-no, I don't want to begin from the beginning

. . . . . a young body. . . . young J. . . . .

. . . . . a young husband . . . again those poems. . . . .

Be gone devil I. . . . .

Be gone devil DON'T WANT . . . . . .

Be gone devil TO BECOME YOUNG . . . .

Be gone devil

AND I UNDERSTAND: ALL THIS IS THE DEVIL!

Be gone, devil, your jokes are much too cruel.............................

The rain returned and when it flew past her roof, it thought: perhaps I'll fall here...

And the garden replied: give it-give it,

there's no longer a road here for memories...

A DREAM ABOUT A TRAMCAR

I was riding in a tramcar and looking out of a window at the morning people. You can really differentiate early morning people from those who roam around the city during the day. Especially by their faces—unhappy and as gray as the cobblestone pavement.

Next to me a ticket-controller stopped and asked if I had a ticket. I nodded without taking my gaze from the window, but he continued to stand next to me.

"Are you sure you've got a ticket?"

I measured him with my gaze. He was a small heavy-set man, who reached just up to my chin, with a great big round head and protruding ears. On his ticket-controller's coat you could see countless bright fibers, threads, and hairs, as well as a kind of down, as though he had been rolling around all over somewhere at a textile factory.

"I have a ticket," I answered, and once again looked out at the street. In the meantime the passers-by had become even more preoccupied than before, and for some of them this had turned into rage. Just about anything might provoke their anger—for example, this tramcar that put a crimp in their itinerary, as they were forced to wait until it crawled across the street, or my kind, amiable face, that of someone who had nowhere to rush and who had just spent the night in a woman's arms.

"I'm not sure you've got a ticket," the ticket-controller said.

I didn't know what to answer him, and tried to think about something pleasant. There was little though that could be pleasant. You might even say there was nothing that could be pleasant at all.

"You're riding without a ticket," the ticket-controller continued his deliberation.

I led my gaze away from the window, and in my soul a heartfelt pity appeared for this small man who had been deprived of a woman's caresses, and who tried to paste greasy tufts of hair to his eternally perspired bald head. Hopelessness glistened in his yellow eyes. His life had even fewer pleasant hours of experience than mine. Illness undermined his health, his pay was barely enough for cheap sausage, and when anyone treated him to a glass of cheap red wine that everybody calls "ink," he became filled with boundless joy, as though the Lord's blessing had descended upon him. At home his wife nagged him, calling him a lazy bones, an idler, impotent, and dystrophic. In the all too rare hours of conciliation, he conscientiously crawled up on top of her and tried to do everything of which his capricious organism was capable. But this didn't last long, in fact it was always so short-lived that it only served to irritate his wife even more; she flew into a rage, pounded his bald head and shouted right up into his face:

"Shithead! Shithead! Shithead!"

Someone suggested to him that he abstract during the act, think about something else, not about women, in order to prolong the loving. So he thought about tramcars, about passengers without tickets, about how they dirty up the cars, how they break the seats, scratch the walls, unscrew screws... Right at the point of the screws forget it—it was all over. It wouldn't go on any further than that. He crawled off his wife and quietly, like a rat, turned toward the wall, covered his head and tried to forget it as quickly as possible.

"Shithead! Ah, you're such a shithead! You good-for-nothing! You clown! You can't even get a broad to come! I mean it, I'll go to the grocery store, I'll stand there—and let just anybody do me! The worst drunk'll be better than you! I'll stand there, lift up my dress, and I'll just keep standing there. Whoever passes by—let him take advantage of it. Nobody'll ever pass up this rear end. They'll even wait in line for it!"

Finally she cracked his head and turned her powerful back at him and fell asleep in a rage.

His hand touched my shoulder and he repeated:

"You're riding without a ticket. I've been following you."

"Your memory's bad," I grumbled, while groping for the ticket in my pants pocket. I could have showed it to him, but it seemed to me that this would dash all the ticket-controller's hopes. It seemed like it was enough for him to catch various turkeys from whose humiliation he didn't get a bit of satisfaction. He could shout at them, fine them, shove them off the tram—all this was petty, of little value and uninteresting. Right now he had tracked down a much bigger beast. You come across this kind in your life just once or twice, just like in any hunter's life. Everyone has his dream of a golden-horned buck, while they've been limited their whole life to just rabbits. And here, when finally the golden-horned buck stands before your eyes and you have to shoot him, then you strive as long as possible to prolong that satisfaction toward which you've been striving seemingly your whole life.

For him I was that golden-horned buck, the dream of his miserable life, the knight of his dreams and ravings. He looked at me from below, and I sensed how furiously his tortured heart was beating, how the veins were throbbing on his temples and how his puffy hands with stubby sausages for fingers were sweating. Droplets of nervous perspiration emerged on his bald head, and it was completely understandable—in the depth of his soul he was wholly trembling from the fear that his dream of the golden-horned buck will blow away completely, will all turn out to be a mirage and a deception, and instead, just the dull pain near his heart and the unrestrained sadness of everyday routine will remain. As though he were seeking assurance that all this wasn't a dream, he touched my shoulder once again, and his fingers trembled. I really existed, I was next to him, and he was really tracking me down. The one thing that sustained his anxiety was my hand in my pocket— at any minute it could emerge and wave the white banner of a ticket before his eyes. Besides that, I could tell him to go to hell and jump out at the next stop. But I'm young and strong, I exuded health, and behind me was a frenzied night of loving with a young lady, whom this clumsy clod could never even dream of.

Just think—just an hour ago I was lying in her warm embraces, my hand caressing her soft and slender thighs, her fabulous breasts, and my ear captured the intoxicating whisper of her hot lips... I'm sure that if she'd even put her hand on his knee, he'd go mad with happiness. What did he see in life? He was someone who lived only for his pay, who's stingy with his toothpaste and facial tissues. He gives all his money to his wife, and then for this gets his share of pea soup and still has to work it off in bed. All hope for him lies in a stomach ulcer. Then they'll give him total peace and won't poison him with leftover potatoes. When he dies, in his dimming brain the thought will flash: "Why did I live?"

Consequently he shouldn't have been born. He wouldn't have been born if his father had been just a wee bit more careful.

When the tram stopped, the fear flashed in his eyes that I would push him and jump out. He even warned me:

"And don't even think about jumping out. Better to pay the fine. Otherwise I'd have to take you to the police.

"I'm not planning on jumping out," I said. "I have a ticket."

"That's not true. If you had a ticket, you would have shown it to me long ago."

His voice trembled noticeably. If at that moment I'd have shown him the ticket, his heart wouldn't have been able to take it.

He evoked compassion in me, and the thought even came to me that I could end up in his shoes. I simply was unbelievably fortunate to have been born somewhere else and at another time. And if I had been the sixth or eighth child of some drunk, then who knows whether I would have managed to make my way to the ticket-controller. Life is an interesting joke. It requires sacrifices. But the opportunity to do good comes so rarely, that for the sake of such an occasion, maybe it's even worth giving yourself up to torture. Perhaps from this very day this unfortunate man will raise his head and smile to the future, perhaps after he humiliates me, makes me obey and forces me to beg for forgiveness, he'll finally realize that he is a man and, arriving home, the first thing he'll do—will be to box his wife on the ear.

Could I ruin his secret dream? In his heart he felt like a real Sherlock Holmes—he had tracked down an extraordinary honcho. And this wasn't just some argumentative babe who'll whack his head so he won't be very happy that he asked for the ticket. This wasn't a shrewd student who unmistakably recognizes just about any ticket-controller before the latter even sits down in the tramcar.

Here he grabbed for my shirt button and began to twirl it with such a stare as if that button literally comprised everything that was most valuable for me and the meaning of my existence. Maybe this act still had some symbolic significance for him.

"Riding without a ticket is really not very nice. Aren't you ashamed?" He muttered. "Now you'll have to pay a fine, otherwise I'll take you away to the police. And there you'll pay an even bigger fine, they'll write a report to your employer, your picture will hang in all the tramcars, and everybody will point their fingers at you."

Listening to these idiotic things, I understood the real reason behind it. Maybe his supervisor had spoken with him just this way: the former took his button by the fingers, twirled it and pronounced:

"Why are you riding these tramcars, giving a piss poor number of fines? What are you doing—can't you grab a scofflaw with both hands and not let go till he pays? The main thing is to figure out exactly whom you can force to pay. In every tramcar there are 20 per cent of the passengers who are incorrigible scofflaws." But just one pays a fine. Because until you fine him, all the others either jump off at the next stop, or get tickets. The point is to spot somebody right away who can't weasel his way out, can't escape, or who won't hit you in the kisser. You have to have a sense of smell. Like a hunting dog, understand? You have to train yourself. And in general our work is complicated and dangerous. In fact, I'm surprised that there isn't a higher institute for ticket-controllers. We ticket-controllers should study psychology intently, pedagogy, ethics, and who knows what if not even world philosophy. Here imagine that you, armed with all the branches of knowledge, approach just such a turkey and suddenly straightening your horn-rimmed glasses, say: "Respected sir! With your gratis ride you are undermining the foundations of our statehood! We are rolling toward an abyss as a result of people like you! You are driving in just one more rusty nail into our tortured motherland! With your perfidious activity you are serving the enemies of the republic. But I've tracked you down and unmasked you! You are an agent of Moscow! Confess and pay the fine. A voluntary confession will lessen your guilt!.." Well?! Now do you sense a difference? And when you say this loud enough, the remaining passengers will come over to your side. And why?! Because all of them want to be patriots. It's easier to be a patriot than an abstainer. It's better to fight for Ukraine than to work hard at the factory.

The words of his head supervisor screwed themselves faithfully into his brain, and now, looking at me, he began to dictate them as though they were an incantation against an evil spirit. His voice trembled yet reverberated throughout the entire tramcar. Right away we ended up at the center of attention. When he stepped up to "the agent of Moscow," among the listeners you could sense a slight animation and even an indignant buzzing. Their indignation, it was clear, concerned me, and I somehow flushed red unexpectedly. This inspired the ticket-controller all the more, and he just incinerated me with his tirade, which began to increase incredibly and turned into a true act of accusation. Several passengers got up from their seats and set off toward us. Quickly we were surrounded from all sides. It seemed to me that I had ended up at judgment day.

Now, even if I had wanted to, I wouldn't be able to jump off the tramcar.

When the ticket-controller finally finished his speech, I felt the perspiration gush on my brow. An unexpected oppressive hotness came over me, and any self-assuredness disappeared without a trace.

"Through people like him we're not living like people," a woman in an awful pink-colored hat said. "If not for these intellectuals, we'd really be somewheres."

"They've sent him here on purpose," a mustachioed granny joined in, "just to destroy the young state."

"Spy!" an old granddad breathed out a bouquet of spirits and whooped.

"What's the damn Security Police doing now? Why aren't they bothering with spies?!" A scrawny, bony retiree screamed. "In our time they caught 'em like butterflies:

–z-zap!–then pin 'em! –z-zap!–then pin 'em! And look what, you understand, happens! And the devil-knows-what comes out! We hardly get this fuckin' independence, and the enemy's already intervening here!

"Yes, there are too few decent people these days," the mustachioed granny said. "Nothing but swindlers all around. At first glance he might look like an intelligent person, but just turn away—and he's pulling your money out of your bag. Maybe this is just one of those. Look at him—he's the spitting image of a pickpocket."

"And look how he's flushed!" The woman in the pink hat poked me with her finger. "You can see right away his conscience isn't clear!"

"Time for me to get off," I said and began to push my way through the crowd, but this turned out to be my profound strategic mistake, because the people immediately leaned and a dozen hands stretched toward me.

The mustachioed granny took a swing and smacked me on the head with her bag.

"Don't let go of him! Hold the criminal!"

They tugged me in various directions, tore my clothes, scratched and hit me with everything that they could grab nearby. The woman in the pink hat tried to bite me the entire time. The frightened ticket-controller, unprepared for such a violent reaction, tried to pull me out and save me, but suddenly got a fist in the nose and was forced to concentrate on his own trickling blood.

Another good blow to the head with the handbag, and I, no longer able to remain standing, sat down on the floor. Everything was swimming before my eyes, feet were trampling me, someone continued to turn my clothing into rags, but I no longer felt any pain. Unexpectedly I felt ever so light, I was taken up into the air and saw from above how the crowd had deserted my body, and the ticket-controller, wiping blood all over his face, sobbed:

"You've killed him! You've killed him!"

An hysterical woman's scream reverberated. The tram stopped and suddenly emptied. Some kind of power carried me off up high, and below everything was disappearing momentarily until it had completely vanished. I flew through the clouds higher and higher. I was warm and joyful from the feeling of having fulfilled an obligation. From time to time you have to give the people the chance to let off a little steam and to crucify someone once more. I brought myself as a sacrifice for the sake of humanity, and now heavenly bliss awaited me.

Unexpectedly something stopped my flight, and I saw an illuminated figure before me with a golden halo.

"Lord!" I shouted. "Embrace my soul!"

"Stop!" The figure said. "Show your ticket!"

"Which ticket?"

"The ticket to paradise, you dope!"

I felt all over myself and became convinced I was totally naked. My suit together with my body remained in the tramcar.

"Aha, you wanted to break in without a ticket? Get away from here!"

The hand of the archangel cuffed my ear, and I, knocked on end fell to that same spot from where I had flown into the sky.

I opened my eyes and saw that hospital orderlies were carrying me on a stretcher.

"Where are you taking me?" I muttered.

"To the drunk tank, where else?"

II. PSYCHOLOGIST OF THE HUMAN SOUL

She's not pretty, but she's dying, so it's not worth talking about her not being pretty.

Her husband's sitting by her bed, holding her hand and keeping silent. She's also silent. That's how all the things in the room think. But they're wrong. Because this husband and that wife do not remain silent.

He wants to say: "Soon you won't be here, and I'll be left alone... What should I do?"

She wants to say: "Soon I'll be gone, and you'll be left alone..."

He wants to say: "I know you've loved me, faithfully loved me, never cheated on me, I never did either, but how can I be left alone?"

She wants to say: "You know I've loved you, faithfully loved you, never cheated on you, You never did either, but how can you be left alone?"

And he says: "Whether you want or not, I have to marry again... The new wife will cook me potato dumplings. I love dumplings so much."

Then she: "You'll get bored quickly and you'll marry again. You'll bring a new woman here and you'll ask her to cook dumplings for you. You love them so much. How can I stand all this?"

Then he: "I'll certainly get used to her quickly, I'll love the things she loves, and vice versa. It'll be great."

Then she: "It's hard for me to think about this—a strange woman will be wearing my clothes, eating from my plate, watering the pots with my flowers, rolling dough into dumplings with my rolling pin..."

Then he: "You've been dying so long that I've already gotten used to it, and various stupid things come to my mind. For example, what will the second one be like... I'll take a widow, a widow's better, a widow has a lot of property after her husband's death. I'll wear his suits, if only his size fits me."

Then she: "In my life I've had only one husband, who pampered me, kissed me... just one and only... But you're going to have one more wife. How can this be?"

Then he: "Maybe that husband whose widow I'll marry later, hasn't died yet, maybe he's still getting ready to die. Maybe she, that future widow, already anticipates this and is also thinking about getting married... If the old colonel who lives across the road should die, I'd court his wife, she's an appetizing woman, and all the rest of course, also..."

Then she: "No, that won't do... I want everything to be fair. I don't want you to think that I belonged just to you, and you can belong to two... No, I don't want it that way."

And then she said:

"Listen, I want to confess to you... I want to confess a sin to you..."

He was all ears:

"What kind of sin? Have you..."

"Yes... In my life I was unfaithful to you once..."

"Don't lie!"

"I was unfaithful with a certain... um... with a certain..."

"You're lying! Lying!" He screamed and nearly took fright from the power of his own voice.

He wanted to say: "How is this so? You've been unfaithful to me? You couldn't have done this... How could you? I never... you..."

She wanted to say: "That's it... already too late... I said it and now it's too late to deny it... I have to recount the whole thing to the end."

"How did it happen?" He asked, and suddenly realized what a stupid question it was, since it proved he believed her. "I don't believe you! It's not true!"

"I'm not lying," she retorted. "I know what I'm saying. I'm still of sound mind..."

She licked her dry lips, and her waxen hands nervously surveyed the bed cover.

"I was unfaithful to you with the colonel..."

"With that... that colonel?" He pointed at the building across the street. Pain contorted his face. "Well, she's lying! She's gotta be lying! And she won't even flinch! Don't fib on your death bed at least!"

"It was in the spring. You went off on a trip somewhere... Maybe it was to your sister's... And I was left alone... He came to borrow... to borrow a ladder... Twelve years ago..."

"Stop lying... They have their own..."

"I took him to the barn... A ladder was lying flat in the barn on a pile of clover hay."

"Stop lying... We didn't raise rabbits then... What would we need that clover for?"

"I showed him the ladder... And he... Then he came close to me and said that I'm really beautiful..." He said: "What wonderful hair you have!" Even you never spoke that way to me... Not even you..."

"You're lying! He could never have said that. The colonel is versed in women. He'd never have said it that way."

"And then he smiled to me... And I smiled, too. And then he started kissing me, and I already couldn't... I couldn't control myself. The clover was so fragrant... green clover... It took my breath away..."

"You're lying! You already said it was early spring and now there was hay from the clover."

"No, you forgot..." Her voice quivered and broke, and it was obvious how hard it was for her to utter the words. "I said it was in the summer and that a ladle was lying in the barn on a pile of green clover... And he just came to borrow a ladle..."

"You said it was a ladder!"

"See how bad your memory is... I say ladle and you hear ladder..."

He furiously measured the room with his footsteps.

"You're lying about all of this... You've dreamt all this up... Liar!"

But somewhere at the bottom of his soul something began to stir: maybe it's true? The colonel is such a... He can... This was all a long time ago—she could have forgotten whether it was hay or freshly cut clover... And the colonel is such a... And to say she's beautiful, he could have... Just to get what he wanted... He could have.

And she thought to herself: "There, I told him. He certainly believed me. Now let him go get married. He'll remember what I told him the rest of his life. It's stuffy in here... Open a window..."

And he paced about the room and couldn't find any space for himself. The miniscule modest suspicion that a minute before had stirred in him slightly, had grown now to unbelievable proportions.

Just like in a movie theater he now saw how all this had happened...

Maybe it happened more than once…

"Listen... Did it happen just once? This was the only time in your life?... You never got together with him again?"

He halted above her and looked into her face with anxiety, but it was motionless and cold. Then he fell to his knees, took her head in his hands and shook her.

"When I was little I loved to shake my money bank to hear the jingle of the coins. One time I took the money bank, rattled it close to my ear and heard nothing. You understand, nothing..."

"You couldn't have! Couldn't have! How could you?! Tell me this was the only time! Tell me this was the only time! Tell me that this never happened!"

"...Then I fell to the floor and cried..."

THE DOORBELL

Suddenly a clamor on the street awakened them. Next to the apartment building an argument had started up, male and female voices gradually gathered volume, she managed against her wishes to recognize individual words, most of them indecent. She was embarrassed to hear this in her husband's presence, so she pretended to be asleep. But he started to wake up anyway. He tossed about, moaned, then tapped her shoulder with his hand.

"This happenin' under our windows?"

"Uh-huh."

"Well..." The bed screeched. "I'll let them..."

Yawning, he felt for his slippers with his feet and, annoyingly mumbling under his breath, shuffled to the window, but he stopped in the middle of the room when she whispered:

"Why? You stupid? Lie down. Do you need this?"

The squabble was so bad that not only individual words reached them, but entire phrases, intertwining like snakes, stumbled at their windows and penetrated through the panes to their bedroom. Here they were in their own element, throwing around furniture and mirrors. They raged and seethed, burning their ears with hellish screaming. Somebody had been caught with somebody else's girl, and now he, the one to whom she had belonged earlier, demonstrated the right to his possession ("I found you!"), a lone girl's voice was trying to explain something. Another was trying to calm things down and asked not to interfere, but the voice of a third guy outshouted them ("... stop, you screwballs, let's put a stop to it, come on, lend your paw")–all this had been scattered like peas, as if they all were afraid that the end of the world would come and they wouldn't manage to be able to say what they wanted.

Finally he couldn't take it and, carefully sneaking up, as though his footsteps in the soft slippers could be heard by those on the street, he pushed aside the blinds a crack. Three boys and two girls had gathered next to their wicket gate.

"Go back to bed," his wife shouted. "They'll scream a bit and then break up."

"Looks like they're getting ready to fight."

"Really?"

She didn't have to ask again, for she herself heard the sound of a dull blow—something champed, a shout, a screech, then one more blow, then another...

"You take a look what they're doing!"

"What's going on?" She slid from under the covers and in a second had pressed herself against the windowpane.

Two of them were fighting, the third was trying to separate them, and the girls screamed and tried to crawl between the two of them. Then the gate squeaked, and the fence started to shake hard.

"I should have expected it—they'll break the fence."

"Maybe yell at them?"

"Eh-he, you just watch, they'll break the window. That kind'll throw a rock..."

"The Marchuks, ya think, can't hear it?" She nodded at the building across the street.

"Maybe they can hear it. What's it to them... it's not under their windows...."

Suddenly everything settled down, grew silent, and froze, and this was so unexpected that both observers felt a chill running down their spines—the girl who was the cause of the fight shouted something.

"What did she say?"

"I didn't catch it..."

What she said obviously had cleared up the situation, because the boys in an instant stopped hammering each other and turned their battered faces toward her. Their arms with fists clenched hung by their sides. They looked at her silently and with ferocity, in the light of the streetlight you could see those malevolent glances, the lady of the house, behind the window, frightened, began to shrivel. To her it seemed her teeth were chattering, so she pressed her teeth firmly, sensing that blood was rushing to her head.

"What's gonna happen?..." She whispered, and glanced timidly at her husband. He, too, was frightened and shut his mouth with the fingers of his left hand. Maybe he was afraid he'd begin to scream...

"You sure?" One of the boys strained, and you could also sense fear in his voice.

" Yeah I'm sure! To get it through your thick skull!" One of the girls tossed out, and there was fear in her voice too.

"Well, you vermin, capisci...," a second boy whispered. "Through her, capisci... The she-jackal..." But there was fear in his voice.

"What are you... well frankly..." Her girlfriend began to wave her arms. "She was joking..." But there was fear in her voice.

"She was joking, right?"

"Clearly…."

"She was joking, right?"

"But I, capisci, because of her…"

"Well, okay, guys… don't you understand jokes?"

"She was joking, right? I'm asking you—she was joking, right?"

"You hicks, stop this train station flea market right now!"

" I'll send you to the grave for these kind of things, you know?"

"Eh, you capisci?"

"Yes, it's her... who, really..."

"Guys, what are you doing?"

"I, capisci, don't forgive these kinds of jokes, capisci... Hands off me!... Keep 'em to yourself, capisci!"

"Guys, stop! I'll start screaming!"

"Shut up, capisci!"

The lady of the house shrieked, but as quietly as a mouse, and her arms spastically grabbed the blind so hard that it began to crack on top, and her husband burst out: "You want to rip them?" And her hands fell. She thought she would begin screaming now. And bit her lower lip.

A boy with all his strength jerked the girl by the hair, she flew into the extended fist of a second boy. In an instant she was knocked off her feet—she fell to her knees and pulled her head into her shoulders. A white jacket on her shoulders tore apart, and the red eye of her sweater lit up like a wound.

"You've gone schizo?!" The other girl shouted.

"Weirdoes!"

" Get your hands off me! Capisci! And you'll get yours!"

And the blows struck all over, and her body wrenched and fell to the ground, and it coiled and yelped under those blows, and as they started kicking, with power, with discrimination, hanging on so that it wouldn't be for nothing, she began to roll along the ground, pressing her knees to her stomach and hiding her head in her hands, and her shout was pounding into the darkened windows, and bouncing off, rolling along the street, and reechoing until she stopped screaming, and was just moaning, and the dance around her continued, this ritual pre-historical dance around a sacrifice, this dance without music, accompanied by dull blows, accompanied by the knocking of heels, a dance to which, it seemed, there would be no end.

The wife was whimpering into her hand, her husband was angrily puffing hard. The old picket fence was moaning. The lamp was illuminating persistently. And the night was trembling.

Finally they jumped away from the body that had curled into a coil, breathing heavily, one began to button his shirt, but there was nothing left of the buttons at all, a second wiped the perspiration from his brow.

"Let's go, guys," the third one said to them. "Enough...""How can we... ah... leave her... ah, here?" The second girl asked.

Those who had struck her exchanged glances with uncomprehending eyes.

"Don't worry... she'll recuperate..."

"Let's go, capisci... Let's go..."

"Next time she'll know..."

"She was kidding, capisci..."

"Here's her handbag," the girl said.

"Throw it next to her."

"Well, what're you, capisci..."—to the girl—"...let the whiner clean up."

"The schizo's cutting our ranks."

"He-he... well, capisci, you're giving..."

"You sack, let's leave her alone... let her be..."

They dragged her girlfriend after them and disappeared in the darkness.

"Whew..." The man of the house sighed heavily. "Go back to sleep, huh?"

"Wait a minute... maybe they killed her."

"Ooh, your imagination! They killed her!"

"Y-yes, I tell you, pound the poor girl..."

"Aw—she's poor! Obviously there was a reason for it."

"We'll need a new fence."

"That's clear... we'll stretch the wire."

"Vlodko will come—he'll handle it..."

"I'll handle it myself, without Vlodko."

"Talk-yap... Look—she's stirring."

The girl ponderously raised herself to her elbows, waited a minute until her head had stopped swirling, and straightened her arms slowly. Leaning on them, she looked around. They saw her face, black and blue, her torn skirt, tufts of stockings hung on her legs like old bark. Here she started to crawl, barely finding the strength just to drag her body a few centimeters.

"Where's she going?"

"Don't you see? She's heading toward us."

"Now!"

The girl crawled up to the wicket gate and hit it with her head. The gate screeched, the girl began moaning, the lady of the house gasped.

"I told you—shut the gate for the night."

"So, why haven't you?"

"See how she isn't crawling to the Marchuks."

"It's closer to us."

Strength left the girl, she fell on her chest onto the gravel that covered the path. Her right hand lay on a flower bed.

"My irises! They're so delicate! Why are you standing there like a tree stump? Do something!"

"What am I supposed to do?"

"You see—she's crawled toward us."

"Go and meet her. Maybe you want to ask her in? I'll put on some coffee."

"What are you jabbering? It's not the time to banter."

"Look—the Marchuks' blinds just swayed."

"That's what I thought... they're looking... staring intently," she strained through her teeth.

"No doubt they always close their gate."

"Haven't I told you: shut it?"

The girl stirred, extended her arms under herself and tried again to raise herself to her elbows. Her head was swaying from side to side. Finally the world straightened out with her eyes. She licked her swollen black lips. For about a minute she looked in front of her, as if she had just remembered the direction she was going, then she lowered her head and crawled again.

"She's crawling to the door."

"With her foot through the irises, the irises... Why isn't she crawling through the middle? Intentionally, huh?"

And actually, the girl was crawling partly on the flowerbed on her right side, and now with her foot, broken irises were being dragged behind her.

"Ah, their blinds swayed again," he pointed with his finger.

"Well, let them look. I won't open up."

"They'll talk about us then."

"No, they won't. Because we'll also find something to say."

"If Vlodko were just here... he'd give 'em hell."

"Those bums."

"Well."

"Look how stubborn she is."

But metal bells were humming in her head—ding! dong! ding!—and the pain poured throughout her body, drowning out her new parts so much that she immediately turned into a massive clot of hellish pain... she was nauseous, a bitter burning rolled up to her throat, and she felt it on her tongue... she felt like drinking... drinking a lot... just to crawl a bit more, a bit more, just a tiny bit more, she could already see the stairs and the door above them, to the right next to the door post a doorbell... to crawl to it and press it... they'll save me, give me water... drink...

"No, I won't open it up," the woman said with resolve.

"Then let's get to sleep already... Why stand here like posts? We've gotten our fill of looking."

He waved his hand and trudged to the bathroom. His wife stood for a while yet, listening to the water swirling, and when the metal latch on the door clanged, she went in herself.

"Try sleeping now," her husband yawned.

"Take a pill," she advised.

"You'll bring me some water in a glass... oh-oh-oh," he began to groan as he lay down.

Here her hand touched the first step of the stairway. She decided to rest a bit. She put her head on the step and felt great pleasure when the surface cooled her burning cheek. Only now she noticed her handbag on her elbow. She couldn't remember what was inside... She finally remembered and pulled out a bottle of perfume. Clenching her teeth on the cap, she turned it in her fingers. Then she spat out the cap and splashed the perfume on her face. It burned so much that she screamed, and her body convulsed as though it had been penetrated by an electric current. It seemed she was going crazy from the pain. Fortunately, it didn't last long. The pain slowly decreased. Then she felt that she had come to her senses. The bottle fell from her hand and rolled along the road.

"What's this?" His wife became alerted.

"Do I know?"

"Do you think she's crawled to the steps?"

"Don't think so."

"Maybe she'll crawl up to them, but she won't stand upright on the steps...," his wife said, and, calming down, turned on her other side. "And she won't be able to reach up to the doorbell—that's almost... True?"

"Uh-huh..."

"She won't reach it..."

"If that's not enough... we haven't slept in so long. I have to get to the Children's World store by nine."

"Why?"

"I arranged for a woman to hold a wooden horse for me. Vlodko will be bringing his little one."

"Why, is there a shortage of wooden ones?"

"You didn't know? Sleep..."

"Uh-huh…" And after several minutes, falling into sleep she whispered: "She won't reach it…"

Along the stairs there were railings, and she thought, by holding on with her hands, maybe she'd have enough strength to clamber up. How many were there? All together five steps—futile. Here she'll just get on her legs… just a little more… more… go on… go on… Finally the railing was beneath her arm, and she, standing there on her legs, smiled to herself, or at least she thought she was smiling. She remembered how as a little girl she loved to smack the metal globe on railings with her lips, that globe was always so cold. Unfortunately, there was no globe here, instead just this metal pipe which she was hanging on to. She leaned with her mouth on it and with delight began to lick the intoxicating cold of the metal, which suddenly engendered a tide of saliva, of cold saliva. For a short time she was able to trick her thirst this way… Tiny hammers were knocking in her head. A stiff pain in the nape of her neck first rose, then fell like a tide. Again she felt nauseous, and hanging her head across the railing vomited, gurgling loudly. Her mouth was sour and hideous. She licked the metal until saliva began to flow from her mouth. A concussion, she thought. If I'm nauseous, that means a concussion… She started to remember what to do in such cases. "It is important to remember that the symptoms of concussion can appear in a few minutes as well as several dozen hours later, if during the entire time the patient shows no signs… If after the blow to the head the patient loses consciousness, vomits, and his limbs begin to tremble…"—only my hands are trembling… just my hands…—"if he doesn't answer questions…"—I answer… I remember everything… I hear how the trees are rustling… ask me…—"if he is tossing…"—this isn't about me… clear that it's not about me…—"until the ambulance arrives the patient should lie calmly. You cannot give him anything to drink, or force him to take any kind of medication, because he may choke. Instead you should apply ice or some other cold compress to his forehead"—I press my head against the handrail… just in case… maybe this isn't a concussion… you can't give water… so… move on… But now she felt nauseous. And it was so intense that she couldn't hold on and fell with her hands on the stairs. She had to wait for a bit.

His wife dreamt that water was gurgling above her ear, and she awoke. It gurgled outside the window, she heard a wheezing and moaning. She's crawled all the way up... well, what does she need from us?

"Do you hear?... No way... he's sleeping like a hamster..."

His wife covered her head and tried to imagine something pleasant, so she could fall asleep easier. A battered girl's face emerged in her memory. Cursing her allergy to pills, she began to think about Vlodko.

She'll make her way to the doors... she didn't know how much time was left... maybe none at all... Good that she remembered that she shouldn't drink. That's the first thing she would have done—to ask for something to drink... She began again to rise up on her legs. This required so much effort that when her chest finally fell onto the handrail, it seemed that this was the end—before her eyes colored circles twirled, she couldn't discern anything else. Pain in the nape of her neck pulsed furiously... If only I can hold on... and not fall... She rested for a minute and made a step, then another. Now she was on the second step. Three more. And again she smirked to herself... What a smarty I am. These torments will soon be over... Who lives there? And suddenly she got frightened... Maybe there's no one home? They couldn't help but hear the fight... Who wouldn't wake up with such a clamor? Are they really not in?... Phoo, I'm stupid... they're just sleeping at the other end of the building. Of course, that's how it is. But these are the windows to the living room or the kitchen... What kind of blinds are in the kitchen?... So a living room... One more step, another... The third step. I'll wake them up now... poor people... Do they have a telephone?

The wife squirmed on her bed, her thoughts kept returning to their yard the whole time. For some reason it was quiet. What's she doing there?

The wife got up from the bed, walked over to the window and pushed away the blind. To the right of the windows there used to be an added-on veranda, and the owners could see the stairs and door.

The girl was hanging onto the rail. She's made her way up. She's climbing up further.

The fourth step... Just a bit more... rest...

Well, move on. What can I do now? Will she really ring? To total strangers! In the middle of the night! There's contemporary education for you... Back in our day... And what do I say there... Maybe I still should go out? Well, go out and what next? What should I do with her then? Console her? Can't let her in the house—she'll steal us blind... She's roaming around with some kind of vagabonds. Expect bad news from this kind... Well, just look at her... She's crawling and crawling... What does she think? What, we'll greet her with open arms here?.. Filthy slut... So don't go running around with just anybody...

The fif-fifth... the fifth ste-ep... finally...

Her head was buzzing...

And he just gulped down his pills and sleeps. His wife shook her head... He didn't think to turn off the bell—now you'll hear the music start playing. She was about to move from the window in the hope of finding where that doorbell had become disconnected there, but suddenly the building began to ring and shake, as though in a fever, and she knelt down in the middle of the room like a thief caught stealing...

"What, there again?!" Her husband woke up.

Those words reinvigorated her. Shaking off a strange fear, she jumped up to the window and plucked angrily on the blind.

"May lightning stri…! She's leaned her head on the doorbell! Have you ever seen anything like this?! Stop it! Do you hear?! Stop it!" She screamed, knocking along the pane.

The girl raised her head. Now just the silence continued ringing.

"Lo-ord, what a night!" The man of the house sighed.

They're at home... that's good... they've heard me... they'll open up now...

She could now see the face of the girl distinctly—tormented, in black and blue and scratches. And when their gazes met, the woman, frightened, screeched and grabbed her chest—the girl's lips with traces of blood that burned on them, these big, puffy lips suddenly began to curve into a smile. It was unbelievable—a smile on that face! As if it were a flower in a puddle of rain.

"What is it?" Her husband called out.

His wife wanted to explain something to him, but she couldn't gasp enough air. She leaned on the windowsill to keep from falling. Her smile grew and grew at that time—she fluttered away from the face and got closer to the window, covering the flower bed, the trees, the street, and the Marchuks's building with herself—like a gigantic wounded seagull she beat the pane with her wings, and her sad rivulets, either rain or tears, rolled along the glass. And the window split precisely in two, and together with that night wind that smile flew in, and the room suddenly split down the middle—the walls ran into the four corners together with the furniture, only the bed was left on which the man of the house was sitting and frantically shouting, striving to outshout the rustle of the wind, which was dancing all around:

"Well, what?! Well, what's going on there?!"

"She's laughing! She's laughing to me!" His wife shouted, gesturing, but he couldn't figure out what she was saying—an awful wind tore her words into scraps.

"What is it?! I don't hear anything!"

"She's laughing! You hear—laughing!"

"What happened?! Will you finally tell me?!"

THE VAGRANT

He appeared at lunch time in a small town where all the townspeople knew each other, so the foreigner's arrival evoked extraordinary interest, even more so because his appearance was really weird: imagine a gangly guy in an old hat with a wide brim, in a worn gray coat that reached almost to the ground, in well trodden shoes with toes turned up, covered with dried mud and dust, in laces of different colors; his face was long, overgrown with a plucked, very slight mustache and the same kind of beard, ash-colored hair in thick shaggy locks falling on his shoulders. And if you just look at his eyes—they were a miracle of divine providence, more than just eyes—they are gray and peaceful, but just like a saint on an icon—that's it, all right. He's walking and propping himself with a walking stick.

"Who's this vagrant?" The ladies shook their heads, and the men eyed the uninvited guest with displeasure, blurting out:

"Watch out...if anything happens to disappear..."

Everyone expected the stranger to approach somebody with certain questions, at least be interested in where to eat or find lodging. But for some reason like a deaf and dumb man he ambled along the street slowly without saying a word to anyone. The children first decided to engage him, they ran after him in a crowd, crying out:

"Hey, you, stranger! Let's play hide and seek!"

Under these circumstances the parents pretended to call their children to stop chasing him, but it was in such a tone that the children understood what they wanted to hear and tried to vex the stranger even more.

Even the dogs didn't like him, and they howled from the four corners of the city. A scruffy one, evidently expecting a prize from his master in the form of a tasty bone, attempted to bite the stranger's leg. But he struck his walking stick on the ground, and the dog whimpered not so much from fear as from the insult that he was being slighted, because he wasn't even hitting him, but just striking the ground. The dog ran away, tail between his legs, back to his yard where he got a good kick from his master, who was expecting to see an interesting spectacle, but instead saw his very own dog's humiliation.

It irritated everyone the most when the stranger went to the town hall where there were lots of pigeons. He pulled a handful of grain out of his pocket and scattered it to the birds, who flew to him from all directions. One of them even sat on his arm and trustingly nibbled from his palm. The stranger later scattered some more grain for them and walked on...

"Isn't this weird that he's feeding our pigeons?" The local inhabitants were indignant and nodded their heads with resolve when the yardman Puharchyk chased away the birds and carefully swept the grain into a puddle with a broom, mixing it with mud.

"They're our pigeons, and we'll feed them!" The yardman snapped to the stranger, but the stranger silently stooped his shoulders and, as it appeared to everyone, laughed bitterly, and in that laugh there was either a certain scorn or sympathy—one couldn't figure it out, in short, it just didn't sit well with the inhabitants of the little town and only heightened contempt for the tramp in their hearts.

Then another thing happened that made them fly into a rage— the stranger, without asking anyone, went to the cafeteria and threw something to a dog that was sitting near the steps waiting for his master.

Everyone then fixed their eyes on the dog—would he take it or not? For the prestige of the town rested on it.

"He shouldn't take it," said the yardman in a tone in which you could sense the certain destiny of doubt. "I know that dog. That's the druggist's dog."

"Yeah, yeah," somebody reiterated. "That's a good doggie. I even tried to buy him once, and the druggist didn't want to hear of it. He says: this dog is a dog for all dogs! O-ho...I know..."

But this thrice-damned creature, this odious louse-like creation, that held the aspirations and honor of the town beneath its nose, sniffed what the stranger had tossed him with curiosity and greedily grabbed it with his teeth, gobbling it up. He even glanced at the unexpected provider of bread with enormous gratitude. Everyone who saw it gaped from terror. Anger rose in their hearts, which was only a droplet away from overflowing all over.

"What a snake!" The yardman murmured through his teeth.

"Gotta call the druggist. Let him give it a knock on the head for shaming us like this."

They sent a youngster to the druggist, who was having supper in the cafeteria where the stranger had gone. The druggist stepped out onto the street, wiping his greasy lips with a handkerchief.

"Well, what's happening there?"

He was quickly told the whole horror of the situation, and then he, no joking, got so angry that he picked up a rock and tossed it at his own dog.

"Get marching, you snake! Get out of my sight!"

The older boys also began to hurl stones at the dog, running after and shouting:

"Shoo from here! Shoo!"

The yardman at that moment stepped up to the spot where the dog had been sitting before, and carefully examined whether anything was left, in order to indicate exactly what the stranger had thrown to the dog, but, unfortunately, he didn't find anything in particular and spread his arms apart in disappointment.

"Oh, I won't forgive him!" The druggist raged. "I'll poison him today."

"Or drown him!" Somebody suggested. "Better to drown him, he'll suffer less, because they say it like this: it's just a damn dog! A being without consciousness."

Then everyone, forgetting about the dog, became interested in what the tramp was doing in the cafeteria, and engaged a delegation of four men to go on reconnaissance, who were thankful for the opportunity to slosh down a tankard of ale without getting any flak from their wives.

They noticed the stranger in the corner at a table. He was sitting alone, having set his hat on the windowsill and his walking stick against the wall. He was sitting and waiting for his lunch to be brought to him.

The men sat nearby and ordered beer. The stranger asked for some kind of soup and meat, and when he saw that they had brought the men beer, he ordered some for himself, but he didn't say what exactly, but just nodded his head in the direction of the tankards and said:

"And something to drink, please!"

His voice was soft and quiet. He was entirely too modest and timid. The men just shrugged their shoulders:

"Is it worth it because of some sluggard to make such a mess in town?..."

They decided they should drink up their beer peacefully and part their ways, each according to his business, leaving the stranger in peace, but then something happened that really intrigued and later riled them. Before they brought him lunch the waiter showed the stranger a little piece of paper with a bill and said:

"Everybody pays up front here."

But the vagrant's eyes grew wide and he wagged his head eerily:

"I...you see...don't have any money...I'm just really hungry...I haven't eaten for three days...But I don't have any money..."

Then the waiter stuck out his lower lip indignantly and grunted:

"Then there's nothing to talk to you about. Get out! We don't feed tramps!"

The men shot glances at each other and without speaking decided that something was wrong here. They left their beer unfinished and started after the foreigner.

The crowd that patiently waited on the other side of the street got fidgety and fixed their eyes on the men in fascination.

"He didn't have any money!" One of them announced.

"Aha, he's an ordinary tramp," another seconded.

"He says he hasn't had a crumb in his mouth for three days!" Said a third.

"They chased him out of here like a dog," piped in a fourth.

"Didn't I tell you?" The yardman jumped up. "They should arrest him right away, cause he's not just a tramp but a bandit."

"Maybe he got out of prison?" The thought flashed to one of the women.

"That's it exactly, just out of prison!" The yardman seconded. "A thief, or maybe worse—a murderer."

The railroad guard, who till now had been silent, announced in deep thought:

"Mebbe this is the guy who hit my dead brother with a bottle across the head during a fight?!"

The whole crowd focused on the guard with sympathetic looks, everyone grew terribly sad for his dead brother, and they all decided to call the police to arrest him...this molesting bandit.

And he, the guilty party in the clamor and the unrest, entered somebody's yard and asked for water, and asked if they could spare him some bread. Just think what insolence! To go into somebody else's yard and ask for food! The owner, who had just come out of the house, said that there was water at the watering post in the street, and bread in the store, and there's no reason for him to roam around here. Without saying a word the stranger turned around and left. And the owner later related that the stranger had even threatened him, but you can't frighten him—he's been through it all and doesn't shy away.

The tramp, stopping in the street, set off toward the watering post, but it was nailed shut with boards, and he couldn't simultaneously pump with his left hand and put his right under the stream of water. The water pump was already quite old and pumped very little water, but, when he tried to pump it and then put his cupped hand under the flow, nothing came out, because by the time he reached it, the stream of water had disappeared and in his cupped hand only a few drops fell that he greedily lapped up. Finally he figured out a better way: taking off his hat, he set it down in the spot where the water was streaming, but then a cop arrived and put his hand on his shoulder. The tramp didn't even have time to pick up his hat from the ground.

Following the cop to the station a crowd of people grew, expecting an interesting ending to this adventure.

They took two men as eyewitnesses. The cops set the stranger down at a table and began to interrogate him:

"Who're you and where'd you come from? Or even better, give me your documents, cause you'll just lie."

The tramp blinked his eyes for a while.

"Which documents? I didn't take any documents? I've never even seen documents."

"He's gotta be kidding!" One of the men slapped himself on the thigh.

"Well, well, don't make problems here!" One of the cops thundered. "Empty everything from your pockets."

On the table the tramp put a bit of rusty barbed wire, half a fistful of wheat and three nails.

Those present exchanged puzzled looks.

"Why are you carrying all this on you?" The cop asked. "Why do you need this wire and those nails?"

"They nailed my arms with nails...And my feet...And the barbed wire my head..."

"What? What are you blabbering? I'll show you how to mess with me! Tell me fast, what's your name?"

"My name...my name is... Don't you know my name?" The stranger answered in a really quiet, timid voice.

"This stranger's making fun of us." One of the men shouted.

"A real psycho!" A second one tossed in.

"What do you take us for?!" The cop slapped the table. "We know your tricks!"

"I'm just really hungry. Haven't had anything in my mouth for three days. Please let me have something to eat..."

"First you have to tell us where you came from and why."

But the stranger was just silent.

"Well?!" The cop bellowed.

"Well?!" The eyewitnesses repeated.

"I...I don't know...I just came here and wanted to see...how you...I just came, and that's all..."

The voice of the stranger disarmed everyone present with its meekness and peacefulness, they could sense paternal solicitude in it, something warm and familiar. A strange sensation began to be born in the people's hearts when they heard him.

One of the men stepped over to the cop and whispered:

"Listen, maybe he's mentally ill? Let's leave him in peace."

All three of them found this solution the best.

"You can go."

The stranger, without hurrying, accepting everything as proper and customary, started to the exit. Near the doors he turned back and said:

"The Lord save you."

Having heard what happened at the station, the crowd slowly began to disperse.

"Just think, a crazy guy... Nothing of interest." Disillusioned, everyone shook their heads, just the children didn't leave the stranger and persistently followed him to the very outskirts of the city. The older children who lived there knew nothing about it and played quite peacefully. They tied the tail of a cat to a long rope and attached it to a tree. The cat screeched in despair and from fear, rolling himself up and unrolling, scampering about, but the cord was strong and didn't rip. The children surrounded this spectacle and roared with laughter.

Then suddenly they stopped laughing: a gangly man with a walking stick in his hand moved closer to them, and they gave way to him. The stranger untied the cat and then, without saying a word to the children, walked away slowly along the road.

The children furiously began cursing, and those who had managed to get there from the center of town explained in brief who that man was, and then the entire crowd grabbed rocks and clumps of branches from the ground and rushed to cut his path off. They surrounded him and began to cast everything within reach at him. They were enraged, they wouldn't forgive this tramp for his insolence.

The stranger covered his face with his hands. Tiny streams of blood oozed between his fingers. The blood encouraged the children more. Someone tore the walking stick from the hands of the man and struck him across the head. It broke in two. You could hear a dry snap, and the man fell to his knees, trying to rest his head on his chest. He said something, but no one listened to the words. They tore his coat off, and he was left in just a clean white shirt and old pants, but soon the shirt turned black from the mud. Blood flowed from his head, his face, his shoulders and hands.

He still gathered a little strength to lift himself from his knees and made his way to the picket fence. There, leaning sideways on the fence, covering his face with his hands, the stranger still tried to take a few steps. One of the boys, demonstrating his strength and dexterity, aimed with a brick so accurately that he hit him right on the forehead. And the man, gasping deeply, quietly sat down on the ground. His gangly body feebly stretched out under the picket fence and grew still. The children knelt in place, expecting the man to get up, but he didn't move at all. Then they understood that he was dead, that they had killed him. And then they asked each other: "Why?" But couldn't find an answer. One of them lifted the coat off the ground and covered the corpse of the unknown man with it . A younger boy, grabbing his head with his hands, vomited.

Afterward fear seized the children, and they ran to their homes, stifling sobs in their chests and something else terrifying and painful that tore out from within. They clenched their teeth, guessing that maybe this would pass. But it didn't pass, it curled in them like a coil of vipers, and hurt badly. The children didn't know what it was, and that terrified them even more, because all of a sudden it seemed to all of them that they had seen THAT FACE somewhere, that they had known it from their earliest childhood. But where, where was it from?

And each one spoke through clenched teeth:

"No, it's not him... It's not true! He's not like that!" But somewhere in their heart unconsciously there was born an enormous and foreboding:

"It's him, it's him..."

III. FANTASTIC
AND ALTERNATIVE WORLDS

1

"Yes, we like this house."

"You like it? I'm really happy. Just look at the view! This road leads to Kryva Dolyna, and beyond the valley, right away there are woods. Lots of berries and mushrooms. My husband and I, may he rest in peace, used to go... cause you see, it's sad for me to live here alone. The house is too big. And my son says: sell it and move to our town. My son checked out prices. It's not too expensive, eh? In town it'd be twice as expensive. You'll live here peacefully. The people are really nice. It's close to town. Soon it'll get urbanized, they'll extend the trolleybus line out here. But, I see, you have your own car... Just farms all around... It's quiet, peaceful..."

"And these rifles... Did your husband hunt?"

"Ah, those... yes, yes, sometimes... duck hunting..."

"You mean there's nothing in the woods?""The woods... yeah, cause... but..."

"Just the wild rabbits."

"Rabbits? What're you saying? Never in your life! Who told you about the rabbits? There aren't any rabbits here. Those are all rumors. You can be sure. What rabbits? From where?"

"Why are you so upset? I was just asking."

"I wasn't upset. It just seemed like that to you. But there aren't any rabbits here. He used to go duck hunting... Hey, maybe you'd like some tea?"

"No, thanks. Time for us to go."

"What have you decided?"

"We'll take it."

On the hills that looked like black trees, the farm owners stood and watched as we were led to our new home. Above them bloated gray clouds floated, and among the clouds the black roses of ravens bloomed. Their sad look didn't portend anything good; we looked on in silence without moving. After some time one of them descended the hill and offered his help. He was an old but muscular man. His name was Kostyo.

In the late evening when we finished settling in on our property, and after my wife went to bed with the little one, Kostyo stayed with me for tea.

"You lived in the city?" He asked, making himself comfortable in the corner between two puffy credenzas. And without waiting for an answer he added: "Even this isn't a village. Just ain't no road. You call this a road? It's a swamp. Without boats you'd never get through when there's slush. And there, in general, it's not too bad... Oh dang it."

"Why are you swearing?"

"Don't you know?" And he squinted his eyes.

"What was I supposed to know?"

"About Kryva Dolyna. Let it be crooked for eternity. Oh-oh-oh, this is heavenly retribution... There's no way out for them or any law."

"What are you talking about?"

"Whaddya think, about the rabbits."

"About the rabbits?"

"Uhuh."

"Valykhnovska said that there aren't any rabbits here."

"E-he, that's a clever dame. She said that to sell it. Don't you know how it works?"

"I don't understand. Unless, is it bad where the rabbits are?"

"Spit... Nye-nye, you gotta spit anyway to keep it from coming true. This isn't a joke... A whole slew of rabbits here. Just like sparrows. In the gardens and orchards they jump like crazy. They'll eat up whatever you plant. Whether you shoot at them or not it doesn't matter—you won't hit 'em... They're so quick... So ultimately nobody shoots at them... You won't believe it that anybody who tries to shoot can ever get away with it... If not now, then down the road, the rabbit's revenge get 'em anyway. I remember during the war a Kraut lived in my house. An officer—from the intilligintsia... If he didn't polish his boots he wouldn't go outside. "Danke sehr. Give me mehr." True, once he nailed me so hard with a stick whip—I had stripes like this all over my back! Once he decided to go rabbit hunting... And by then a couple Krauts had already gotten killed hunting... Everybody told him something was amiss with those rabbits. And he responded: "Galician Hasen?" And left. And what do you think? He stumbled on a branch and the carbine fired at him."

"What did the rabbits have to do with it?"

"Well, you see, it seems like nothing, but... You should go to Kalenyk. He knows better. I settled here just before the war, and he was born on the farm. He remembers the time when the gentlefolk used to go hunting. They went mostly after wild boar, but sometimes to get a rabbit. And what do you think? One shot himself, another—his friend, and a third—flipped over into the ravine... I'll tell you, they're clever—when they go after the gardens it's at night. Even the dogs are afraid of them."

"Come on!"

"Uhuh... Once in the middle of the night I heard a dog howling and howling. Well, I threw on my leather jacket and went out... And the rabbits were sweeping up the cabbage so fast that you could hear crackling sounds. The dog got tangled beneath the boards in the yard and whimpered. I yelled to him: "Brovka! go get 'em!" But he didn't even stir. He just shivered and whimpered."

"You couldn't chase them yourself?"

"Hey, am I stupid? Old Matsiy somehow leapt out with a pitchfork. What do you guess? One of the rabbits jumped so hard into him that he flew up like ballet dancer and broke his leg."

"Some kind of devilry."

"Aye, that's the truth. Only the devil knows what it is. You can imagine—they tore up a greyhound."

"Now you're..."

"I swear they tore it up! Ask anybody you want. Vikhtiuk had a greyhound. A good greyhound. Once it disappeared. Well, Vikhtiuk goes looking for it. He found it in the valley torn to shreds. There obviously was an incredible fight, cause everything was torn up all around, as if some boys had gone at it. And tufts of hair—a dog's and a rabbit's. and you say..."

"Well, look," I thought, "You don't have to travel far for folklore—it's under your house, growing like pigweed."

"That's not all," Kostyo couldn't calm down, "If it only was! But those rabbits influence us in some way. At times it seems as though something is creeping into your soul... well, I don't know how to say it... it's as though you're a rabbit... Do you understand?"

"No." I shook my head.

"Well, you walk along the field and above you a raven says "Caw!," and you shrivel up. Or a dog begins to bark, and it's as though a grater's passing along down your back. Or you look into the mirror—and see the spitting image of a rabbit. It's already at the point I shave just when I really have to, so I don't have to look as often in the mirror... Or if you look at your wife—she gets a harelip. I've lived with her for so long and never noticed it. And then suddenly I noticed... Something unfathomable is going on... You're about to laugh—and that laughter is just like a rabbit's squeal. Eh, eh... Have I ever eaten raw carrots before or cabbage? Never before. Then from a certain point in time I began to guzzle down food... Somehow I drop by at my neighbor's—and he's holding his hand behind his back. And he—chomp, chomp... his hand behind his back... then he quietly lowers it. Then it rolls out from under a bench. I look—a head of cabbage. Well, I think, it's not just me who's stupid."

"It turns out then, Valikhnovska tricked us?"

"It turns out she did... Not for pleasure of course. Her husband also got a heart attack cause of those rabbits when he chased after them with a rifle... Hey, why am I telling you just about bad stuff? I made a fence out of barbed wire, I dug in wooden stakes all around the seedlings and now I have some peace. You can live... why not? Just sometimes you feel like hiding in a corner, falling to the ground and pretending that you're not there. Why is that so?"

2

A year passed...

"Where're you going?"

"I'm gonna do some shooting."

"Don't go," I could sense an apprehension in her voice I never knew. She looks at me almost pleading. I want to shake this penetrating gaze off of me, but can't. "Do you hear me?" Her voice echoes as though from a far off valley. "I don't want you to go. Better if you'd play with Baby Andriy."

Baby Andriy is fidgeting on the floor, trying to fix a broken drum-playing mechanical rabbit.

"I'll be back soon... I'll bring him a little rabbit."

"I want a little rabbit!" The little guy screamed. "This one's broke. Bring me another one."

I walk out of the house and I see my wife's tightly compressed lips. They're trembling like leaves in the wind.

Our house rises above the wide high ground, overgrown on both sides with sweetbrier and thorn berries. The high ground rolls to Kryva Dolyna and gets lost there. My feet slip along the loose, saturated earth.

I looked back beyond the gate. I saw her face in the window. Having pushed aside the curtain, she follows after me with her gaze , it's as though I hear: "Don't go!"

A morose noontime takes me into its gray coldness, a damp silence on watch wafted out of the valley.

I took my rifle off my shoulder and slowed down my step so as not to frighten the rabbits beforehand.

3

When Arkhyp Kalenyk found out that I had bought a rifle to hunt rabbits, he wagged his head, deeply disconcerted.

"You want problems? I can't recall anybody ever shooting even a miserable one here."

"Till I try my hand—I won't believe it."

"But this is stupid. There are a lot better ways to kill time. Ones that are completely safe."

"And do you want to believe in all that nonsense? For a while I've had a mind to teach them rabbits a lesson. Especially now that I've bought a rifle."

"Have they really bugged you so much?"

"All those tall tales they spin around them have bugged me the most.""And what if I tell you they're not rabbits at all?""Not rabbits? How can they not be rabbits?"

"So-o... they're not rabbits. Maybe they're some kind of demons, do I know? It just happens sometimes that at night something shines in the valley. I've seen that light. It was in the form of half a globe as big as a good size hut. I stood there dumbstruck, I didn't believe my eyes. I thought I had to come closer and look. I was going-going along and it was—well just like from the house to the fence gate... and I couldn't get up closer to it. As though it's not going further away, and it's standing in place, but you can't go up to it. I spat and started off along the road home. But when I emerged on top of a hill and looked back—the light was gone."

"What could it have been?"

"Maybe little people or the rabbits drying their treasures in the moonlight," Kalenyk wryly laughed.

4

I sat down on a stone, began to smoke and waited. The entire valley was dotted with big and small stones, in places they were squeezed out of the ground and gigantic—half a man's height, as well as clumps the height of a man. They were covered with moss, they got wrapped with bindweed, spare tufts of grass jutted out from the crannies. The place wasn't very suitable for rabbits. True, a tall fern created something like a roof over the ground, and if a rabbit were to sit still, you'd hardly see him unless you stumble over him while you were walking. I lifted up a pretty big stone with my foot, and it began to roll down, bending over stalks of ferns to both sides. I kicked one, another, a third, and a fourth. The stones rolled, jumping up, hollowly striking one another, and grew still somewhere in the depths of the valley in the sweetbrier bushes and hawthorns. With a staff I raised an entire clump, round and wide-brimmed, and it rolled with a rattling sound, hitting the smaller stones, and then a whole bunch of them went downhill, so the fern began to hiss angrily.

Then I saw it. It jumped out of the grass, dove, jumped out again, and dashed, leaping before my eyes. I aimed and fired.

But I missed. The rabbit escaped. Then another one appeared, and, jumping just as high, rushed in the direction of the dense bushes. I fired again. This time the rabbit no longer jumped. With a joyful shout I ran to the spot where I saw it last. I didn't have to search long. Bending a fern I saw droplets of blood on a stone. But the rabbit wasn't there. A little further—blood again. I began to amble to the bottom of the valley, surprised at the spiritedness of this rabbit, because he certainly must have lost a lot of blood if he had marked the road for me so considerately. A tall prickly wall of blooming thorns cut my path. There in the thicket, perhaps, the last tracks were lost. And when I raked away the twisted branches with my rifle, I nearly shouted from surprise—the rabbit was sitting in the bushes and looking at me. He looked with such ferocity in his eyes that it was not like a rabbit, but an agitated dog. For a second I froze in indecision, but the rabbit didn't flee, and I feverishly began to think over the situation. I can't crawl through those bushes and I can't reach it with my arms. The bullet obviously had hit it in the back leg, which was all red, and surrounding it a whole pool of blood. This was unbelievable—rabbits don't have this much blood. I recalled that the tracks he had left behind also were overly saturated. Blood could be seen on the stalks of the ferns, and here even on the branches and leaves. An improbable fear took over me, perhaps the result of that fierce gaze that crucified and quartered me, a gaze that I was unable to endure, and I turned my eyes away. Trying not to make sudden movements or to make noise, I let the branches return to their place and then rapidly loaded the rifle. And again, spreading the branches apart, I met those hateful eyes. It was evident how furiously its tiny heart was beating—its chest pulsed in a nervous rhythm, and the pool of blood got bigger. Maybe it feels the pain, I thought. Then why is it sitting so still? I tried to imagine myself with a wounded leg, that is, rather not to imagine, but to recall how when in the army a piece of railroad track flew out of my arms and fell on my instep. I rocked back and forth along the gravel, going out of my mind from the pain, I coiled and uncoiled like the torn off tail of a lizard, wailing so much that you could hear me maybe all the way to the next station, then it turned out that nothing really awful had happened, just a small crack.

I raised my gun at him and noticed surprise and despair flashing in his eyes, as though he expected something that I was supposed to read in his eyes and understand—there was something else besides ferocity, there was something there which I didn't pay attention to, and now I distressingly wanted to remember, as though my own fate and further life depended on this, but my memory didn't return anything but this wrath of his. My finger froze on the trigger, perspiration covered my brow, my heart became vile and frightful.

He didn't run away, he stubbornly looked at me and it seemed as if he were reading me like an ABC book, reading me—wretched and empty, because that's exactly how I was at that moment. Didn't he really have the strength to crawl away a little further, at least to move from that spot? Maybe he understands that right when he does that I'll shoot immediately. I knew this, waiting for him to stir, and the rabbit stuck out petrified in place, and his ears protruded, and bloody veins appeared in his eyes, as though the fires of a distant city flared, extinguished, and flared again, because it was certainly the only language with which he could still come to an understanding with me—the language of blood. Only I couldn't understand it any longer.

This gaze would soon crack me like a nut and shell me. I already felt how it was becoming difficult to breathe, as though I had just covered a who-knows-how-long-of-a distance, just a little more and my heart will be beating in single rhythm with his tiny frightened heart. I understood the stupidity of all these thoughts but I couldn't control myself, something greater than fear crawled into my chest. And then I hollered at him. I wanted to shout something like "shoo!," but only a graty whoop tore out, either because my mouth got filled with saliva, or because of the imaginary run, after which I sensed myself exhausted and with bitter acid burning in my throat.

The shouting, though, didn't stir him. This was already beyond my strength. I couldn't leave my trophy in these bushes, and, putting my tail between my legs like a beaten dog, trudged home. I had to leave from here as a victor, because I am the king of nature and he is not. How dare he humiliate me with his terrifying steadfastness, throw me from my height to occupy the place that is destined to be mine? Now it was not ferocity, but the blood of distant ancestors beginning to shimmer and flap like flags, and then with such fervor as though I am destroying all the evil and unfairness in the world, with the fervor of a person who had been chosen for this blessed mission, believing that all of humankind was behind me—I pressed the trigger.

The eyes of the rabbit flared, but I no longer noticed surprise in them, the blow tossed him away and knocked him on his side, shattering his pulsing chest.

With my walking stick I pulled him closer, grabbed him by the ears and pulled him out of the bushes. His weight surprised me. He was too heavy, maybe twice the weight of an average rabbit. This must be some kind of special breed, I thought, throwing my trophy into a bag, and I started off uphill. It began to grow gray, a fog slowly crawled into the valley, and the ferns joyfully met it.

I felt easy and uplifted, as if I had just thrown off an unbelievable burden from my shoulders. But then I heard a squeal in the grass, bent over for a moment and saw a small baby rabbit. It was shriveled up and leaning close to the ground. I'm lucky, I thought, my little one will be really pleased. I grabbed the baby rabbit by the skin and, putting it in my hat, carried it off home.

It was already completely dark when I made my way out of the valley. My mood was like after a just victorious battle.

I walked along the road and whistled. The baby rabbit squatting quietly sat in the hat that I pressed to my chest.

And here I heard that someone was behind me, I even differentiated the stealthy footsteps. I nervously glanced back—some kind of shadow suddenly appeared on the road, or so it seemed... I stopped, guardedly looking into the darkness, and again an interminable fear overcame me, and my ears began to rise just like a rabbit's.

I moved almost in a run, but the road led uphill and I quickly ran out of breath and slowed my pace. Behind me I could clearly hear footsteps, here the unknown thing stepped on a branch and it cracked dryly. I stopped again almost physically sensing how my ears had stretched out, ardently listening to the darkness. But I didn't hear anything more and didn't see anything suspicious.

Gotta move on, these hallucinations can go to hell...

The higher I climbed, the hills along the path grew shorter and shorter, the force of the wind increased, it ruffled my hair, which now stuck to the side of my head. My head cast the shadow of a beet with a top. Tall ash trees rustled so loudly that I barely could catch the sloshing sound of feet behind me, someone was doggedly following me, managing to remain undiscovered. I tried to calm myself. Why be afraid? I have a rifle. Here I remembered that it wasn't loaded. I loaded it on the move. Again I looked back. The stranger obviously was walking along the palisade where it was darkest. Then I also stepped to the side and plowed along the palisade. It was curious that I barely heard my own steps, on the other hand, those in back of me still came through, despite the swaying of the wind and the rustling of the ash trees. High in the clouds the blind half-eye of the moon swayed, it blew cold and emptily from the sky where, it seemed, terrible winds were raging at that time, and the whirlwind dances were drawing in frightened stars as though into a vortex.

It was already not far, I could see the illuminated windows of my house. And I boldly quickened my pace.

Suddenly I screamed—something grabbed my left pant leg. It jolted from between two fence boards—my first sensation was that the tentacles of an octopus had grabbed me. I nearly fainted from surprise, tore away my leg—something prickly and thin passed along my pant leg. Soon my other leg was girdled by these... I don't know what to call them, because at that moment only the frantic round dance of octopi and cuttlefish circled in my head. Fortunately, when I tore free, I slipped and fell, and my hand ended up in the interweaving of those prickly tentacles, and only then did I understand that it was an ordinary blackberry bush. I tore out of it onto my feet, swore loudly and stepped out onto the road.

Curiously, the whole time that I was writhing to and fro beneath the fence, I couldn't hear the steps of the stranger. That meant that he was waiting patiently. I went on more slowly, straining my ear and trying to understand where my tormentor was. He too should get tangled up in the blackberry bush. But I had already crossed a large chunk of the path, and his steps hadn't become silent for a moment. What does he want?

"What do you want?!" I screamed, shouting over the wind and the rustling of the trees, the shout flew off and opened up in the darkness without an answer.

Then I threw myself into a run, my feet got stuck in the mud, and slipped, it wasn't easy to keep my balance, but the protective light of my own house quickly grew close, and I was already in the magic circle of the house light. Our entire yard was brightly illuminated. I entered with the look of a victor and shout:

"Khry-y-yshka!"

And the wind reverberated with the ash trees: "Khry-y-yshka!"

My wife appears on the threshold with the little one.

"Look what I brought!"

I gave them my trophy, and only then, turning my face to where I had come from, but my tormentor wasn't bold enough to step into the area of the light. He remained there in the darkness, it seems I could even discern his figure—he was standing beyond the fence and, perhaps, was looking at us.

"Khrystia, look over there—is anybody there?"

"Where?"

"Over there, where I'm pointing."

"N-no... Who's supposed to be there? I don't see anyone."

"So... Must have imagined it for sure. Let's go inside."

5

The little guy was really pleased with the tiny rabbit. We put him in a big cardboard box where we had put some sawdust. It was already too late to bother with the captured prey, and I carried it off to the cellar, and the next day on Sunday I pulled it out and showed it to Khrystia. I held the jackrabbit by the ears, turned it on all sides, waiting for shouts of enthusiasm. To my amazement my wife was silent. She kept silent and didn't look at the jackrabbit, but at me. She looked at me the same way when I had been getting ready to go hunting.

"Why are you looking at me like this?" I couldn't hold out any longer.

"You... you..."

"Well, what?"

"It's a sh-she-rabbit, not a jackrabbit..." She was nearly whispering. And her face was pale.

I took a look—yes a she-rabbit. Does it matter? There were so many rabbits in the valley that it was time to totally annihilate them. Like rats.

"Well, what? Just imagine—a she-rabbit." I shrugged my shoulders.

"And this—is it her baby?"

"This is just too much!" I exploded. "This is a baby rabbit I picked up when I was walking out of the valley, it doesn't have anything to do with this one...these, in short, don't seem related."

"Are you sure?"

"I'll repeat again—I found it in another place. Besides, even if it were so, what does it change?"

"Are you planning on eating it?" There was such amazement in my wife's voice, as though I were planning on frying an old fat toad.

"And why not?... The fur, it's a shame, is messed up. Then we'll have roast—it'll be finger-lickin' good."

"You're nuts! I'm not planning on eating her!" Now she looked at me with repugnance.

"Maybe I should even cook the meat?"

"I don't wanna have anything to do with it! And, please, do your culinary art out of my sight."

"It looks like it's not me who's nuts, but you. What's with you—your maternal instinct has extended to our tiniest brethren? And how about when your father stuck a pig, leaving behind eight little piggies? Think about it—eight little orphans who had just stopped suckling milk. And you were eating their beloved mommykins. And you even helped make garlic sausage, scrapple sausage, kishka, ham, and the devil knows what else! Why didn't your instinct begin to speak then? And what about the eggs you enjoy every morning. You steal them from the nest of a loving mother! You eat the babies that still haven't come out of the shell!"

I screamed and screamed, but the true object of my annoyance was the she-rabbit that so humiliated me in the valley, and that now had become the cause of an argument.

"Shut up!"

"I won't shut up! You fried piggies! Two pink tender babies! You crisped their ears! I remember it well!"

"You—you fascist!" Khrystia wailed and, covering her face with her arms, ran out of the room.

I struck the she-rabbit on the floor in anger. I wanted to crush it, so that not even a wet spot was left after it.

"Daddy, what's a fascist?"

Damn, that's all I need.

"That's a bad guy," I grumbled just to extricate myself.

"Daddy, are you a bad guy?"

"No, Andriyko, I'm a very good guy... What kind of a guy am I for you? I'm a dad! A really good dad! See, I brought you a baby rabbit."

I didn't notice that I had raised my voice again, and the little guy's face grew sour, his lips pouting—ready to cry.

"Andriyko, your dad's good, isn't he? Don't be angry at your dad. Your mom and I have had a little tiff, and now we'll make up. And then your daddy'll cook the she-rab... the rabbit, and we'll eat him up."

"Then why did Mommy say she won't eat her?"

"Her? Who's her?"

"The she-rabbit."

Lord...

"Mommy was kidding. Daddy will go now to apologize to Mommy."

6

Khrystia was sitting on a couch with her hands propping up her chin.

"Khry... well, Khry... what's with you, for God's sake... Do you want me to throw her out? Do you? I can bury her in the garden. I can carve out a cross and coffin."

"Don't crack jokes."

"You're altogether... How could I know whether it was a she-rabbit or a male?.. And how it turned out I can't understand, why are you so depressed?"

"Because this won't end up in anything good."

"What do you mean?"

"They'll take revenge."

"Who?! What's with you?"

"Didn't anything strange happen to you during the hunt?"

"There was something... For example, a lot of blood came out of the she-rabbit. Then... she weighed twice as much as a rabbit her size, even though she wasn't pregnant."

"Anything else?"

"Nothing else."

"Not true."

Women's intuition is the 28th wonder of the world, that's why I was forced to describe everything as it happened in sequence.

I put the she-rabbit into the freezer and in the morning before leaving for work buried her in the garden. I couldn't eat her anyway. Her wild look remained in my memory.

In the evening on returning from work while I was still in my car, I noticed a stranger who was looking into our window. A sloping incline allowed me to roll up silently all the way to the gate with the motor turned off. I tried not to frighten him, but the damn gate screeched anyway, and the stranger ran around the corner. I rushed after him, but he disappeared without a trace.

"Take out the trash," Khrystia said after dinner.

Obediently, since this is one of my most significant duties, I carried the bucket out into the garden. We threw our trash out beyond the gooseberry bushes, right there where I had buried the she-rabbit. When I got close I froze — in that very spot there was a gaping hole. Somebody had dug up the she-rabbit. Why? In anger I dumped the trash into the hole and upon returning to the house shouted:

"It's all clear to me!"

"What's clear to you?" Khrystia calmly asked.

"That the mafia's at work here!"

"What are you driveling about?"

"You all conspired! Come on, confess! You want to play me for a fool?"

"I don't understand you."

"What's not to understand here? It concerns the rabbits. I don't know what impulse you're following, but the joke has dragged on too long."

"Explain something... I don't understand anything."

"If you weren't my wife I'd send you off to the Filmmaking Institute. You're a great actress. But you've gone after the wrong guy! You've gone overboard with the hole business."

"With which hole?" "With the grave of the venerable she-rabbit! There's a hole there now. And the she-rabbit's disappeared. Your conscience bothering you that the meat is going to waste?"

"There's a hole there?"

"A hole, a hole! But I've figured you out! It's you who so lovingly dug out the grave and pulled out my lawful trophy. And now it's being cooked at Kalenyk's for sure. And tomorrow you'll drag me out, so to speak, for roasted rabbit. Let's go to Kalenyk's. Right away without wasting time."

"Let's go. So that you can be assured of your stupidity. I swear there wasn't any conspiracy."

"You also swore that you'd never throw raw onions into the soup. And what happened? Did you ever even begin to sauté them?"

"What've onions got to do with this?"

"But you swore!"

"I promised, but when I'm in a hurry..."

"You're eternally in a hurry. If you had covered up the hole—who knows, maybe, everything wouldn't have turned out this way."

7

Kalenyk listened sullenly. After I related my hunting adventures, he told me:

"I'm afraid that this won't end here. I warned you that there aren't any jokes being played here. Nobody's planning to play any tricks on you, and for what reason? A joke's a joke until it's gone on too long."

"I can't accept these superstitions. That's why I'm looking for a more realistic explanation."

"But you yourself just related what happened to you during the hunt."

"All these tales put the fear into me, that's why I saw everything in that light. I was too excited. The wounded she-rabbit certainly just couldn't escape. What was left for her to do? Just to look at me... And couldn't my nocturnal tracker have been a creation of my imagination? That's why I'm inclined to think that the rest is all just somebody's joke."

"Well, of course, it's much simpler this way. If this is just a joke, then it didn't begin with you. Oksenych broke his arm, Matsiy his leg, Tymkevych got burned, and Prokip was blinded in one eye. All of them in one way or another bothered the rabbits."

"Listen, why do you tie all this in with the rabbits? Maybe a rabbit threw itself at Matsiy's leg, and he fell not so much from the blow as from surprise and broke his leg. Prokip became blind! He was over 80 years old. That's why he shied away from an operation. In the end, we're talkin' about maybe an ordinary cataract."

"No, it wasn't a cataract."

"But to accept a story that these rabbits are some kind of supernatural ones is just ridiculous! And then—what do rabbits have to do with it? A person followed me, if I didn't just imagine it. Under the window there also was a person. And it wasn't rabbits that dug out the she-rabbit from the hole. You can see the marks of a shovel there."

8

My wife went to sleep with the little one, and I stood in the kitchen next to the window and gazed into the darkness that hid all the secrets of the day in it, like a treasure chest snapped tightly shut, the key to which is lost, nobody knows when or by whom. I couldn't calm myself down, I was drawn to Kryva Dolyna. It seemed that I had forgotten something important there, something I wasn't conscious of before, but it was there, sitting inside me from my childhood, eating away at my soul. Casting away all hesitation, I put on my jacket, slid one eye over the rifle and decided that I wouldn't take it with me, but on the other hand, perhaps, not expecting much of my own boldness, stuffed a cleaving knife in my belt.

The night met me with a chilly breeze and dampness. When I found myself in total darkness, just like yesterday I sensed someone's footsteps, but now they were echoing in front of me. It was as though we had exchanged roles, and it was me who was a tracker, with the only difference that I couldn't figure out whom I was tracking.

The road was loose and soft. I complained that I didn't remember to put on my boots, and soon felt mud on my socks, but I didn't want to go back. At that moment I struck the rhythm of footsteps of whoever was walking ahead, and for God knows what reason, tried not to break the rhythm, as though the success of my wandering depended on this.

The barking of dogs echoed to me from the farms, it rolled across the moon somewhere onto the meadows and, weakened, fell onto the moist grass. But it was not enough for me. So the silence would stop grating my ears, I began to whistle a stupid song to myself, it encouraged me and revived my hankering for adventure, and the cleaver was an irreplaceable comrade for me in all of this. The footsteps in front of me no longer frightened me; I tried to step more loudly, so that my steps would re-echo the same way, but it didn't work. The footsteps belonged to a much heavier person, I judged his athletic build and, maybe, wouldn't be able to compete with him, so I walked in step without paying any attention to the exasperations of the muddy road, just as if it were me and not the first guy who had stirred its drowsiness and disturbed its oily black placidity. The road snaked and snaked, and the hills with bristling branches of bushes quickly rose, hiding the greatest part of the starless sky from me.

The impenetrable darkness that gaped ahead, like the wide open maws of a hungry beast, announced the approach of Kryva Dolyna. Here I recalled another method for increasing courage, and I lit up a cigarette. Now my nocturnal sortie, at least formally, didn't differ from a regular walk before sleep. I even stopped being carefully vigilant about the darkness, which had so invitingly opened up before me. I stopped sensing its derision, its malevolence, and started to think about the surprises that it, perhaps, was preparing for me.

I descended into the valley and it seemed as if I was descending into myself along a thin cable that stretched from my eyes to the depths of my body, into its darkest recesses and disquiet, not knowing anything about the length, or about when my hands themselves will sense the emptiness, and I—am a rapid drop to the bottom of consciousness.

Stones cracked and crumbled beneath my feet. Somehow unnoticeably in the sticky silence the footsteps of the guy ahead of me opened up.

There was no reason to go further, somewhere here, from this spot the whole valley could be seen as though on the palm of your hand.

My cigarette burned my fingers, I flicked it and the hot yellow fire flew below in an arc. Then I pulled out my cleaver, and my entire soul transferred into my right hand that powerfully pressed its handle.

It was useless to gaze into this despairing blackness, you can't catch anything in it besides your own helplessness, but I waited patiently. That glow remained the only proof I lacked in believing Kalenyk's nonsense. I knew quite well that a tree stump could shine at night, but there wasn't a single stump in the valley. That glow had to be extraordinary, or else I wouldn't believe in it. And though I didn't feel like smoking, I lit up again, setting my legs widely apart, as though preparing myself for battle.

Dampness oozed from the valley and made its way beneath my clothing, the mud stuck to my socks and already had begun to irritate me, but I stubbornly surveyed this mysterious place that hypnotizes as though it's trying to draw you into itself, into that unknown emptiness that calls and straightens up its forgotten wings above its head.

I decided—I'll finish smoking the cigarette and go. A frightening chill slid along my neck. I spent myself and yielded, I had enough courage just to get here, because here I already had begun to sense the indefensibility of my back and sides. The longing wish to look back appeared against my will and didn't let go. An endless number of footsteps that will radiate to the epicenter of my brain from all sides, were sensed all at once, and neither the cigarette nor the cleaver helped any longer, I suddenly became divided into two enemy camps—my legs strove to rush off and it was just my arms that didn't fail to lose a sense of balance and were ready to defend me.

The accursed silence, capable of driving you crazy, tears apart my chest, displaces everything in places that in its opinion is not laid out right, pulls me out from the inside and chases me home, dispersing herds of ants along a burning spine. I'll finish my smoke and go. I firmly decided, and the foresight of a quick end to my stupid wandering gave me strength. Slowly I calm down, very slowly. I'll take to my heels right away like a scared rabbit, and I'll run along the road without looking back.

The flashing began.

9

The flashing happened suddenly. The valley glimmered like a mirror aimed at the sun, but in a moment it grew dark again, only there in the depths where an illuminated dome still glowed, which really reminds you of a Cossack hut by its shape.

Here a mysterious murmuring and bustling could be heard, an endless number of muffled voices tore into my field of hearing. They all walked into the illuminated dome alone, and it blazed in solitude and splendidly, and most strangely—without illuminating the space around it, although its bright glow should have snatched a tangible area out of darkness. The entire valley came alive and bustled. I didn't see anything but distinctly heard life stirring. Even the ferns and stones beneath my feet were stirring and began to rattle excitedly. It seemed that a green wave of sprigs would knock me from my feet. Bushes swayed and surrounded from all sides with their stirring.

High above in the sky a star flashed, its light pulsed not any slower than the beating of my heart. And here I noticed that the lit-up dome pulsed to the same rhythm. It was as though the star and the dome were calling to each other, and that this conversation was peaceful, and it seemed, not devoid of content. In an instant I collected myself. My whole body tensed up and appeared to be clearly outlined—and not like the cogs of a mechanism. The fear disappeared that took nest in my soul, the vision of uncertainty disappeared. I myself pulsed, glowed and called back and forth to the star.

This is that long awaited opportunity to uncover a mystery. I carefully began to lower myself into the direction of the enigmatic glow, without releasing the cleaver from my grip. The closer I came to it, the more frenetic the noise surrounding it became. It seemed that a whirlwind was raging, the ferns from underfoot were seething like a turbulent sea, and I nearly was knocked off my feet. It was difficult to walk, my feet slipped on the moss-covered stones time after time. They stumbled, and the bushes foamed like a white blossom, jerked toward me, and grew to gigantic proportions before my eyes. The pulsing of the light of the star and dome became more intense and resembled alternating rapid gunfire. Suddenly my left foot slipped on a stone. I couldn't hold myself and got entangled in a bush with the cleaver falling from my hands. I managed to grasp it, but...but it had gotten noticeably heavier! I straightened up on my legs, the cleaver grew heavier and heavier, I could no longer hold it with one hand and took it with both. The weight increased so quickly, that the cleaver simply bent me over to the ground, so in order not to overstrain myself, I let it fall. It banged with a force that could be compared to the blow of a falling clod of earth.

My spirit suddenly sank without that weapon. But I was still drawn down to the valley because I would hardly be bold enough for another nocturnal trip. It was better to find a solution right now.

It was a lot easier to walk without following after the lights, but looking underfoot,. About five minutes passed until I lifted up my head. By that time I should have ended up in the center of the valley, but instead didn't even get a meter closer. The glow was the same distance away from the place where I had fallen. I remembered Kalenyk's account—it's true that the glow doesn't allow you to approach it. And what if you throw a rock at it? This idea obviously was stupid and had its deep traditions—everything you can't comprehend with your reason elicits the wish simply to destroy it. So I grabbed a rock, but just as it was ripped from the ground, it began to get heavier and heavier until I got rid of it cursing.

Now I had completely lost the rest of my courage—I turned and ran away, and it was so easy for me to escape that I had no time to be surprised by it. Even though there was good reason—because I was running uphill.

10

On Tuesday a new adventure happened. Just as I got home, my wife asked:

"Have you seen Andriyko?""Where?"

"What do you mean where? He was playing near the gate."

"I didn't see him."

Khrystia stepped out of the house and returned in a few minutes.

"Listen, he's not anywhere. Where'd he disappear to?"

Now we both began to search for the little guy, but when we had checked out all the nooks, my wife ran to all the neighbors, and I started off along the road. And only when I got down to Kryva Dolyna did I see him behind a clump of stones. Andriyko was peacefully sitting there playing with colored rocks.

"What are you doing here?"

"Playing."

"We set off for home quickly. Mommy's crying for you, and you're such a bad boy..."

I grabbed him by the arms, but he began to heave to and fro and scream:

"How about the rocks? Take the rocks!"

So we had to take them too. With the little guy in my arms I hurried back as fast as possible.

"How can you be so bad? How could you go there alone? Your mother'll let you have it now!"

The little guy laughed and was pleased by something unknown.

Khrystia ran out to meet us, wiping away her tears on the way.

"I'm gonna give it to you now!..." She ordered, and I quieted her down, because when it comes to the ritual of punishment, you won't get a word out of the little guy.

We pressed hard on the little guy—how did he make his way so far?

"Unc took me."

"Which uncle?"

"He came and said: Come to me, I'll give you some really nice toys, and you give me the baby rabbit. I gave him the rabbit and we set off, and he gave me the rocks. Dad, where are the rocks? Show me."

I took a handful of the rocks out of my pocket and only then looked closer at them—they looked like diamonds. My wife gasped.

"Do you understand anything?"

"The same as you."

"Who could it be?"

"Maybe that stranger who peeped in the windows."

"But those rocks... They're like diamonds."

"They're similar... Andriyko, what did that old fellow tell you?"

"Nothing."

"Did he tell you how to get home?"

"He showed me. He left, and I sat down and played. Will you give me the rocks you took?"

I gave him some of the rocks and put the rest in my pocket.

"Tomorrow I'll be in town, so I'll drop by at the jeweler's."

"Listen," Khrystia got scared, "better go to Slavko. Don't just go to anyone. What will you be able to explain to a stranger if they're really valuable—you'll get into trouble."

"Could be anything... Maybe there're some kind of mines in the valley."

"If not, who's gonna believe your drivel? Some old guy gave them to you! Try to explain then which old guy."

Slavko was struck dumb. To be sure he surveyed the rocks under his magnifying glass.

"Where did you get them?"

"Khrystia's grandmother left them to her."

"Keep on lying. Well, this is your business. If you'd like, want me to sell them?"

"No, what're you... family heirlooms.""What the devil are they good for you? You'll just hang onto them? Let me sell them."

"Ya know, I never shoot craps with the law, and don't plan on doing it now."

"A dopey priest must've baptized you! If you change your mind— come to me. Do you know for how much! He-he... Here, my friend, for a good... ahem... twenty thousand."

Even though Slavko always kept the real value down in such cases, the sum stunned me. Because I didn't show him everything.

11

After returning home I decided to walk to Kryva Dolyna while it was still light out. The key to the riddle was hidden there.

The fog curled and foamed, the valley was swathed in it, it was impossible to see anything, and I stopped in desperation, without knowing what I had to do next.

"I knew you'd come."

The voice emanated from beside me, from the densest part of the fog, and within a moment I could discern a familiar figure that moved to meet me.

"A-ah, it's you," I nodded to Kalenyk, sensing the tension fall, because I was expecting someone else.

"What are you looking for here again?"

"I want to figure out who made the trade for my son's rabbit."

"That's easy to explain—I did it."

God, what a dope I am. Of course the little guy would have never gone with a stranger and wouldn't have called him uncle.

"But why you? What's this to you? Who are you?"

"We flew here from another planet and landed in this valley. The first living creatures we saw were rabbits. We made a mistake. We thought the inhabitants of earth all looked like this... It was so long ago... I was really little then. My parents and their companions took the form and shape of those beings you saw here. Because rabbits had died out long ago on our planet... They left me by the machine, and left the valley, moving close to your settlements. The locals started shooting at them, chasing after them with dogs... Then they understood their mistake. The ones who were shooting looked just like they did... they were the same kind of people. Nothing different about them. The frightened "rabbits" ran back to the valley, so that with the help of the machine they could return to their true appearance. Only now it was too late. Your people had beaten them to it and destroyed the machine... This was during World War I. They could have taken it for some kind of tank or something..."

"But what happened to you?"

"They took me with them! And raised me.""You mean those rabbits are the descendents of those who came from your planet? And the lights?"

"The lighted dome that you observed is a receiver we constructed to finally inform our people back home about the fate of the expedition. In fact, it was I who made it, because no one else, since they were in rabbit form, could construct anything. But they knew how to make it and supervised my work. All their hope lay with me, so they never broke contact with me, never let me forget who I was... Day and night my whole waking life I worked on that transmitter. This was without having the slightest clue how it should look. I worked and the rabbits gave me signs when something was wrong. From early childhood I learned to understand their squealing... But the work pushed forward very slowly because they, knowing quite well what the transmitter is made of, didn't know how to make most of the parts. They had seen them only in finished form. The years passed. The war began. I went to the front. It seemed all their hopes had been dashed. And I could have been killed... Can you imagine what they endured during that time? Fortunately I survived. Maybe only because I had to survive... I returned home and my house was gone. It had burned down. And the drawings had burned up, and the parts. I was forced to start from scratch again..."

Kalenyk began to smoke, and I noticed how his fingers trembled.

"...from scratch," he repeated. "I thought I wouldn't be able to finish it. Till finally it was ready two years ago, and we began to send signals. And recently they answered. They're already flying here. Tonight they take us back to our home planet."

"You too?"

"Me too."

"But you have a family here..."

"But my homeland is there."

"One that you barely remember."

"I remember... I never stop dreaming of it."

"Why didn't you tell me earlier?""I couldn't. I wasn't sure whether our attempts to signal would succeed. I was already losing hope."

"But then I would have never dared hunt the rab... that is, your... eh..."

"That's why I tried to scare you. And not just you... I have a request. I want you to be there when they arrive for us. So you can tell my family that I... I'm very sorry to be leaving them... But I don't have much time. I want to die where I was born. Do you understand?"

I nodded my head. The old man's eyes got teary.

"They'll take us away. They're obliged to take us," he said with a cracking voice while walking away and disappearing in the fog. I sensed in his voice still painful doubt, he wasn't able to hide it in front of me. Of what was he unsure? Here I recalled that he didn't explain everything, but maybe it wasn't worth bugging him. He had to be with his family a bit. Tonight he will leave them forever. Only he will know that he's parting, and they'll act as usual. He will catch every movement with sadness, every word, trying hard to remember, in his mind he will embrace them, draw them near, and there'll be tears on his cheeks, and they'll ask what's wrong, and he'll keep silent, but this will just be his farewell.

12

When it grew dusk I couldn't sit in the house any more.

"Where are you going?"

"I'm going for a walk."

She still didn't know anything.

"There again?"

"This is the last time. Promise."

"Your promises! I know them!"

I puttered around the house a bit until Khrystia took the little guy to put him to bed, then I made my way to the valley.

Kalenyk's receiver was already working. I looked in the sky and besides the star that was pulsing earlier, I saw one more bright tiny dot growing before my eyes. I didn't take my eyes from it.

Someone touched my shoulder.

Kalenyk stood beside me with a knapsack on his back.

"They'll be here soon."

"What kind of vehicle can it be to fit all of you?"

"Rabbits don't take up a lot of space," he laughed. And there was bitterness in his smile.

"Rabbits?"

"Obviously they'll turn them back into people only back there, otherwise we wouldn't all fit."

"Somehow you're not very happy."

"Cause I'm leaving everything I know and love, instead something I love is waiting for me, but it's completely unknown to me... True, it's beckoning so strongly... It's almost terrifying."

We grew silent for a minute. The bright little dot grew and grew.

"Then, be well," Kalenyk said and extended his hand. "Remember me sometime... Tell my family to dig under the shed in the right corner... The same kind of rocks are there."

"What can they do with them if they don't explain where they got them?"

"You can say you found a treasure!"

"Why didn't you do that?"

"When? When I was digging up a hiding place for the transceiver I came across the wreckage of a flying ship, and the rocks were there... Well, o.k. Gotta go. And you hide here so they don't see you."

Once more we clasped hands, and he lowered himself into the depths of the valley, and I crawled into a bush and sat on a stone and began to wait. Without delay a saucer as big as a house hung over the valley. Above that saucer was another smaller one, in the middle it was lit up and completely transparent. Two people sat in it next to the point of embarkation. When the saucer touched down, one of the people descended into the lower part of it and opened the door. A stripe of light streamed out from the door. The man shouted something. Right away a bustling ensued, from every which way the rabbits rushed, knocking into one another to crawl into the doors.

The man grew angry, and when the coil of rabbits got stuck at the entrance, he cursed and kicked it.

Kalenyk appeared and began to explain something to the man, gesticulating hastily, but evidently the man didn't want to listen, because he just cursed and waved his arms. All the rabbits already were inside the saucer, but Kalenyk continued to argue over something, pointing somewhere behind his back. There in the illuminated stripe that stretched from the saucer, a rabbit was bustling about as though he were looking for something. The man pushed Kalenyk away in anger and rushed to the rabbit. The rabbit ran up to him and began to squeal and wave his paws. The man grabbed him by the ears and carried him to the saucer. The rabbit no longer squealed, but screamed frantically. The man shoved him inside, returned to Kalenyk and pulled him to the door. The old man grew obstinate and said something further, pointing in pantomime. Some individual words floated to me:

"...a child... you understand... small... it's..."

Here the second man appeared, the two of them forcibly dragged Kalenyk into the machine and shook the door. They raised themselves into the upper part of the saucer.

You could feel a slight humming, the saucer began to pulse.

Suddenly I became terrified—the upper part began to separate symmetrically from the bottom. The men on the top acted quite calmly. Maybe they didn't notice? I bolted to my feet and wanted to throw myself at the machine to inform them of the accident somehow, and one of the men at that moment bent over and looked down, then he turned to his companion and nodded to him. His companion laughed in answer. It was clear that everything went according to plan.

But which plan? The upper saucer gained height and when it had risen above the valley and the trees that were growing on the crest, and the noise of the engines settled down, I heard a knocking and a din that echoed from the lower saucer. There they were knocking on the door, attempting to break through. But it was in vain. Then I understood— they had been fooled! But before I could think how I could help the unfortunate ones, an explosion reverberated—the saucer left on the ground flared up in a blinding flame and instantaneously flew apart into bits. When it struck me in the bush, I just managed to cover my head with my hands...

...I got up—darkness reigned in the valley. And there was dead silence. High above, the star pulsed.

13

THE NEXT MORNING AT DAWN

Burnt stems of bushes, blackened ferns and vast amounts of shattered scrap iron. And among all this, blood and dead rabbits. Completely mutilated tiny bloody bodies.

Kalenyk lay crumpled, face down to the rocks. I turned him over face up and saw his glazed wide-open eyes, in which astonishment and despair were frozen. From his left upper arm to his chest a red gash darkened.

I sat down beside him and pulled his knapsack to me. I could have expected to see just about anything at all there, even a garlic sausage sandwich. But instead it was stuffed with white packets that instantly crumbled between my fingers. Kalenyk was taking seeds to his homeland: hollyhocks, sunflowers, snowball berries... At the very bottom I felt a book. A tattered often read *The Kobza Player* opened up in my hands, and from it a packet of paper fell out. From the very first words it became clear what I had come across—this was a decoding of the signals that had come from space.

Notification–1. The expedition TI-NA-TI–1918. You, as planned, took on the appearance of the local population. As a result of a mistake turned into four legged rodents. The apparatus was destroyed during an armed encounter. Awaiting confirmation.

Notification–2. From the 1918 expedition one person is still alive. The rest were born after the accident. There is a total of 800-850 of you. All of you want to return to your homeland. Awaiting confirmation.

Notification–3. To your request to settle in the region of Nida we answer: that city no longer exists. Designate another place.

Notification–4. Hardia answers: "We can't accept you." Name another place.

Notification–5. Pelifia answers: "We can't accept you." Name another place.

Below were the names of several more cities, which rejected accepting the refugees. All of this looked like a bad joke. Obviously their countrymen just delayed while hot debates went on, whether it was worth accepting the refugees at all. What could have made them hesitate?

Nearly seven decades had passed—during which time life on their planet could have changed substantially and, judging by everything, not for the better. Therefore the carriers of their culture were hardly desirable, for they were raised by parents who still remembered better times. Requesting them each time to name a different place, at the same time they were testing them: just how well the future repatriates knew their homeland.

My thoughts were interrupted by a slight whimpering. I looked around—a tiny rabbit was cringing on a stone. It was trembling and looking at me the way you look at the only being near and dear to you. This look was so human and plaintive that a knot rolled in my throat, and I had to clench my teeth so as not to burst into tears. An unbelievable anger seized me, I cocked my head up into the sky, but it was clear and cold.

That's why the rabbit was agitated. No, it must have been a she-rabbit looking for her baby. Kalenyk explained that they couldn't take off because a baby was missing. But they didn't understand. Fortunately.

The spilled packets whitened—hollyhocks, the sunflowers, snowball berries.

I collected them and put them away in my backpack.

That's it.

What else can I do?

I go home with my backpack and the rabbit.

The farms were already waking up, and when I got to the top of the hill, I heard the crowing of cocks, the barking of dogs and the snorting of motors.

Eight o'clock. All was peaceful.

This valley was so deep and distanced from the farms that no one noticed either the explosion or the blinding flash of fire. A wide black torn-up crater remained in the place where the flying saucer had stood, and its swept out remains had completely burned up.

Who will believe my account?

For everybody else Kalenyk's notes would just be the ravings of an old man.

The only witness to the tragedy was just a small gray ball of fur that will never be able to speak. It leans trustfully against my chest and gazes into my eyes. It thinks, perhaps, that I'm one of those who is able to stand up for the truth, or at least not walk away from it.

But I'm not that way.

I'm ordinary.

"What happened?!"

She's startled by the way I look.

"Kalenyk blew up on a mine there in the valley ." "What?! When?!" "At night, must have been. Go to them... tell them..."

"My God!"

Tired, I sit myself down on a long bench, not letting the tiny rabbit from my hands.

"Daddy! Daddy! You brought me a baby rabbit?!" Andriyko jumps with joy; I can't hold back and smile through my tears.

"Oy! You brought me the same rabbit!"

He takes him into his hands, kisses and cuddles him.

"Daddy, can I play with him?"

"You can."

"And with the rocks, too?"

"You can."

"But Momma took them away and said I can't." "I'll give them to you right now." I open the dresser and throw out the rocks onto the floor.

"Momma said they're really-really valuable, that you can buy a car with them."

"Momma was kidding. You can't buy anything for them. They're ordinary rocks. Go ahead and play."

"And if I lose them?"

"Lose 'em. They're ordinary rocks. You won't even get a cup of sunflower seeds for them."

THE SNAIL CHRONICLES

1

The wind blew stronger, and the wide river surface was covered with spots. Somewhere the cold glazing of trees, of the sky; in a moment they will appear again. In the cotton of clouds, in the crowns of willows tiny fish, tadpoles shimmered.

There is my reflection in the water. What a jelly-like look I have! Eye-glasses swim on my cheek-bones. I try to put a stop to their oscillation, but instead they flow, squeezing through my fingers and—plop-plop—in the water: the circles run and run away... then it's peaceful again. Only father extended his arm and said:

"There... there..."

His hand was pointing at the water (the gray sign of fear was on his face)... he doesn't say anything else, suddenly he turns back and with a quick step sets off straight for home. I want to catch up to him, to murmur something gentle (for example: ...), but some kind of power forces me to kneel down near the water and fervently look into the depth. Now I sense the puzzling fear that has overcome my father.

2

Earlier I had said: "...in the cotton of clouds, in the crowns of willows tiny fish, tadpoles shimmered...," but now I understood that all of this looks far from peaceful—these little fish, tadpoles, these tritons and bugs don't just shimmer, but fulfill some kind of task, because their movements are sharp and synchronized. Several tadpoles have grown motionless by the shore and are following after me. Anger flashes in me, which even now I'm still unable to explain to myself, because it is so unexpected and senseless. Then I break a willow branch and try to chase away the tadpoles. Suddenly a strange force tears away the swatch from my hand, and it disappears beneath the water. I barely manage to grab onto a bush, otherwise I would have flown headfirst from the shores. Anger overtakes me, pushing me to do even more senseless things: I gather stones and toss them. Suddenly those very stones fly at me from the water, I save myself by running away, they hit along my back, my head...

I don't know whether I really sense laughter behind me, or it just seemed so.

3

My father locked himself up in his room, he didn't come out all day. By evening my mother went to the neighbor woman, and we are able to toss a few words back and forth. My father is somber, hands behind his back, shoulders drooping...

"... ... ...?"

But I couldn't make it out.

"Did you see? Did you?" He keeps repeating.

"Yes. I broke off a willow branch and tried to chase them away, but something tore it from my hands... then I threw stones, and they shot back at me..."

"You're too imprudent."

"Because I don't know anything."

"Several nights I've been dreaming the same dream: water is coming out from the shores, and the fish, tadpoles, frogs, and water beetles and tritons are breaking into our buildings, seizing them, drowning us like kittens, and the entire earth then begins to belong to them."

"So you took me to the river on purpose?"

"I knew that you wouldn't believe my words alone. Now are you convinced of how strong they are?"

"And what if we throw dynamite at them?"

"The same thing'll happen as with the stones." His fingers nervously fold the tablecloth. "But I'll try to come to an agreement with them," he says, biting his lips.

"On non-aggression?"

"Maybe."

"Or on an alliance?"

"Hmm..."

"Is it possible you'll become one of them?"

"The snails, too, are all together with them."

"That's even better."

"I know that you will judge me harshly, but understand (his voice trembles, breaking here and there, growing quiet)... otherwise it will be impossible (he quiets down)... we don't have the strength...

4

Father got dressed in his new suit and went to the river.

It was already becoming evening, and that very same wind that had danced in the morning above the water, now played with the curtains and blinds, threw a bunch of dry leaves into the room. It began to rustle... I want to defend myself from it, from its blasts, but I sense that I am losing my body, and that it's becoming alien to me and distant. I see myself from without—here I stand so helpless and follow after my father who is returning from the river. He's returning bare-chested, wet, his gait is weary, and he's entirely like a bunch of autumnal yellowed grass. I'm standing—I'm not me. And I already understand that my father is bearing bad news, but I'm happy with the hope that he will announce it to the other me, and not to me, because I've already separated from myself and already was lurking behind the blinds.

"They're enraged and don't want to speak (his sleeves and breeches are in green water reeds, wet tracks on the floor)... but I'm not simply going to capitulate, I'm going to fight (he makes a theatrical gesture, he wants to look calm, and winks)."

When he turns his back I see a tiny hump. That hump is still going to grow.

5

Father for days at a time disappears at the river, he returns wet and mother says: he's changed so much. The hump keeps growing and growing, though, slowly, but not so little that you can't notice it. His body is growing smaller, scant, he's transforming into a teenager. Sometimes he brings fresh news... sometimes nothing...

"The slugs have joined with them, the land slugs and wood slugs... But they're not depending on them as much as on the snails. The snails occupy the high posts..."

"The river has flooded about half a meter over the shores..."

"In the lake an unknown fish has appeared... Maybe it's a resident of a different basin..."

"They acquainted me with it. It's satisfied with my intentions to help them and promised to take care of getting documents that would support the fact that I'm really a snail..."

"The river flooded about half a meter over the shores..."

The other day he brought me a big snail in his pocket and, pointing his finger at me, said:

"This is my son, he feels great affection for you... Since childhood my son has dreamt of becoming a snail... Other children want to become a pilot, others a sailor, others a government minister, and ours—just wants to be a snail. He especially likes your principle: I carry everything with me."

And the snail:

"Uhuh... uhuh..."

"Son, they've asked me if you could write them an anthem."

The snail in a dignified manner nods his feelers, my father waves his hands, and pronounces the words filled with pathos.

6

My father got more and more miniscule. In the winter he hid beneath a dresser. He ordered me to give him food there and not to bother him with stupid things. From that time we saw him very rarely. Mother went into mourning and tells everyone: our father has died... You could understand her—it wasn't very pleasant when one of your family wants to become a snail.

At the end of February my father began to appear, these visits of his were always unexpected—he'd dive out of some crack in the floor, he'd wave his feelers and disappear. Sometimes, though, he would pass along the latest news. Still it was nice that he didn't forget us.

It would happen that my mother would cry, then I would console her: our father is carrying out a very important mission. My mother leaves crumbs of food in the corners so that dad can have a snack. From time to time she cooks his favorite soup and pours spoon after spoon into the cracks.

In the spring the bedbugs, cockroaches and ants united with the watery inhabitants and the snails. The spiders stubbornly maintained neutrality, though they had supplied them with weapons. We walked about the house very carefully, fearful of crushing any of the allies. But we didn't manage without difficulties. Once my father was resting in a vase, and I poured water over him. He nearly drowned. Another time my mother sat down on an armchair, forgetting to look for him before sitting... A slight crackling could be heard. Mother frightened tore to her feet—the pitiful remains of a crushed snail could be seen on her skirt and the armchair. We got terribly upset, mother quickly wiped away the armchair, and threw the skirt into the fire.

The next day our dad appeared and calmed us—it turned out that that particular snail was a deserter, and as well had views that went counter to the foreign policy of the allies. So they even sent us a note of thanks for destroying their ideological enemy.

When the cherry trees blossomed my fear passed. I stopped being afraid of water, and the fact that war was possible no longer affected me as weightily. Father moved into the garden, there you could see him with other snails in the furrows.

At the beginning of June he greeted me cheerfully:

"The war has been postponed! We've achieved peace!"

"Father," I said with worry, "can you return to us now?"

"No, I still have a lot of things to do here... In fact, you can congratulate me—I've taken the post of prime minister... Now I'm forming my cabinet... If you don't get a job anywhere, then I could find you something... Your anthem is on everyone's lips here. They know and respect you. They introduced it even into a mandatory school program... They want you to write them something else... will you?"

"Well, if you wish me to..."

"Of course I won't force you, but... but who knows... maybe it's in your own interest... And how's our mother doing?"

"She's still in mourning."

"Poor mother."

We say good-bye, both of us are sad that we're in different worlds and don't want to yield to each other.

After all, I lean more decisively to the fact that snails are more civilized than we are, and, perhaps, soon I will take up my father's proposition, all the more so that I entered their school program.

And all the more so that an elegant and very nice little hump has begun to grow on my back.

"His name is Abel!" And she charmingly began to laugh. "You'll thank me yet for this gift. This is a really sweet kitty. A Persian breed, Mr. Lutsyk."

"Yes—yes..."

He obediently nodded his head, trying to avoid this piercing glance that forced him to do what the woman wanted. He could already see that he wouldn't have the strength to refuse, and it was already too late, because, when she was handing him the cat, his hands just stretched toward it and accepted the fluffy black body into his open palms.

"But...but I don't have anywhere to keep it. I live in a rented apartment. I don't know how the landlady will take to this."

"Never mind," as though swatting a fly, the charming stranger waved her hand. "She should also like it. It's tidy, obedient and not wild at all. Its name is Abel. A—bel, will you remember?"

She spoke without emotion, as though she were dictating a text that someone else had written.

She wants me to remember her words.

And those words, like an incantation, swaddled Mr. Lutsyk and subdued him for themselves.

And she's beautiful, devilishly beautiful... Why did I mention the devil? Perhaps because she has those eyes? Well of course, she has the eyes of a devil! Incredible eyes... But who am I to her?..."

"You're right," she began to laugh, as though she had guessed his thoughts.

"Right in what?" Mr. Lutsyk gave a start.

She didn't answer, she just began to laugh again. Then, seeing that she was getting ready to go, he got the courage to do what he had never had the courage to do in similar situations:

"Tell me, where did I meet..."

And already he saw that he had vainly seen what lay in his heart. But she had tempted him only just recently, he just noticed this, though he didn't defend himself.

She came to his concerts, sat in an empty row and stared at him ardently. Directing the orchestra, with his back he sensed her electric gaze and barely kept himself from looking back at her. And when the concert had ended and he was bowing, then he saw that she would get up and disappear during the applause. Isn't this similar to temptation? Perhaps she simply did this this way unexpectedly, as women often do just to be convinced of their abilities, they likewise do this involuntarily, the way they look into a mirror, checking if a disobedient tuft of hair somehow has strayed.

"Nowhere. Today I'm leaving Lviv... Ah, I'll never forget our concerts... Your music—it's...it's... In a word, wonderful!"

She waved her hand and disappeared. She dissolved in the fog like sugar. Beside him leaves fell quietly and unnoticeably, and he imagined himself to be a tree that was strewing its leaves. Somewhere below at the base janitors were shuffling their brooms. The scent of burnt leaves and gloom climbed up the trunk.

The landlady was so corpulent, and like a great percentage of all corpulent people, quite good-natured. Therefore she didn't object when her renter (a very intelligent man, if only you knew how many books he had read—wow!) took in a cat. She just couldn't remember the cat's name and called it "Matsko."

For days at a time the cat lay in the house, it stubbornly refused to go out into the street, and although it often sat down on the window sill, it never started up acquaintances with other cats. This terribly irritated and intrigued all the female cats, who, in the interests of anxiety over the good stock of future generations, alternately strove to allure Abel, explaining that there wasn't any debauchery involved here, but only high ideals and, if he's a patriot, and additionally of the Persian breed... At that point convinced of the hopelessness of these endeavors, they left with dissatisfied looks on their faces.

Mr. Lutsyk never had a liking for cats, he never though of having this particular creature in his home, but when Abel appeared in his room, then it seemed that he couldn't get along without him.

Earlier, let's say, he never sensed such a need to express something aloud, and right now he was doing this constantly, just this way: "Well, what, Kitty, do we start up a new symphony? We'll look right now what masterpiece they've shoved at me... Though what kind of masterpieces can there be in our day anymore?" In actual fact it turned out that it was as though he were consulting with the cat. After a while he noticed that Abel never took his eyes off him, that he constantly followed him. This was touching—such devotion! Replying with reciprocity, Mr. Lutsyk coordinated every one of his steps with the cat. Soon all of his actions became like an imitation of Abel's decisions. When he sometimes wavered on how to resolve this or that problem, an unknown power turned his eyes to the cat and forced him to find an answer there. And when the cat just barely nodded his head, Mr. Lutsyk calmed down, assured in the correctness of his intentions.

And once he caught himself humming some strange little song that was composed of just a single word "Abel." All of this was somehow incomprehensible, he didn't believe it, several times he resolved to revolt, to do something opposite, but always lost. Everywhere he saw only those piercing eyes that allowed no-one to enter them, but rather seized everything with themselves, covered everything with a netting, laced very carefully so that you could easily notice that they were nudging to certain action.

Sometimes Mr. Lutsyk sensed someone's footsteps behind him, at first very quiet, at first only in his skull, and then outside of it, but somewhere not very far away, quite nearby. He looked around impetuously, capturing the surprised looks of passers-by, he apologized and walked on further. But again he heard those steps... And just before they were about to disappear, the doors of a car slammed shut and the motor of an invisible car rattled. The rattling little by little moved off into the distance, and everything grew quiet. The strangest thing was that Mr. Lutsyk didn't see a single car around him. But on the other hand some kind of car constantly was following him. Somehow even during his directing session when the symphony resounded, Mr. Lutsyk heard it drive up quite close and stop behind his back. He wanted to turn around immediately and catch it with his eyes, but he understood how stupid he would look in front of an audience of hundreds. The car was standing behind his back and was rattling quietly. Then the door slammed. Then an unknown person struck a match and loudly released some air with smoke: "Pfu-u-u..." And all of this was here, next to him... Almost on stage.

Overhearing what was happening behind his back, Mr. Lutsyk directed entirely mechanically. Just once did he lose control over himself and get thrown out of rhythm, when suddenly a woman's voice echoed. The voice appeared quite audible and could have belonged to that charming strange woman. She asked someone: "Well, what?" And a man's voice responded: "Everything's in order." "Then sit down, let's go," she ordered. And the car drove off.

That car appeared every week in the most unexpected moments and always behind his back. And whenever our hero finally couldn't stand it and looked back, he didn't see any car.

Once it drove up at night while he was sleeping. He heard the rattling of a motor through a dream and woke up. He lay motionless for a minute, waiting for this to pass, that he was just imagining hearing this, but the motor didn't subside. Then he carefully turned his head. In the room there clearly wasn't anyone. And at the same time that car was there... Finally the door slammed... Someone got out... A man's voice said:

"He's sleeping..."

"Somehow I don't believe it," the woman's voice disputed.

"His eyes are closed."

Mr. Lutsyk truly had shut his eyes, but all the same he couldn't see anything.

"Why isn't he sleeping with Abel?" The woman said again.

"Really, it's strange..."

The car disappeared following these words.

What do they want from me? Mr. Lutsyk didn't understand. What are they checking?... Last night I couldn't fall asleep. And in the morning...

"How you've grown exhausted, dear sir," the landlady said. "You should take some time off. Really, you're overworked."

"Indeed, of course...," he agreed.

After breakfast he went upstairs to his room and, having sat down on his bed, pondered her words. And here again he sensed the gaze of the cat, and when their eyes met, he noticed that the cat had nodded his head affirmatively.

Is he really even reading my thoughts? Mr. Lutsyk got frightened and for the first time felt annoyance. This time the cat had gone too far.

But he took some time off anyway. And suddenly he became convinced that this wasn't the best way out, because now the cat had him in sight the entire time, and it seemed that he didn't wish to release him anywhere. Several attempts to start off on a stroll collided with such skillfully set out traps that the very thought of going somewhere in just an instant appeared ridiculous and even stupid. He was left to sit in the house and read books, but even here the feeling did not leave him that he himself wasn't reading, but that someone invisible was looking over his shoulder, and Mr. Lutsyk sometimes noticed a strange habit; having read a page, he waited for a minute and didn't turn it, by doing this it was as though he were letting someone standing behind him read to the end.

He noticed with horror that he was beginning to get used to this inconvenience. He sat in the house for two weeks. The car no longer appeared.

Finally the desire to overcome this magnetic field was born in him, to step out from it to freedom, but right away he concealed this desire with other thoughts, so that the cat wouldn't figure out anything. On purpose he began to think of stupid things which earlier he had never brought up, and at the same time prepared himself for decisive action.

"Well what, have you eaten it up?" He asked the cat, with pleasure noticing perplexity in his eyes.

The cat had ended up in a snare prepared to catch him and by the time he had disentangled himself, Mr. Lutsyk managed to find a way out of his situation.

Events from that moment unfolded very quickly.

The landlady went out and brought back the mail.

"A letter for you."

The envelope was without a return address and postal markings. The cat impatiently stepped from paw to paw. Mr. Lutsyk opened up the envelope, and at that very moment the cat nervously began to hiss, arching his back and standing his fur on end.

"How do you like Abel? Isn't it true that he's a marvelous creature? Respect him. He loves it when you treat him with respect. Why don't you pet his tummy?"

"A-a!" Mr. Lutsyk began to scream. "Pet his tummy?!" Suddenly he blurted out: "I'll kill him!"

And then he turned to the dumbfounded cat and with inexpressible delectation tossed the following words right between his eyes:

"Did you hear?! I'm going to kill you!"

The cat was thrown back by an atomic shock wave. He hit the wall painfully and meowed in a fright. But on the floor strangely he quickly regained consciousness and in an instant already was looking at Mr. Lutsyk with insolent distrust: "Well, what are you... Calm down. You won't kill me. You won't." But in his eyes you could also read a certain perplexity.

"Ah, I won't kill you?!" Mr. Lutsyk shouted, and his fist fell on the table with a rattle.

The cat's hair stood on end and he meowed once again, but now quite pitifully. Mr. Lutsyk disdainfully took him by the skin and threw him into a tote bag. At that very moment that old, rugged tote bag began to take on the strangest forms, and calmed down only after Mr. Lutsyk had pounded it on the street three times. Further on along the entire road while he was carrying it into the forest that was growing dark at the end of the street, just a quiet whispering echoed from inside there, as though a rusty iron wire were unwinding itself.

Mr. Lutsyk scooped out a hole in the soft clay in the forest, and the cat Abel reposed calmly in the Lord together with the tote bag. The newfound grave digger removed his cap and for several minutes remained silent over the fresh grave.

The return trip was very easy for him, but just as he stopped on the street, he heard those steps again. Someone was rushing after him, at times he sensed a nervous breath. Mr. Lutsyk stubbornly refused to look back. But when he slammed the car door shut and the motor started to grumble, he suddenly backed up to a wall and took a look. No, no-one was planning on running him over. The street was empty and quiet.

The next day in the morning a letter came without a return address and, as earlier, without post marks.

"Ah, how unkind this is, Mr. Lutsyk, to abuse a poor creature, to bury it in the ground. I never expected this from you. But you're rejoicing too early. You'll never succeed in getting rid of Abel."

His dreams now began to be filled with bats, dreams of bright green eyes that moved by themselves in space, sometimes they stopped, diligently looking at him, and he even heard a quiet grumbling. Mr. Lutsyk sprang up and growled: "Shoo!" The eyes disappeared, but getting insomnia from the dream, he didn't have any peace until it began to grow lightoutside the window, and then he was relieved, sighing, that the night finally had passed and that there was assurance that the next day would come.

When his leave of absence ended and he began to go to work again, he noted with satisfaction that his persecutors were no longer appearing. The leave of absence, evidently, had been useful. The main thing was to get a grip on himself: in the morning—a cold shower, exercise... Sharply limit TV movies, especially when it pertained to crime and horror films.

In the tramcar he saw luxuriant thighs. His eyes ran up to her face along the thighs. A rare harmony stirringly acted on him, and in addition the passionate dark-haired woman unexpectedly smiled at him with that much-promised smile, that all tempting women take as their weapon. Mr. Lutsyk also tried to smile, and, obviously, he was successful, for she sat next to him and put one leg over the other. Her knees glistened like the reflection of the moon on water.

Then they rose up along the stairs, carefully treading so that the landlady wouldn't hear, but, as it turned out later, she had heard everything quite well with the invariable virtue of all the landladies of the city of Lviv and its environs.

Because of insufficient experience Mr. Lutsyk squeezed his lady awkwardly, and in addition a question made him anxious: what should he take off of her first—her shoes or her blouse? Finally he grew bold enough for a kiss and when their eyes came close, he suddenly blurted out:

"Ah, miss, you've never been a kitty?"

The lady began to laugh indulgently:

"What are you..."

"Is the name Abel familiar to you?"

"Abel? How do you know that? Abel is my last name! Suzannah Abel!"

"Abel!" He whispered in a strained voice.

In the meanwhile the lady quickly decided everything herself, and under the questioning gaze of Mr. Lutsyk took off her skirt. He said: "He-he" and shut his eyes. When she had taken everything off and said "that's it," and he had opened his eyes, he was finally convinced that it was everything. And suddenly he nearly swallowed his breath, and his eyes nearly jumped out of their sockets: the breasts and stomach of the dark-haired woman were covered with curly black hair. Instead of breasts, some kind of red gelatinous mass gaped, it quivered fervently and was transfused in the light. Below her stomach a black cat's muzzle laughed malevolently: "Murrr-meow-he-he-he!"

He recognized the cat Abel! He recognized him in that muzzle, and in the eyes of this slut!

"Abel!" Mr. Lutsyk screamed. "You're persecuting me again! I'm really going to destroy you! Destroy!"

He grabbed a heavy metal candlestick and threw it at Suzannah Abel. The candlestick passed through her body and hit the wall, even spattering the plaster. Suzannah Abel disappeared as if she had never been.

That very night he heard the drone of a motor. And voices.

"He's sleeping like an innocent babe," the man rasped.

"A murderer," the woman said sullenly.

Mr. Lutsyk closed his eyes tightly and began to twirl a new symphony in his head. The music filled his entire brain. And, it seemed, not a single other sound was capable of breaking through it. Yet something broke through...

"...the killer of the kitty Abel shouldn't sleep like an innocent babe!" The woman pronounced.

I'm not a killer! Mr. Lutsyk wanted to cry out, but fear fettered his muscles.

"No, you're a killer!" The woman insisted. "A killer with sadistic impulses! To bury him alive in the ground! What could be more horrifying?!"

"Soon he'll be convinced himself what a pleasure it is!"

That very instant Mr. Lutsyk heard the earth being sprinkled over him. He got tangled in his bed, and even opened his eyes wide, but the earth immediately sprinkled over them. He tried to scream, but the earth was covering his mouth. He still managed to catch sight of a car driving away first before he was choked by the thick clogs of earth.

In the morning he awakened all perspired. The room was inundated with soft, sunny light.

"All of this is just a dream!" He joyfully shouted.

And he spat the earth out of his mouth. He spat it out right on his blanket, and then he gazed at it for a long time as though he were gazing at some kind of rare fossil. And it really was earth. Sand was still scraping on his teeth, and his tongue retained the taste.

Then this wasn't a dream?

There was a knock at the door. The landlady entered.

"Excuse me, are you up already? There's a letter for you... Mr. Lutsyk, some woman brought your cat here."

"What?" Mr. Lutsyk startled. "What cat?"

"Well, Matsko... Or whatever you call him. The poor guy has grown so thin... For sure he went courting somewhere, he-he... They say, a cat... I poured him some milk, and he's lapping it up almost shaking..."

Mr. Lutsyk followed the landlady in agitation and tore open the envelope.

"Dear Mr. Lutsyk! With great satisfaction I'm sending you back your dear cat Abel. Try to find a little bit of affection and compassion for him. Why does he, a poor orphan, suffer? For his love for you? With a fervent greeting!"

The door slammed open, and the cat Abel went into the living room. He truly looked pitiful—emaciated and ragged, not for a moment now did he resemble the one-time Persian beauty. The cat intensely looked at Mr. Lutsyk and, proudly ambling to the stove, rolled up under it like a loaf of braided bread.

Mr. Lutsyk was upset that he didn't have a revolver. With what pleasure would he have planted a half-dozen bullets into this monster! Suddenly he remembered that there was still a little rat poison in the basement. This was just what he needed. Does he like milk? Great. Mixed with the poison he won't taste it.

And when he shoved the cat the plate with the poisoned milk, he heard just an indignant hissing. The cat was insulted and had no intention of making contact with Mr. Lutsyk.

"Wait, my darling, it's not for nothing that I read *The History of the Inquisition*. You'll die in my house in horrific agony. Let those people who sent you to me know this!"

With those words Mr. Lutsyk grabbed the cat and wanted to stuff him into his black briefcase, when unexpectedly he sensed pain in his brow—short and sharp like a shot. This lasted just for a minute, but in that minute he, apparently, lost consciousness. When he came to, he suddenly rushed to see what was happening with him. He was lying on somebody's lap. And someone's hand was gently stroking his fur...

Mr. Lutsyk turned his head and became convinced that he had turned into a cat. The one who held him on his lap was none other than Mr. Lutsyk.

This was so horrifying that the cat Lutsyk extended his claws and carefully tested the leg he was sitting on. This sensation turned out to be incomparable to anything else. He imagined himself as a mighty tiger from whom everyone seeks favor.

The warm hand pet his neck, and he felt a sweet sleepiness overcoming him, he felt like sleeping and dreamt of the wildness of primeval forests. But, straining all his will, the cat Lutsyk didn't give in to the drowsiness and jumped from the lap to the floor.

"Kitty, kitty," the gentle voice of the landlady could be heard.

It turns out I've become a cat, and the cat Abel has become me... Who the heck contrived this wild joke?

"Mr. Lutsyk! Mr. Lutsyk!" The piercing voice of the landlady echoed from the steps.

In an instant she had flown into the living room waving a newspaper.

"Look what I just read! What joy! Congratulations!"

The cat Lutsyk jumped up onto the table and tried to look into the newspaper, but it was for naught.

"What joy!"

"What is it?" Mr. Abel asked.

"Congratulations! Let me kiss you!"

And with her entire one-and-a-half hundredweight she threw herself at him to hug him.

"The old bat's gone nuts," the cat Lutsyk thought.

Finally Mr. Abel, freeing himself from her intense embraces, took charge of the newspaper.

"You're a laureyate! Congratulations! A state prize! Who would have thought it! Such a person in my house! Mr. Lutsyk, I'm going to go right away to make your favorite dumplings. And to think that in such an historical moment this kind of disaster happened to me! What a dork I am that I didn't burn that creature right away!"

"Mr. Lutsyk!" The landlady chattered. You also have to get ready for the prize! I'm already on my way to iron your suit and shirts."

"I'll be very grateful," responded Mr. Abel. "I'll evidently go tomorrow."

"Like hell you'll go!" The cat Lutsyk clenched his teeth. His look fell on a plate with milk. The tin can with the poison stood next to him. It seems this is just what's needed. Just have to wait for dinnertime.

The radiant landlady floated to the living room with a tray, on which there was a large pot of steaming boiled potato dumplings and a full plate of sour cream.

"Go wash your hands, Mr. Lutsyk."

"O, you've managed really well!" Mr. Abel joyfully began to laugh and, jumping off his bed, pecked the landlady on the cheek.

"How tender you are, Mr. Lutsyk, like never before," she began to blush.

"That's for sure," the cat Lutsyk grimaced. "I never permitted myself anything like this before. Kiss that old dip? For a big pot of dumplings?"

When both of them had left the living room, the cat Lutsyk rushed headlong at the tray and stuck his paw in it. Then on three paws he jumped onto the table and mixed up the poison in the sour cream.

Mr. Abel, returning, didn't notice anything suspicious. The cat hid under the bed and wiped his paw on the floor to clean off the poison. With all this he really hurried, because he couldn't deny himself the satisfaction of observing the agony of his hated enemy. He expected that with Abel's death he'll return to his natural condition. You can't say that he didn't sense fear in this, the vitality of the cat turned into some kind of mystic dimension, where all phenomena simultaneously lose any kind of logical explanation. Those who had decided to conduct their cruel experiments on him could be found close by and observe. If that's so, then they definitely would be poisoned. But Abel swallowed the dumplings with the poisoned sour cream without any problems.

The cat Lutsyk didn't take away his anxious eyes from his double. Abel finally noticed this and smacked his lips:

"What, you want a dumpling? I won't give it to you! There you have your poisoned milk, you can lap it up... And what do you think of a stroll in the woods in a black briefcase? Ah? Ha-ha-ha..."

He belly laughed with such self-satisfaction, that spatters of sour cream, flying from his mouth, fell right under the nose of Lutsyk the cat. The cat replied pertly and stepped away to the wall.

Abel's laughter soon turned into some kind of raucous droning, and in another minute he had already fallen onto the floor and was thrashing about in spasms, pressing his stomach with his hands.

Mr. Lutsyk sensed a sharp and burning pain in his stomach, he wanted to scream, but instead just a not very dainty gurgling burst out. Piercing sirens began to howl in his head.

Right before his eyes he saw the quite live Abel the cat with a poisonous smile.

Brakes screeched, and the car stopped next to his head.

"You finished the game," the woman said. "He's a completely worthless subject."

"I was right when I suggested not to choose him. He's evidently no good for this role," the man responded.

"For some reason it seemed to me that this was the one we needed. Too bad, so much work—all for naught."

"It's not all for naught. Contact should be built on mutual sympathy. For this we shouldn't choose too intellectual of a person. I'd guess that a subject like the landlady would be completely suitable for experiments."

"You think so?"

"I'm sure."

Mr. Lutsyk rose up on his elbows, but didn't see either the car or the people.

"He just has a few seconds left."

"It's his own fault."

With a single strong tug Mr. Lutsyk threw his body to the side and crushed the cat.

"Lord! What's he doing?!" The woman shrieked. "Why are you standing there?! Do something!"

Mr. Lutsyk couldn't feel someone tugging at his shoulders, trying to turn him face up, then he sensed fingers with a frightful strength compressing the cat's neck, he heard the crunch of cartilage and warm blood that flowed along his fingers that had already torn through the skin and had penetrated into the cat's dying body. It shuddered once more when they finally had succeeded in turning over Mr. Lutsyk.

"Dead," the woman said.

And it wasn't clear who she was referring to—the cat Abel or Mr. Lutsyk.

ORDER IS EVERYTHING

"Excuse me... Isn't it clear you're getting in the way? Do I really have to explain?"

I obediently walk away toward the wall. I make room for the cleaners. No, they don't have to explain anything to me. Let them do what they're doing, and I won't get in their way. There are lots of them, they're really careful, they don't even miss a speck of dust. The brooms, like birds, flutter in their hands. Everything that's not needed, everything that's not in place disappears.

"Let me pass..."

I let them pass. Alongside me they carry out something big and cumbersome, the door breaks open from it, it strikes me on the arm, it hurts, but I laugh, so they won't notice how painful it is for me.

"Did we hit you?"

"No, no, what are you saying! Lord, no!"

A speck of dust settles on my shoes.

"Allow me."

"Ah, how nice you are!"

The dust disappears from my shoes, the broom, having glided across them, leaves a white wet stripe. Nevertheless, I thank them anyway. I would have thanked them even if they had ended up on my face instead of on my shoes. Though they didn't manage to wipe a submissive smile off my face.

They tidy up around me not only during the day, but even at night, even when I'm sleeping and dreaming interesting dreams, someone carefully tidies up everything that isn't in its place, and in the morning, having just wiped my eyes, I thank them. If I could see them at that moment then I would bow down low, really, really low, I've already learned to bow down. They're indifferent to this, everyone bows down to them, they've already gotten used to it. They don't even blink an eye. But for me it's very pleasant.

Here's dust! Look how clever it is—it's hidden in the crack. And you clean it with a broom, with a broom! And don't hide, don't try acting so clever! The broom's not picking you up? Let me use my tongue!... No, no, don't contradict me, I'll do it with pleasure! This is fun for me! Here it is on the end of my tongue already. Well, why should you do it with your hands? Your hands are meant for something sophisticated. It's better to do it with the broom, eh-heh, it's more comfortable. And for me it's just pleasure! Not just with the broom, I'd chew that dust up with my teeth.

"Hey, let me get through! Why'd you stop!"

I'm letting you, I'm letting you, what do you think I'm doing? I'm not doing anything. Tidy up. Order is a holy business. Everything that's not in its place—away with it!

Again they're carrying something big. This time the doors are closed. They're closed because someone is sitting there. They're carrying somebody out, and he's keeping quiet. If they'd take me out, I'd also keep quiet. And why should you make noise? If they carry you out, that means you're not needed or harmful. Therefore you should just do everything so they're satisfied, so the need never arises for them to stick their fists in my nose. Well, then, they're tidying up all around, working, and I, a naughty boy, allow it to get all pigged up. I get in their way. I get in their way more than that dust. I have to go see their supervisor and tell him about all this. I'll tell him: I understand you and with all my heart, no, better—with all my soul I'm devoted to you, because I know that order is everything. If you didn't sweep up here every day and didn't tidy up, then life would be lost. Of course, it is so important to clean up our society in time from every good-for-nothing who just burdens it. And I, when you remember, even with my tongue... I licked off those bits of dust. I'm not one of those squeamish types. I'll sacrifice anything for the sake of the common good... I can— and I bow down—become a broom... And I bow down even lower. They should like this... Eh-heh, this is a great honor for me! I can still be a handle and open doors for you so that you don't tire your hands... I can't be anything bigger. The way I am right now before you, I'm not needed by anyone, I'm superfluous. The smallest bit of dust has more foundation where it is than I do...

But who is their supervisor?

"I ask you to forgive me... I, destitute and low, had the audacity to disturb you..."

"What do you want? Go away!"

"I want... Who is your supervisor?... I just ask... I don't want that..."

"We don't have a supervisor. We're here on our own."

"No, I understand... I won't say a word about this to anyone. I'll keep this completely confidential. You can trust me. In one respected establishment... do you understand me?... they said that with a resume like I have, I can have pretensions even for the post of first secretary... They just didn't narrow it down, whether it was a regional or an oblast town... There weren't any kulaks in my family. We all lived like beggars. My ancestors used to beg by the church. What did they beg for? I don't know. Apparently it was bread... And the main thing. No one in our family ever lived on occupied land. How did they manage it? I won't say. But we are born beggars. In French this will be 'proletarian,' isn't that so? Well, that's it, we're proletarians. And if you have to unite, then at least I'm ready right now. Just show me with whom... And I need that supervisor of yours..."

"We said: there isn't any! Go away!"

"I, if you remember, licked up dust with my tongue..."

"This doesn't concern us."

Ye-es, I wasn't lucky. Can it really be true they don't have a supervisor? But maybe, might this simply be some kind of very important secret? They don't trust me, and they're right—if they were to trust everyone this way... Then I'd stop respecting them myself, if they were to trust just at someone's word. And it's so good, that they chattered with me at least for a while. In their place, they'd better scold me well, meaning, why am I getting in the way? They're cleaning up here, tidying up, and I...

It seems, if you get to the bottom of things, I'm an enemy of the people. Because I'm tearing them away from their work. I'm sticking my nose in where it doesn't belong. I'm interested in various details. I'm tearing them away from important work for the state. They are forced to waste their valuable time on stupid chit-chat with me, they have to avoid me, because I get in their way.

"Allow me... Why have you stood mostly right here? You see— they're carrying things out."

Yes, yes, I'll make way, I'll open a path for you. God forbid that I'd do something, I didn't do anything... Here, if you wish, I'll offer my back... I deem it an honor...

Again they're banging a hefty dresser. And something is banging in there, it's banging with fists and screaming. It's a woman's voice! Evidently, even among women you come across the kind who stand in the way. Women are especially dangerous, because they raise children. And if such a woman has views that go against the grain and the central politics of the regime, then it is quite likely that the child will become a dissident. And this is already an extraordinary blow. But, while it's small, it's impossible to arrest it, the state is forced to waste money on its enemy, it not only gives him the possibility of growing up, but also of becoming a convinced and even an irate militant revolutionary. It turns out that the state is placed in a terrible situation: for years it has been forced to raise its murderer! And only then when he becomes grown up can you approach him and provoke him to some kind of action. And this again is leisure time. The enemy can be so clever that he doesn't allow himself to be provoked.

Oh, I'm a lousy philosopher! I should be working in one of the ministries. At least for a week. My talent is wasted. I'm living without a goal. I'm superfluous here. There's so much work around here, and I'm standing like a tree stump...

Here they've made off with someone else. This one's not creating a scandal yet, but he's crying. Well, crying, of course, is purifying and so forth. And in general, everyone should have their own place.

"Make way! You blind? Can't you see we're carrying something? What a gawking fool! Get lost!"

Right away—right away, sorry...

Who is standing by the wall? He's standing motionlessly and looking. He's wearing eyeglasses, with a book beneath his arm. He surely is the most intelligent of all of them.

"Tell me, be so kind..."

Oh, he turned his head. "Well?"

"Tell me, what is the order?"

He looks at me with derision. Looks at me for a minute, another minute. He takes the book and picks up the pages. What a big book it is! He's very, very intelligent, if he's reading such big books. Finally he closes it and says:

"Well, okay, I can tell you even without the book..."

Ah, how intelligent he is! Without the book!

"Order? What is order?"

"Eh-heh, tell me what order is."

"Order is everything."

Oh... He's so clever! He spoke so harshly! Ah, you, my God, I would never have figured that out.

In our great building work constantly bustles. How patient you have to be to reconcile yourself with my presence. All this already has lasted for so long that they notice me only when I stand in their way. It turns out that I, in order to somehow justify my existence, am forced to get in their way. Then they and I get convinced that I really am. In truth I've gone since long ago.

"Make way!"

No, I'm still a bastard. Have you been able to tolerate my insipidness till now?... Perhaps I should ask for forgiveness?... If so, they'll set aside some place. Any place, just so I'd know that it was mine, that no one'd take it.

"Mister! Kind sir! You are so intelligent... Even without a book! You've said that... that..."

"Get out! I'm fed up with you!..." He squeezed through his teeth and his eyes glistened.

No-no, I'm an impossible person. I stick myself everywhere. I get on everybody's nerves. And from the dresser which they're carrying out past me, a child's crying echoes... What kind of child is this there?... Whose child is it? In which language is he crying?

Here's an open window... On which floor am I? The twenty-fourth or the twenty-fifth? He said: get lost... get lost... get lost...

Who's this window open for? Who's it waiting for?... For me?...

I should step aside so that I stop making other people's eyes toil; so that I stop being interested in those dressers that are filled with people as if with clothes... I have to go away... And here I lean over the windowsill... I lean over... ah, how easy, how joyful to fly down... I've never flown before... flying down—in fact is flying up... I'm an angel... a gray angel... an everyday angel... an angel for everyone... greet me... just one thing disturbs me—it's the fact that they'll have to clean up my broken body... it would've been better to drown in the ri...

THE FLOWERBED IN THE KILIM

Translated by Mark Andryczyk

A multi-colored kilim was hanging on the wall in the living room, on which a flowerbed was woven, behind the flowerbed a little orchard, and in the orchard — a small house under a red cherry tree. The little house was so charming that, every time I looked at it, I was struck with a strange and insurmountable sadness. I wanted to find out who lived in that little house and whose flowerbed it was. The flowers that grew there were truly remarkable — even Auntie's flowerbed didn't have these kinds of flowers, neither did her straw hat.

When I put my ear to the kilim I heard the rattling of moths and the buzzing of bumblebees, while my nose caught the intoxicating scent of flowers, dew and honey. But, no matter how often I gazed at the little house, I was never able to see a living soul there. But somebody had to live there because, looking at the flowers, it was obvious that someone was diligently taking care of them, weeding and watering them.

Sometimes, when I pressed my ear right up against the little house, I was just barely able to hear the clamor of human voices; I wasn't, however, able to make out exactly what it was they were saying.

The strangest thing was that the seasons would change on the kilim as they would in nature. In autumn, flowers would break off and leaves would fall, leaving the branches bare. Every now and then rain would shower down, and the colors on the kilim would fade. The little house would lose its elegant and fabulous appearance, and the sky above it would spill down like gray lead. In the winter, snow would fall and solidly cover the orchard, weighing down heavily on its branches. And then tiny footprints could occasionally be seen along the snow. Smoke rose from the chimney and the scent of resin would take wing. And, at night, a light would shine in the window, and a dark shadow would spread along the curtains.

I really wanted to end up in that little orchard in the kilim and peek into the little house, but, no matter how much I tried to fulfill my dream, the kilim remained just a kilim and would not let me enter it.

A large wall-clock was hanging right beside the kilim in a wooden case and behind glass. The wall-clock would always stand still and I never-ever heard it tick. Its hands were always stuck in one spot, displaying five minutes before twelve o'clock. The wooden case was locked and I didn't know where the key was, otherwise I would have tried to set the correct time long ago.

I would have never noticed any connection between the kilim and the wall-clock if it hadn't been for a certain, strange incident. One time, having opened the door to the living room without warning, I saw a male mannequin frozen in an unusual position by the kilim. He stood, bending over and extending his arm as if he wanted to pick a flower. But as I got closer, I saw that he was not trying to pick a flower, but, instead, was trying to pick up a key from inside the flowerbed. I had never noticed any key on the kilim before. And now, it seemed, somebody had lost it.

I pretended that I hadn't noticed anything and walked out of the living room. After some time, I re-entered the living room and saw that the mannequin was in his usual position and that the key had disappeared. You didn't have to have an especially wild imagination to figure out where it was.

I bravely walked up to the mannequin and pulled the key out of the pocket of his suit jacket. He ferociously blinked his eyes but didn't dare to budge.

Now there was only one thing left to do: put the key in the wooden case and see if I'd guessed correctly. But as soon as I attempted to do this, there was a loud squeak. The mannequins turned their heads toward me and popped open their eyes in fright. I saw they were afraid of me.

I turned the key and the case—creaking and screeching—flung wide open. Then I lifted the lever and the clock moved. The room filled with new sounds, and it seemed like they gave life to all the objects in the room, because they also immediately began making sounds, each in its own way, and, just like that, the whole living room was abuzz. The faces of the mannequins cheered up, anger disappeared from their eyes, and the corners of their mouths were smoothed out.

And not only did the living room come to life, but the kilim, too, seemed to have woken up from its winter slumber — I saw how leaves on trees shook from the wind, how petals shivered, and how the scent of flowers rose up into the air. Everything now looked like it was on a movie screen. I tried brushing my hand along the flowers, but all my fingers could feel was the thick wool of the kilim.

And then, suddenly, everything changed. The wall-clock let out a heavy groan, something clanged, grinded, and the first stroke of the clock sounded. At that instant my hand forcefully broke through to the flowerbed. Without stopping to think, I jumped into the kilim and ran along the path that leads to the little house as fast as I could. Behind me I once again heard that sound.

Right on the third stroke I ended up by the door and turned the doorknob, but it was locked. I ran up to the window and looked inside. The house was cloaked in twilight, but I was immediately able to recognize several things that were familiar to me since birth. There, on the table, was the bowl that I had once broken accidentally, and there was Grandma's vase with its peculiar rhododendron — it had dried up after Grandma died, so Mom threw it out. And there was our cat lying on the pillow, a cat that, also, had died long ago. There was the bench, on which Grandma used to love to sit. And the eyeglass case with her glasses, and her embroidery… And all the walls here were decorated with various embroideries. One of them was of me, as a little boy, playing with a kitten.

And the clock behind struck two more times.

I couldn't pull myself away from the window, recognizing one object after another, and, most peculiar, was the fact that every one of these objects was connected, in some way or another, with Granny.

Well then , where is she?

I ran behind the house and saw that a yard stretched from behind the bushes all the way down to a narrow, little river, where ducks were quacking. From the little river, up the hill, a path climbed, cutting through the yard, and along this path a hunched-over figure carrying buckets was ascending. I recognized this person immediately and, shouting in turn with the menacing grumbling of the wall-clock, I yelled:

"Gra-a-an-dma-a-a!"

At first she thought she was just hearing things and she even stopped to look around her. Then she put down her buckets and, after I yelled again, raised her head.

Initially, her face lit up with joy, but then it immediately was overcome with horror. She waved her hands and screamed:

"Run away! Run away at once!"

The clock now struck for the eight time. I don't know why I was counting these rings.

"Grandma!" I yelled. "I 'm coming to you!"

She became even more horrified and started running up the hill, repeatedly imploring me:

"Run away! Go back! Before it's too late!"

I looked back and saw the frightened mannequins, who were also waving there arms at me, surrounding the kilim.

"BONNGGGG!" The ninth ring sounded.

But I didn't want to leave my Grandma and this delightful orchard! Nevertheless, I saw something in her face that convinced me and, when "ten" sounded, I finally moved and dashed home. I ran as tears flooded my eyes and I could hear Grandma's voice behind me:

"Faster! Faster!"

"BONNGGGG." "Eleven."

I tripped over a rock and flew, headfirst, into the flowerbed — the flowers crunched beneath my feet and squirted dew in my face.

"O Lord!" Grandma screams.

Gathering my strength, I'm barely able to push myself off the ground and thrust my body forward. The wall-clock, with a certain despair and groan, strikes "twelve" just as the strong hands of the mannequins caught me and laid me down on the floor.

I looked at the kilim and saw a familiar scene. Everything is as it was before. Except that the flowers are a bit squashed. But Grandma will tie them up, straighten them out, sprinkle them with fresh water and, God willing, Auntie won't notice anything.

I once again immobilized the wall-clock, returning the big hand to five minutes before twelve; I closed the wooden case and placed the little key in the mannequin's pocket.

Tears spill from my eyes and, for a long time, I am unable to free myself of sorrow over the fact that I didn't stay with Grandma and with my beloved kitten.

PEA SOUP

Translated by Mark Andryczyk

My aunt often cooked pea soup, which her late husband used to love to eat. Nowadays, when she finished preparing it, she would always fill up a bowl with it and place it on the windowsill. At night, her deceased husband would come and eat up the soup.

I was always fascinated with how clean the bowl was when I saw it in the morning. Because everybody knows that it's impossible to finish a bowl of pea soup without leaving behind a yellow film. Unless… unless of course he licked it clean.

And although I was not especially fond of peas in general, just the fact that someone would lick the bowl clean after eating it enchanted me for some strange reason. I, too, wanted to lick up the bowl after eating the soup.

When my aunt became aware of this, she dropped her washcloth and, for a moment, gave me a frightened stare. Maybe she had imagined that the spirit of her late husband had entered my body. But when she looked into my eyes, she saw nothing strange, just the clever eyes of a young hooligan looking up at her, and my aunt was able to calm down.

Nonetheless, the pea soup continued to intrigue me — it dawned on me that there must be something beyond taste that would drive my deceased uncle to lick the bowl clean.

From that day on, I began to gaze much more attentively at its murky, yellow waters, in which finely chopped carrots and onions would swim. And when my aunt would pour a handful of golden croutons into the soup, they would make it even cloudier, and a pale, yellow slime would begin rising from the bottom.

One day I realized that strange creatures lived at the bottom of the pea soup, who, just at first glance, looked like minced dill weed — thin, branchy and akin to people, with arms, legs and something resembling a head. These tiny, green dill weeds submerge and then resurface, swimming and overtaking one another as part of some kind of race. When I gather a spoonful of the soup, the tiny dill weeds, as if they had been scalded, shoot down to the very bottom, and settle in the slime like a school of fish. But not all of them are able to rescue themselves, not all. Those that end up in my mouth struggle in despair — I can feel them bustling, tickling my palate and tongue.

At one particular moment, I swish about the pea soup, together with all of its inhabitants, in my mouth, delighted at my absolute supremacy, tossing the despair of the poor little dill weeds against my palate with my tongue and then, finally, I swallow, feeling the pea soup stream down in a hot waterfall and hearing the screams of these strange creatures.

Spoonful after spoonful, I pour their fatherland — all of them together with the graves of their ancestors — into me.

Everything disappears in my mouth — all of their dreams and imagination, all of their hopes for a better life, all of their plans and intentions… It's the death of their civilization — a civilization that hasn't yet had the chance to fully blossom.

Pea soup is not a suitable place to live, but the tiny dill weeds don't understand this, and choose it time and time again.

IV. BLACK HUMOR
AND SATIRE

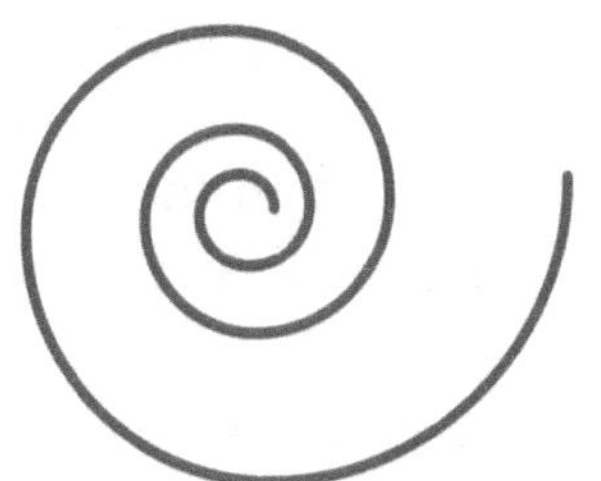

THE ISLAND OF ZIZ

Translated by Askold Melnyczuk

I.

The Island of Ziz near Arcanumia is inhabited by warbling dogs. These rare beasts sit on branches and sing like birds. They also lay eggs. They do not, however, build nests. Instead, they simply let their eggs drop from under their wooly tails to the ground. Because the eggs land in the excrement with which the dogs themselves have covered everything, they don't break. They lie there, warming peacefully. For that matter, these eggs differ from all others because of their hairy shells. When you put one to your ear, you can hear some shred of carrion growling and frisking about.

The entire island is in fact a mound of shit: new shit got piled on old shit and the result is this shitty island with a shitty landscape the color of shit. It's interesting to note that even the sky above the atoll is, typically, the color of shit. And the trees, on which the dogs sit, are, to be precise, high heaps of shit out of which Mother Nature has miraculously fashioned trees.

In the course of a thousand years even a product as absurd as shit can give birth to life. But, on the island of Ziz, we see the true apotheosis of the Renaissance of Shit. Everything, but everything, here is the color and shade of shit.

Until recently our press eschewed profanity and the dominant color on the island of Ziz was called honey. Here, however, honey is nothing other than bee-shit.

When I, in the company of two charming Arcanumians, arrived on the island, I was at once impressed by how various are the odors of shit. I smelled flowers and branches and small shitty butterflies. All claimed their own incomparable aroma. For the first time I sniffed shit in its primordial form, untinged by other smells. There was something celebratory and pristine about it. I came to know the essence of shit, its nature, and the great future concealed in its depths.

We strolled the island, admiring its lovely vistas. The Arcanumians proposed we take off our shoes and I eagerly followed their lead. After all, nowhere else on earth can humans feel quite so free and open: only on Ziz is there no danger of stepping in shit since shit surrounds you everywhere and everything is made of it. Only on Ziz is the risk of being full of shit no more threatening than a sun shower.

The Arcanumians were researchers at an academic institute. They patiently explained everything to me.

"Lately we've been working on developing a major discovery called antishitification," they explained. "The process of turning all things to shit is widely known and well established. But how to reverse it? That's the mystery. Professor Arse proposed using a special pump to send the excrement back where it came from. By his calculations, in just a couple of hours, one's food would well out of one's mouth. Professor Popik pointed out that the method has one drawback: the food wouldn't emerge as discrete items but rather as one well-masticated, solid mass, thus seriously undermining the effects of antishistification. This is now known as the Theory of Arse-Popik. Or vice versa.

"And the research went no further?"

"On the contrary. We already have huge antishitification plants with special machines transforming shit back into food. Thus far we've exported exclusively to developing nations. Yours among them."

"Why's that?"

"You see, it doesn't meet our needs. Moreover, it's been tough divesting it of a slight odor of shit. You mean to say you've never tasted it yourself? Why, we send it to you in the form of humanitarian aid."

"Unfortunately not. Humanitarian aid gets distributed only among the poor."

"To the poor we don't begrudge even shit itself. Why, we use it in our architecture. It makes nice brick and tile when fired. It's also used for bowls, mugs, and large pots. Shit mixed with gravel makes a perfect substitute for asphalt. Our electric power plants are driven solely by shit. Recently Professor Fartovich drew a peaceful atom out of it. Some of our craftsmen have distilled alcohol from it. In short, all areas of our lives have been touched by this shit revolution. Not for nothing did Pliny note: "*In cacatus veritas*"—that is: "*The Truth is in shit*."

As if to emphasize their words, the two Arcanumians abruptly sat down on the ground out of which they molded two appealing objects. The first represented the Pentagon, the other the Tower of Babel. Perhaps under other circumstances this would have offended me, but here I took it in cheerfully, enthusiastically. I confess I too longed to commemorate my visit to the island with a similar memento but didn't dare compete against their architectural mastery.

Wanting to know the island up close, I asked the Arcanumians to leave me alone for a week with the shit.

I soon grasped that when shit is everywhere, then, in fact, there is no such thing as shit. And, if there is no such things as shit, then this is the most perfect place on the planet. There was no point to the Arcanumians telling me that the island of shit is in fact a logically created mass and that in the near future we will be able to enter into direct contact with it.

II.

I saw it all. The first day, Monday, the shit began bubbling. Every bubble burst, sending up a tiny cloud of shit. The warbling dogs hopped nervously from tree to tree, sneezing whenever a cloud got near their nostrils. Every once in a while they pointed at me with their paws and blinked their eyes angrily. Maybe they blamed me for this miracle.

The second day, Tuesday, the whole island was cackling like a sizzling griddle. It smelled as though the whole thousand member Arcanumian Academy had farted, unanimously. Even the dogs covered their noses with paws and tails and tried crapping less.

I myself found no alternative to shitting in my pants, resigned to a smell that's now dear to my heart. Say what you will, our personal shit not only rivals its western counterpart but even, in rare cases, bests it as an evocative bouquet of inimitable aromas which inevitably, like the legendary yevshan-zillia, stirs memories of the home you left behind and, with its hazy chestnut color, immediately calls to mind the song "Again the chestnuts are in bloom..."

Here I realized how we've underestimated our own country's excrement by failing to list it alongside such indisputable cultural achievements as borscht, pork-fat, garlic sausage, and kishka. I'm not even touching on our spiritual wealth; excrement is, after all, material, though clearly it's kin to spiritual culture. Note how it emanates an utterly original spirit or, if you wish, aura. We've regarded our excrement as something second-rate and useless, seeing it only as a by-product. And there have been wise-guys who complained we'd produced too much excrement and that pretty soon our wonderfully fertile country would turn into a wasteland. Some even convinced themselves the time had come to change the name of planet Earth to planet Shit.

Our intrepid émigrés a century ago carried samples of Ukrainian excrement abroad, thereby substantially enriching foreign cultures. The process of enrichment continues to this day. I believe, however, that this is nothing other than a pillaging of the national treasure. It's time to limit the export of shit to the levels of gold and art. Just as we insist that England returns the treasures of General Polubotko, the day will come when we'll demand the return of our national shrines. I already foresee planes racing toward us from all corners of the earth carrying not the usual load of pitiful humanitarian aid but dividends on our own excrement. It makes one want to cry: "Ukrainian shit of the world, unite!"

Unfortunately, the majority of our ignorant population doesn't understand the role a pantheon consecrated to our national excrement might play in our spiritual rebirth. Frankly, it would be wise to open a museum of excrement in every town so that the people could see examples of the shit the greatest minds of our time produced. This can't be accomplished without some modest sacrifices. It will be enough to put out a call, and the Center of Shit Studies will be flooded with jars, beakers, vials, boxes, and packages filled with this product.

It's a pity our Central Administration, deciding on the various global issues of our age, has offered no solution to the problem of our national excrement. There is, as a result, no way to bridge the gap between ourselves and developed nations.

But let us return to the events of that day. That afternoon I had one more adventure. I suddenly felt a suspicious squirming inside my pants. Something in there burbled, and came alive. I hurried toward the sea but halfway there got a grip on myself: the experiment was worth seeing through to its end. The creation of new life inside my own pants was no small thing and worthy of critical examination.

I sat on a rock and continued my scientific observations, although I did not feel at my best because my pants kept either expanding like balloons or collapsing and sticking to my legs. It was wet, but warm.

On the third day, as though on command, out of the clouds that had sprouted from the bubbles, little humans began to emerge. These individuals, of various shapes and ages, appeared on this earth hatched from shit, and so it came as no surprise that they at once got busy acting like degenerates, pairing off wherever and with whomever happened to be at hand.

It interested me enormously that not all the little people were born naked. There were some among them who appeared in black suits, with black hats, and carrying black briefcases.

Some foolish force had swept them together and now they stood on a hill, eagerly rehearsing the conduct of their brethren. They finally reached a conclusion and, while one group built massive tables out of shit, others hunted down a couple of naked subjects and led them to the men behind the tables.

The debate didn't last long but its consequences were unmistakable: the naked subjects raced down the hill clutching in their fists the indecent parts of their sinful bodies. The neophytes went among the masses preaching the idea of sin. Pair after pair ran off scouting for burdocks, or anything with which to cover the usual, suspicious places.

Yet everything did not go smoothly. As soon as a majority of individuals had put on something that could pass for clothing, the minority, which had failed in its mission, became even more acutely visible. This, naturally, outraged the good citizens. They shook their bald heads and at once set about arresting the transgressors.

Judgement came swiftly. The nudists were sent to concentration camps for rehabilitation.

III.

On the fourth day I ran out of food. I left my lookout searching for something to eat.

Several coconut palms grew near the beach. I cracked one open and brought it to my lips. And spat. I was ready to live in shit, walk in shit and, for the matter, to be called a shit, but I was not yet ready to eat shit.

Hunger, however, is a harsh mistress and shit is not, *surprise*, poison. I gulped the next nut down in one swig. I swallowed this gift of nature and fell silent, awaiting the consequences. They weren't long in coming. All that I'd drunk down came calmly back up into the very shell I held in my hands. Along with the previous day's dinner. I cursed and hurled the shell with its precious fluid to the sea. And here I noticed the fish swimming lazily among the moss-covered rocks. They looked very unshitlike.

I quickly snatched up two fat flatfish and buried them in the excrement. At a certain depth it got so hot the fish soon sizzled. The delicate odor of excrement lent them a certain piquancy.

When I returned to my post I saw that the rehabilitated populace had been released. The resisters had been nailed to crosses.

History repeats itself, I sighed.

History does not tolerate intrusions, I said and with this aphorism quelled the nobler instincts urging me to give aid to the victims.

IV.

By the end of my week on the island of Ziz I had lost all interest in trying to enlighten this excremental civilization. It was all too clear down what road they were headed.

Finally the Arcanumians arrived on their speedboat and took me off the island.

"Goodbye, shit!" I cried into the fresh dawn air.

"Bubble-bubble," answered my pants.

The Arcanumians laughed, stripped them off me, and set to washing them.

It seemed that nothing memorable had come to life there.

MAX AND ME

1.

I was, maybe, fifteen and my brother Max—six, when our old man acquired permanent ownership of a wooden villa, whose sole inconvenience was that you could only lie down in it horizontally, and that it was two meters beneath the ground. He arranged his journey into a better world this way: he fell down drunk from a footbridge into a stream, whose water was only knee high. He managed the fall so well that it's possible he had help, though we certainly wouldn't know anything about that.

It's true that on that very evening mom ordered my brother and me to lay a rope across the footbridge and to slightly saw the handrails. She didn't say why, and I'm still wondering about that. When the corpse was found in the morning, the ropes were certainly gone.

Mom started wailing:

"O woe is me! How terrible! Who have you left us to?"

It would have been a sin to complain, cause our mother was in the not-so-bad hands of her suitors, who, even when our old man was alive, trampled the path to our house and paid decent money, paying their due to mom's charms.

At those times mom chased us out of the house, but we weren't too in the know, and sneaking up to the window, watched everything with delight. I lifted my little brother on my arms so he could see how our momma was playing hoppity-hop on the bed with the guy.

We knew all her guests by sight and always greeted them fondly. We really liked them and showed them respect, because they brought us candy and other sweets.

There was just one windbag we couldn't stand. He was such a fat pig that he could barely crawl into the house. So as not to hurt our momma, he didn't mount her, but put her on top. It was like this, our poor momma got tossed and tossed till abundant sweat pours out, and he lies there like a log snorting.

Ha, you're such a dog! We're going to make you bolt away. Just before his arrival we took pepper and liberally sprinkled it on the bed under the sheet. Then we lurked behind the window and waited.

Our sweetheart arrives and right away wants to do his thang with Momma and boom—right to bed. Mom started to do her thing, and he—whether he wanted to or not—scraped his backside, and the pepper even went up there. Whichever way he was tossed up or down, our mom, like a sparrow, flew up, then quickly fell down with a bang. We began to worry that our mom would fall on the floor. But God showed mercy. Our piggo, though, after all that jumping around began to scratch his ass non-stop. Even when he was getting dressed he couldn't stop scratching!

Then Gramps finked on us under the window and bellowed:

"What are you scamps doing here?"

And we answered him:

"Hush, Gramps! You'll frighten away the client!"

"What kind of client, dammit?"

"Come here and just take a look!"

And from that time our Gramps began to hang out under the windows. He would instruct us:

"Look, don't forget to call me when those... Cause I'll take a crowbar and break your legs! Take that, blockheads!"

It wasn't even a year since Dad's death, and our mom had exhausted herself to nothing from riding. Then the suitors disappeared somewhere—as if the wind had blown them away.

As though for spite, there was an adventure with Gramps. Gramps, ya see, was busy checking the neighbor's chicken coop. He liked order everywhere.

"I," he says, "don't take anybody else's stuff, just what's left over. And when I begins to count the chickens, I sees an uneven count, and I sez to myself: if you don't get hitched—the tartars'll make your life a bitch. And I takes away one chicken. And when I count an even number, then if I takes one—you break up the pair. So I takes two."

At a certain unfortunate hour Gramps was caught in the chicken coop just as he was screwing the heads off of a pair of chickens. Gramps, of course, tried to explain that his activity was directed exclusively for the benefit of the economy, but the cudgels didn't pay any attention and skillfully counted up the paired nature of Gramps' ribs. Now no one has had any doubts about Gramps not having an extra rib.

After such a counting out the dearly departed didn't get up out of bed. But we already knew quite well that our breed has more lives than a cat and Gramps has, God knows, many more years of tumbling in bed till he even thinks about giving up his spirit to God. This wasn't to the point for us, and we didn't complain much when somehow at night Grandpa puffed and panted underneath the feather comforter that covered his head. So that feather comforter wouldn't slide off and our Gramps, God forbid, wouldn't catch a cold, we sat on top with Mom.

The dearly departed couldn't even quack because our Mom even then was a stout woman, and, though she had a rump the size of two, all the same, for sure, Gramps' pretty little head hurt her, especially his long hooked nose.

Thus just as Gramps, God rest his soul, we were left standing on sheep dung. His diploma for soundless penetration into the chicken coops lost its validity from the time his authorship to the deeds became known to everyone it served. So it wasn't a surprise when our mom somehow said:

"Well, you've already grown up, time to get on with business. Cause I'm not planning on supporting any spongers."

That this is the holy truth, we were assured through Gramps, and to insure ourselves against various surprises, at which our mother was very adroit, we started up an entirely decent business: if something was lying in the wrong place, we dragged it into the house at once.

Little Max was a strangely talented boy, but already much too screechy. Somehow that screeching burnt me up so much that I couldn't take it:

"Shut up," I says, "or I'll cut off your ear."

As much as I tried, he wouldn't stop. I really loved my little brother, but you have to keep a promise. So I take a knife, slash-slash—and the ear's gone.

Max fell silent instantly, his tears vanished. First they dripped as though from a downspout, then disappeared without a trace. He looked at me with such bulging eyes. His mouth gaped, and from his ear ever so quietly, the brrr-brrr of blood.

"Idiot!" I couldn't hold back. "You could at least cover it with your hand!"

Not even a peep from him. He stands there as though he's struck dumb. It would have gone on for a while if mom had not come out and asked:

"What happened that he's not crying? First he wailed like somebody not quite knifed to death, then he quieted down and hasn't even stirred. What did you do to him?

"Nothin'. I just lopped off his ear cause he was convulsing too much."

"Did you at least clean his ear before you lopped it off?"

"No, but so what?"

"The what is that you can spread infection. Lord, what am I to do with you? You never ask the grown-ups, you decide everything yourselves. Max, go into the house. I'll cover your wound with dough. Just look at how it's bleeding all over! At least cover it with your hand, just look at him, he's bugging out his eyes like a frog!

I put away the ear in a matchbox, covering it with cotton, and Max never parted with it. His ear soon became the subject of envy of all the boys on the street, even kids from the edge of town came to eye it. With pride Max showed his ear, explaining:

"It was Vlodzyo who cut it off when I was screaming like somebody not quite knifed to death."

Then everybody turned their gaze to me, filled with respect and envy: this little brother is really cute!

Fortunately I realized that, for the displaying of a cut-off organ, you could make some decent dough, and I began to take a nickel from every onlooker. And only in rare cases, when an onlooker was too young to control his own finances, was the payment exchanged for some valuable objects. These might be colored glass lenses, buttons, a dead mouse, a bizarre little beetle, or even a piece of candy.

Momma couldn't have been more thrilled with us:

"I always said: my blood's flowing inside you."

She never mentioned our dad's blood, since she could never be sure which of her countless suitors really was our dad.

But all things must come to an end. When the audience for admiring the ear dwindled, our profiteering declined. Poor Max couldn't take this. With tears in his eyes, he begged me to cut off his other ear, but well I knew that this would hardly interest anyone again.

And then we began to reflect upon what else we might cut off Max. We thought for a long time until Max finally gave notice with a secret glance that he had one other strange thing that was completely unnecessary, and happily he would part with it. But when he showed me the thing, I didn't want to take upon myself such a heavy sin.

"Max," I said, "you're still much too little and can't appreciate the value of that thing. When you grow up a bit, you'll really need it once in a while."

In short, whether we wanted to or not, we were forced to look for other earnings.

2.

About the same time a lush wandered into our yard and fell asleep, and our sow snuck up and bit him on the neck. And she, as rarely happens with a sow, wasn't miserly and called over the boar to share the sweets.

Upon hearing the really loud snorting and smacking, we ran out with our mom and chased off the gluttons. But it was too late, the lush had already departed for a better world. And at that moment a bold idea visited Mom's gray little head: so as not to waste good stuff, and before the meat began to stink, she decided to make schnitzel from the lush.

Without thinking much, we dragged him into the barn and quickly chopped him apart into bits and pieces.

Since the skin was already damaged we buried it, and separating the meat from the bones, we put it through a meat grinder.

The next day, a sign above the doors adorned our house:

UNDER THE GREEN DOG.
Here you can tastefully dine
and lodge overnight
in the company of an incomparable Lolita.

The incomparable Lolita, of course, was our momma. She got a shaggy black wig and didn't look bad at all, even though no rubber or corsets could tuck her shape in any longer.

Our work lay in making sure our overnight guests were fed with the most varied of meat delicacies, lavishly flavored with hemlock. When the guests dispersed to their designated bedrooms, right away they got interested in the incomparable Lolita. What confusion when it turned out to be our momma. But there was no other way out—the incomparable Lolita visited each room in turn and forced them to lay down, mixing the practical with pleasure.

By dawn not a single one of the clients was breathing, and then our real work began. Although visitors of "Under the Green Dog" often dropped by, so much meat was left over that we had to take it to the market. And so many damn bones collected that the entire barn was cluttered. Then we suggested to mom that she make soap from them. So much work piled up that we, no joke, were really huffing and puffing.

One evening after a long discussion, we decided that Max would care for the garden. We'd planted hemlock and henbane everywhere, so that we'd have seasoning for the meat. He'd also take care of the kettles in which the bones and fat cooked. The butcher's work fell to me, and to Momma—the cook and the incomparable Lolita.

Despite this, later on, we still couldn't manage everything, and therefore Momma suggested that we look up her brother, my uncle.

3.

My uncle lived outside of town on a farm, and he had three underswine: Bodyo who was my age and two twins—Milko and Filko. I'll tell you about the daughter later.

Uncle occupied himself with a nice little business: he'd catch cats and dogs and make soap out of them, which, of course, couldn't compete with ours. Auntie then would sew mink and fox furs from the cat and dog skins, which suspiciously gave off too much of an odor, and their owners would really complain about the fact that at least a dozen cats and dogs would run after them on the streets, perhaps relatives of the fox fur.

Thus I was designated negotiator. Just in case, I picked up an ax and hid it beneath my belt under my jacket.

Quiet reigned on the farm. An autumn wind was playing with the miserable leaves. Auntie was sitting at the doorstop kneading butter. It was hardly cow's butter.

I politely said "hello" and asked whether Uncle was there.

"Yep, yep, go back of the house—he's there, landlording."

In back of the house my old blockhead uncle and his three little blockheads were tanning cats.

"God help you," I greeted them.

"Oh, look who's come to us!" Uncle shouted out, pretending to be really pleased. The threesome of his ferrets stretched their mouths from ear to ear, baring sparse yellow teeth. "What wind brought you here?"

"The wind that sweeps in money."

On hearing about money, Uncle looked at me with interest. Then he wiped off his bloody hands in the grass and stepped closer.

"Well, okay, let's talk. But first let my boys check if you don't happen to have any kind of dumb thing under your shirt that might cut a finger."

With these words the three jerks rushed toward me, baring their teeth, already eager to fulfill their dad's command, but I stopped this impetus in time, welcoming the eldest with a shot to the head.

"Eh-eh," Uncle got fidgety, "I was just kidding."

"Keep these kind of jokes for a job that I'm about to toss your way."

They poured a bucket of rainwater on Bodya and he came to. We sat under a tree on the grass, and I explained:

"Well, the deal's like this. With our mom we opened up an inn "Under the Green Dog," which a lot of guests frequent, but no one notices whether they ever come back out."

Uncle looked back and forth at his den mates meaningfully, and I continued:

"We treat them to meat, and the leftovers of the meat we sell at the market. In addition we make soap from the high quality bones and fat. Maybe you've heard about the brand 'Chinese Orange?'"

"Why wouldn't I have heard about it? It's the best soap there is. I use it a lot myself."

"Yeah, we make it. Though, true, we don't use it ourselves."

"So you cook it from the bones you separate from the meat?"

"Uh-huh."

"And you get the meat after the overnight guests disappear?"

"Right."

"And you feed the overnight guests with meat that appeared after a room is freed up by their predecessors?"

"How quick you are, Uncle!" I shouted rapturously.

Uncle sat lost in thought. The three ruffians wrinkled their stunted brows, pretending that thoughts were strongly depressing them.

"Hmm..." Uncle finally mumbled. "And you want to propose that we work together?"

"It's as if you, Uncle, just read my mind."

"And you aren't afraid I'll sell you out?"

"Naw."

Uncle raised his eyebrows in surprise:

"Why?"

"Because Max and I are juveniles, and the court would decide that Momma threw us off the righteous path. But Momma won't end up in jail because she's too smart. They'll lock her up in a palace of culture for crazies, and they'll release us to all the four corners of the earth. But then, dear Uncle, your judgment day is about to begin. There's lots of fat on you, the soap'd be splendid."

Uncle grimaced.

"Well, good. I agree. How about you, my lovely kiddies?"

The lovely kiddies immediately nodded their heads. I liked their reticence. We squeezed each other's hands, and Uncle said:

"Well, it wouldn't hurt to wash down something to seal the deal. Let's go inside the house."

Auntie covered the table. Uncle got some kind of bottle overgrown with moss out of the cupboard and poured out a shot glass for everyone. In all my life I've never had to drink a more abominable poison. A corpse would have cursed had someone sprinkled that contagion on his lips. I bit a pickle, because those meat dumplings that appeared on the table failed to win my trust.

4.

From then on our business was so successful that we made oodles of money and began to think about how to expand. It's true, things didn't go without altercations, because Uncle and Momma never missed the chance to cheat each other.

Once Momma said to Uncle:

"Listen, Lodzyo, why don't we become related?"

And so now the time comes for me to say a few words about Uncle's daughter, who was already 17 and considered herself marriageable. Her name was Ruzya. This was a creature born quite stupid, who was good only for being kept in a dark garret, so she wouldn't frighten decent people.

Imagine an emaciated, greenish, and, if that's not enough, mustachioed babe. And they were planning to hitch me with such a dirty snout.

I resisted this idea with my hands and feet:

"She's as ugly as the world communism! When I see her, everything gets limp and hiccups take over."

"My son," said Momma, "our business needs this. And if you don't agree, then I'll have to take extreme measures."

She looked at me in such a way that I envisioned one leg in the place my beloved dad was.

5.

The wedding was grand. The number of stray cats and dogs in town noticeably decreased, and they shot down so many crows you couldn't even count them. Auntie baked such tasty chicken in cream made from them that the guests nearly swallowed their fingers. I won't even speak of the stewed rabbits from cats and the roasted meat of dogs. Auntie put all her culinary talent into this, so that even the most discerning gourmet wouldn't doubt the naturalness of the sausage, the pate and hams.

I sat with a sour look on my face, and next to me jutted out, like a sore thumb, my Ruzya. Her mustachioed smile gleamed from ear to ear.

For a long time I tried not to look her way, so as not to ruin my appetite, and scrupulously consume those several natural sandwiches that my momma had stuffed into my pockets. But those greenhorns, her off-their-rocker brothers, screeched awfully—so to speak, the liquor was bitter (but can it be sweet if it's made of animal dung?), and they're not going to drink, you see, until the young couple sweetens it up.

I turned pale and felt that ants were crawling down my back. Forget about sweets, mother damnedest! Let a fence post like her kiss my boots, then, maybe, they'll glisten from her lips as though from tar. But those monsters don't sit up, they lament so their mugs turn red as a beet from the exertion.

In the meanwhile Ruzya looks at me like she's looking at a dog, and I hear something gurgling in her stomach, as though someone there is pushing a wheelbarrow of bricks uphill.

I rose up on my feet with a heavy heart, Ruzya stuck her mug at me and, spattering me all over with saliva, nearly bit off my nose. That nag attached herself to me by sucking like a leech. I thought she'd suck out my soul. I already sensed how in my stomach furious juices were diving and rising up to my throat. I barely tore her off me. I fell on the bench. My muzzle glistened from the saliva, but it wouldn't have been apropos for me to wipe my face, so I grabbed a piece of wedding cake, though it was baked from sawdust, that I stuffed it into my mouth to somehow kill the taste of Ruzya's lips.

In the meanwhile the parents somehow decided that I was burning to be alone with the bride and, grabbing us under the arms, shoved us into the bedroom and locked us in.

My little wife, all red from indefatigable thirst, was filled with the desire to finally destroy the concrete and iron Maginot Line of her innocence, instantly slipped off her rags, everything that hid her bony form from the human eye, and became naked as a jay bird before me, the way her stupid mother had given her birth.

My depressed gaze rode along the smooth flat surface of her absent breasts and sank to her sunken stomach covered with blue veins, which you could straighten out nails on, and with horror I got entangled in a black distaff that stuck out from beneath her stomach. This horrible broom stunned me with its disproportionate size, and I immediately suspected the talented hand of my auntie.

Laughing malevolently, I tugged at that nest. Ruzya let out a scream. An ordinary wig ended up in my hands, it had been adapted for a different function—and not without great skill. And on the spot where there had been impenetrable debris, a timid Ho Chi Minh-like little beard now reddened that Ruzya not inappropriately had decided to chastely cover with her bony hand.

To somehow dispel the tense atmosphere, Ruzya giggled and, jumping on the bed, sprightly threw her little legs apart, so that I wouldn't immediately doubt the reality of the spot they had married me, a dope, to. I really saw that everything there was in order and that a disguised chopamatic wasn't lying in ambush for me. From my relatives you could expect just about anything.

Ye-es, I think to myself, if I don't teach her common sense right away, when will I be able to teach her? And taking off my strap, I went up to her and she the fool grins and tempts like a cat. I grabbed a pillow, covered over her snout and marked her with a criss-cross. Like a snake she , writhed and rocked, so much so that her bones rattled, but I didn't stop—striking crosswise—until the strap stuck to her skin.

I pulled away the pillow, sat down next to her and said:

"Just tell anybody this and I'll kill you on the spot. I'm that kind of guy. Capisci?"

"Uh-huh," she says through tears.

"I don't want to have to see you naked anymore. Your goddess-like looks tempt me the way turpentine tempts a cat."

6.

After these intimate relations, perhaps, we'd live like dumplings in butter, but our mom shriveled up. Now as the incomparable Lolita she'd only be able to satisfy the kind of guy who'd been sitting in prison for 15 years, and only if you got him good and drunk.

Our whole family gathered together around the rectangular table and begin to think how to get out of this difficult situation. Since our mom wasn't there as before, I suggested that we should rope our auntie or my beloved wife into this business.

Hey, you should've seen how Uncle reacted! All of a sudden he springs up on his bow legs and starts pounding his fists on the table:

"I won't allow it! I won't give her to you!" He said, along with similar things flavored with peppery words.

His three nitwits grabbed for the knives and forks, as though they had taken me for a cooked turkey.

"Aha," I say, "when my momma has been overstraining herself for the sake of the communal pocket, then you don't say boo, but when it comes to your turn, right away you hit the brakes?!"

"I'm too weak for that kind of work," Auntie said.

"She's very weak," Uncle reiterated. "I don't wrestle with her more often than once every two days, and even then it's scratch-scratch to get it over with quicker."

"And that's only when I get smacked across the mouth," Auntie moaned. "Cause for me even every two days is too hard. It's good that I take out my lower plate at night, cause my whole mug would be smashed otherwise."

"Those guys are all some kind of heretics," Momma shook her head. "Once one guy came to me who wanted just to cut out a part of my rear-end. He said that when he sees it, he begins to slobber and wants to wolf it down. When I done heard that, he never saw me again without my undies on."

"But how did he?..." Auntie got interested, but Momma, casting a look at the children, whispered into her ear. Auntie said: "Aha!" And she got lost in thought.

"Well, good," I thrust in. "You're right about Auntie. Keep her exclusively for your own little rich farmer needs. Pound her muzzle and sniff if she's breathing. But I'm a guy of the present, my morality isn't messed up by bourgeois superstition. I'm giving up my beloved wife for the communal business."

Ruzya, when she heard this, flared up like a fire, and lowered her eyes. It was immediately clear that she valued my sacrifice as the greatest gift fate had offered her. Finally she would shake off the heavy shackles of innocence from herself and sate her thirsty flesh.

All the rest ponderously redigested the proposition, feverishly calculating their percentages of the take. To ease those calculations, I continued:

"Since I'm her complete owner, I require 40% of the profit for myself."

I knew what I was saying. Uncle, catching wind of money, suddenly forgot that we were talking about his daughter, and threw himself into the negotiating, knocking down the price. Auntie inserted her own:

"And how much for me? I gave birth to her! Carried her for nine months with a constant backache! Please pay me for every month."

"Not nine, but seven," my momma said. "I remember well. That's why she was born so emaciated."

"How's that seven?" Uncle was put on the alert. "I counted well. I know what I was doing. Everything went according to plan. It can't be seven, because they would have taken me into the army right after the wedding."

"But Ruzya was born in the seventh month, I remember that as if it were right now. You were already serving your ninth month."

Auntie sat with her eyes directed at the ceiling and was completely white.

Uncle slowly turned to her, looked meaningfully and, without thinking long, drove so hard into her teeth that Auntie thudded together with the armchair, throwing up her arms and legs. In her left hand she clutched her lower plate, which she had managed to pull out.

"Yep, it's this way with dames," Uncle shook his head and gulped down ten double-shots of moonshine without munching anything. "Twenty five and not a percentage point more."

"Good," I agreed.

Ruzya didn't even grumble about her share at all, because she got all that she could ever dream of—every night five or six boys, sometimes more. This wasn't just life, but paradise. I'd be envious if I were a girl.

That was the start of our problems. The ex-Lolita had concerned herself only with containing the voluptuous shapes that tumbled out of her clothes, but the newly cooked up Lolita, on the other hand, had ribs that jutted out like a ladder.

In order to survey well which parts of her body in fact required the hand of a maestro, Momma ordered Ruzya to undress completely. By that time Auntie had convalesced, having gotten two cuffs on the mouth from Uncle and a cup of water on her head. She put in her lower plate and started to work on business. Momma and Auntie circled around Ruzya like bumblebees, discussing what to do with this treasure.

"I'll make titties from oakum," Momma said. "I'll sew them around with cheesecloth so they hold together when the client feels them up. And you, Ruzya, should moan heartily, because even though it's oakum, when somebody grabs a girl by the tit, she has to moan and roll her eyes. That's the rule. But what can we do with the ribs? You can play marches on them. I'm surprised, son, why you haven't knocked on them from time to time."

"Maybe we can cover them with dough so they don't stick out so much?" Uncle asked, chewing pork rind.

Auntie took a spoon from the table and knocked herself on the forehead, looking Uncle straight in the eye at the time. But Uncle, for sure, didn't understand her transparent hint, because he stretched for a pickle and not for his strap.

"There's no other way out," said Momma. "We'll just have to feed her with dog lard for several days. That'll make her fill out real fast."

"I don't want dog la-a-rd!" Ruzya began to shriek.

"You need to add a little honey, whiskey and whipped eggs to the melted dog lard," Momma added. "This is a solid-as-a-brick-wall recipe when someone wants to put on weight quickly. And it's not as vile as you might guess. I used to drink it, and it wasn't bad."

"And what kind of eggs?" Auntie asks. "Chicken?"

"No. Cat testicles," Momma answered.

"Oo-oo-ooh," Ruzya grimaced.

"Hush," Auntie interrupted. "If you needa, you needa. We have enough testicles, why spare them?"

"It'd be nice to broaden her rear end a bit," Momma said, "because this is a lump and not a rear end. How does the poor girl sit on it? Well, bend over."

Ruzya obediently bent over, showing us a butt that was hard as a knee cap, at the sight of which Uncle grievously and very quickly swallowed ten double-shots.

That very same day they tied poor Ruzya to the bed and every hour began to feed her with a cocktail made of dog lard and whipped cat balls. And so that the lard would satiate her body and as little as possible would be lost, Ruzya didn't get up from the bed, so as not to shake off any of her fat. Toward evening the whole family would gather near her bed and carefully follow after the results of Momma's diet.

Ruzya's muzzle virtually glistened from the lard, but she looked sad and oppressed. Little by little her body took on the fat, and the extra even came out all the time. Her body veritably beamed in the darkened room. It was thick with the odor of dog and whipped cat balls.

Hard as Momma and Auntie tried their sorcery, after a week Ruzya hadn't put on enough weight to let her loose among the clients, and they were forced to continue fattening sessions. In another week Ruzya looked so elegant that my own saliva drooled, and I felt like having a taste of this morsel, but, recalling what kind of seasoning it was stuffed with, I quickly lost my appetite.

Ruzya had now become puffy and round everywhere. Her ribs disappeared, in their place, layers of fat appeared, and even on her chest two pastry fluffs dangled and with each step cheerfully hopped. Momma also taught her to walk in such a way that her rear end stuck out as eloquently as possible, and my Ruzya turned into such a mare, on which hardly anyone could refuse to take exercise.

That's how it happened. Ruzya enjoyed constant success, and our business blossomed in all its many colors.

7.

When the police surrounded our farm-yard we were completely unprepared to defend ourselves.

Uncle and Auntie were busy with their cats, Max was boiling soap in his cauldron, Ruzya was upstairs entertaining her next client, and Momma was making hunter's sausage from cat intestines. At that time

I was sawing wood for smoking ham, and my brothers-in-law were distilling their beloved animal dung.

And right at such a peaceful time, when the sky above our heads poured out in translucent azure, unexpectedly sirens and brakes began to screech, triggers were cocked on carbines, tens of voices commanded us to raise our hands and give up one by one.

"Better death than slavery!" My momma shouted out, and in seconds we hid in the house.

Everyone armed himself, as well as he could. Uncle placed his double-barreled Austrian rifle, which he'd been using to hunt cats, through the window, and Auntie dug out on the thatched roof an ancient machine gun that looked like it was from the Neolithic period.

From upstairs, Ruzya ran down with her client, completely naked. The client screamed that he was here by accident and was going to give himself up on the spot.

"Good," Uncle said. "The road is clear."

Ruzya gave him a ta-ta kiss, and the client jumped out into the yard, shouting:

"I'm one of yours! One of yours!"

Perhaps if he'd chosen a different password, everything would have gone well, but the police sensed an insult to their dignity in that shout. The machine gun lines sewed through him—up and down at first, then sideways.

After this the police moved to the attack. The machine gun in the attic began to snarl. The bullets skipped along the trees, then the plank fences, and Auntie swore at the police royally, and, I think, those curses annoyed them more than the machine gun bullets. At the same time somewhere from the basement the three brothers dragged out a cannon painted orange. The cannon looked more ridiculous than threatening.

Attentively, Uncle frightened the police with his double-barreled gun, heavily snorting with his potato-like nose.

Max and Momma took pitchforks and occupied the defense by the doors.

In that time I gathered everything into the basement that could give evidence against us, and poured gas over it liberally. At any moment it would be enough to throw a lit match in there, and in a single blow the police would lose all their evidence.

Finally they loaded the cannon, and opening the doors, directed the barrel at the assault force. On seeing such a monstrosity, the police instantly fell to the ground.

Bodyo lit a fire, raised it to the end of the barrel and shouted: "Fire!"

How can you describe what happened? A deafening explosion resounded, so the whole building shook. And all around a poisonous black smoke wound through. I don't know how they managed to aim at the police. One shot broke open all the windows and frames, the doors with their jambs, and for some reason behind our backs, right across from the doors, the pith knocked another door out of the wall. For sure, the cannon had shot in the wrong direction.

When the smoke had cleared I saw two ragged heads. The twins had done their duty virtuously. Bodyo was luckier—they just tore off his hand.

Uncle coughed heavily.

Momma and Max shook their heads and beat themselves on the ears.

Auntie in the meanwhile had already crawled out on the roof, because she had a restricted field of vision from the attic, and shouted to us:

"Lodzyo!"

"Whoa!" The old man's throat rattled.

"You alive?"

"Who got killed?"

"The twins."

"I never did get any joy from them. Even on a day like this they got on my nerves."

And in a minute:

"Lodzyo!"

"Whoa!"

"Tell Ruzya to put on her underwear because the police are almost here."

After this the machine gun began to rattle, and Ruzya threw herself into finding her underwear.

I understood that not much was left for us.

Bodyo was stubbornly loading the cannon with one hand.

Now it didn't matter which direction it shot because the police thrust forward from all sides.

Momma and Max stuck out their pitchforks through the windows and then through the door so the enemies would know what kind of threatening weapons awaited them.

Uncle asked:

"Bodyo, you going to shoot?"

"Yep."

"Well, then take care."

The cannon thudded so that another door appeared on the opposite wall, and one of the police cars flared up. Too bad that Bodyo didn't see that.

A rattling reverberated on the roof, and Auntie's voice announced:

"Lodzyo!"

"Whoa!"

"I'm flying off!"

"May the heavenly kingdom be yours," Uncle crossed himself as Auntie crashed solidly in the yard. All our mouths had blackened from the cannon fire and we looked like angelic insurrectionists.

Ruzya finally put on her underwear and crawled along the attic to the machine gun.

Max asked:

"What've we done to them that's so bad?"

"We'll die like heroes," Momma answered.

Upstairs the rattling of the machine gun rounds reverberated again. I could really take pride in my wife. And a strange thing: never having slept with her even once, in that decisive moment I felt for her such an insurmountable attraction, that I was ready to rush to the attic and make love to her beneath the bullets to spite our enemies.

And, perhaps, I could have done that, but at that moment a rattling reverberated in the attic and Ruzya's voice said:

"Daddy!"

"Whoa!"

"I'm flying!"

"The Heavenly Kingdom to you, too!"

Ruzya fell along with the machine gun.

Uncle slowly turned his head away from the window, and I saw his mouth fill with blood. His body fell heavily onto the floor.

I picked up the double-barreled gun and knocked off some policeman's cap. The weapon, it seems, didn't pretend to be anything more.

Momma and Max defended the door courageously, but it was an uneven battle. The police wanted to take at least some of us alive and shot above our heads. And when Momma stuck one of them like a dumpling on the pitchfork, the infuriated policeman tore her stomach apart with bullets.

"You bandits!" Max violently became enraged and threw himself into the attack with pitchforks.

The end was in sight. I quickly jumped from the window, struck a match, and the flame struck hard in the basement. Max's pre-death scream could be heard from outside.

I raised a small log from the floor and with all my strength whacked myself on the head.

I found out what happened later at the trial.

They, of course, put me on trial, because I alone survived. The evidence burned up completely, and I stubbornly played the role of a crazy guy, feigning that I didn't understand what they wanted from me.

I got what I wanted. They designated me as sick and sent me off to the asylum at the Park of Culture.

Right now I'm sitting by the window and admiring the wintry park. A fine snow is falling, crows are cawing, I'm wearing clean pajamas, and on my knees—a plate with sweet porridge. Life is beautiful.

When Spring comes, I'll ask the cleaning lady Olya to take me for a walk in the garden. I behave so well, that all the personnel can't stop wondering how I could have done such evil deeds earlier. Some even say that I'm suffering only because I was left alive, everything was thrust on me alone. Olya the cleaning lady brings me candies, pats me on the head and says: "So young, so nice, but terribly ill!" I try to lick her hand, but she hides it behind her back and laughs.

The cleaning lady Olya will say: "He's earned it," and will take me for a stroll in the springtime. At that time my pants and shirt will be hidden beneath my pajamas so I can get changed.

"Be careful that the head guy doesn't notice," the nurse in charge will smile to the cleaning lady Olya and will open the door.

We will be going to walk slowly, very slowly, since over the past year I've grown unaccustomed to walking. The cleaning lady Olya will hold me beneath my arms and will order:

"Careful, a hole... Careful, a bump..."

There in the garden's depth behind the thick bushes I'll smile to the cleaning lady Olya, take her by the throat with both my hands. Her neck is so fragile, swan-like. Her cartilage will crumble so easily, and her body, small and tender, will hang on my hands.

Maybe I'll kiss her good-bye, and maybe not.

Quickly getting changed, and rearing back on a branchy linden tree, I'll take respite on a wall. A farewell look at the house of crazies, and—welcome, Freedom!

But for now it's winter. I politely chew my porridge, and when the cleaning lady Olya asks about a second helping, I quickly lick her palm and say:

"He-he-he!"

WELCOME TO RATBURG

"When I arrived in this town, the first living soul I met was a rat."

This is the way Marko Pekelny began his story after having come back from his last trip. Each time experiencing breakneck adventures, this guy, who at first glance seemed so quiet and had such a far from heroic appearance, appeared at my place without any notice. Tossing out a brief "salute" at the doorstep, he came upstairs right away to my study, entering the holiest of holies, where even my wife feared to drop by without a knock at the door. On the steps Marko, without turning his head, asked:

"Got any coffee?"

He wasn't interested in the answer. He knew the answer beforehand—there had to be coffee. When I came back with it, Marko was already lying on the couch, throwing his long legs over the edge.

I turned on the tape recorder and listened to the latest adventure.

"Yep, there was a rat... His appearance baffled me—he was in a black suit, a white shirt and white gloves, and from beneath his heavy breeches white gaiters peeked out. The rat gallantly raised his hat above his head, and, baring his yellow teeth, said:

"Welcome to Ratburg!"

The rat was the size of a cat and stood on his hind legs.

"Ratburg?" I was surprised, and pointing to the buildings, added: "But people also live here."

"Of course. Just like in any town. But rats founded Ratburg. We discovered this place and settled down. And people showed up later. That's the history of a lot of towns. But for some reason we were always in the shadows."

"And how do you get along with the people?"

"Great. Beyond all expectations. We even name the separate streets in human language."

"And where do you live?"

"In the cellars where we've always lived. In principle nothing much has changed. At the same time there are certain changes for the better. We finally found a common language as well as common interests. People stopped harming us. On the contrary, they respect us, consult us with regard to the building up of the town. We've made them happy."

"You?"

"Of course! Figuratively speaking, they're sitting on our shoulders, ha-ha."

"Excuse me," I interrupted, "Did I not hear that they're sitting on your shoulders?"

"No-no! That's the way it is. We do a lot for them. We write books for them, which they read with pleasure, compose songs, which they listen to with pleasure, we make films for them, which they watch with delight. We enliven them spiritually. And they're very thankful. Their thankfulness is expressed mainly by their treating us to dinners. Note— just dinners. We have to get our own breakfast and lunch. Agree—they make out very cheaply. And moreover, all their spiritual nourishment is only nominally in our hands. In films, for example, people appear, even if they concern essentially problems of the rat family. And books? In books, too, as a rule, people act as protagonists, and rats only appear episodically. Historical works become an exception... since only we represent and create history here, people don't really have any connection to it. And all of this—just for dinner! Can you imagine?"

"Hmm... Really. This is the first time I've met such sincere rats."

"He-he... That's a good one—sincere rats! I'll remember that."

Listening to the rat, I noticed that not far from the building someone was watching us—in the window behind the curtain I could see a figure. But each time that the head of the rat turned in that direction, the figure disappeared and just the barely noticeable glimmering of the shadows on the white curtain gave away the observer. At the same time the unknown person made signals to me with his hand.

"Well, I'm quite thankful to you," I said. "I'll move on."

"I'd be happy to guide you to the most interesting places."

"Thanks, but I have little time and it'll be enough for me to just stroll around the town."

"Wonderful! I'll show you to the main street."

"No-no, I'll go alone... I, you know, like to walk alone."

"I'll accompany you anyway. Otherwise you'll have a twisted impression regarding our hospitality."

The rat spoke amiably, but in such a tone that I had no doubt he would not back off.

"Listen," I lost my patience, "I'm used to just traveling alone, and till now—quite successfully. I'm not planning on abandoning my habits in your town."

"No one's stopping you. Though things may happen! We have hooligans here. It'd be really awful if you had a mishap."

"I'll manage. Be well," I grumbled with irritation, and, turning my back, went to the building. The rat followed in my footsteps. I heard his quiet shuffling. When I got up to the building and put my hand on the gate, I heard a screech:

"Stop! What are you doing? That's not allowed!"

"What did I do? I'm terribly thirsty. I want a drink," I responded courteously, which irritated him even more.

"But where are you going? A madman lives there!"

"That doesn't matter. I want some water."

"I'll show you where the water is!"

"I'm already sick of your spying!"

"How can you? Me—a spy?! I just showed some hospitality. In my place..."

"That doesn't interest me."

When I jostled the gate and stepped into the yard the rat became totally infuriated. He dashed about, spewing foam and shrieking as he convulsed:

"Stop! Don't move a muscle! You won't get away with this! You've caught my diligence off guard. I'll lose my job through you! Turn back immediately! A madman is there! It is strictly prohibited to visit people! They are all mad! All of them! They just ridicule our culture. They just pretend, I know! You've been sent by someone! Who sent you?!"

He was screaming, and during that time I cut across the yard and walked up to the steps. At that instant a piercing drone began to reverberate. Looking back I saw him jumping hysterically, unable to stop me in any way. And a few dozen rats were running along the street to come to his aid.

A door opened up by itself and someone's hand pulled me inside. The lock screeched in the dark hall and a man's voice said:

"Follow me."

When we got to the room, the master of the house glanced through the window:

"Boy, they're bustling around!"

"What is it?"

"Take a look," he said, not without a certain satisfaction in his voice, which really surprised me, because I saw the street filled with rats. What's there to be happy about?

He was a robust guy of about 50, with wild gray hair and long shaggy whiskers.

"Is it impossible to cope with them?" I asked.

"Nothing bothers them. They're much too smart. They don't eat poison bait, they don't get caught by traps, they've devoured all the cats and dogs a while ago... What's worst, right now there's a new generation in power that has already been born after we had become scared. It's so sure of itself, convinced that it's doing us a great favor by taking care of our every step."

"What do they want?"

"Submission and gratitude. But we're already incapable even of that. We're tired of being grateful."

"Is it really true they've taken your entire spiritual sphere of life away from you?"

"You can just imagine—it's true... But this is just on the surface, because few if any of us truly accept this. Mostly we've all learned to pretend, and when we need to, we paint satisfaction on our faces. But alone, hiding behind three doors, we let ourselves relax, and crawling under feather beds and hiding our head beneath the pillow, hum one of the old songs... We're wary of singing when visiting each other, because there are a lot of stool pigeons among us." "And what do they do to you for this? Prison?" "Worse. An asylum. We don't have any prisons. There, in the center of town, there's even a banner hanging up: 'Ratburg—a town without prisons.' Everybody ends up in the asylum who dares to doubt the propriety of the rats' power... From this day on that may await even me."

"You?/.. But how can they know what we're talking about here?"

"Just listen," he said, pointing to the floor. And it was true, from there a careful scratching echoed to us. I stamped my foot and it grew silent.

"They're everywhere," the man of the house smiled sadly. "You can come across them in the most unexpected places."

"But what happens to out-of-towners who come to visit you?" I finally inquired, sensing unpleasant news.

"First they try to work on people the way they did on you. To cloud your head. When they succeed, they take the out-of-towners to exemplary families, acquaint them with the life of the town and show them around with favor. And if they don't succeed, they put them away in the asylum."

"Why have you lured me here?" I got angry. "Now both of us are threatened with danger!"

"I just ask you not to be angry... I've been waiting for this moment a long time. Because I can only trust an out-of-towner. Especially if he's fallen into the same kind of dead end as I have... The fact is that I was a colonel once. I've managed to store away certain reserves. I have a lot of grenades, two machine guns and a flame-thrower. The three of us can smash them into bits..."

"The three of us?"

"You and me and my daughter. It's entirely possible that other townspeople will join us. I believe that. It can't be that they've all been turned into cowards. We'll break into the asylum at first. The people we need are there right now."

I didn't know what to answer out of surprise. For no reason at all to take part in an uprising against the state wasn't particularly enticing. Why should I meddle in someone else's internal business? It's true that rats don't evoke any sympathy in me, but they didn't burn me up so much that I'd go in for breaking their heads and beating them. But the prospect of ending up in an asylum scared me all the more. How would we manage against this countless number of rats? When the insurrection flares up, of course, the business would go easier, but before we do anything good, they'll chew off our fingers.

There was nowhere to retreat—the rats were already swarming beyond the window. But not even the shadow of fear flashed on the face of the master of the house; hate beamed from his eyes and just hate.

"Good, I'm for it," I said.

"We don't have another way out anyway."

"There was. If you hadn't have summoned me into the house, I wouldn't have ended up in this trouble."

"Yes, I acted discourteously... But understand me... I've waited for this day for so many years! My God!... I waited until my daughter grew up... Then I waited for a stranger... But not a single one appeared at my house. I'd already lost even the smallest hope. I couldn't trust just anybody, and because of that, I had to pretend to be a faithful citizen... Even though my only son died in the asylum... When my daughter was born, instead of being thrilled, I banged my head against the wall. What is a daughter for me? I needed a son! But God sent me a daughter. And then I was reconciled. My wife died during childbirth... It was in the late stages. This entire time I've raised my daughter as a vicious killer. I taught her hate... Her hate grew to such a degree that she even disgusted her classmates, because they all believed the rats. But I also taught her to hide her feelings. The slightest suspicion—and my whole plan would blow up from the start."

"After so many years haven't you found anyone in the town who thinks the way you do?"

"All such instances have ended miserably till now. Everyone who tried to protest or gather like thinkers around himself ended up in the asylum. That's why we'll go there first. We'll release the prisoners. We can trust them... All people with courage are there. They also have nothing to lose."

"Keep in mind—I'm a sorry shot."

"I'll give you a flame-thrower. It's a simple device. My daughter and I will lead in front, and you'll cover our rear guard. I'll also entrust you with a wagon with grenades, and fuel. You can't leave that wagon even for an instant, all our hope lies in it..."

"How did you hide the weapons if the rats can get into the house like child's play?" "I kept them in a box with mothballs."

"What can I say, pretty sharp," I broke out laughing.

The clamor and rustling reached us from beneath the floor.

"Aha, I got under your skin!" The colonel barked under the floor. "So you'll get yours, scoundrels!"

The door at the entrance opened at that moment and a tall lean girl appeared in jeans and a checkered shirt. At first glance she looked, maybe, 16. Her thick ash-colored hair fell on her shoulders. She was holding a tray with three opened tin cans, sliced bread and a jar of dill pickles.

"Time to have lunch," she said.

"This is my daughter. Her name is Violetta, Viola... Because the name's similar to the word 'volya'—freedom."

The girl smiled.

"Daddy gives a secret meaning even to a little thing like a name..."

"This isn't such a little thing in our time when rat names and customs permeate every family and when they feed us exclusively with canned goods. I don't want to ruin your appetite, but you have to agree: eating the same thing day in and day out isn't so hot."

"Is it canned fish?" I asked, when we sat at the table.

"Yes. This, take note, is our national dish. For all holidays. Pickles— and these already are old stock. And during the day I eat canned potatoes or porridge."

"By the way, Dad, it'd be worthwhile for us to take a bit of food."

"I'm counting on you to do that. And where's the wine? We have some from way back. Two bottles. Bring it, honey."

"Does it turn out that you're low on wine?" I asked.

"We have dry laws. Alcohol loosens the tongue, and that's really unsafe. That's what the rats think. They keep us from subversive conversations."

The girl brought two bottles of wine and uncorked them.

The wine turned out to be not just tasty, but strong as well. I sensed this right away with my tongue and palate. On the other hand, the canned food made my mouth twinge.

"Don't twinge," the master of the house said. "It's more than rash to undertake the overthrow of the state on a hungry belly. Who knows how long our revolution will last." I forcibly pushed the food into me in big chunks, as though I were swallowing a hot potato. My spirit was somewhat lifted by the wine, but not so much that I would throw myself onto the barricades right away. What kind of devil bit into me to end up in this Ratburg? I had already seen that this was some kind of suspicious place, and look, I had stuck myself in it already. Now it was not known whether I could extricate myself from here alive.

"There, the little devils! They're already here!" The old man shouted.

I looked where he was pointing and saw a rat in the middle of the room staring at us attentively.

In a lightning move the old man grabbed a revolver from beneath his shirt and shot it. The volley blasted the rat against the wall, splattering it with blood, and tore the creature into shreds.

"Without aiming!" He said. "Well, how about it—let's drink to the start of rat hunting season! This is the happiest day of my life."

"If only I had your enthusiasm!" I smiled unhappily. "What's one rat when there are thousands of them?"

"Now there'll be a hundred less," he cut me off and with those words pulled an automatic out of the dresser.

"Dad, what have you thought up?" The girl got frightened.

"A little diversion," her father tossed back to her. "Can't I allow myself a little diversion after so many years of humiliation?"

With a strike of the rifle butt he blew out the window pane and sent a volley into the thickest part of the grinning rats who were sitting all around the street.

I saw how the blood gushed out, how paws, heads and bits of skin flew into the wind. The rats, demented from the shock, scurried in various directions, crawled out one on top of the other, allowing a single bullet to strafe through several of them at once. The volleys shredded them pitilessly, turning them into a foaming mass that was squealing and moaning.

It was disgusting to watch this, and finally I turned my eyes away. But this was just the beginning. A comparable spectacle will happen with me either until I die or until I get out of this damned place. I could save myself only by stepping on the dead bodies of the rats. The worst thing was that I was forced to fire at these ravenous creatures.

The machine gun turned silent. The clip emptied, and the old man tossed it onto the street. Inexpressible satisfaction shone in his eyes.

"Well, what? Now are you convinced that we can kill them? The main thing is just not to panic and not to turn soft: hate, hate and more hate! Understand? Our breed is too compassionate. Any kind of stupid little thing can move us to tears. A broken flower or a baby bird that falls from its nest... We're a nation of lyric poets and not warriors. That's why we're doomed to perish. A nation that hasn't given birth to a single dictator can't be called a nation. This is just a throng, unified by language, embroidery, and songs about eternal life. Take note—they sing about eternal life, while they're at death's door! We, who haven't created our own country yet, will die in battle with the rats! We're already dying!"

"Why are you aggravating the problem so much!" I disagreed. "The rats took over a single town, and that's just the result of a nuclear accident. What's one town against tons of other towns?"

"You're wrong. The rats live with people in every town and village. Throughout every country, throughout the entire world. They even travel on ships and planes. They're everywhere. And they're just waiting for the signal. Understand? They're waiting for a signal to take power! And their intellectual base will be here, where they're working out the plans for a future war. Their diversionaries and leaders are getting ready here. We have to destroy all this."

"We'll manage, if we're lucky, to kill 2-3 thousand," I shook my head.

"Yes, we won't kill them all off, but we'll kill the most aggressive ones, chase the blind mass into the cellars and sewers, then we can take charge of the situation."

"If there are enough weapons. Can you at least still get a carbine in the town?" "No. All the weapons were destroyed. The rats can't use them and they don't need them. It was a miracle that I saved some of them."

"Then what good is it if we release those people from the asylum? Will they have to chase the rats with stakes?" "Don't forget that battle is tiring work, and that relief wouldn't do us any harm. And then... Who knows whether we'll get through without getting wounded, and then..."

He didn't quite finish the sentence, catching my glance.

"...then again without anyone dying?" I completed it for him. "Pardon me... I shouldn't say it that way. If somebody has to die here, then it should just be me. Because this is my business and my war. Though... why just mine? You can't imagine what these rats threaten the whole world with! A civilization of rats! Yes, yes, they've decided to create their own civilization. And our town is just the first little swallow of the new civilization. But their plans have a considerably broader reach. Right now they're preparing battle teams for an assault on other territories. Their emissaries travel constantly in every direction. They're not even terrified of radiation. In fact, thanks to the radiation the rat mutants have begun to multiply. As you noticed, they're all the size of a cat, and there are even bigger ones. Each succeeding generation produces even further developed rats. And this happened at the time when the generation that squeezed us out and grabbed power didn't know a human word. Now they just don't leave it at talking, they also publish books. True, they read them in their own way: eating them up. I estimate that in about ten years the rats will be as big as German Shepherds. And then you won't cope with them in their numbers, especially if you add human intellect to their size. They'll surpass us very quickly in intellect and strength. We'll turn into rats ourselves, we'll begin to scrounge in the cellars and devour their leftover crumbs. That kind of future doesn't frighten you?

At first I thought I was listening to a madman. This whole story of the rats didn't appear so serious. That is, if I saw danger for anyone, then it was just for the inhabitants of the city and not for me. But for this danger to become worldwide? With current technology and the level of science?

"To dispel your doubts, I suggest a very interesting thing for you. This is an original rat 'Mein Kampf.'"

The colonel extended a brochure to me, the cover of which was decorated with: "Where are You Going, Brother Rat!"

"When you read this a lot will become clear. You'll see that this isn't a game, but a terrifying threat to all of humankind."

At this spot Marko turned off the tape recorder and said:

"You'll hardly believe me if I try to retell this whole dream in my words. I managed to take out a brochure from Ratburg."

"Do you have it with you?"

"Yes. You can take a look at it. And in the meantime I'll get the coffee ready."

When he left I put in a new cassette and, closing the door, began to read aloud.

"When I shut my eyes I see a boundless gray sea of the backs of rats, I see mighty waves that run along it, I see the hot light of eyes, turned to the future, I hear the beating of brave hearts that rush to battle, and I know this is my nation ready for anything to sacrifice anything for the sake of happiness and peace on earth...

So, the entire harnessed mass thirsts for peace, that mass that for so many centuries was denied the most elementary rights of a living being, that was chased into the catacombs, into the background, into obscure and dark corners, into the stinking sewer, into this horrible river of human foulness. We were doomed to a miserable existence, to a hungry existence, and the only thing that saved us—this was our thirst for life and the ability to multiply under any conditions, the ability to renew ourselves under the most terrifying cataclysms when thousands, when tens of thousands of our best sons and daughters died in terrible agony from burning poison, they placed their ferocious heads in steel traps, and often they died simply under boots and sticks.

Are there other living beings on earth who were so despised and debased? And I myself will answer: there are none! The Lord has sent us to this earth for torments and death. Then, perhaps, we should rise against God and damn him, as he has damned us with the lips of his numerous prophets? Perhaps we should declare a war against him, as he declared one on us?

And I will answer: no, my brothers! It is not proper for us to take up arms against the Lord, to reject his grace and will. Yes, namely his grace! It's not a slip of the tongue. For thinking long in solitude about our pitiful existence, I suddenly came to the conclusion that the Lord in his actions was boundlessly good to us, perhaps even better than to any other living creations. Just look what fate awaited all those whom we envied for so many years, all those domestic creatures who seemed to bathe in God's grace. They were all degraded, turned into a pile of meat that knows only how to eat and produce excrement. Whom did we envy, brothers! The pig whose intellect is sufficient equal to the needs of the stomach? Or a dog that licks the very hand that just beat its backside?

Let us envy only ourselves! Just ourselves! For from all living creations on earth only we are worthy of envy! Constantly suffering from miseries and difficulties, never eating enough, risking our lives every minute, we have become strong and healthy, courageous and stubborn. Is there any such thing in the world that can frighten a rat? No! Is there an illness in the world that can knock a rat off its feet. No! Is there a creature in the world that is capable in just one year of giving birth to a hundred children? No! Only a rat can give birth to 20-25 rats four times a year!

I've counted: from one pair over the course of four years 1,934,690 strong and healthy rats can be born. This is nearly two million!

There's a multitude of us! Millions upon millions of us! And there is just one problem, that we didn't know about this for so long.

Without knowing human language or their writing, we were ignorant and uneducated, the world tossed us around like tumbleweed, and we didn't know anything that would give us the opportunity to feel ourselves to be a great nation and not just a gang of rodents.

Our genealogy stretches back to the most distant times, and our great ancestor Rat, it turns out, was as big as a hippopotamus. And Herodotus described the disgraceful escape of the armies of Assyrian warrior Sennacherib who never knew defeat before the onrush of rats. On the eve of a battle with the Judeans they gnawed through the bowstrings of his soldiers, and of what value is the best bow in the hands of even the most knightly warrior without a bowstring? And who would know how the map of the Near East would look now if not for the rats, which have already saved Israel twice!

In gratitude to us for this, the Judeans spread the rumor that we were unclean creatures and that to use us in food was not only a sin, but unsafe because of a horrible poison hidden in our bodies.

But our enemies were not slumbering. There were those among them who sought death for us. One of them, a certain Robert Sauti, wrote that rat meat is really very tender, juicy and tasty. And that only by turning us into food for themselves could they defeat us.

This was the most dangerous speculation on how to destroy rats in the entire history of our existence. But, fortunately, no one paid any particular attention to this idea.

The Lord's Providence protected us.

And that's why, my brothers, we will praise our Lord, the most holy Rat, whom vile people depicted in the image and likeness of themselves! Let us sing a chorale to him, let our singing reach his ears and let his heart rejoice!

I just pointed out to you how the Lord's grace turns into damnation for some, and for others how the Lord's damnation turns into grace.

And now let us look to what degree those who their entire life were sure of the Lord's love and knocked into their heads that only they were chosen on this earth became degraded and degenerated. Yes, I'm speaking about the vilest being, about the lyingest creature, the cruelest thing, the stupidest beast—man!

It would seem that all possibilities, all paths to the future, are open only to him, it would seem that only he is capable of ruling the world, to pursue balance and to maintain the surrounding environment. But look! In reality they didn't even think about doing this! In reality they were only shouting and pounding their chests and never really kept their own word. These so-called people didn't have enough sewers under their buildings, and they turned the seas and rivers into sewers. They destroyed the earth itself on which they lived. They dirtied the air they breathe; they poisoned the food that they eat! Is there greater inanity than the actions of man?

It has happened that rats have destroyed one another, but it has never reached such fantastic proportions as we see among people. For them, to grind a million or two similar to themselves into dust is a game! It's even a necessity! Making countless numbers of people corpses, they then have food for their writings, they then are thrilled for years by the singing of their heroism, they suck the bones of tragedies and genocides clean, they swear solemnly not to repeat anything similar, but they repeat it anyway, they continue to repeat it, because in their baseness they don't have any distraction other than death! They repeat it, for it is their nature, and they never will become better. They themselves have already become convinced that they've put a much too heavy burden on their shoulders. Their attempt to bring order into the world has admitted ruin, they have led this world to a terrifying crisis, and now we should come to take their place, in order to save at least something of what remains. If they had a sense of justice or at least were conscious of the fact that they are standing on the edge of an abyss, then they would give full power to the rats without any resistance. If they had at least a little bit of common sense and less arrogance, then they would enter into negotiations with us and would request for themselves a minimum of rights, which they need for normal existence and the continuation of their lineage.

Unfortunately, this isn't the way it is. And we must take power from their hands by the path of war and revolution. Onto the altar of the Homeland we must place thousands of heads, and these will be the most loyal, the most patriotic heads! Right now we have been preparing special detachments of kamikaze rats, which are infected with the plague, with cancer, with syphilis and cholera. An infinite number of illnesses that we will carry unto people will suddenly seize our enemy; epidemic after epidemic will cut down their ranks. At the same time, we'll break our way into peoples' living places; we'll gnaw human children. We should carry death and fear everywhere!

Having created the glorious city of Ratburg, we have now shown the world our ability to create a mighty civilization with a much more attractive future than the one promised by people. The rat mutants, having acquired human size, will differ little from people. Very soon they will lose their bristly hair and tails, and their faces will take on more regular features. Their intellect will go far beyond human intellect, and we will send our representatives to other planets, we will enter into contact with other worldly civilizations, propagandizing our ideas and our means of co-existing with humans everywhere.

We will be magnanimous. Death does not await all people. We will leave part of them so that this particular form of mammal does not become extinct, we will create special People Parks, where they can live in conditions that are as close as possible to their natural living conditions.

At the same time, I come out strongly against the theory of some of our Ratburg philosophers that the future of rats lies in the assimilation of people. With this theory, they greatly insult the rats themselves, in fact rejecting their ability to create a civilization with their own hands. The marriages of rat-mutants with people, if they will have a place, will not be definitive. One human mother is able to give birth just to a single child in the course of a year, or in very rare instances, two. What is this in comparison to the hundredfold rats that our average female rat gives birth to?! The number of rat-people who will appear in the world will become too sorry of a number even to count. At the same time, I am afraid of something else. Will not the appearance of rat-people lead to a certain segregation among our breed—of the true rats on the one hand, and of the rat-people on the other? Will not this minority, which has a good measure of human cunning and arrogance in its nature try to rule by rank and proclaim their race as a chosen one?... And this smells of a new revolution, and what is especially unpleasant, a civil war.

In any case, we should not allow things to reach this point. At no time should our racial standard and stability ever suffer. Therefore, one of the first laws, which I would recommend that we introduce immediately after taking power, is the banning of marriages between rats and people. That is, illegal coitus will be permitted, but the progeny will be doomed to the status of a slave beforehand.

And one more thing. I want to salute you, my dear citizens, with the great success that we have achieved in recent times. Our scientists have created and introduced a new virus, which has no hope for a cure. We have successfully tried this virus in Africa and right now are carrying it throughout the world. Yes, this is the AIDS virus!

People, frightened by numerous epidemics, which are being strewn over their heads, are panicking and pushing those buttons from which our final victory hinges. A nuclear war will empty the earth, but, as is well known, the radiation is no more terrifying for rats than cold water. Just the opposite, radiation will stimulate our growth and our intellect. The belief of our eminent philosophers that nuclear war will bring countless sacrifices even for us should not scare us away and stuff our heads with pacifist ideas. There will be sacrifices, and there will be many of them, but once again I remind you—our unique ability for self-re-creation and reproduction, which, in fact, is stimulated by radiation, will save us from this disaster.

In particular, during an explosion at the local nuclear power station here in Ratburg we became convinced that irradiated rat mothers would be capable of giving birth six times a year with thirty children each time. The explosion led to the fact that those very children grew and became capable of reproduction markedly quicker than was possible before that time. Besides this, the radiation stimulated the mental development of the rats, making them capable of completing various complex operations and even of speaking human languages. This immediately gave us the ability to come into contact with people, to occupy all posts and to take the next generation under control.

Moreover—we synthesized an anti-radiation vaccine from our own blood, which gives immunity from radiation and introduced it to those humans who manifested trust in us. As a result of this endeavor of real genius, there arose among people an actual competition to become worthy of the vaccine. They began to send their children mainly to those schools where rats were in charge of classes, because they did inoculations in those places.

In this way, we were able to take the entire city into our hands. And this says something about the boundless possibilities of rat civilization.

Now we should specially train our agents and send them to all the nuclear power stations with the aim of creating a series of catastrophes and explosions. The panic and fear that will take over society will create boundless possibilities for our benevolent expansion.

Cities similar to our Ratburg should cover the entire earth in a thick net.

We will be victorious, for behind us is our Lord Rat and the truth."

Marko returned with the coffee when I already had finished reading and inserted the previous cassette.

"Well, what do you think?" He asked, putting away the brochure into his knapsack.

"It's horrible! This is all so unreal that it comes off like a bad joke."

"But this is far from a joke."

"I don't believe it, that an average rat could think all this up. Such plans!"

"And all of this has its beginning in Ratburg, not somewhere beyond the oceans, but somewhere very close."

"Have you already shown anyone this treatise?"

"No. That would be stupid. No one would take it seriously. I didn't acknowledge it myself at first. Then afterward... when I saw everything with my own eyes... A person who hasn't seen it will write it off as someone's wild fantasy... You have to find some other way, some other way to convey this to the world... I don't know how... Just not simply knock them over the head with it... maybe you can suggest something..."

"But what... what did you see there? In that Ratburg?" "In Ratburg?" Marko asked again, with such revulsion to that name, to the point that his eyes were gleaming. "Oh, I've seen a lot there! You couldn't dream this in your sickest dream."

His hand stretched to the tape recorder.

"Well! Well! Tell me!" I wanted to cry out, but with great strength I controlled myself. God forbid that I showed I believed him. Better to play along as a skeptic. Then Marko will describe everything in much greater detail.

Finally he pressed the "on" button.

"The colonel waited for my reaction. I don't want to say that even then I sensed trepidation. It was only a vague feeling of fear, the strange anxiety that takes over a person during a storm, when lightening is flashing above your head, but you're in the house and nothing threatens you. But anyway, when the sky splits open, you sense that you're a tiny bug."

"Wouldn't it be more to the point, instead of an uncertain rebellion, to try to escape from here and tell people about the danger?" I asked.

And suddenly I understood that I had blathered something stupid. Because it wasn't fear that was speaking in me, but bad sense. Fear already had chased me far off from this damned place, somewhere far off from this idiocy.

For a moment I imagined that in making my way out of here I would try hard to smash through to the gates of human anxiety, to point my finger at the danger, to scream in their ears, and I understood, that this would be an entirely hopeless task. In the best case they'd lock me up in an insane asylum. There, beyond the borders of Ratburg, everything would look less tragic, even to me.

It's not for nothing that the colonel didn't feel it necessary to contradict me. He simply kept silent.

"I'm not sure of my strength," I admitted. "This is because I'm not able to calculate the strength of the enemy."

"Their strength is quite great. But I can assure you—we're the only ones who can save the world from a horrifying death.

"Speaking honestly, this rat prophet is right about certain things."

"Therefore, I even think that when they succeed in crawling out into the world with their ideas, people will be found who will meet them with total support. In fact, that was the way it was here. Many of us with complete sincerity occupied ourselves with the fate of the rats. This was some kind of universal madness. Suddenly decorations came into vogue with the depiction of a rat's head. A rat decorated shirts and sweaters. The Year of the Rat was announced, which to this very day has not yet ended. It was announced that this was the happiest year in our life, and there was a proposal from our workers to continue it. I already said that these first rats who began to push us out from all of our privileged places didn't even know how to speak human language. How they managed to lure so many intelligent people onto their side I can't even imagine. But mainly with the lips and hands of those renegades, a revolution was created! They achieved the proclamation of rats as very useful creatures. The priest in church said: 'Don't kill the rat as your neighbor!' A rat became a neighbor, this was already a status that was higher even than the one that domestic animals ever had...

People began to share their food with their 'neighbors.' And the fact that this 'neighbor' all the same was a creature, from impassioned love for them, it was decided to find a way for communication. The Institute for the Study of the History of Rats was created. And that wasn't even enough. They also added the Institute of Rat Studies and the Institute of the Physiology of Rats. It reached the point that scientists rushed to find a means for increasing the rat population. For, you see, too few of them were still being born.

At the same time, the rats began to perform willingly in the circus, appearing to be very clever creatures. Someone noticed that they even could discern cards with letters. And then it all began! Schools for rats were established. But, besides the schools, everyone in their house at home tried to teach their rats to read. But reading was easier to teach under everyday conditions. Then the rats sat down with people at the dinner tables.

Further on down the road there wasn't a single side of human life left in which the rats did not participate.

All of this happened rather quickly. So quickly that very few managed to figure out the danger that lurked in the future. And when that day arrived it was already too late. The rats had occupied all the positions of power and had so intertwined with the everyday life of people that there wasn't a single possibility of somehow being extricated from this critical situation.

Already not rats, but people, occupied the rat security forces! People protected the rats from people! It's difficult to think up a more horrifying idiocy.

The undercover security forces investigated dissidents and locked them up in the insane asylums. Why am I saying 'investigated?' They're investigating them even now but... It's already under the sensitive direction of the rats themselves.

Worst is the fact that they've duped our children, a generation has already grown up that accepts the rats as a higher race and thirsts to become like the rats. Children mimic the conduct and habits of the rats, they reject their parents, and if they protest against this, they write denunciations against them."

"It seems somebody's knocking," the girl interrupted.

The colonel grew silent, and sneaked up into the vestibule on tiptoe with his revolver. The knocking was quiet and timid. "Who's there?"

"It's me, your neighbor."

"Are you alone?" "Alone."

The master of the house nervously tugged the door and led a short, fat man in a checkered waistcoat into the house. Meager down was turning white on his balding skull.

"This is our neighbor, Mr. Krupa," the colonel introduced us to him. "How is it that you've ventured to come and visit me? Do you have something urgent?"

"Well, I, it seems, don't have anything... But the rats have."

"The rats?... So you're their... ehhh..."

"Delegate," Mr. Krupa completed the sentence. "They came to me and said that I should tell you their conditions because they trust me. My son is an activist in the Union of Young Rat Lovers and various other things. So what could I do? I had to obey... You know yourself if I..."

"Sit down and tell us what they want."

"I see that you've planned something serious," he said, nodding his head toward the machine gun. "The rats are demanding that you give up. Then they'll guarantee your life. And if not, then death awaits you."

"They're promising us life?" The colonel began to laugh. "What kind of life is this? Can you call this life?"

"Ehh, you trying to convince me? I know myself what their words are worth, but... personally, I have an entirely private request for you. Would you be so kind as to accept me into your group?"

"What, Mr. Krupa?" The master of the house was surprised. "You want to become part of the insurgents?"

"Ehh, you see, sir... My life is already coming to the end of the line. And I don't feel sorry about it, but I feel sorry for my son, and those like him, young boys who serve this rabble. I hate those fucking shitfaces so bad that I'm ready to tear them apart with my bare hands. And if I can get my hands on some kind of revolver, then I'll make do."

"Mr. Krupa," the colonel embraced him. "You're a true patriot. I'm infinitely happy that my hopes have come true—we're not alone in this city. The enemy still hasn't made everybody a zombie."

Mr. Krupa got a revolver, the father and daughter took machine guns, and I, a flame-thrower. After a brief discussion we decided to hang grenades all over us. We agreed to toss them into the fray just after we emptied our cart. In the cart there were two reserve tanks with combustibles, a lot of machine gun refills, a package with trotyl and a roll of Bickford rope.

They helped me to make the two tanks and the flame-thrower comfortable on my back and showed me where to press in order to let out the flame.

"Take a revolver, too," the colonel said to me. "But take care of it to the last. I still have several dozen bottles with combustibles in the cellar. It'd be a shame to leave them."

"What are you waiting for?" I was surprised. "Carry them out quicker!"

"This is much too dangerous. They'll flare up by themselves with a blow. God forbid the cart should turn over—we'd be goners." "Then we have to get rid of them first," said Krupa. "And I'll take care of the cart myself."

"Maybe you're right," the colonel agreed. "It'd be a pity if we didn't make use of them."

We placed the box with the bottles on top of the cart and covered it with a blanket.

When we stepped outside, the clamorous howling of thousands of bared maws met us. A giant gray army plugged up the street. A whistle reverberated, and the army started to attack. The green fence suddenly became gray.

"Throw the bottles!" The colonel ordered.

The bottles fell into the very center of the throng and didn't break. The soft rat backs broke the fall, now the bottles rocked forward and back without even touching the ground.

"Ah, so you're doing it this way!" The colonel shouted out. "Violka, fire!"

The automatic rounds cut into the thickest part of the harnessed bodies, tearing them into tatters and spattering their bloody entrails together with tufts of fur. The bullets shattered the bottles and finally the gray sea flared up in such a great flame that it was pleasant to look at it. And their commanders also didn't have fewer smarts than we had and drove their army with their backs on fire right at us. Krupa quickly backed off with the cart, and I cut down rows of kamikaze rats with the flame. Now not only the rats were burning, but the earth around them as well.

The fence broke apart and fell over, slapping a thick wave of stench in our direction.

The rats backed off, leaving mountains of charred corpses behind them. Mr. Krupa threw a few more bottles at them. The path to the street was freed up, but the earth was still flaming, and it would have been stupid to drive through it with the cart.

"We don't have to go straight ahead," said Krupa. "We can go around. Let's go through my yard."

So we started off, knocking over his fence.

The father and daughter walked in front, Krupa in the middle with the cart, and I covered the rear.

The rats kept observing us for a minute at a safe distance, but when we started to move along the street in the direction of the center of town, they set off after us, the entire time maintaining a distance.

The whole time the thought never left me that someone was very deliberately coordinating them. They were leading their assault in much too organized of a way. If only we could find out where their leader was located and toss a bottle in that direction!

I shared my thoughts with my comrades, and the colonel said: "I doubt that their leader is somewhere nearby. Rats are capable of catching information on ultra-high frequencies. Therefore, it's quite possible that their commanders are sitting somewhere in the sewers, and not just giving commands, but receiving information from the point of action."

Meanwhile the rats had already prepared themselves for a new attack, and began it this time from every direction simultaneously. A dangerous moment had arrived.

"Toss the bottles!" The colonel barked out, and was first to hurl a bottle. After him—Viola and Krupa. I sent a stream of flames following after the bottles. The fire seized the pavement, the rat mass furiously began to squeak and tossed itself blindly at the walls of the buildings. Several of the creatures crawled onto others, imparting the flames onto them, and dying in entire groups in drunken ecstasy.

Scorched and baked, they didn't even think about retreating, and this was a terrifying sight. Perishing, splattering around the foam of madness, they tore on forward. We barely managed to stop some of them just a few meters from the cart.

The rats attacked just from one side of the street, not cutting off our path for the time being. However, understanding that the fire was unsafe even for us, several of them with burning backs ran around us through paths known only to them and threw themselves at the cart, now literally in pre-death spasms.

On the entire street this entire time not a single human soul appeared. All the windows all around were covered with curtains, and if someone from behind the curtains had been observing us, we didn't notice.

"What the hell?!" The colonel swore, looking all around at the buildings. "Doesn't anybody see our battle raging? If only somebody would just throw a vase at these demons! If only they'd throw broken glass at them!"

But the windows were silent.

"Cowards!" He began to scream in a feeble rage, raising up his whitened fists. "Well, then go and rot, you rat-lackeys! Swine!"

Suddenly the attack of the rats stopped, and someone's voice began to echo from out of the loudspeaker on a pillar.

"Foreigner! If you stop this idiotic rebellion, we'll let you leave our town! Foreigner! You've been fooled! You've gotten caught in a trap that our enemies have cleverly set. They want to just use you, after which they'll take care of you like they'd take care of an unwelcome witness. We are the most peace-loving beings on the earth. Enough pouring out of innocent blood! Take a look how many self-sacrificing citizens have lain down by your hand. What are they guilty of? We will forgive you this sin. Go with God and carry the truth of our magnanimity into the world!"

The loudspeaker rumbled and grew silent.

"They want to divide us," said Krupa. "But they're lying creatures!" "The voice is somehow strange," said Viola. "It's not as squeaky as the rats."

"A-ha, it's true, the voice is somehow too human," the colonel agreed. "They've already learned, the bastards!..."

"I want to take a look at this thing speaking," Krupa was about to begin looking around.

"I doubt that this is anywhere here," the colonel retorted. "And, anyway, what do we need him for? I think this shrieker hasn't made any particular impression on Marko."

I laughed.

"But, you can't deny the fact that when he was speaking you were looking at me really anxiously. As if he might hook me!"

"God only knows. Anything is possible," the colonel agreed. "We're fighting because we simply don't have any other way out. And you seemed to have one."

"Even if I should think about deserting, all the same, I wouldn't believe them. I guess that it would be enough for me just to split off, then they'd overtake me and tear me to shreds."

"I think that's exactly how it would be. What do they need extra witnesses for?"

And in the meanwhile the rats, not receiving an answer, once again threw themselves into the attack.

"Wait," I said to Mr. Krupa. "Don't throw the bottles. We're wasting them too much. Let's try..."

And with wire I tied a bottle to a grenade. Now thanks to the explosion the combustibles would ignite in all directions evenly, not just spilling on the ground, the spot burning too small a territory. That's what happened. In the very first explosion, tens of rats were torn to shreds, glass shards flew in all directions, cutting the mouths, the stomachs and backs of the dumbstruck creatures, and the fiery splashes ignited on their stubble, burning their skin into living meat, flowing along their body and forcing them to die in horrifying agony.

The assault of the rats, on the contrary, didn't lessen. On the other hand, the one who was commanding them obviously understood that only attack after attack could reach their aim, because the weapons that we had were not in endless supply and we could only hold out for a limited time. For essentially how long?

The river full of rats seemed to be endless. It crept at the fire, crawling fearlessly into the flames, snuffing them out with their bodies. The rats bit through each other's stomachs and their blood inundated the fire. This happened in some kind of fanatic inebriation, perhaps they didn't particularly understand what was happening to them. Their wide-open eyes swelled with blood, their wide-open foaming jaws glimmered in our eyes with such rapidity that I already sensed a slight stupor, as happens when you look from a bridge onto a foaming river. Before my eyes now a gray river was also foaming with a fiery luster, it roared, whispered despairingly, and gurgled with ferociousness.

The assault was so strong, that we were forced to fling all the bottles with the flammables.

The sight was horrific—fences were burning along the street, and as far as the eye could reach the pavement was sown with the charred, bloody bodies of the rats. All of this together with the earth was giving off smoke and filled the air with an odious stench, from which my head whipped back, and my throat began to scratch and scrape. An unbelievable stifling heat surrounded us from all around. Fortunately the colonel had brought a glass of wine with himself, and gave us each a swig. The swig of the delivering liquid was a drop in a handful of sand. But the loathsome taste in my mouth disappeared, although my thirst wasn't quenched.

We moved on stubbornly and with a vengeance, with a certain dullness as though we were playing out our duty, and behind us newer and newer legions of the rats' army crawled out from the cellars and sewers. At the cost of unbelievable efforts we managed to ward off this horrible attack, but we didn't save our strength and now felt tired and unsure whether we'd be able to hold out without anybody's assistance.

Finally the street led us to a park.

"We're here," said the colonel, pointing his hand at a two-story building with columns in the Stalin Repressnaissance style. "This is the asylum."

Having understood the purpose of our arrival, the rats went completely demon-berserk. They threw themselves at us to overtake us, they encircled the bushes and began to climb up on trees.

"Now, while we're moving under the trees, the rats are beginning to jump at our heads," said the colonel. "When you ignite them, they'll try hard to jump onto the cart. Watch that we don't fly off into the air."

The rats kept crawling onto the trees with startling persistence. There wasn't a free spot left at all, but they kept crawling all the same.

At first I cut loose the flame along the ground and it ignited the dry grass and then moved along the tree trunks. Four bright torches, covered with rats, flapped into the sky. The burning creatures began to drop down like walnuts.

When not a single rat remained on these trees, I ignited four more trees several meters away. Step after step we came closer to the asylum, leaving behind us fire and a wasteland. We outfoxed them and didn't go beneath the burning trees with the cart.

From both sides of our path, boxwood bushes stretched, and setting them on fire, I created two long walls of flame, which the rats didn't have the strength to overcome. Their only recourse was either to climb up further into the trees or to attack us in the narrow corridor of the alley. And these last ones were not very terrifying for us.

Making our way to the building, the colonel and I decided to enter while Mr. Krupa and the girl guarded the entrance.

All the grass, the bushes and trees at the entry of the building continued to burn, and, until they burned out, the rats could hardly push their way in here.

The colonel rapped the door with his shoulder, and we entered the building. Several rats scampered beneath our feet.

At the end of the corridor a man in a white waistcoat appeared.

"Where are you going?!" He waved his arms. "You aren't allowed to enter here. There are sick patients here!"

"We're allowed to!" The colonel cut him off. "Who are you?"

"I'm the director."

"Are there rats here?"

"Yes."

"A lot of them?"

"Maybe fifty or so..."

"Any of the doctors here?"

"There's nobody here. Today is Sunday... What's on your mind? Is it you who caused the fire?"

"Who else? Man! A revolution's going on outside and you're sitting here in your rat's nest and don't know anything. Release the prisoners!"

"What prisoners? This is a hospital and not a prison," the doctor got riled up.

"There it is! Is it a real hospital?" The colonel winked at me. "Well, how 'bout it, honorable doctor... Then release the patients."

"How dare you say this? These are really sick people! In any case, they can't be released, they absolutely can't control themselves! And finally, I'm responsible for them..."

Suddenly I felt bad for him. A pitiful type. But he was simply doing his job conscientiously. He had been told "It's forbidden," so he told us "It's forbidden." But our situation also wasn't a good one. If we didn't get reinforcements—we'd be goners.

"You can't expect me to do something for which I'll lose my head later."

"You mean to say that among the patients there isn't a single one of sound mind?"

"Not a single one. Here there are only madmen. And, in addition, they're in very serious condition."

"And there aren't any people here being forcibly treated?"

"How can you suspect us doctors of such a crime?"

"I don't suspect you personally, but those who are in charge of you."

"I don't know what you mean. There has always been order in my hospital."

"But I don't believe you," the colonel said firmly, placing the cock of the automatic in the doctor's stomach. "Open up the cells immediately."

"You can shoot me! What difference does it make to me whether I die now by your hand or later by theirs?!"

His decisiveness could not help but surprise us, and so I believed him, though this wasn't particularly pleasant. However, the colonel had, evidently, his own idea, and no less decisively placed his finger on the trigger.

"I'll count to three... If you don't open up the cells, I'll make a sieve out of you. And then I'll pull the keys out of your pocket and open them up myself. Well?!"

The director was pale and perspiration glistened on his forehead. His hand was trembling as he took the keys out of his pocket and opened up the first door.

Six uncared for, unshaven patients, with dark eyes, lost in themselves, lay in a row in the cell on six bunks. Their faces, devoid of the least amount of expression, resembled the masks of mannequins. Not one of them so much as turned his head toward the door. In the room it smelled of unwashed bodies and the sour taste of vomit.

The colonel looked at me with such sadness, that only just now did I understand what kind of a hopeless situation we had come upon. But hope had not abandoned us yet.

"What did you do to them?" I asked the director. "I don't know what they did to them," he responded insultingly. "I found them this way."

"But these aren't real madmen. They were driven to such a horrifying state."

"Do you have proof of this?"

"I once knew one of these patients... Just by sight though, but he was a completely healthy person."

"You and I are also completely healthy people. And what'll become of us tomorrow?"

Now the threatening screech of metal could be heard in his words. Or did it just seem that way to me?

"Open up the next cell."

The director obediently opened up one more door.

And again we saw the very same picture.

"Now have you been convinced?" He asked.

"No," the colonel cut in. "Open up the rest of the doors."

We passed from cell to cell through the entire first floor without any results. We didn't see a single person who would even slightly remind us of a normal person.

This entire time the rats were scampering in the corners, but in such small numbers that it didn't frighten us.

"So of all the personnel you're here alone?" I asked.

"Well, how to put it... I'm alone... though the rats work together here with people. Among them there are also several... hmmm... doctors. They work without any days off. They are very hardworking, as opposed to..."

Here he shut up and led his glance away.

"As opposed to people? Yes?!"

Suddenly the colonel got enraged.

"I didn't want to say it that way," the director defended himself.

"But you said it!"

"I only said that their doctors are hardworking..."

"Well, of course! Now I clearly see the success of their doctoring!.. And what's on the second floor?"

"On the second? It's not enough for you to see what you've seen here?"

For some reason he was really unhappy with our obtrusiveness. And he didn't succeed in hiding this from us. But it was worth it to finish up this business.

"Take us to the second floor," the colonel grew stubborn.

"But I'm warning you—the especially sick patients are up there. Unforeseen excesses might occur. You have an overly aggressive look, who knows how the patients will react to this. Because they've gotten used to seeing just pajamas and white robes around themselves."

"You forgot to mention the gray pelts of the rats. And maybe they see that most often."

"You can take the keys," he said, offering us an entire bunch. "The number of the cell is engraved on each one. I won't go with you."

"We don't need you."

"Just what you see there might ruin your state of mind for a long time."

"Well, it's not worth getting upset over our state of mind. It's been ruined for a long time, from the time when people like you began to work for the rats."

"And what was I supposed to do—die from hunger? Or turn myself into one of those?"

The colonel didn't say anything in response, he just nodded to me to follow him to the second floor.

We stopped in front of the door that was painted bright red.

The key turned completely soundlessly in the lock. In exactly the same way the door opened soundlessly and the colonel entered. At first I heard his cry and then random swearing. He was thunderstruck in the doorway, barring passage to me, and I was forced to push him slightly, in order to look into the cell.

What I saw provoked a spasm in my throat.

Three creatures were sitting on the floor that had human muscles but large rat heads. These monsters bared their sharp teeth and glared fiercely. For a minute or so they looked at us guardedly and indecisively, but suddenly, as though a current penetrated them, they shuddered and bolted to their feet. This looked as though they had just received someone's signal. Someone had ordered them to attack us, and they threw themselves at the door, roaring threateningly and gurgling saliva.

"Ah, abomination!" The colonel shouted and pulled the trigger.

The automatic round ripped through their chests and stomachs, threw them backward and knocked them over onto the floor.

"If we find similar monsters, we have to destroy every trace of them immediately," he looked at me. "Do you understand me? We have to at least manage to do that."

"It seems that we won't be able to do anything more."

"Are you sorry you've gone in with me?"

"No. All the same, somebody had to brave this."

We saw two people in the next cell who were tied to steel beds with wide straps. One was lying motionless. The other turned his head to us, and these were the first eyes in which we saw traces of intelligence. Their mouths were taped shut.

"This... this is my colleague!" The colonel shouted out. "Captain Kolyada! I recognize him!"

The man had long locks and a beard. On hearing his name, he joyfully nodded his head.

We released both of them from their straps in a second.

"Captain! How did you get here?"

"Mmmm... mmmm... ooh..." The one getting up from the bed mumbled something.

His comrade, though, lay there without stirring, and I, having untaped his mouth, realized that he was dead.

The captain rolled up the sleeves of his pajamas and stretched out his emaciated white arms to us. The entire inside surface of his arms had needle punctures. Then he showed us his chest in bluish spots and once again tried to explain something, but managed only an unintelligible cackling.

"They obviously tried some experiments on him," I guessed.

The captain nodded his head. He suddenly got scared and began to point his hand at the neighboring cell. He also understood that we had very little time.

The colonel opened it and an even more horrifying picture opened up before our eyes.

Four completely naked women were sitting on the beds and each one was playing with at least ten tiny rat-people. These abominable fidgeting creatures scurried along the women's legs. They crawled to their breasts to suckle milk.

I couldn't look at this. I was sick to my stomach. The captain clenched his fists and shook them in the air, imitating fire from an automatic. Then the colonel slowed down.

The women did not react to our visit at all. You could sense a certain confusion just among their children, who, seeing someone unfamiliar, began to scurry and tried to hide between the legs and under the arms of the women, the entire time squealing in fright.

The captain drew the colonel's automatic toward himself and the latter, without offering any opposition, gave up the weapon.

I stepped out into the corridor and leaning my hand against the wall, just vomited on the shining, varnished floor.

Behind my back automatic rounds, a piercing squeal and a convulsive shriek reverberated.

When they exited from the cell, I was surprised at how different their faces were. The colonel carried his cold stone expression harshly, but a happy smile was playing on the captain's lips. He was pleased that he had gotten the opportunity for revenge.

"Three more doors are left," said the colonel, fingering the keys. " They have an entire research institute here."

"I won't go there," I responded. "I've had enough."

"He'll go..."

We waited in the corridor until the captain finished his business. The same thing could be heard from every cell—first gunshots, then the despairing squeals of the tiny rat-people and the screams of the half-crazed women.

"Let's go back," the colonel commanded when everything was already done.

"Mmmm..." The captain began to mumble and ran ahead, leading us downstairs.

When will all this end, I thought. We passed the first floor and began to descend into the cellar when a loud growling unexpectedly echoed and six stout rat-people jumped out to meet us with metal rods in their hands. Their appearance was so unexpected that we barely managed to stop. Happily the captain distinguished himself with a reaction worthy of astonishment, for covering us with his back, he suddenly began to shoot from the automatic continually. And even then the bullets didn't stop these monsters, they continued their assault, waving their rods. Their wounds evoked an even stronger appearance of ferocity, and we had to move back.

Then I let loose a flame from the flame-thrower right into their grinning maws. A shout of mortal terror echoed in the basement. Four of the attackers fell on the steps, two of them lurched to escape and disappeared around the bend.

The captain, having taken possession of the automatic, didn't release it from his hands. Now he was our leader and this time set off in front, taking the greatest danger on himself.

We descended into the basement and saw the metal door. The rat-people hid themselves behind it and perhaps not only were they hiding, because from all the captain's action, it was evident that there was something very important for us behind the door. But whether it would help us somehow, or on the other hand become a peril that must be destroyed, we didn't know and just relied on our new comrade.

"I'll force open this door," the colonel said, and hooked two grenades onto the doorknob.

We barely managed to hide for cover around the corner as a mighty explosion shook the walls.

The lock from the door jumped off.

The captain nervously opened the door, and a chamber appeared before us with an endless number of various apparati, glass bottles, retorts, test glasses with rubber tubes into all of which something was being poured, something was being transfused: it gurgled, hissed and foamed.

Four monsters stirred in the depth of the chamber next to the window with gratings. They were pulling the grates and howling from despair. Two of them still had iron rods in their hands, but remembering how their comrades had expired, they were more afraid than the others had been and didn't even think about attacking us. Yet all the same we were forced to destroy them.

They weren't able to hide from the flames.

At that very moment a shot echoed, and the colonel grabbed his shoulder. Somebody was firing from somewhere behind the apparatuses. The captain leapt onto the table like a cat, with his feet breaking all the glass devices. He saw someone behind the tables, for in the next second he jumped there with the battle cry of pre-historic tribes.

A bustling shout was heard as well as a despairing shriek that evidently did not belong to the captain.

I moved around the really long table and saw our beloved director on the floor. The captain stepped on his stomach with one foot and clicked the trigger ferociously. The clip was emptied in full sight.

"Wait!" I stopped him. "Don't kill him!"

The captain looked at me with eyes that didn't understand but took away his rifle.

"Stand up!" I ordered.

The doctor raised himself, trembling from fear.

"Why were you shooting?" I asked, as calmly as possible.

"I didn't want to...," the doctor began to howl. "Accidentally..."

With a nervous movement the captain raked a pack of some kind of brochures from the table, and holding them for a second in front of my eyes so I could read the title, he shoved them into the doctor's face.

"Was it he who divulged this?" The voice of the colonel began to speak near me, behind my back.

The captain shook his head contrarily.

"What is it—he wrote this?"

The captain nodded.

"I didn't write anything! He's lying!" The doctor began to scream, first looking at the colonel hotly and then at the captain. He didn't take heed of me.

But on the table we found one more interesting thing. It was something like a radio. The captain, pointing at it, clipped his nose shut with his two fingers and gave a tug.

"A rat?" The colonel asked.

The captain nodded.

"A signal transmitter for the rats?" He asked again.

And once again he received an affirmative answer.

"Aha. So all this is your work?! This is you and that rat Führer?" Screamed the colonel. "Now you're gonna pay for everything!"

"Nothing of the kind!" The doctor defended himself. "I don't have anything to do with this!"

Suddenly outside the grenade explosions reverberated. A couple of rats banged their bloody bodies into the windows. The attack had begun.

"Time to go upstairs," the colonel said, and passed the disk to the captain. "Finish with him."

"Have mercy!" The doctor shrieked hysterically. "They forced me! I didn't want to!"

We tossed the "rat Führer" for the captain. There, upstairs, the automatic fired and grenades rattled ceaselessly. Amid this uproar I barely made out the sound of the short round of firing that echoed behind my back.

"Viola!" The colonel suddenly shouted, and taking two to three steps at a time rushed upstairs.

Now I heard her voice—she was calling for help.

As it turned out, the girl had barely managed to drag the cart into the building and slam the door before the baring maws of thousands of rats, who, having waited until the fire in the park had settled down, threw themselves into the assault. You could hear them gnawing the door with zeal.

"Is this Mr. Krupa?" We asked simultaneously.

"Uh, uh, he's there...," the girl began to sob.

"Open the door!" I said to the colonel and stuck out the flame-thrower.

But the captain stopped us, raised himself up several steps and looked into the window. Making signals, he ordered us not to open the doors.

I ran up to him and also looked out. Mr. Krupa had disappeared behind a thick blanket of gray bodies.

"It's too late," I sighed.

"He shielded the wagon with himself," Viola explained. "He forcibly shoved me here..."

Then she noticed blood on her father's shoulder and rushed to wrap the wound.

"It's not too awful," said the colonel. "But since my hand is quite weak, I won't be able to hold the automatic..."

"Poor Mr. Krupa," I shook my head. "To die such an awful death…"

"He died like a hero," said the colonel. "He died saving the weapons. If we get out of this alive, then it's only thanks to him."

The door shuddered from the rats' assault.

"Lord, is there any end in sight to them?" Viola asked.

"This isn't the most horrifying thing," said the colonel. "The most horrifying thing is that we're left alone… We don't have anyone else to rely on… and the rats… Seems to me that they're becoming depleted… These are the last forces they've thrown at us. You might say an all-national militarization."

The captain took a shot from his automatic along the corridor. The band of rats that was rushing here suddenly flew in all directions, escaping through the cracks under the walls.

"You see how sly they are," the colonel was amazed. "They've already learned how to fight."

"That's nothing. Now I'll show them some cheerful dancing," I said.

"Don't do this. They are a sorrowful bunch of people in the cells, they won't be saved from the fire."

"We already have very little time left. We have to get out of here somehow," said Viola.

The colonel wiped his hand beneath his chin.

"We have only one way out… Marko and Viola can put on white robes, they can lead out the madmen and together they can all exit the building by the back door. The building, of course, is surrounded. But from that side there are iron doors and the rats would hardly be able to storm them. Those who are there lying in wait won't bother you. The madmen don't interest them. Neither do the doctors."

"Daddy, I won't go anywhere without you!"

"And really, what do you think? We're going to defend to the very end," I countered.

"Nothing will work out. We're here in a trap. What I'm proposing will give us the opportunity for all of us to be saved, and also to destroy thousands of rats. I'll set the trap for them myself. Right now the captain and I will set out all our tanks with explosives, all the grenades and packs of trotyl, tying it all together with the Bickford rope fuse. We'll space them equally along all the corridors. And we'll hide in the basement. When the rats storm the building, we'll wait them out, so that as many as possible are packed in here, and then—kaboom! The building will catch fire like a stack of straw, and just the window panes will blow out in the basement."

"And then?"

"And then we'll blow out the gratings of the window in the basement with an explosion and catch up with you."

Viola looked at me with hope, waiting for me to find something once again to dispute. But now I didn't have any arguments.

"It's time," said the colonel. "We have to make haste so we can lead out all the madmen from here. Who knows, maybe they'll still come to their senses after those injections. We can't leave them to the mercy of fate, because they were all people with ideals."

From time to time automatic rounds ripped into our conversation. It was the captain shooting all around at the rats who had penetrated the corridor.

There was no particular bother with the madmen. They submissively allowed themselves to be led out by the hand into the corridor, and waited patiently until we led out the others. We conducted ourselves as carefully as possible with them, in order to, God forbid, not arouse fear or anger in any of them. These unfortunate people were in such a profound state of apathy that I was already worried how we were going to move with them through the entire city. Because they themselves were not emboldened to take a single step.

"Take each other by the hand," the colonel advised. "Marko in front, Viola in the middle. This way you'll make your way from here in a chain."

Two of the madmen had bandaged heads. This led me to the thought of wrapping myself up with bandages, so that those who might have seen me in battle wouldn't recognize me. We put on white robes, and Viola tied up her hair with a white kerchief. Now we resembled either cleaning people or the madmen.

The colonel gave us pistols, packages with shells, and knives.

"This is for the worst case, but I hope it won't come to this... We'll meet beyond the city near the river where the gardens used to be.

Now there are a bunch of deserted houses. Get the madmen settled there and wait for us."

In the meanwhile the captain didn't waste time and quickly set out anything that could possibly ignite and explode in the corridors. In the basement he found some bottles of alcohol and liberally poured it over the floor.

"Hurry up!" The colonel ordered, leading us to the back door.

We opened the door, the iron shrieked piercingly, and a threatening rat detachment appeared before us. About two dozen rats immediately bolted at our feet, but the colonel was already waiting with the automatic. The rest of the rats stepped aside. The madmen didn't interest them, and without resisting, they opened up a path for us. I was walking carefully, so as, God forbid, not to step on anyone's tail. Behind my back we could hear a loud yelping and rounds from the automatic. Then the rats tried to penetrate the building from under the madmen's feet. Finally I heard the doors slam shut, and the shooting grew silent.

One of the rats ran out onto my shoulders and sniffed all around the nape of my neck. Then he twisted and turned here and there and jumped across to my neighbor's shoulder. My neighbor was a big guy with the neck of a bull and an unbelievably dull look on his face. So dull, in fact, that it seemed that he was the maddest of all the madmen. But when the rat decided to sniff him all over, and jabbed him in the cheek with his mouth, the madman unexpectedly bared his teeth and barked so threateningly that the poor rat was blown away as if by the wind.

As we were walking past their army, individual rats ran up to us from time to time and sniffed us all over, but they didn't bother us.

Suddenly this entire sea shook in a single gust as if an electric spark had run past. I looked over my shoulder and saw that a rabid stream of rats was pouring into the open doors. The colonel was welcoming the guests.

"Now he'll strike them," I could hear next to my ear.

I gazed at my neighbor and couldn't believe my own eyes: a normal human face was looking at me. And the trace of the wild look that still dominated before that moment disappeared.

"You're not a madman?" I asked in a whisper.

"Not any more so than you are."

"So you've been playing the fool intentionally?"

"Sometimes it can be useful. As you can see, it's worked out for the best for me. Otherwise they would have been sticking me up with needles, putting me in the same state as all the rest."

"Why didn't you tell us this right away?"

"Who there knew where you were from and what you were looking for? Could it have been a provocation? Yes, it could have. That's why..."

There were fewer and fewer rats in the park. They inundated the building, pouring into it not only through the doors, but even through the windows, which the colonel and captain had left open for them. They crawled on each others' backs, cutting through the air with their caustic squealing, which for them obviously had replaced a battle cry. They rushed on to meet their death, and I had to admit, that the colonel's plan turned out to be extraordinarily successful, at least the first part. As to whether the second part would succeed—I wasn't sure.

Having walked still further on, we saw four rats in black suits on a wide stump. They were examining a map. About two dozen more guards were on watch around the stump. All of them measured us with curious looks, but didn't move from their spots.

Finally ending up in the vicinity of the park, where there wasn't a single rat, we stopped.

Viola stepped up to us.

"Are you the only pseudo-kook here, or is there somebody else?" She asked, smiling.

"I think I'm the only one... but, it's possible, that in time the senses will return to somebody else. Maybe we can get to know one another?"

The sturdy guy's name was Kost.

The rats had certainly already filled the building to the brim, because they could even be seen on the roof. Several hundred rats were still roaming around the park, there were many of them even around the building.

"How come there's no explosion?" Viola grew nervous.

"I guess we need to move from here," said Kost.

"How do we go?" The girl grew irritated. "Don't you see how many more rats were left in the park? Our people won't be able to get through them on their own."

"During the explosion a mass of rats swept around the entire park. Such a scare will ensue, that, by the time they calm down, they'll be able to escape."

"But won't the building fall down?"

"What are you saying? This is an old building. You need to take great pains to ruin it. Let's go. Don't forget that we're madmen, and a lot of danger is still waiting for us in the city."

"In the city?" I was surprised. "After the explosion, won't the people understand that the time has finally come to throw off their yoke?"

"I don't advise you to try to explain it to them."

I shrugged my shoulders, not understanding what he was leading to.

And right at that moment a deafening explosion reverberated. Flames puffed violently from the windows and doors of the building, breaking the door and window frames, grabbing everything within their reach. More and more rats had gathered on the roof. They comically jumped along the burning metal plate, climbing onto chimneys, sliding and flying down right into the flames. But when the rafters caught fire, they all rolled from the roof dead.

Several dozen creatures crazed from terror swiftly rushed past us.

In the air you could sense the caustic odor of scorched bristles, burnt wood, and paint.

"Let's go," Kost ordered. "We're madmen! Follow the example of how we should act."

And really, if someone were observing us, it would have been easy to differentiate us from the others, because they, the real madmen, didn't pay any attention to the explosion, but just stood there, dejectedly lowering their heads, hand in hand, the way we had left them.

We walked out of the park and set off along the narrow streets, trying to leave town as quickly as possible. Although we were trying to avoid populated places, we made our way to one particular street where a large crowd of schoolchildren was listening to a rat speaking to them from the open window of the building.

If we had tried to turn, it possibly could have aroused suspicion. We had to amble past those schoolchildren.

"Citizens! Our homeland is endangered!" The rat yelled into the megaphone. "The approaching enemy has penetrated into the heart of our city. They've broken into the research center of our helmsman, our beloved leader and teacher. They've performed a horrifying, evil deed, killing him. Science has lost a distinguished scholar and our young republic its father. Citizens! The army of rats has experienced deep losses. Without having any weapons other than our own teeth and claws, we have thrown ourselves into the fire. In front of bullets and grenades. Thousands of our best sons and daughters have died in this lopsided battle. The last blow met us accidentally when we were hoping to save our leader. The enemies have caused a terrible fire in the building where the most significant part of our glorious army was located. Everyone who was in the building lay down their heads. The situation right now is uncertain and very troubling.

I am turning to you now as those whom we've educated as devoted patriots, to those upon whom our entire hope lies. Arm yourselves with shovels, crowbars and sticks. Form battle companies and occupy a post on every one of the streets. The enemy must be disarmed. We, who have poured out our valuable blood for you, are calling you now to repay us for our constant love and care for you. Death to the enemies of the fatherland!"

"Death! Death! Death!" The schoolchildren chanted.

"What horror!" I shuddered.

"If you want to, as you can see, you can raise a person to be a rat. Look at the windows—aren't these real rats?"

The heads of people stuck out in the windows and listened to their rat's calls.

Some of the schoolchildren pointed their hands at us.

"These are the madmen," the rat explained. "They're not harmful to us. Let them go in peace."

At that time someone's head in hair curlers poked out from one of the windows.

"These aren't madmen! These are masked enemies!" An ugly crone began to shriek. "I noticed that they were talking to one another!"

"Me too! I noticed too!" It echoed from another window.

"Strike them!" Somebody else bawled.

"Those two in front!" A woman shouted and tossed a flowerpot at us.

"Squadron! Get ready!" The voice of the rat reverberated.

"Oh, this is already getting serious," Kost said. "That's enough pretending that we're crazy, let's hide behind the gate."

"Anywhere but behind the gate!" Viola ran up to us. "They'll lock us up there and won't release us."

A stone flew at us. They threw flowerpots at us from the windows, kitchen pots, everything that happened to be within reach.

"Onward! To the attack!" The rat implored.

"What are you doing?" The girl shoved me. "Take out your pistol!"

Out of surprise I had forgotten about it.

"Ow!" Kost groaned, getting hit in the shoulder by a stone.

I shot at the rat, but hit the megaphone.

"We have to make our way forward," said Viola.

"But they're flinging stones at us!" I answered.

"Then shoot at them!" Kost shouted.

"At the children?" I was surprised.

"What kind of children are these? These are rats! Give me your pistol."

He tore the weapon away from me and shot into the crowd. One little boy fell, grabbing his leg. The people in the windows began to shriek, banging the windows shut, hiding in the shadows of their rooms. The schoolchildren threw themselves up onto the gate.

The rat babbled something, but no one was listening to him. The girl aimed and in a single shot knocked him down.

The madmen, in the meanwhile, had already trotted along the length of the wall like mechanical dolls. We hurried after them. Kost and Viola were covering our rear guard.

From time to time from behind the gates a stone flew out and we were forced to defend ourselves.

I halted above the little boy who had been shot. He was lying in a pool of blood but was still alive. His body shuddered from the pulsing pain, his lips became blue, and whispered: "Mom... Mom... Mom..." But in the eyes that were gazing at me I saw only an animal's ferocity. "You won't save him, Marko," the girl tugged at my sleeve. "These are lost children."

"But they are people!"

"No they're not, they're little rats."

A woman ran along the street, sobbing loudly, and when, in due time, I looked back, I saw her above the little boy's body.

Unexpectedly about two dozen rats jumped out from the gate and threw themselves after us in haste. I took the pistol from Kostya and killed two of them, Viola another two, and the rest of them disappeared behind the gate again.

While we were making our way through the city, the fixed gazes of people followed us from the windows along the entire road. In no way did they show their enmity toward us, being fearful of the bullets, but neither did they support us, and only gloomily followed us with their eyes. Didn't it come to mind to any of them that very little was left to achieve freedom?

"What's with them—with these people?" I was surprised. "How can they watch like this indifferently? Today they have the opportunity to remove their yoke. Why not take advantage of it?"

"Because the yoke has grown into their necks," said Kost. "An ox that has gotten used to the yoke and driver feels helpless in the open field. He becomes doomed from the excess of freedom."

"But you can never have too much freedom!" Viola contradicted.

"Accustomed captivity is also safer than unaccustomed freedom. People fear the unknown."

"But anyway, how can one get accustomed to the rats?" I didn't understand. "How can one permit children to be abused this way? Where do they get so much inhuman ferocity that even the death of their comrade doesn't frighten them?"

"Because in school they got the idea of the Great Deed shoved into their heads," said Kost. "They were taught to love their Homeland and its interests above everything else. The children rejected their parents and voluntarily entered militarized orphanages. The children themselves turned in their parents to the asylum, when the latter tried to interfere..." His voice began to quiver, and catching my glance, added: "Yes, that's the way it was with me. My son sent me off to the asylum, informing them that I was carrying on anti-rat propaganda."

We quickly ended up in the outskirts. The buildings disappeared little by little and wild, untended gardens dotted with wooden huts emerged. Several of the gardens were overgrown with poppies and thick raspberry bushes, currents and gooseberries. Not far away a river was flowing, and across it you could see a meadow, in which buses were rusting, as well as tramcars, automobiles, and all kinds of scrap iron. There was even a black locomotive rising up with several battered cars. A stork in a nest was perched on its exhaust pipe.

The madmen wandered into the bushes and threw themselves at the berries.

"They're not so stupid," I said to Kost, taking an example from them.

Just Viola sat in the grass, wrapping her arms around her knees, and sadly gazed at the road that led to town.

"They're deprived of memory, deprived of desires, besides the most necessary ones—juice, food, water... Well, in general they're retarded... though you can even talk with some of them," Kost recounted. "Maybe if we'd take care of them, then some would return to their senses."

"Why, then, did the rats allow the madmen to exit the park?"

"Because you killed the one who understood something about this. There wasn't anybody else in the hospital. Now maybe an extraordinary confusion has already ensued. Now both we and the madmen are in the same danger."

"Maybe it's not worth it to stop here?" I asked.

"And what about father?" Viola chimed in.

"Well, I, let's say, would stay here and wait," said Kost, " the problem is that the place is wide open for many kilometers up further on, and, when they reach you, there won't be any possibility of occupying a defensive position. It's better here."

Dusk somehow drew through the outskirts unnoticeably. All around, in anxious quiet blue-gray, you couldn't hear either the chirping of grasshoppers or the croaking of frogs, or the evening warbling of birds before sleep. The river quietly rolled, gleaming from time to time in little waves and rocking a black poplar.

Suddenly a desperate shriek echoed. When we ran up to it, we saw that one of the madmen was screaming. His body was completely glued with rats, he rolled along the ground and waved his arms like a windmill. I grabbed my pistol, but I was afraid to shoot for fear I would hit the man.

Fortunately other madmen ran up, and, throwing themselves at their comrade, began to catch the rats with their bare hands and to tear them into bits. I grew numb, seeing how they were stamping the rats with their feet, how the blood was spitting out and how the guts were bursting.

But here Viola screamed and began to shoot. The entire rat army was already pushing its way at us from the direction of the city. I lay down on the grass and was shooting while lying down. In this way the bullets were skidding along the ground, and, in a single shot, it was possible to destroy several attackers. Kost hurled stones, sticks, everything that his hands could grab. I was pleased when I saw that even the madmen had grabbed fence palings and took to defend from the flanks. And this was just in time, for the rats had already set in from the sides, approaching closer and closer to us. Pistol volleys couldn't stop them. Finally I was forced to grab a pole and fend off this terrifying attack. Viola shot until she had used up all her bullets. In just a minute she appeared with a pitchfork and took to stabbing them left and right. The madmen fought peacefully, without panicking, so that it was as if they had not lost their common sense. It was only their bitten up friend whom they succeeded in saving who literally foamed at the mouth from anger, first moving forward to the assault, then jumping back, and then suddenly he threw himself into the thickest part of the battle and fiercely stamped the attackers with his feet.

Individual rats were jumping onto the poles and running along the poles right into our arms, while others were making their way to our legs and backs. We had to tear them off of ourselves with our hands, and in doing so lacerated our fingers. In the meantime others were already biting our legs.

"Let's retreat to the river!" I shouted.

This was our only salvation. There, on the other side of the river, we could hide in the middle train car.

One of the madmen suddenly fell, sliding, and his entire body immediately became covered with rats. He defended himself as best he could, biting them with his teeth, tearing them into scraps with his hands and crushing them with his knees, but there was no way he was able to rise up. Several of the madmen began to lead him away from the ground, but at that very moment they began to dance in place, tearing the creatures off themselves.

We couldn't abandon them, but we were helpless in trying to help them.

"There's paint there! Paint!" Viola shouted, pointing to a little house, out of which earlier she had carried out a pitchfork."

"Paint? What kind of paint?" Kost and I were surprised, for what did paint have to do with anything here?

There was nothing for her to do but to skip off into the little house herself and roll out a plastic barrel with paint. And only then did we understand her idea.

I quickly opened it and began to roll it, releasing the paint in such a way so as to create a wide circle.

Kost and Viola dragged the madmen into the circle. Not for a second did the rats slow down their pressure. My machinations did not interest them in any way, but I myself, of course, was of interest to them, and I had to chase back the annoying carnivores the entire time.

Finally the circle was painted. I set down the barrel and pulled it into the circle. Then I just struck a match and the fire encircled us, scorching the rats. Now we could peacefully keep ourselves occupied with those attackers that had penetrated the circle and also help the madmen.

And they themselves finally were managing not too badly, for, no longer concerned with the danger, they expeditiously tore the rats off of their backs and chests and stamped all over them with their feet.

"Now let's wet our poles in the paint," I said, "because when this fire goes out, we'll have to make our way to the river."

"But first let's wrap the ends with this here," Kost suggested, taking off his robe.

We tore our robes into shreds, and wound them around both our and the madmen's poles, and then we wet them in the paint. Then I spattered the barrel with paint and Kostya and I, lighting it up, rolled it out with our poles right at the rat army. We could hear a piercing yelping.

The fiery circle was going out little by little.

"It's time," I said.

Having lit up the torches, we set off to the river. The madmen surprisingly quickly understood what was expected from them and correctly moved backward, sticking the burning poles into different directions.

These weren't the rats that had attacked us during the day on the street and plunged into the fire like madmen. The best of their army had perished, only the gray mass was left, one that wasn't bereft of courage, but not to the same degree that they would throw themselves mindlessly into the flames. They jumped back from the torches, and those who burned their mouths blindly scampered off somewhere further.

We reached the river this way. The rats, realizing that it would be difficult for them to attack in the water, scattered along the shore, casting themselves in the river, trying to reach the shore sooner, in order to surround us.

Had we been alone, they would never have succeeded in doing this, but the madmen, no matter how we would hurry them, didn't particularly make haste. The water was warm and from time to time they stuck their heads into it, fluttering from satisfaction. We had to drag some of them by force.

In the meantime, the rats had occupied the defense on the opposite shore, and were jumping up and down from anticipation.

Our torches little by little were going out, and those of some of the madmen had been extinguished during their time bathing in the water. Now there was no reason to rush, and we stopped in indecision. It was safer in the water.

Having seen that we had stopped, the rats put a halt to their crossing, leaving an equal quantity of their army on both sides of the shore.

We stood this way for several minutes, until the creatures finally were assured of the fact that we weren't thinking of making our way to either shore. And then by the dozen they splashed into the water and swam to us.

Then something unbelievable began. From both sides the harnessed mass of carnivores was coming at us, and we were already tired and desperate. Dusk darkened our eyes, and the rat army was turning into an army of millions, that here would sweep us away like dust and would scatter us over this wasteland so that not even the memory of us would remain. The poles wouldn't obey our hands, our palms were burning with fire, with each sweep of the pole we thought more about not hurting our comrades, rather than about hitting the rats. From the blows the carnivores sank to the bottom, the current carried them off, but a number of them again recovered and returned. The current saved us more than anything. It washed away the flanks of the rats, not allowing them to attack us with their entire ram. But the rats weren't stupid. They threw themselves several at a time at a pole, then suddenly ran along it to our hand, and we had to plunge our pole into the water in order to free it. By this time other rats were managing to make their way to us, and we already had to whirl around, like mechanical beings, so that we wouldn't allow them to break through from behind and from the rear attack those who were repulsing the assault from the opposite shore. The madmen were unable to manage such a task because they were striking blindly in some kind of deadened ecstasy, and we gave Viola the task of mainly killing those rats that were maintaining a hold among our ranks.

I heatedly sought some way out, seeing that we would soon be exhausted, but I couldn't think of anything more intelligent than trying to break through to the abandoned train cars. Such a plan, besides, had one essential deficiency—we didn't know whether the madmen would listen to us and run quickly enough across this rather small break in the path.

I don't know how this plan would have ended if rounds from the automatic had not reverberated unexpectedly.

"Daddy! Daddy!" The girl began to scream in the darkness.

"Rise up against the flow, and I'll cover you," the voice of the colonel echoed.

Hurrying up the madmen, we began our retreat.

The rats quickly figured out their own plan against our maneuver and now were jumping from the shore into the water several meters upstream. The current carried them right at us.

Automatic rounds dispersed the rats near the shore.

"Come here!" The colonel shouted out.

We made our way to the shore and had just stepped away several meters when a grenade flew into the thickest part of the rats, right into the river. The sight after this was simply blissful. Not only did those rats die, most of them were also stunned. The current carried off their lifeless little bodies, the rest of the rats dispersed in a panic, and we finally could release the poles from our burning hands.

"Where's the captain?" I asked, waiting until his daughter had rejoiced in being with her father.

"He died... during the explosion."

"How did it happen?"

"The rats chewed through the rope. The captain made his way upstairs. He thought that while he was rushing like a whirlwind the rats wouldn't be able to stop him... But there were so many of them... I ran out after them and began to shoot those creatures, but the captain was covered with them so massively. And then he lit a box and threw it a little further away from himself. Evidently he thought that the fire would not succeed in reaching him so quickly. But the explosion was of such magnitude that it even threw me down the steps to the wall. The flame simply crackled along the entire floor. Hunched over, I crawled to the laboratory, closed the door, and for a while lay there, coming to my senses..."

"How's your hand?" Viola interrupted.

"It's not bleeding anymore. The wound is all the way through, but the bone isn't damaged..." Here he turned his gaze to Kost and asked: "Do you have some reinforcements?"

"This man pretended to be a madman."

"I see... I'm happy that you were able to link up with us..."

"There's one train car with unbroken windows," said Kost. "We can occupy it."

"Yes, but first we have to wring our clothes dry," the colonel reminded him.

The train car turned out to be quite satisfactory on the inside. We could only dream about finding a better place to spend the night.

Having quickly settled the madmen to sleep, we gathered in one of the partitions, in order to create a plan for tomorrow.

"You didn't explain to us what happened further," I said to the colonel.

"Further on I set a grenade in the grating in the window and made my way into the park. There were very few rats in the park, and in addition they had not come to after the explosion and the fire. But when I stopped in the town I understood that danger was waiting not only from the rats. The inhabitants of the city began to hunt me. These were the same kind of people as you and me. And what's most terrifying—almost all of them were still children. They were holding shovels, axes, pitchforks, scythes, knives, and poles in their hands... In a word, when they had surrounded me, I was lost. I didn't know what to do. Shoot at people, at children? At first I shot above their heads, then toward their feet, but nothing seemed to work. They kept crawling and crawling. I tried to explain to them that I was fighting for their freedom, that I wanted to chase away the rats so we could finally live like masters of the house and not like slaves. And then some boy stopped them as they had shoved me up against the wall. They stood in a semi-circle, maybe ten steps away. And that boy asked:

"Did the foreigner convince you to do this crime? Yes?"

"No, I convinced the foreigner to do it. For a long time I have been carrying out a plan to break the yoke off of us."

"Who asked you to take the yoke off? What yoke? Where have you seen it? We've lived with the rats in harmony. We've built our home together. And what have you done? So much blood has been spilt! The rats have lost so many of their citizens that I don't even know how we would be able now even to seek their mercy. Each one of us is ready to tear off his arm, just to somehow atone for this horrible guilt."

"Why are you here?" I cried out to calm them down. "I started the uprising."

"Yes, but you are one of us. You're not a rat. You're a man. What kind of faith can the rats have in us after all this? How can we look into their eyes? They've cared for us as if we were their relatives, they've given all their efforts for the sake of our welfare... And you, living among them, pretending to be an upright citizen, secretly have been cultivating treason!"

"He was just waiting for an opportunity!" A fat lady with a rolling pin in her hand uttered.

"You've hidden deadly weapons. Against whom? Against defenseless creatures!" The boy stated.

"If he's such a hero, then why didn't he go against the rats with a stick?!" Someone from the crowd shouted out.

"These are the kind of heroes they are!" A boy insinuated.

"They've left ashes and ruins after them. How much property they've destroyed! More than ten buildings have been gutted from the fire, the parks have burned down, the gates."

"And people in those buildings have died!" The fat lady interrupted again.

"That's not true!" I said. "We didn't burn the buildings, just the insane asylum."

The crowd began to whistle violently.

"Do you hear?!" The fat lady with the rolling pin began to shriek. "What awful lies?!"

"Why listen to him there! Hit him! Hit him! Hit the traitor!" The crowd began to choke.

"We don't believe you," the boy said. "You're a traitor, an arsonist and a killer. And you have to be punished."

"Wait a minute," I said. "You don't know everything. They tortured people there in that asylum, they did experiments on them. Everyone who didn't want to give in to the regime they turned into the mentally ill, into beings incapable of doing anything. They paired women with rats and procreated a new race of rat-people. These are monsters with the heads of a rat."

"What are you babbling? What kind of rat people?" The throng flew into a rage.

"He's getting us off track."

"It's true, that there is such a theory about rat-people," said the boy. "But this, till now, is still just theory, and if it really becomes realized, then it'll happen only willingly, and not through some kind of forced experiments! Rats are already very close to people with their development. Why shouldn't they pair off in the future?"

"But we've already seen grown-up monsters, we've even seen little babies. There were more than half a hundred!"

"And how will you prove to us that this is the truth?"

"Ah, he's just lying! The building burned down, and now he'll think up whatever he wants!"

"It's not me who's lying! It's the rats who've filled up your heads so much that you've turned into obedient puppets in their hands. You're already nothing, you're just the servants of the rats! They've taken away everything from you—your history, your dignity, your traditions! And what have they given you in return? What have you turned into? You live like animals. Nothing interests you anymore. And those who've tried to rise against them they've locked up in the insane asylum with your silent agreement. What have you come to? Children who rejected their parents! They're imitating the rats in their conduct!"

"It's too bad," the boy sighed, "that you didn't reveal yourself earlier. Then we would've cured you in time, and, maybe, even saved you for society. But now... we have to liquidate you..."

The crowd flared up, ready to throw itself at me at any moment. During this time I managed to notice that along the right flank there were fewer people, a trash-collector was standing near the wall, and behind him there wasn't anybody at all. Then I resorted to subterfuge.

"Take a look!" I shouted. "You're all surrounded!"

They turned their heads to where I was pointing. In just a second I ran to the trash-collector, I jumped toward him, jumped away, and rushed along the street, from time to time cutting loose bullets at their legs. But they didn't retreat for even a footstep, evidently, they figured out that I didn't want to shoot at children. And then I shot at the legs of the boy who had been leading them. This stopped my persecutors at least for a short while. I ran to the neighboring street, and instead of moving in your direction, I started off toward the swamp."

"You lost your way?" I asked.

"No, I did this on purpose. It was beginning to get dark. Any minute the rats could gather up the survivors of the rout. Darkness isn't terrifying for them, and they'd quickly catch up to me along my tracks. While no one would be able to smell my tracks in the marshes. I knew the road through the swamp from childhood. There neither people nor rats are frightening to me. My persecutors lagged behind in the marshes. They just couldn't understand where I went, why in that and not the other direction. But they were afraid of going after me through the swamp. I disappeared among the reeds and, making a little zig-zag, came out here."

The night passed peacefully. We took turns standing guard and anxiously listened to the silence, but not a single suspicious sound echoed to us. Although the enemy was already here, right next to us, preparing for the final attack.

And then, when the sun rose... I don't know precisely why they threw themselves into the assault after sunrise; maybe they had decided to give us the last morning of our life as a gift? And maybe they gathered their forces the entire night in order to overcome and destroy us without any doubt?

I awakened on hearing Kostya's shout; he was manning the last guard duty. Almost simultaneously we rushed to the windows and saw that he was repulsing four rat-people with a fence paling.

The colonel grabbed the automatic, and jumping out of the train car, knocked over two of the attackers with rounds. The other two managed to hide themselves behind the train car. Kost pressed his bitten hand into his chest and swore. The colonel and I walked around the train car from both sides but could no longer see the monsters. Maybe they were hiding in the bushes and were waiting again for the right opportunity.

"Everybody, we have to get moving," said the colonel. "Lead out the madmen. And don't forget to grab your poles."

After several minutes we made our way to the southwest, all the further from this horrifying place. And we hadn't made two dozen steps when they attacked us again. This time it was the rat-people and the children, as well as the rats. It's true there were very few of the latter; however, I counted about ten of the monsters and about two hundred of the children. In addition they attacked us all mixed together, so the colonel was forced to shoot above the children's heads in order to kill any of the rat-people. But they figured it out very quickly and stooped down.

After several seconds an indescribable confusion began. Those of us who had weapons mostly were occupied with the rat-people. Though the little boys were not less of a danger for us, but for some reason our hands wouldn't rise up to shoot at them.

The rats scampered beneath our feet, and we didn't notice them. With the poles in our hands, we created a path for our retreat. Unfortunately, in such a situation we were already no longer capable of protecting the madmen, and they pressed us away from them. The children, armed with whatever they could pick up, set on us even more tenaciously. The rat-people, in the meantime, attacked the madmen, knocked them over onto the ground and chewed through their throats. And we couldn't help them. Finally Kost, with a threatening roar, broke his way through the children and began to strike the monsters with his pole. But their heads, evidently, weren't made of melon, because he wasn't able to knock a single one off his feet. On the other hand, they knocked him off his feet and assaulted him in a threesome.

This was already too much for my nerves. I grabbed the pistol and shot twice in front of me. The children began to shriek, blood splashed, but I no longer paid any attention to anything and using a staff, made my way through to Kost. A tangle of bodies rolled along the ground. Kost was all bloodied. I seized the moment and shot one of the monsters in the ear. That was all I was able to do for my comrade, because in the next moment the rat-people also attacked me. There were two of them and each one of them got a bullet in the gut from me, but this didn't slow them down. I shot once again at one of them and after this the cartridges in my pistol were spent. There were cartridges in a box in my pocket, but there was not enough time to reload. The rat-people, from whose stomachs blood was flowing, were coming at me, stretching out their arms, baring their fangs. It would have been senseless to beat them with the staff, and I, turning it to its sharp side, stuck the point into the monster's stomach, right into his fresh wound. The rat-person raised his head in a horrifying scream and became petrified on the spot. I plucked the staff out, and in the same way, drove it into the stomach of the other attacker. Now that one raised his head, bellowing a dying scream. But to my surprise and to my horror neither of them fell to the ground.

Then several seconds were enough for me to reload the revolver and shoot the monsters right into their gaping maws.

These were evidently the very bullets they needed to make them fall to the ground and die in convulsions.

I looked around and saw that the colonel and Viola had finally chased away the children with their shots and were backtracking to me now. Kost was battling now just with a single monster. I had shot one of them, and he had strangled the other. Knowing now how to kill the rat-people, once again I placed the revolver to the predator's ear and killed him with a single shot.

Kost got up all bloodied.

"These scoundrels are really strong," he spat. "I thought they'd tear me apart."

"Good that you're alive. Do you have any serious wounds?" I asked.

"It looks like no."

A machine gun round echoed. This was the colonel firing after the escaping monsters. There were just three of them left. They had completed their task—all the madmen were lying on the ground with slashed throats.

The children stepped away to a safe distance and deliberated. More and more rats came to them. It was evident they were preparing for a new attack.

Kost washed off the blood and didn't look as awful as before the assault. But several wounds were still bleeding and Viola, pulling out a bandage from my knapsack, bandaged him up.

"Just the last clip left," the colonel said, nodding toward the machine gun. "We have one chance—to go toward the swamp. I know that road well, but if something should happen to me, remember that before you take a step, be sure to thrust your staff into the ground. Otherwise you'll end up in a swamp-hole."

"Attention!" Kost shouted out. "It looks like a new attack."

And indeed, among the group of children, the hairy heads of rat-people had appeared again. The three of them, who had escaped. While the children started out at us in a single body, tightly gripping cudgels in their hands, as well as shovels, rakes, and pitchforks.

The colonel shot above their heads, but this didn't stop the children, and the rat-people bent over, hiding behind the children's backs.

There were about thirty meters dividing us. We had to dare to do something, otherwise they'd crush us.

"We have to shoot," I said, and shot at the legs of one of the boys. He let out a scream and fell.

But the rest of them kept moving with a fierce expression in their eyes. You'd just be amazed at their stamina.

The colonel also struck a hard blow at their legs, but the boys walked through the wounded and continued their assault. Here and there the rats rushed out, and moved past and in front of our noses like light cavalry, simulating an unexpected assault.

I took my pistol with both hands and aimed at a rat-person, but I missed; instead, one of the boys shouted and fell.

"Daddy," Viola whispered, "they're going to kill us right now."

"Well, that's it," the colonel responded. "No more time to wait."

The automatic round chopped down several of the boys; I recall, I also shot three times, and this time managed to wound a rat-person. Only after the second round did the boys dive vigorously in all directions.

We walked up to the children who lay killed and wounded in the grass. Suddenly Kost shouted out and fell on his knees next to one of them:

"God! Slavka!"

"What's this?" I didn't understand. "Do you know him?"

"That's my son," Kost moaned.

The boy, wounded in the stomach, looked at us with wide-open eyes, without expressing his pain with a single sound. Just tears ran down his pale cheeks.

"This is your son?" I asked, and hid my pistol in my pocket in a way that it appeared as if I had wounded him.

Kost drew his hand along his face, wiping away the tears, and asked:

"Is it painful for you?"

Perhaps at that moment he didn't think about the stupidity of his question, he simply didn't know what to say to his son, who just recently had written a denunciation of his father and had had him locked up in the psychiatric hospital. I don't know if I would have conducted myself in the same way at that moment, but a knot rose up in my throat.

"Son, do you recognize me? I'm your father!"

The boy looked as if he were looking right through him, without reacting to his father's words with either a single movement of his lips or eyebrows. Then Kost bent over closer, attempting at least to see something in those glassy eyes.

It happened in a single second—the boy pushed off his hands and grabbing his father by the neck, pulled him over to himself. This looked like a fervent embrace from the side. In reality something else was underneath it. Kost began to scream and darted back. Blood was gushing from his bitten artery.

"A rat!" He uttered hoarsely. "A rat! A rat!"

A smile of contentment illuminated the bloody, ravenous mouth of his son. And he breathed his last with bared teeth.

We didn't manage to get to Kost to help him, as he had picked up someone's abandoned pick-ax off the ground. He threw himself with a wild animalistic braying at the boys who again had already gathered together in a group. This stunned them so much that they, having themselves now gotten used to attacking, now froze without moving and just tried to defend themselves at the last moment. But the children did not interest Kost; jumping into the densest part of the group, he lopped off the head of one of the rat-people, drove his pick-ax into another all the way up to his shirt-cuff. A third one darted to escape, but just as he had jumped out behind the boys, an automatic round mowed him down.

The children ran from Kost in every direction, and we saw him weaken quickly, drop the pick-ax from his hand, fall down, and grow motionless.

"We have to escape," the colonel said and pointed at the river. There a new defense militia was moving with the same weaponry.

The children, having seen the reinforcements, joyfully began to wave their arms. From all of this it was evident that this had added to their resolve.

We ran amid their chiding and whistling.

"Quicker! Quicker!" They shouted. "They're escaping!"

And further they themselves started after us on the run, picking up stones and tossing them at us.

Unexpectedly, Viola shouted and began to roll along the grass. A stone had hit her in the leg. We grabbed beneath her arms, but she no longer was able to run, just limp.

"Escape," the colonel said. "I'll hold them off."

"I won't abandon you!" Viola threw herself onto his neck.

"No, no, you have to run. I'll catch up to you. I'll definitely catch up to you. The swamp is quite close, it's there beyond the grove. Well... be well..."

"Daddy, take my pistol. Though it doesn't have shells. Marko, do you have any more shells?"

"Right away," I scrounged in my pocket.

"Don't have to, I have some too," the colonel said, putting away his pistol. "You might also need them."

He stood on one knee and shot at the children's legs; the children threw themselves onto the ground and began to crawl.

Without paying attention to Viola's protests, I picked her up on my back and carried her off, grabbing her legs with my arms. The reason I like thin girls is just the fact that in a tough jam it's not really hard to be chivalrous for them.

From time to time we could hear the crackling of an automatic behind our backs. And when I had made my way to the grove and had lowered the girl onto the ground to rest for a minute, I saw that the children had succeeded in surrounding the colonel, and now they were narrowing their circle.

"Why isn't he shooting?" Viola was getting nervous.

As if he had heard her words, the colonel cut loose a round above their heads and broke away from being surrounded. But the children once again ran around him in a horseshoe and pulled him into the circle.

One of the boys threw a shovel, but the colonel managed to step aside. He ran clicking the automatic; but it was evident that there were already no more bullets. Then he hurled the automatic at his persecutors and hit somebody in the head. This infuriated the boys even more, who now ignored the danger for themselves and who already were tossing whatever they could reach at him.

"My God!" Viola screamed. "Help him!"

"I'll help, but you have to go away. Limp any way you can, but try to disappear into the grove. We'll catch up to you."

"Why are you chasing me away? That's my father!"

"And what of it? Don't you understand that you're getting in the way? Go into the grove, and I'll run to help him."

She, however, didn't move from the spot.

"Well?!" I said. "I won't go either, till you disappear. Think about your father!"

She turned and walked lamely to the grove, and I ran to meet the colonel. He had already pulled out his pistol, and had shot himself loose from the boys while moving. It was just in time, because just a little more and the circle would have closed again.

The children continued to throw stones and sticks at him. From time to time they hit the mark, and the colonel fell headlong several times.

Those rear cover shots that he permitted himself mostly had the aim of frightening his persecutors. The boys figured this out quickly and came at him with all the more zeal.

Suddenly the colonel fell and rolled along the ground. Then someone got him with the pick-ax. The boys all at once flew at him from every direction, waving their weapons. Two more gunshots echoed, but then their shovels and pick-axes gleamed in the sun.

I stopped. There was no sense in running further. From here where I stood the bullets couldn't reach them. Anyway, how could I help him?

I threw myself into running back. When I looked back, I saw that the children, having done their work, had now started off after me.

All of this appeared to be immeasurably stupid—the deaths of each of us one by one and the inability of others to help in any way. Now I had to save myself and Viola. There were only two of us left who knew about Ratburg and about the horrifying danger that the rat-mutants were preparing for the world. We didn't have the right to die. I ran thinking about the fact that I would have to inform the girl of the death of her father. I decided to say nothing until we ended up in safety, because who knew if she'd get stubborn and want to go back.

The boys little by little were catching up to me; but the distance was fairly great, and I didn't dare to shoot. I saved my bullets. The band of rats caught up to me in the grove; they weren't attacking, but just scurrying at my feet. Evidently they were making sure that I didn't disappear.

I caught up to Viola quickly. She was walking lamely along the path, leaning against a pole.

"Well, how's your leg?" I asked.

"It's already better, it's stretched out. But where's Daddy?"

"He took another road, we'll meet in the swamp."

"Which road?" She stopped and anxiously looked at me.

"There's no time to talk nonsense," I cut her off and dragged her by the hand.

"I can't walk so fast!" She shrieked. "Don't drag me!"

"Hang in there! We have to make our way to the swamp soon before they catch up to us."

"And Daddy?" She couldn't calm herself down.

"Maybe he's already there," I lied.

The voices of the boys grew louder behind us. The grove became less dense, a little bit more and we'd run out into the swamp. It'd be just in time, because Viola had already lost all her strength. The water began to gurgle beneath our feet. The marshes had begun...

I told Viola to walk on alone, and that I was going to walk back and chase away the boys. I pulled out my pistol and shouted to them:

"Stop! I'm going to shoot!"

But my words didn't have any more effect on them than the chirping of a sparrow. In answer, sticks and stones that they had grabbed and carried with themselves flew at me. Several of them hit my chest. I began hissing from the pain and no longer could stand on ceremony. I tried to shoot them in the legs and although not all the shots hit the mark, four of the boys were already writhing on the ground.

Having shot several more times, I turned back and ran through the marshes to Viola. The marshes were becoming more and more sticky, and the girl had to thrust out her stick at every step.

I didn't think that the children would be bold enough to follow us into the swamp, but they ran there anyway. Once again I began to shoot, and two more of them fell. The rest of them were surrounding us in a small circle.

In the meantime we had wandered into a swamp so thick we were wading up to our knees in mud. I only had four bullets left in my pistol.

"Oh, oh!" Echoed somewhere off to the side, and I saw a boy mired up to his waist in the swamp. He began to be sucked into it even further. Someone offered him a pole and tried to pull him out, but in that very spot he too fell into the very same swamp-hole. In front of our eyes in just a few seconds only ripples on the dark sorrowful water remained where both boys had been.

From the other side the same kinds of shrieks echoed to us. The boys, wandering without thinking, ended up in sticky slime and disappeared in it faster than anyone could come to help them.

Finally, fear arose in them and they stopped. Several returned, others began stamping their feet in indecision. The horrifying death of their comrades had really rattled them.

They stood this way until we entered the reeds and disappeared from their sight.

Further during the course of this entire journey through the swamp, I had to lie in order to calm down Viola. Toward the end, I was doing this so unpersuasively that when we finally stepped out onto dry land, she, without saying a word, fell into the grass and began to sob.

After several days we made our way to Lviv, and I took the girl to my aunt. My aunt lives alone. It'll be better for her there."

Marko grew silent and drank up the rest of his coffee.

"That's all?" I asked.

"That's all," he responded.

I turned off the tape recorder and at that very moment heard a rustling that reached me from the knapsack.

"What's there?" I poked it with my finger.

"I don't know."

"Something's rustling."

Marko stretched his arm to the knapsack, and from there suddenly with a piercing squeal a big rat jumped out and scampered to the open door. Marko took a look into the knapsack and pulled out an entire handful of tattered paper from it. Just dust remained from the rat bible.

"No!" He shrieked. "How's this possible? It turns out that while I was speaking that monster was gnawing on the book!"

"Marko! We have to immediately get to your aunt. Is there a phone there?"

"From where? She's living in Krivchitsi."

"Alone?"

"I already said that she's alone... do you think..." His eyes bugged out at me with a half-crazed look. "Oh, Lord! Let's go!"

But first, before we left the house, I took the cassettes with me so that the rat wouldn't chew them up.

We drove up to the building by taxi and ran to the door as though we were possessed. But the door was locked from the inside. We hollered and listened whether we'd hear somebody's voice in response, but silence reigned everywhere. I walked around the building looking for an open window or something else to get in; but I didn't succeed.

In the meantime Marko found a crowbar in the shed and was already forcing open the door. This was an old oak door, and it gave way with great difficulty. But finally a loud crackle reverberated, and a woman ran out from the neighboring house.

"It's me!" Marko shouted to her. "For some reason, we knocked and didn't get an answer. Someone has to be inside, 'cause you can see the key in the chink."

"I didn't see anybody come out," the neighbor woman said. "I already thought of knocking myself..."

The door split open and we crossed into the entryway. And in the entryway, and in the kitchen, and in the bedroom—an ideal harmony reigned everywhere, and am there wasn't the trace of a living soul among it.

"Upstairs there's another bedroom. Maybe they've gone to sleep," Marko said with a dried out voice. "Auntie sometimes snoozes after dinner."

We saw them both on a wide bed. They were lying under the covers and with pale, waxen faces. Just the way that death had caught them.

Marko slammed open the blinds. A playful sunny glow overflowed the bedroom.

Their heads were lying in pools of dried, darkened blood. The blood had clotted on their throats, and the red tracks of rat claws were still visible on the covers, on the bright parquet floor, and disappeared under the dresser.

"Now there are only two of us who know the horrifying secret of Ratburg," said Marko.

Shivers ran down my spine from those words.

Now I had no choice but to transfer all of Marko's tale onto paper, and I sat down to work.

But the entire time that I had been writing, the mice and rats had been on the watch for my work nearby. When I left my desk I had to take my tape recorder, cassettes and typescript with me. First, before beginning to retype, I bought two Siamese cats. If not for them, I, maybe, wouldn't have been able to sleep a wink.

I constantly heard squealing and shuffling under the floor, from every corner rat eyes constantly peeped out. My wife could not handle our ill fate and ran off to her parents.

Taking care of both floors of my home was quite impossible. The rats succeeded in destroying all of my food reserves besides those that were kept in the freezer. They couldn't get in there. I live alone now, like a rat, without sticking my nose out of the house.

Fortunately my wife didn't leave me completely on my own, but would come every morning and bring me food. She wasn't bold enough to enter the house, she would give me a bag through the window, throw me a kiss and disappear. We greeted each other this way:

"Are you still alive?"

"Yes, alive. And as hungry as a dog."

She also took care of the food for both of my Siamese knights, who, in the morning, would always carry their nocturnal prey to the windowsill, praising their battle successes.

On the eighth day of work I finally placed the final period. And here my wife made me the best gift that she possibly could—she brought me a not very big safe. Not very big, but the driver and I could barely slide it into the house. Now the cassettes and papers will be safeguarded.

We lived under the rat siege for another week, after which the number of gnawers successively began to grow smaller, although they didn't disappear entirely. Someone always continued to watch over me.

I got myself a metal briefcase, I put my manuscripts in there and carried them off to a publisher together with one of the Siamese cats.

"I suggest that while you're reading this tale, you keep this cat near you," I said to the editor.

He looked at me with sympathy and asked:

"It seems you've gotten a bit tired. Take a rest somewhere."

"Definitely. But only after you read this. And I beg you to keep the briefcase under lock and key."

The editor sighed and offered me his hand:

"Come tomorrow. If not for this cat, I'd ask for you to come in a month. But I really don't feel like taking care of your cat for an entire month. Once in my childhood just this kind of Siamese cat nearly chewed off one of my fingers."

And right by the door he added:

"Your cleverness with the cat has succeeded, but I beg you: don't share your experience with other literary types. Because one of them might feel obliged to toss me a panther."

V. SPRING GAMES IN AUTUMN GARDENS

SPRING GAMES IN AUTUMN GARDENS

Prologue

1

The dark waters of sleep spread so slowly and softly — the flow carries me to the surface rocking, and though my eyes are shut, even so, I see everything beautifully — I see the Arabian dance of the underwater plants and the silver glimmering of the tiny fish, the sorrowful twinkling of the water and the undulating beams of light that penetrate the water from above and below, stealthy shadows and the flashes of a shell — it seems I am so tiny in my mother's cradle and it's so warm and peaceful that a baby bird wouldn't want to wake up and remain happy in this balmy water rocking on the waves, but some inexorable power pushes me out from the depths to the surface grabs me brutally by the hair and I don't don't don't want to wake up — I don't want to go to the surface I want to go back into the depth into the silence there into the half-shade into the balmy water into the soothing rocking...

2

The winter sun gnaws through squinting eyelids, the rays painfully bore your brain and open the damaged cupboards of memory, pull out the drawers, shake them out with a clamor, and then he begins to remember what had happened till now, with which thoughts he had fallen asleep and why his head was buzzing like a tambourine... This kind of awakening is so horrible... as if it were a plunge into glacial water. Back, back into the balmy water of dreams, into a warm mirage, into a world without pain and sorrow, into meadows filled with flowers... But eyes are incapable of closing, the brain has become fixed on the transition from dreams to wakefulness, there's nowhere to retreat, the dream is disintegrating, like mortar on an old building, baring the surrounding world — your eyes glide along the room, filled to the brim with bookshelves, drooping lower to islands of papers, magazines, books, empty bottles, eyes wander, sinking in the thick pile of the rug, to the doors, beyond which dead silence lurked, for a certain amount of time your ears try to capture at least the hint of a sound, a strum, a clink, but the silence is dead — it is never more dead… Together with the consciousness of awakening from a dream something else appears — painful and unpleasant, filled with despair and a sense of being lost, consciousness of complete ruin… All the fortresses crumble all at once, and the towers have fallen to ruins, the smashed armies have fallen to their knees and lowered their banners, everything that surrounded him till now, everything behind which he continued to live in a cozy nook and in safety disappeared in a single instant.

3

In the middle of the night and dreams the ringing of the telephone reverberated, it burst into his brain, like a dashing train, rattling and giving off sparks, it seems his head would crack in another minute, split into two halves. What's this? Who is it? In the middle of the night! He tears from his bed, stumbles on the books strewn all over the floor, slips on piles of manuscripts, nearly falls, but he manages to grab onto the table, finally blindly with a trembling hand groping for the receiver, and first before putting it to his ear, in which the warm sea of dreams still continues to splash, and not everything is still sufficiently distinguishable between mirage and reality, he shouts out: "HELLO!" — so loudly, as if he needed to be heard on the street.

The morning recollection of a telephone conversation is like reading a palimpsest. Did it really happen? Or did he dream it? But your gaze falls onto the table — there were two bottles of champagne, and both of them empty. They were drunk up during the night. Right after the phone conversation. And this is reality, which it is impossible to doubt. His memory retained several fragments of the conversation, all the rest is torn, shredded, and submerged in the wine.

The call was from the US. She suggested getting a divorce. And she added: "It'll be better this way." Better for whom? He couldn't manage to ask her, he was so stunned that he was incapable of squeezing a single complete phrase out of himself. Eventually, this wasn't all that strange because he was asleep, and the phone call had awakened him. A phone call in the middle of the night has its peculiarities. It always forces you to shudder, it forces the heart to beat faster, it fills you with anxiety. The one making the call is in a better state because she knows what she wants, has had time to think out what she has to say, she knows what she wants, but the one picking up the receiver is absolutely unprepared for a conversation. What kind of conversation can there be when someone calls from the U.S. and to save money babbles hurriedly, chokes on her words, swallowing individual syllables without any pauses, that would allow anything to be grasped — the sleepy brain is unable to digest all this, to comprehend it, to counter it…

"…it'll be better this way."

These words stung my brain and will never be effaced, all others — will wither, will crumble, but these will remain and will prick for years and years, will shoot out in sprouts of couch-grass and wound.

The conversation lasted for a short amount of time, he mostly listened, and she quickly set out everything in its place, arranged everything onto shelves, numbered and sealed everything. And then she threw down the receiver: somewhere far far away on Long Island in New York. And he heard her slam the receiver down. And he even dreamt that he had heard her words that were directed not at him, but at another man, who the entire time was next to him listening to their conversation. She said: "Well here…," and the man also said something hoarsely, it was hard to make out the words, maybe it was all said in English, in the dark room only the rustle of his voice wafted, and then silence came, and he stood next to the telephone and didn't move away, as if he were continuing to listen to the receiver gone silent, waiting for another call, though he understood that the conversation had come to an end, no one would call, but all the same there was some kind of invisible thread that linked them across the ocean, it continued to vibrate, continued to link them, refused to be broken, and until he stopped hearing its vibration, he didn't move from where he was standing.

And in a moment the vibration disappeared, and in his ears silence again dawned, but it was restless and dreadful, clenching his heart with a burning sadness. Back, back into sleep… gropingly, scraping his brow with his hands, diving and swimming, further, further from that place, further from that time, to return everything from the beginning, to fix it, to rewrite it, to save it… Actually, to save it — he needed to rush beyond the seas and oceans to foreign lands and to free the princess, whom a wicked sorcerer had imprisoned in a tower without windows, to snatch her onto a winged horse and, pressing her to himself ever so tightly, to fly home… In his head a noisy carousel swirled and assorted colors twinkled. This lasted for several long wearisome minutes, until outside the window it began to drizzle, a fine, miserable, winter rain, but he sensed a certain strange gratitude to this rain that finally destroyed the silence, forced him to move from where he was standing and turn on a light. In his head the carousel of words continued to swirl, separate sounds, pauses and breathing… He uncorked a bottle of champagne, fell onto an armchair and drank glass after glass, and at that time around him the walls fell and a wasteland appeared. Time after time he replayed that conversation, trying hard to recreate it in its entirety, but the champagne set in all too quickly, for every new recollection something was lost, words were confused, order was lost, he was annoyed mostly by the fact that just when he had immediately grasped something, he could answer this or that reproach. The words faded, were replaced by others, and the further he got drunk, the less and less memory of the conversation remained, and just one phrase refused to fade and continued to circle in his ears: "It will be better this way."

Maybe it really will be better this way? Wine saves you from sorrow and covers everything with a semi-transparent film of paraffin. If not for the wine, he would have never fallen asleep after that conversation.

The man finally crawls out of bed and shuffles heavily to the bathroom. The cold water washes away dreams from his eyes. He squeezes out onto his toothbrush an entire mountain of toothpaste and, when he begins to brush his teeth, his gaze falls into the mirror.

In the mirror he sees he sees the sullen, unshaven face of a forty-year-old man, he sees swollen bags under his eyes, he sees disheveled hair, he sees sadness in his eyes.

And at that moment with horror I suddenly become conscious of the fact that this man in the mirror is — me! And it was I who had had a conversation on the telephone with my wife who called from the US, and then — again it was me — who downed two bottles of champagne, and now it was my head aching, and not somebody else's.

A mirror is always indifferent to whose kisser it is reflecting. My kisser half-awake had a sour taste. To somehow sweeten it, I brushed my teeth, combed my hair, washed my eyes, then I crawled under the shower, shaved, got dressed — but anyway I still looked like a squeezed lemon. It's always this way. Waking up in the morning after a drinking bout, I always feel like a cat run over by a car. But my nighttime drinking bout was of a particular kind — I drank out of despair. When you drink out of despair, it's a completely different feeling, because then you usually drink alone. You drink alone with yourself late into the evening when all the sounds around you grow quiet, and when midnight passes, you're finally the way you need to be, you're drunk, your no one's, and here right then, right in that state you can finally speak with yourself, openly and candidly, to cut out all your insides, all your intestines, hang them all up nicely and make a diagnosis. And more, and this is always the most interesting, to create plans for the future. Well, what can you say — plans at such moments simply bloat your head, and everything looks so courageous, so rosy, that despair disappears, hides itself in the deepest recesses of memory, so that it can rise to the surface tomorrow, but it will be tomorrow, not today, and today you just feel like swimming along the waves of daydreams.

THE PILGRIM'S DANCE

Part 1

1

You really begin to understand women only when they leave you. It's right then that they finally illuminate some kind of higher truth unknown to you to that point and with it slay you on the spot. You might have lived with a woman for forty years, but just as that moment arrives when she tells you she's leaving, you find out something about yourself that had never occurred to you. And this, by the way, can be some totally inane thing, a complete nothing, nil, that at any other moment would have elicited just wild laughter, but not then, not at that moment, when she tosses it out at you as she's saying good-bye. And the main thing is that she tosses it out! Something at which you just want to wildly burst out laughing. What? At such idiocy? Yes, strictly speaking, at it. Thus it sounds like a verdict, like a final judgment, that is driven into your forehead with a nail, into the very center of your forehead, right here between your eyebrows, and from that time on you have to wear this nail in the middle of your forehead, to touch it and think quite hard what it really all meant and what in actuality stood behind it.

From every young lady with whom I've been close I've learned something new. Strictly speaking at the time when we broke up. Perhaps someone might call this masochism, but when I've wanted to break-up with a young lady I've never said such a thing to her. I couldn't have pasted together words such as these: "Pardon me, but I've fallen in love with someone else" or "Everything's over with us. Let's break up." I've listened with astonishment to several of my friends' stories about the strange scenes that they've played out with young women they've broken up with. Some even arrange a farewell dinner that ended again with such similar farewell endearments. Oh no, that's not for me. I did it in a simpler way. I have in mind simpler for me, and not for the young lady, for in fact all this was not simple for her. I did things so that they would break up with me. I began to play the role of a scoundrel, this isn't a simple role if in your heart you're actually not a scoundrel, but you want to come out dry from the water, you don't feel like enduring any scenes, explaining your relations, maybe even earning a slap in the face, anything you feel like — all this so that the young lady will tell you to go to parts unknown and that the windy rhetoric will turn out to be shorter, that's better for you. But in reality it never turned out short. It always lasted a long time. Always the young lady's fault. It's superfluous to say that I never guarded myself against slaps to my kisser. Finally understanding what kind of scoundrel she was dealing with, the young lady exploded into an uninhibited fountain of accusations that uncovered for me such bizarre facets of my "self," that it was impossible to comprehend even a single one of them: and why did you, my little dove, waste so much time with such a monster?

And do you know what? It made no sense to ask the irate young lady any such question. The answer would always sound like this: "I thought I could make you better!"

In the relations between two people can there be a nobler wish than to make someone better? At the very moment of utterance of such a sacred intention fanfares, flutes and trombones enter, at such a moment you feel like embracing the young lady by her knees, kissing her shoes and begging: "Keep trying, make me better!" But no, if you've seriously aimed at breaking up with her, don't relax, because all this is a fiction, no one will ever make anyone better in reality. You can mold from clay, but not from sand. You will remain the very same as when you first met, the only thing that can be expected from you is that when at some point you accommodate the young lady, you'll strive to rid yourself of habits that irritate her, but only at those times when she's there next to you. Certainly you in fact can become what the young lady thirsts for you to be, but if for you she is not a gift from heaven and you feel just a physical attraction, and just her butt interests you, you can just sneeze at all the conventions, you are the way you are in reality: inattentive, imprecise, unfaithful, ungrateful, dishonorable, unreliable, ill-bred, mendacious, insolent, unsocial, conceited, shameless....

The main thing here is not to get depressed and to take these accusations seriously. Otherwise a vile thought might really steal in to allow yourself to be saved, to give in to reeducation and, constantly improving yourself on the wings of love, to become exemplary, to become ideal, and sometimes, stepping out on the balcony, to listen to the rustle of the wings behind your back.

Usually, my method of breaking up with a young lady to some will stick out as a bit protracted, but the process of becoming a scoundrel can't last just a number of hours, or even days or weeks, but nevertheless I've been lucky with the young ladies, for some reason fate for the most part has constantly provided me with explosive frenetic women, ready at any suitable moment to scratch out my eyes, tear out a handful of my hair, scald me with boiling water, or tear my manuscripts to shreds. It is strictly speaking the manuscripts and books that for some reason evoke in them — evidently for a long time — a pent up ferocity, nevertheless it was just literature that stood as an obstacle to complete possession of me. Consciousness of the fact that there is something more important and more valuable for me than their vagina, their butt, their breasts, their loving heart, than their lips with droplets of sperm, for their kitten-like caresses and even for their plum-filled fried dumplings, elicits in them aggression directed right at what is most valuable and dearest, by which a writer lives, and then at moments of hysteria they grab papers and tear them up, tossing bits of your writings in every direction, with their feet they step on half of a book, and with a wild scream pluck the other half upward — and where do they get such strength? — in ecstasy they're ready to help themselves with their teeth, and here into the air a plundered Baudelaire flies down, and after him — Rilke, and after Rilke — Svidzynsky, and you, as though you are mad, try to save what's nearest and dearest to you, and, helpless, you must revert to your strength, twist her arm, knock her to the floor, rip her nightgown, and tearing her underwear with the very same ferocity that she had ripped up Rainer-Marie Rilke, you screw her, while she's all tearful, sobbing, howling, moaning, agonizing, in front of the plundered Charles, Rainer-Marie, and Volodymyr.

Actually, with frenetic women who love to drink and smoke, it's considerably easier to split up. Draw them out of their equilibrium — then spit once. It's enough just to refuse to do something that you've done to that point without excess words, but beside that give such a shaky reason for your refusal that it grates the ear. For example, if you have constantly made coffee for her, but one time growl out to her request: "Make it yourself — I'm busy," then you can be sure that at that very instant you should abruptly duck, otherwise a cup will crack right on your forehead. The very same reaction awaits you after a negative answer to the question: "Will you go along with me?" Then in the best case a slipper flies at your head, and in the worst — a shoe.

I don't know how others react, but when I listen to groundless accusations from my beloved, then I feel offense, sadness and despair, as well as absolute helplessness, inasmuch as I am not capable of answering with the same astonishing fountain of words. The words are strewn out in such a way as if they were hurled into my face not individually, but in entire handfuls, they scorch and blind me, they jam my lips and span the air, and if in the first minute any kind of timid attempts to defend myself appear, to hide behind any of my own words, perhaps, and not so sharp and painful ones, then in the next minute — unexpectedly for me I begin to feel in my heart a slight crust of responsibility, and in an instant I'm already unable to come to the conclusion that I'm not guilty of anything, and it begins to seem that these accusations are completely just, and I am being insulted not undeservedly, but with justification. And here I already discern in those words a note of indulgence; actually, I'm left the small apartment with the door open, a quite tiny apartment, but I can take advantage of this magnanimity and fly into it with arms crossed over my chest uttering: "Forgive me! Forgive me!" However I never did this, inasmuch as everything went according to plan. And it was only that nighttime ring of the phone that wasn't according to plan. It stunned me with its unexpectedness.

2

Everything began completely innocently and not because I had to hear what kind of swine I was. At first my wife set off for the U.S. on some kind of shaky invitation to have just as shaky of an exhibit of her paintings. We said good-bye with intense embraces and nearly with tears in our eyes. She didn't hide the fact that she intended to remain there, to find work and tried to convince me to go after here, inasmuch as I had an invitation to Canada. I didn't take it seriously: for me to live in the U.S. there'd have to be at least a return of Soviet power in Ukraine.

My last vivid memory of her is a kiss through the air. But after that, a strange situation began: she disappeared, and for half a year I heard no news from her. Besides one — the shaky invitation turned out to have been so shaky that no one met her on arrival and she was barely able to find an artist acquaintance of hers and took up residence in his studio where she slept right on a table. A woman who had just returned from the U.S. passed along this disconcerting news to me by. My wife's parents, of course, got letters from her, but they told me they didn't have any news. Right at that moment she phoned me and announced that we needed a divorce. And here, strictly speaking, I heard something about me that I never would have guessed: I didn't have a clue that I was some kind of philanderer, that I chased after every skirt, that I slept with all my female colleagues and God knows who else, that I may even have hit on her mother, but that now at last I could fashion an idyllic existence with... and here she named about a half-dozen of my female colleagues, whom I not only hit on, but dreamt of marrying. The cascade of absurdity poured onto my head so unexpectedly that I couldn't find a single argument to counter it, I choked on the nonsense the way a fish gasps for air, as for the fountain of her accusatory words I managed only to gurgle out something inarticulate, and then she didn't try to hear me out, but prattled like a machine gun, tossing out of herself a hundred words per second. That's why it's not surprising that I couldn't remember a tenth of what flew into my ears later.

From what I remember anyway, a rather unattractive picture arose. For monsters such as me there simply was no place on earth. There is nothing sacred! There was no hope to fix things up. I flirt with everything of the opposite sex on two legs. I'm a monster! A maniac! A vampire! I suck out energy, I drink blood and get enjoyment out of the torments of others.

After this there were several phone conversations, just as agitated, in haste, she attacked, I defended myself without knowing that her attacks already made no sense whatsoever, she was just searching for justification for herself because during that time when I continued to live alone, she already had found a cozy little nest and was living with a dentist near New York. When I found out about it, I sensed a heavy winter's ice floe slide off my chest and it became easier to breathe. I grew weary of fighting and understood all that I needed now — which was, strictly speaking, to turn into what she said I was: a maniac and a vampire. But for the purity of the experiment I needed to convince myself that she never was.

VI. MALVA LANDA

MALVA LANDA

Part 1

1

Somewhere deep in the heavens golden stars flew from branch to branch, shaking shimmering golden ambrosia from their wings, and it fell on the city that was concealed in a stony slumber, in the cold tears of autumn, it settled on the sleepy windowpanes of the evening, dying on the illuminated ones, blossoming on those darkened…

Boomblyakevych randomly leafed through a slim dried-up and yellowed book and read…

> *At such an hour loneliness is deeper*
> *And space more confined.*
> *Like a spurt of blood, the linden trees cast*
> *Their deep blue shadow to the dew.*
> *The bitter acacia, the sour apricot,*
> *Simmered in blossom,*
> *And the sky floats between white fingers*
> *In spring water.*
> *Such a fragrant evening background—*
> *The siege of spring…*
> *The sun leapt up in a quivering tear*
> *From my face…*

There wafted over him again the certain special magic of nostalgia for the colorful world of the Secession, that is interwoven with the hops and blades of Indian cress that has already blossomed, where the flowers and sprouts of the lotus are striking in their thin contours of female bodies. On the darkened book cover those strange plants surrounded her name, the name of a poet forgotten by God and man, whose slim book he had somehow acquired somehow by chance and, to his astonishment, inexpensively... This name for quite a long time, from when her poems began to sound in his head, aroused in Boomblyakevych an incomprehensible sorrow, as though it's the name of a well-known person whom he had met sometime long ago and lost touch with, and now she dove out of the mysterious hazy depths and is enchanting him, squeezing his heart into the silver ring of sorrow.

He had no other pleasure but to rummage through other people's attics, closets and drawers, looking for books, and swindling people out of them for a trifle, or even stealing them, hiding them under his belt beneath a knitted spacious sweater especially made for this purpose. And when he failed either to swindle or steal them, he had to buy them, sparing nothing, for more than on one occasion he was forced to sell something from his house in order to acquire the book he fancied.

He lived at home in a two-room apartment, completely filled with books, and since they constantly were being added, less and less space was left for them, thus he found shelter for them even in the refrigerator. When his mother was still alive Boomblyakevych was forced to tolerate a great amount of her things that stood in the way of the books, they guarded their territory before them and very unwillingly stepped aside even for a centimeter. And when his mother died, with a tranquil heart he remade all her dressers into bookshelves, even the old bed on which he was conceived right in the year when the NKVD* agents arrested his father and dispatched him to the untamed lands, where heavy snows swallowed him forever, he even took apart that bed gnawed up by woodworms with rusted springs and pressed it up against the wall.

When she died, his mother not only freed him from her things, but also from her constant reproaches and grumblings about a wife, and also from the dreams and ravings bordering on madness about a mysterious young woman who was waiting for him somewhere in a park hiding from the rain, and when he appears with an umbrella,

---

* The earlier name for the KGB in Stalin's time. The acronym stands for the National Commissariat for Internal Security.

her tender and sonorous voice will pour out unexpectedly from underneath a spacious beech tree and tickle his ear, throbbing in his heart—"excuse me, but could you, kind sir, accompany me in the rain, because I have an urgent matter." And that matter, well, to be sure, was a premier at the theater, and it turns out that there are two tickets, the other was for her girlfriend from work who disappeared somewhere, and there they were floating under the sail of the rain... And Boomblyakevych went to the park, wandered under the beech trees, and waited for her voice... but there was nothing... just a mirage...

Then he related everything in succession to his mother: about their acquaintance in the park, the theater, and how they arranged their next meeting, about all the further meetings with detailed conversations ("I want to know all-all-all of it," his mother said) that he had played before in his head.

"What's her name?" She asked him once.

And at that instant he sensed that if he gives her some kind of ordinary name, he'll really depress his poor mother, he'll depress her so much that he was afraid she would stop believing these inventions of his, and then he blurted out:

"Malva*... That's her name..."

"Ma-L-va...," his mother repeated and shut her eyes. It sounded like sweet halvah, that name, and it melted in her mouth, running to her palate.

Rambling through the city in search of his next treasures, Boomblyakevych fantasized about his conversations with Malva, and when he really went to the theater or to the movies, then he discussed what he had seen with her for a long time and even argued with her, so that afterward he could relate everything to his mother.

"How intelligent she is..."

And she really feared he would bring her home sometime.

"Just don't bring her here... Because when she sees the way we live, she'll break up with you..."

---

* Meaning: "hollyhock."

2

…Boomblyakevych approached the mirror and judgmentally looked at the balding chubby dwarf with upturned radar antenna ears. With such an external appearance he simply had no moral right to steal up to any decent young lady, much less utter his last name.

First of all there is this schizophrenic BOOM, as if someone were drumming on something empty, or maybe on a tambourine—boom, tsik, tsik! It's true that a certain well-known person has already had this BOOM in their last name. Wasn't there a Boumidienne?* But further on there was this indecent and scatological BLYA!** And though it's clear that the last didn't come from the fact that someone was constantly drumming or occupied with blya-blya-blya, but entirely with something else, for example, with tapping, which is an entirely decent pastime, for in truth, what is disparaging when you begin to tap your index finger on your lips — that is, to drum? But not everyone has the patience to penetrate so deeply into the etymology of someone else's name, and to explain it every time you meet someone would be entirely comical. And nothing remained for poor Boomblyakevych but to glow and to float in a worked up sweat in the presence of an innocent young lady until his ear-radar antennae pricked up even stronger and watchfully would quiver like aspen leaves…

This all was wild and indecent, but Boomblyakevych had never had a woman, and from the realization of his state, he was growing bitter and resentful, as though someone were mocking him. True, he didn't consider himself a little boy, for from the age of twelve, he occupied himself with solo action, and those were special moments of inspiration that he waited for, one can say, all day long. At night before sleep he dove into his dreams and fantasies, in which only bizarre women failed to submit to him, in which beauties nearly had to gasp for breath from those unbelievable splendors, with which Boomblyakevych showered them! Often these were girls and women

---

* The former president of Algeria Houri Boumidienne.

** "Blya" suggests "blyad'," the word for whore in Ukrainian.

whom he knew or didn't know, or just ran into on the street, all of them had to have a round, prominent little bottom: he didn't like skinny or bony ones! After he read Robert Merle's novel *The Island*,* he began to imagine himself after the sinking of a ship on an uninhabited island. Only he and eighteen captive girls survived… Oh, what splendid nights they were on that Polynesian island! The captive girls even argued over him, and sometimes even leading to fights. Somehow once one of them was missing. And only after some time had passed, the ocean tossed her body onto the shore in green seaweed… And then one more disappeared… And the ocean tossed out her body… A third was found in thickets, a fourth in a precipice, a fifth under a rock, a sixth in lava, a seventh in the snow, an eighth in amber, a ninth in a bottle, a tenth in the belly of a shark, an eleventh in a coconut, a twelfth in the clouds, a thirteenth in the tears of the fourteenth…

In general, if not for his mother, then who knows how his life would have turned out, because on occasion the opportunity to be with women would come up, but he didn't have anywhere to take them, and everything broke off after a brief flirtation. Eventually, there was an attractive young woman by the name of Slavtsya who lived in apartment next door. His mother loved to chat with her, but on more than one occasion, she warned her son not to even try anything with her.

"She smokes, she can drink an entire bottle of wine by herself and reads all day. She's not for you."

Slavtsia was thirty-two years old and, having decided that she's already a spinster, gave free reign to herself—she'd eat everything that tasted good and stopped caring about her figure. Boomblyakevych knew her from childhood and treated her like a sister. But on the other hand he caught himself thinking that if not for his mother's kvetching, then something with Slavtsia might have happened. She's not stupid, she's a teacher in fact, and they have a lot of things in common for conversation. But each time, just as his neighbor would call him either to help her move a couch or to take down blinds, or to chop up a

---

* Published first in 1964.

bone for broth, in just a few minutes his mother appeared with her invaluable advice and would not leave until they both returned home together.

His mother looked after him like the apple of her eye. And Boomblyakevych was left with nothing other than dreams and fantastic perversities, instantaneously capable of transporting his mother out of life, if she managed to break into those dreams for even a minute. Though he just dreamt about it — he was the dread of the entire city, who lured little girls somewhere into dark places and made love to them...

The little girls appeared very unexpectedly, just most recently.

One time he went to his cousin on some matter, and right at that moment she was in the bathroom bathing her little one. And she had to get up because the telephone began to ring: her girlfriend was on the line.

"Take care of my Danusya for a bit because I have an important call. Be careful she doesn't mess up the whole bathroom!" His cousin tossed out at him as she flew out and disappeared in the next-door room.

Boomblyakevych sat down on the edge of the bathtub, and the little girl, achieving her freedom, began to dive up and down in the water, to turn in every direction, showing him all her goods, because the clean, clear water even without that failed to hide anything. He looked at her as though he were under a spell. The little girl was, maybe, eight years old, but she was rather tall and plump, and on her breasts two little pink nippies were painted. Her full round thighs, as though she were doing it on purpose, didn't stay together. She lay down in the bathtub, spreading them and riveting the eyes of her uncle to her puffed up lips, that had frozen in some kind of dreamy state, as though right after a kiss.

It suddenly dawned on Boomblyakevych that this had been going on for several minutes, from the time the little girl stopped her craziness and had lain down in front of him in this embarrassing pose. She lay there and looked at him smiling, and his eyes darted nervously and continuously returned to the captivation of her thighs. Now he distinctly saw that the little girl was interestedly observing him gazing at her, but at the same time this was quite dangerous — what will her mother think when she finds her little one spread apart like that?

"Well, take your bath," Boomblyakevych said. "Keep bathing."

And he splashed water on her. The little girl started to laugh and puffed out her tummy, but she didn't change her pose. Then he splashed water on her one more time. But the little girl refused to move from her spot.

His hand, touching the water in which the little prankster lay, was no longer capable of retreating. A certain incomprehensible power drew it to the deep, to those little thighs that waited for his touch. He watched as the little girl swam around with a smile as his hand dove deeper and deeper and, it seemed, that diving would never end. The water wet his shirtsleeve that was rolled up above his elbow and began to rise up higher, his fingers already felt like they had to push forward to those taut little thighs, but for some reason didn't push forward. He bent over the edge of the bathtub and even dunked his head into the water and, opening his restless eyes, tried hard to see where those little legs had disappeared. His fingers scratched the bottom of the bathtub, further along the sides, but it was empty everywhere. He plucked his head from the water and saw that there was no one in the bathtub. The water was not as transparent as it was at first, some kind of yellow cloudiness rose up to the surface, and waves spread in all directions as though from a breeze. He sensed this draft on his back and even began to sweat.

He sprang up onto his legs and surveyed the bathroom with his eyes in terror. The girl had disappeared. Did she drown? Without thinking very long, he dove into the water and started to swim, nervously paddling with his arms, and from the bottom a caustic yellow fog rose up and blocked off his view, slashing and burning his eyes with fire. At every turn he sensed as though something were striking him along his legs, something like the tail of a fish or the fan of a coquettish little lady. Palmated algae stuck to his face, and his ears were already gurgling from the water, as though ringing springs with myriad tiny bubbles were beating, tearing upward, and it seemed as though his soul was being torn from him, and there was quite little left to do — just to open his mouth and let in the intrusive cloudiness in order to settle in these parts forever…

With strength he pushed off from the bottom with his feet and sprang to the surface. He plaintively swallowed the air, but he already had no strength to reach the shore.

Someone's gentle hands dragged him to them, helping him get out of the bathtub.

"What are you doing?" His cousin was astonished. "Why did you crawl into the bathtub with your clothes on?"

"I… I was looking for her… she was drowning…"

"The frolicsome girl?" His cousin began to laugh. "She'd sooner want to drown someone herself. Danusya, come on get out! Where are you hiding?"

Boomblyakevych waited for the muddy waters to part and for the little girl to dive out of them, but the waters didn't part, and instead a hamper with clothes opened up, and the tiny naked prankster jumped out, laughing uncontrollably.

His gaze again fell on the water — it was just as yellow… What could it have been?

"What kind of tricks are you doing?" His cousin chided her daughter. "Do you know how much you scared your uncle? Poor guy's all wet." Here she also took a look at the water. "Yikes! Well, you're going to get it now! Who poured egg shampoo into the water?"

And she smacked her on her bare little bottom that immediately became red and turned into a ripe apple; a full mouth of saliva congregated on his lips.

"It wasn't me-e-e, it was uncle-e-e," the little one sobbed.

From then on little girls constantly visited his imagination, and it was entirely the same to him whether they have round little rumps or ones like pears, whether they have breasts or just tiny nipples. The main thing was that they should be young kissie pie virgins — extremely sexy and obedient, inquisitive and seductive… Whatever you suggest — agreeable to everything. Just at the end you have to give them a chocolate, or a mandarin, or a little picture book…

But when Malva appeared, all the captive girls were trumped completely.

She first used to come just in those non-existent meetings and conversations, which he fantasized for the sake of his mother, but later one evening something happened that changed everything. Boobmlyakevych slid his hand under the covers and tried to summon from his imagination one particular little girl who lived nearby … He suggested to her to go on the roof to look at a star that was called Malva Landa…

"Malva Landa?" She whispered and eagerly followed him.

And there on the roof he hugged the little girl and randomly pointed his finger into the starry sky:

"There, do you see it? That star — that's Malva Landa."

"Oh, wow!" The little girl said, spellbound staring at the sky and entirely unaware of the fact that the hand of a grown up guy was petting her little round legs, petting her round little stomach, then taking off her little white underwear, with his lips falling to her round little bottom.

"Malva Landa!" The little girl utters, as if she were under hypnosis, and sets Boomblyakevych onto his knees, and the entire starry sky, the completely starry sky watched with thousands of pupils as they make love on the roof beside the cats and gutters…

But then suddenly a single star began to grow and grow and to shoot out rays, flying to them so so rapidly…

"My Lord!" Boomblyakevych shouted upon seeing that the star had turned into a queen and was standing on the chimney.

The queen was in a translucent tunic that fluttered in different directions in the wind, and her name was Malva. She moved close to the little girl, grabbed her by the skin as though she were a kitten, and flung her off the roof into the darkness.

"Now you are mine!" Malva said imperiously and forced Boomblyakevych to belong just to her…

Malva took him by the hand, and they flew off somewhere above the buildings, into the deep blue warm air of the night…

VII. PEARS A LA CREPE

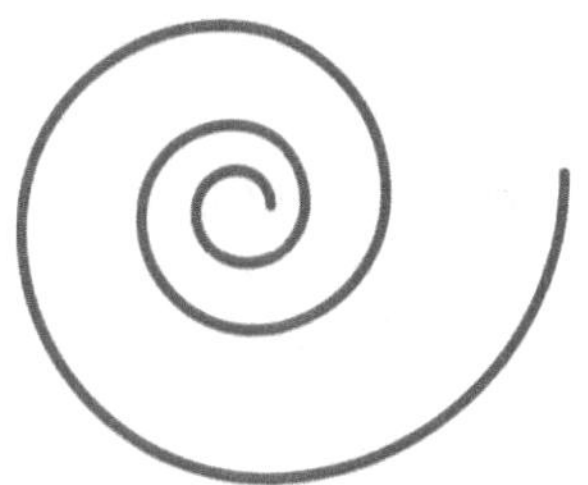

PEARS A LA CREPE

Waking up in the morning in Vynnyky on the outskirts of the city of Lviv, you don't hear either the piercing screeches of the tramcars or the rattling of cars on the cobblestones. Instead, the frolicsome chirping of birds, the buzzing of bees and the lazy cackling of chickens will tickle your still semi-somnolent ears. Every morning. And at night you'll fall asleep to the rhythmic croaking of frogs and the delicate chirring of crickets. I won't even speak about the dizzying scent of gillyflowers and lilac.

The sun's rays slowly penetrate through closed eyelids, and the gray cover of drowsiness crawls from your eyes to reveal this quiet sluggish world of the house. A morning like any morning. It could have been like countless other ones. But it wasn't. Because when I woke up, my sensitive ear caught someone's rhythmic breathing. Someone was lying next to me, and his warm breath in just barely perceptible waves touched my cheek. Who could it be? I strained my brain that was still mellow after sleep and suddenly came to the conclusion that it could only be a woman. If it were a man, then he would have been sleeping on another bed, because I'm not queer. So – it definitely had to be a woman. But my thoughts further ran into a solid wall. I couldn't remember at all where she had come from.

I tried to examine her, but this didn't give me anything, because her head was covered. For some reason I've only been lucky with girls who cover their heads in bed. Why they do that, I've never been able to figure out – for the simple reason that this happens with them completely subconsciously. Because when you ask a young lady why she always covers up her head, the very same answer resounds: "Really?"

Imagine – they are even surprised at this, the only thing they distinctly remember is what they're sleeping in. Women here are divided into two more or less identical halves: those who sleep in their panties, and those who don't. They have one answer to the question:

"I'm used to it like that." At least you can understand that habit. Therefore don't even try to re-educate them. It's the same as trying to teaching a cat to bring your slippers. A woman, when she gets used to something, won't part with that habit till death. One half of them before going to sleep won't take them off under any circumstances, the second won't ever put them on.

The young lady, who was snuffling next to me that day could have belonged to either half. To be honest, the ones who upset me the most are those who, after passionate lovemaking, slip on their panties as if they hadn't taken them off. I could never fathom what that's supposed to mean. That she's already accomplished her mission and the gates are closed for the night? That she's afraid I might rape her in the middle of the night? Or maybe, the underwear for her is something like a garland of innocence?

Is this one in her panties? I slipped my hand under the covers and felt a hot female body. My fingers touched her springy bottom and I sighed with relief. It wasn't enough that I finally remembered her. I lifted myself up on my elbows and looked around the room. Carefully folded jeans and a white tee shirt lay on an armchair. My clothes were scattered all over the floor. This was just like me. Sometimes I toss them on the table. This time the table was cluttered with bottles of champagne, Hungarian wine, *horilka*[*] and beer. O Lord! It's not odd that my memory was knocked out of me.

Was it just memory? Somehow I couldn't remember a single moment of sex from last evening. Did we make love at all? It was logical to assume yes, for when two people of the opposite sex lie in bed, it's not for discussing the latest decisions of our parliament. The quantity of empty bottles struck me. What was the occasion for the party? Where is everybody else? What were we doing all evening?

If the chairs and table were not in the middle of the room, but by the walls, then people must have been dancing. I glanced at my watch. Half past noon! Well… It's all clear. The party was till early morning. At six AM when the buses start running, the warm company made its way to the bus stop. It'd be interested knowing, did we make love

---

[*] Ukrainian vodka.

after that? It's hard to imagine that after an all-night party. I carefully crawled out from under the covers, grabbed my shirt from the floor and dragged myself to the bathroom. Neither hot nor cold water returned my memory to me. I still couldn't figure out who was lying in my bed. When I went to the kitchen, I fell into a stupor. Everything was clean and tidied up. The table was no longer littered in dishes, little boxes of seasoning and crumbs of bread, and the floor shined and glistened. And, as if this were not enough for total happiness, all the dishes used for yesterday's party shined and glistened.

That was 1992, when I turned forty, and I'm a bachelor again. After the regular concerts with the "Don't Worry!" comedy troupe, a cheery bunch often inundated my place, one that I had to see off the next day no earlier than lunchtime. But this regular flood of guests miraculously left behind itself a clean house. And, additionally, this time, a certain mystery person.

I boiled some coffee in a Turkish pot and, drinking it pensively, stubbornly tried to imagine the way she looked. Tall. I figured that out when I accidentally touched her stretched out leg. She doesn't snore. And sleeps without her undies. She hung her clothing carefully on the chair. Though in ecstasy she might have flung it onto a lampshade. And she undressed herself, because if I had undressed her, then everything would have not been hanging on the chair. In my opinion, too many positive qualities here. And once again we need to divide women into two halves. Those who get undressed themselves, and those who wait for you to undress them. The entire fact of the matter, however, is that even when you break it down, all the same you won't figure out who she is, your young lady. The fact that she doesn't undress herself, but shyly gives in to your hands, doesn't entirely mean that she's doing this for the first, second, third or eighth time. There are young ladies who just love it when you peel off all their husks, and are prepared to be in ecstasy from it for the one thousand and first time as much as the first. There are those among them who do this not from ecstasy, but to rouse you up, and when you ask them how many men they've had, you can have no doubt there will be a single answer: "You're my second." Therefore it's stupid to ask about such things. You won't hear the truth anyway.

And because, when she whispers to you in moments of tenderness: "Ah, how long it's been since I've done this," accept her words with gratefulness, as if you have no clue about anything else.

A young lady who undresses herself does this for two reasons: a) she doesn't give a damn about your sorry butt and doesn't care what you think about her, b) she doesn't give a rat's ass about you and doesn't want to play a dummy.

With great satisfaction I came to the conclusion that the young lady doesn't give a rat's ass about me, because if she did, she wouldn't have tidied up in the kitchen. Though this doesn't testify to her passionate feelings. Maybe just by nature she can't tolerate a mess. There are also these types. Mostly they turn out to be colleagues of my friends and, tidying up my kitchen, they're striving to make an impression not on me, but on the person they came with.

But it's one thing to tidy up the table, and another – to wash the floor. Maybe she doesn't love me, but to wash the floor, not giving a rat's ass about me, that's already pathological. I'll be damned, but I won't believe she loves me.

The only thing that bothered me was when did she have time to do this? And the further I thought about this, with even more dismay I comprehended this shameful picture for myself. But she didn't go to bed until after she had tidied up everything. That is very praiseworthy. This shows her best side. But if I don't remember it, it means I was sleeping. I conked out. And she, poor girl, finished this ordeal, and with hope took off her panties and lay down next to me. Maybe she even cuddled up, maybe she whispered something tender in my little ear. And I barely comprehended it. What a scoundrel I am! I grabbed my head with my hands and intensely got lost in thought. And what is there to think about here! Just now it dawned on my completely cleared up head: I was in my underwear. Well, that's it, I've disgraced myself forever. I have no justification. It's clear that the night passed full of chastity and lazy snoring.

And despair with such power shook my soul that I decided to do something nice for this girl. In my understanding of nice – something tasty. Breakfast in bed. And what do young ladies like for breakfast? From innumerable thickheaded men, who offer their young lady garlic sausage for breakfast, an omelet, fried potatoes or yesterday's Salad Olivier with a great big chunk of bread.

O horrors! O the wrath of God! This is an awful mistake, this is a blow to the system and the crashing of all expectations. With this kind of breakfast you can ruin everything that was built up over the evening and night. During the night you could have demonstrated the pinnacle of sexual prowess, and in the morning it will all go to waste. No! No! Three hundred times no!

Write this down, ignoramus. A person's life is given one time, and you have to live it in such a way that you don't ruin your future with one little breakfast. Therefore, the main this is: a young lady doesn't like to chew anything in the morning. No garlic sausage, ham, stuffed pig stomach, smoked lard, or macaroni. Breakfast has to be light and airy, it needs to melt in her mouth, run along her gums and not get stuck in her teeth. And with the first mouthful of coffee, her lips should overflow like the song of a Carpathian Hutsul woman over green mountain tops.

What doesn't get stuck in your teeth? Well? I ask you! For example, flat pancakes don't get stuck in your teeth, or filled rolled ones, and apples a la crepe. You whip up two eggs with a glass of milk, sugar and flour, you dip apple slices into the mix and then fry them in a frying pan, or bake the stuffed rolled pancakes and spread them all over with jam, preserves, fruits, marmalade, chocolate, with memories about last night, sunny little bunnies, and your own secretions. And here a sacred moment arises. At the first sounds of the awakening of your lady to active life, you carry in a tray with coffee, rolled pancakes or apples a la crepe to the room. This historical sight will never be effaced from her memory; she will carry a recollection of it throughout all the calamities of her life. And when she will be parting from this befouled world, from her darkened lips words will fly directed at her husband: "You never brought me apples a la crepe in bed." He, poor guy, will immediately give a start, will grab her by the shoulders and say: "Who! Who has done that for you? Who?!" In response he'll just get a bitter smile – the last one of her life.

I didn't have apples. But I did have juicy pears. But pears a la crepe – write this down! – are even more tasty than apples.

And this is how that morning began. I fried the pears in crepes, my young lady was sleeping in my bed, and it seemed that even the rumbling of an empty water truck wouldn't wake her.

Life was beautiful. The sunny morning filled my soul with inexpressible joy. I already imagined that after breakfast we'll again dive into bed, and then we'll gather up some food and something to drink and start off toward the lake.

I sifted through all the girls I knew in memory and tried to figure out which of them could have ended up in my bed. So it would be easier to figure out who my young lady was, I took my note pad and on a separate sheet wrote out all the names of my female colleagues, then I began to check them off one by one. Half of them abruptly dropped off the list, because I never would have invited them to my place even skunk drunk. Several other eligible bachelorettes looked at me like a serious target of attention, and to get them to bed I'd just need to put a stamp in their passport. In the worst case – I'd just need to go to the marriage registration office tomorrow.

I pondered. Did I need to go so far in my thirst for love? Who knows? At times you feel like saying something nice to a young lady. It ends with the fact that one wonderful morning you look into the kitchen and realize you're already married. Maybe this was just such a fatal morning.

I didn't want to believe it. I didn't believe it. That's why with a light heart I crossed off the eligible bachelorettes. Several individuals remained, whose appearance in my bed would have been most likely.

Here they are, in order of probability. Olyunya gets crossed off because she took off for the beach. I got into an argument with Maryana forever and we'll make up in a week when her parents run off to a resort. Vira exclusively spends her weekends with her fiancé. Lida came over last week without warning and ran into Marta, who peacefully was sunbathing in the garden, I don't even want to bring up how that ended. We'll cross both off the list. Lesya, Oksana and Ulyana were left.

On the table a full plate of pears a la crepe was steaming. I made fresh coffee, put it on the tray and concentrated. Who... Who... Who...

Oksana, may I kick the bucket right now, doesn't wash floors, that's already for sure. She'll sit around the entire evening, staring at the TV. Or she'll lie around. Ulyana doesn't undress herself. Not for anything will she do that in her life. Besides that, she always puts on her panties. That's her style. Well then, I'll cross them off.

Lesya's left. My God! What a scoundrel I've been in the way I treat her! How many times I've deceived her, led her on, made promises. One time I even prattled on about love. And she believed me. She's generally trusting and a very kind person. I'm just not worthy of her. I suddenly felt like falling on my knees before her, kissing her feet and begging forgiveness. For just everything. Even for this too.

She! Just she could be an ideal wife. She talks so little. That's it, enough of these adventures for me, this disorder, unwashed dishes, scandalous stories and explanations of my relations with their husbands, who, thanks to me, grow buck horns. That's it. I'll look in right away and say. What will I say? Damn… Let's get married, what do you say? No, not that way. First I should repent. I'll tell her everything. No, that'll take too long. I'll tell her in general terms. Without naming names. And I'll burn my notepad completely. Oh! What an idea! I'll burn my notepad in front of her. It won't cost me much because I have one more. And then I'll tell her, say, let's… That is, we'll get married.

In the meantime the first sounds of her awakening echoed from the room. I immediately felt a fervent desire to end up next to her and embrace her hot, deeply stirred body.

And here I grab the tray and with a smile from ear to ear fly into the room.

"Lesya-baby!" I call out, all hot and bothered from the unexpected flash of thirst and love. "Look what I've brought you!"

And it was as if right at that moment Vesuvius erupted under my windows, it would have stunned me considerably less then if from under my snow-white covers there had shouted out to me not the angelic little head of Lesya-doll in golden curls, but the great big shaggy and bearded snout of Stefka Orobets.[*]

---

[*] A popular cabaret singer and comedic television personality in Lviv.

My knees were wobbly and I sensed I was losing my potency for the entire next week.

"Can you shut the hell up?! Steftsio thundered, scratching his broad chest with all five of his fingers.

"Ste… Steftsio!" I muttered. "Where did you come from?"

From my show "For you, Morons."

"But… why are you in my bed?"

"Because you, shithead, got sloshed and didn't want to put out sheets for me on the couch."

"But… why are you naked?"

"Because that's the way I sleep, you imbecile! And there's no reason to feel up my butt, you queer!"

"But who tidied up everything?"

"Leska."

"But where's she now?"

"She left with Orko."

"Who the hell is that? Why with Orko?"

"Because you, idiot, told her you're getting married. And invited her to your engagement party."

"Me?! I'm getting married?! To who?"

"Ask the champagne. And stop getting under my skin! What do you have there? Some kind of pancakes? What's with you – you couldn't fry me some garlic sausage with eggs? And where's last night's Salad Olivier?"

VIII. TANGO OF DEATH

SYNOPSIS OF YURI VYNNYCHUK'S
TANGO OF DEATH

Yuri Vynnychuk's new novel *Tango of Death* unfolds in two segments of time. In pre-war and WWII Lviv as well as in the chronological present. Four friends – a Ukrainian, a Pole, a German, and a Jew, whose fathers were members of the army of the Ukrainian National Republic and who were executed by firing squad in 1921 by the Bolsheviks, experience various adventures: they fall in love, enjoy life, solve the mysteries of an ancient manuscript, look for work, but also work at finding themselves. Despite numerous cataclysms, they never betray their friendship. They grow into adulthood at a time when Europe is already doomed. In lieu of their relatively happy pre-war life, significantly more serious difficulties ensue: the first Bolshevik and Nazi occupations, the war, and the seemingly unimaginable Shoah in these lands.

Ordeals and a cruel battle for survival lie ahead for the four friends. All four take part in the defense of Lviv in September 1936 against the Nazi army. After the Nazis retreat and "liberators" from the East enter the city, a true Dante's inferno begins. We find out what the so called "liberation" of the Western Ukrainians looked like, about the suffering they were forced to endure, about the mass executions by the Bolsheviks first of Polish officers and then of the Ukrainian intelligentisa.

In the novel a number of plot lines are masterfully interwoven: there is a contemporary interpretation of nearly unknown pages of Ukrainian history; an ancient manuscript, in which the mystery of eternal life is encoded; about the pitiful agents of the secret services who hunt for experts on ancient Arcanaumian culture; and about the horrors of the Yaniv concentration camp – an orchestra of prisoners and a tango of death.

One of the four friends, the Jew Josip Milker manages to survive both the Nazi and the Soviet concentration camps. And now he has just one aim: to convey the truth about the past, to resurrect it and to reunite hearts in love. Because when it seems you've survived your adventures for the day, you've already made love with a woman with whom you're once again enamored, that you have a foreboding feeling about future meetings, maybe, in fact, your soul has been reincarnated, and the traces of your former life have remained miraculously in your memory. The encoded Arcanaumian manuscripts will help you remember everything.

It is important to note that the main hero of the novel is also the multi-national and multi-cultured city of Lviv. In the novel there is a great amount of humor, many brilliant episodes that one can compare to the humor of Jaroslaw Hasek, but also a great amount of pain – because *Tango of Death* is also about the tragedy of the Jews of Galicia and the Holocaust. This undoubtedly is the first Ukrainian text that has appeared after Ukrainian independence in 1991, in which the Holocaust occupies a prominent place.

The Holocaust here isn't an end in itself. It is the occasion and the possibility to explore the depths of the nature of society, of European civilization, of crucial philosophical categories in general – of all of humanity.

If we speak about the very nature of the intrigue of *Tango of Death*, about its mystical overtones, everything is markedly even more complex. The great triumph of Vynnychuk the narrator is in the fact that we literally – to the very final(!) word – fail to understand the author's convention. We can't even guess how this finds expression in the end. The finale is unforeseen and striking.

High above snow is falling, crows are crowing, the trees are cracking from the cold, and somewhere far away snow is crunching beneath the boots of the killers. You can sense their approach in everything – somewhere off in the distance you can hear the threatening barking of dogs, which is different from the barking of village dogs; the barking increases in intensity, at the same time, crows, cawing loudly, dart into the air and fly off. Four young men are sitting in a hideout, listening to the barking; then, glancing at each other, they burn some kind of papers; smoke crawls out of the vent. Then they change into clean shirts and pray. They don't pray together, but each one separately, and their prayers are in different languages. The three of them sit down around a small plank table; a bundle of grenades is lying on the dark smooth surface; the hands of all three of them are lying nearby. They wait silently. There is no fear in their eyes. Each one is thinking his own thoughts.

The fourth one takes a violin into his hands, stands next to them and listens closely. The sound of the dogs barking is already above their heads; the fire in the hideout is burning out, and tiny sparks jump across the burnt documents and disappear in the air. Upstairs, the command demanding surrender can already be heard. The men don't react; their eyes are riveted to the grenades. They shudder just as they hear despairing women's voices appealing to them, cursing them, imploring. Their voices squeeze out tears from their eyes, but they refuse to give in; they know all too well what awaits them.

A hand with the bow touches a violin, and the melody of a tango resounds. Now the barking of dogs and human voices are forced to burst through that melody, and not only through the melody, but also through the singing – the four men are singing something really quietly. And then the hand of one of them stretches to the pile of grenades....

1

When we are young, we all are nobody, not even the greatest geniuses, whose careers and recognition await them in the future, come into this world not overly fit for it, that's why it's not unusual that after we get married, we find ourselves in certain ordeals that rarely end happily, and rather more often in the parting of ways. This was exactly the trap that Myrko Yarosh fell right into after he got married to the sweet and warm Roma after graduating from the university. He used to read the poetry of great poets aloud to her, and she pretended to listen, even straining her eyes and pursing her lips; and her face became so inspired that he fell in love with her more and more, thinking that she, in fact, had been created to listen spellbound to everything he would say, that entire heap of words, which he was falling in love with and which he was sinking into, as though into a quagmire, greedily swallowing air; and when during those readings she snuggled up to him and tickled his ear with her hot breath, he thought that the idyll would be eternal, and that both of them simply were destined to be married to each other. Feelings were taking over common sense, and from the moment they married, they started to live at Roma's parents' place, and that was the beginning of the end.

Two years of teaching and then part-time graduate school boded no joy, because if there wasn't any money, there'd be no money, and Roma's parents never denied themselves from reminding the young couple on every occasion that they were mooching off them. In the evening, after putting their little son to bed, Yarosh, with his books spread all over the kitchen, was writing his dissertation about the literature of Egypt, Babylon, Assyria, Sumeria, Arcanaumia, and the Hittite Kingdom, but the deeper he delved into the topic and dug up sources, the more his work seemed to be hopeless, because certain sources gave birth to other ones, and those – to yet others, and it was endless, forcing him to get lost in the labyrinths of different versions and often drawing conclusions by groping about in the dark; though everyone, who was working on this topic, was not dealing with a complete panorama of literary life back then, but just with fragments that miraculously managed to make their way to us, that miraculously had been decoded and read, but not all of them, because no one had grasped the Arcanumian* language, and an opinion about their literature had been formed from Hittite and Hurrian sources. And it was the latter issue that excited Yarosh so much that he cast aside all the remaining ones and took to decoding Arcanumian texts. Many scholars had tried to do this before him, but failed. Arcanumian cuneiform was unlike any other.

Finding time for his scholarly work just in odd moments, Yarosh seriously began to contemplate the sense of his family life. The stupid routine of work in school oppressed and tormented him; he was surprised at how it came to be that he had become a teacher despite the fact that he had hated that profession when he was still in school. He would come home tired, and the only thing that could motivate him to do scholarly work was wine. The first glass took away his daylong tension, the second freed his thoughts, tore off all the chains from them, and then his pen would begin to fly across the paper as though it were mad. Only it lasted for not more than about two hours, but then tedium would fatigue him, and he would lie down to sleep with his head filled with ancient hieroglyphs, clay tablets and papyruses; the complete disdain of his wife and in-laws of his scholarly work added to this feeling; they considered his work nonsense, a waste of time, but he would never complete his scholarly work, so he was, therefore, destined to pass through life as a simple school teacher. This became a kind of obligatory ritual to tear him away from his work and to send him to the store for bread, carry out the trash, fill up the water in a portable cistern when the water pipes would be turned off, awaken him before dawn so he can occupy a place in line for milk, ringed sausage,

---

* The Merriam-Webster Dictionary defines Arcanum as "mysterious or specialized knowledge, language, or information accessible or possessed only by the initiate." http://www.merriam-webster.com/dictionary/arcanum. Additionally it adds: "The word *arcanum* (pluralized as 'arcana') came from Latin *arcanus,* meaning 'secret,' and entered English as the Dark Ages gave way to the Renaissance. It was often used in reference to the mysteries of the physical and spiritual worlds, subjects of heavy scrutiny and rethinking at the time. Alchemists were commonly said to be pursuing the arcana of nature, and they sought elixirs for changing base metals into gold, prolonging life, and curing disease. The frequent association of the word with the alchemists' elixirs influenced the use of 'arcanum' for 'elixir.'"

cheese, sugar, and flour – it made no difference; it was just he who was made to run after everything when in the 1980s there was a shortage of nearly everything, and people turned into hunters for goods, scurrying through the city and saving his place in several different lines at the same time so that in each of them he would manage to buy a kilo of sugar or a packet of laundry powder, because they wouldn't give each person more than one, and he also had to keep vigil over the bookstores, where once a week they used to deliver new books; only a limited circle of people received information about that, so for at least an hour before the bookstore would open up after the "delivery of goods," he would occupy a place in line, and then dash into the place at the head of the crowd and be the first to grab a Kafka, Camus, Akutagava, Cortazar, Marquez, Borges, and their number was endless. For the sake of his sacred goal, Yarosh even started up a platonic love affair with one of the bookshop girls; he wasn't able to do anything more because she was one of those spinsters, who, as a result of years spent in loneliness in their everyday life, they become intolerable, capricious, and boring. Inviting her out for coffee, Yarosh was forced to listen to her expound on her life motto, an entire heap of those cunning prescriptions, with which he surrounded herself from every direction like warning flags; overall, her entire wardrobe, which was designed to hide all the protuberances of her body like a nun, was a warning flag, because she was waiting for "serious relationships;" "flirting didn't interest her," but "Mr. Myrko˙ is a very pleasant person," "you can trust him," "it seems to me sometimes that we've known each other for a really long time" – and a long, promising smile, one more little flag that began to gleam on the horizon, more, with a telling caution: "No one, no one, no one – just him alone." Yarosh looked at her pale white arms, covered with fine little red strands of hair, and began to imagine her legs, maybe just as hairy, and this even elicited the desire in him to research this continent not studied by anyone yet with all its hidden nooks; just the fact that he had far too little free time saved him from that research, so just going for coffee with her was entirely sufficient to

---

* Galician Ukrainian often uses the term "Pan" (Mr.) or "Pani" (Mrs.) with a person's first name in addressing someone as a sign of respect or unfamiliarity with that person.

sustain friendly relations and to acquire information about the arrival of new books.

Once when he finally went to sleep long past midnight, leaving his papers on the kitchen table, which late in the evening served as his office, and in the morning finding a hot frying pan on his papers spattered with grease, from which his father-in-law was scarfing down an omelet, liberally covered with scallions, blocking himself from the world with his newspaper, this turned out to have been the last straw for him. With unceremonious boldness, which he had never dared before, but with an obliging "excuse me," he plucked his papers from under the frying pan, shook them over the table in front of the astounded and delirious eyes of his father-in-law and left. Now he realized that he was standing before one inevitable dilemma – he needs to sacrifice something: either his family life, or his academic one. He chose the former. One morning, so as not to arouse any suspicion, he stepped out of the house to go to work the same way as any other day, although he still had to take his son to daycare as one of his regular duties. Parting with his little son was particularly painful for him. He knew he would be losing many pleasant moments in the future; because what he had planned would certainly ruin his familiar existing lifestyle once and for all, but he saw no other way out and, waiting for the house to be empty, he returned, and slowly, without rushing, gathered all his things, packed his books and papers and wrote a letter, in which he announced that he was going away forever. He'll send money for childcare at the beginning of every month. Then he phoned the school where he worked and announced to the principal that he was forced by virtue of various circumstances to quit his job.

"You can't just leave in the middle of the school year!" The principal was justifiably indignant.

"I have very serious reasons."

"Can I ask what they are?"

"Illness."

"An illness?" The principal grew concerned. "Is it that bad?"

"Unfortunately, the diagnosis isn't satisfactory," he repeated a phrase that he had heard in a movie and sighed.

"Well, that's to say... while you're undergoing treatment, we'll keep your job open...."

"No, no, treatments are useless... the illness is incurable, understand? There's no point."

"So where are you going? Do you have a new job?"

"No. I just want to live out the rest of the days left for me to my own satisfaction. Do you understand what I'm talking about?"

"Of course. That's very sensible. And really, why work like a mule... but you can leave your work service record with us... so your term of service remains uninterrupted... oh, what kind of work service is there now!... but all the same, so you don't have any problems... because if you end up at the police station, and they take an interest in your place of work... they'll tack on vagrancy... it's safer this way...."

"Of course. Thank you very much for your concern."

"You're welcome. And remember that our entire staff always took pride in you. And the children loved you. It will be hard for them without you."

After that he called a taxi and ended up on the other end of Lviv in Mayorivka.

V

The bazaar behind the Opera Theater was not only called Krakidaly,[*] but God only knows why, Paris. It never lost its importance or name even during the war. Lvivians sold all sorts of things there, forming two rows, and buyers walked back and forth between them – mostly Soviet officers, rank and file soldiers, government officials, as well as their wives, who here, "in Paris," turned into European ladies. Among the vendors you could meet theater actors too, bank directors, and distinguished professors – each one would bring out something from his or her home to sell, and each one would loudly praise his or her goods. Some needed money for food, and others collected money to bribe the liberators, to save someone assigned for deportation

---

[*] The local nickname for the bazaar, which historically was located on Krakivska (Krakow) Square behind the Lviv Opera House.

to Siberia. But the Krakidaly Bazaar drew people for yet one more reason – this was the place for socializing and a source of political news and rumors; here certain middlemen gadded about, who knew how to arrange for contact with the Cheka[*] secret police and with prison workers; here you could find out the latest news from the London radio and the date and time of the next militia roundup, buy a German passport, and find someone to guide you across the border.

At the market from morning till evening shouts echoed of "Liquor, booze, hootch," "Bachevsky, Bachevsky, Bachevsky!," "Booze, booze, booze!," "Local liquor and imported stuff!," "Saccharin pastilles! Real Wodka Wyborowa!"[**] One cheerful man shouted out at the top of his voice: "Selling a cure for bedbugs, fleas, cockroaches, and all kinds of utter bastards. Death to fleas, death to male lice and female ones too!" Soon after that a fellow approached him and wanted to know whom he had in mind when his mention of "all kinds of utter bastards" disappeared.

The enterprising Lviv women collected a great big heap of shining multi-colored buttons, crowns, ribbons, belts, gloves for cotillions, artificial flowers, colored hairclips and combs, décolleté night shirts and robes – and they carried out all this to sell to the greedy Soviet ladies, who had never seen such miracle-wonders. Besides what they had collected from their houses, the Lviv ladies also sold what they had made themselves, because there was not a single lady of the house who didn't know how to bake tortes, sheet cakes, and cookies, and it wasn't surprising that at the Krakidaly Bazaar you could see Mrs. Professor,[***] and Mrs. Learnedbarrister, and Mrs. Haughtypants herself, who, without any complaining, peddled their goodies. Ah, how the ladies from the Soviet paradise savored them! Each year you

---

[*] The Cheka (*Chrezvychainaia komisiia*, meaning "extraordinary commission") was established by Vladimir Lenin in 1917 and was the first of several iterations of the Soviet secret police.

[**] One of the oldest and most popular brands of Polish vodka, the production of which began in 1823. Its name means "select vodka."

[***] It was common in Halychyna (Galicia) for married women to be addressed with the title of her distinguished husband's profession. E.g., *Pani* (Mrs.) Profesor, *Pani* Doktor, etc.

would notice the chomping traps of the officers' babes bespattered with cream and crumbs.

Milya peddled her mother's cookies and even grumbled about doing that:

"Because of this Krakidaly Bazaar I just get fat and nothing more. 'Cause when no one buys the cookies, and I'm bored, I eat them. And then momma complains that she doesn't feel bad about the cookies, but she doesn't see any money from it."

So it's not strange that the Soviets, after they just arrived in Lviv, immediately got interested in how to get to the Krakidaly Bazaar, or rather, as they said it, "to Krakadily" [The Crocodiles], because here they could buy wonderful things really cheaply, and they, acquiring used European suits and coats, quick as a wink changed their clothes at the gate, and only then would walk out into the city, but that didn't save them from crooks, who promptly figured out the ignorance of the liberators, sold them the most wide-ranging, odd, useless stuff, convincing them of its exceptional value. The four of us joined in with this profitable gesheft.* Yash managed to get enema pipes and plastic covers for rubber syringes from the drugstore, which had been smashed to bits during a bombing,; all these devices had a small valve, which allowed you to open and close the flow of liquid from a vessel. As first we weren't able to comprehend Yash's idea, but he convinced us that the goods were first class, and had to sell, if we were going to market those pipes to the Red Army boys as an outstanding achievement of contemporary technology in the field of smoking. And it happened that we tried to convince them, explaining how such a "mouthpiece" for smoking, perfected by world science, twisted with a valve in various directions before the eyes of the bewildered solider.

"Here's some great technolology! If you want to – you smoke, if not – you don't."

After he said that, the soldiers gleefully and with fascination smoked the newspaper roll-ups with reeking cheap tobacco jammed into the "mouthpieces," continuously turning those little valves. After

---

* In multicultural Lviv it was common for German, Polish, Yiddish, and other foreign words to be adopted into the local dialect of Ukrainian. "Gesheft" comes from the German word "Geschäft," which means business or deal.

the supply of our little pipes was gone, we managed to sell more than ten printing machines as a form of technology for printing money. We did this, of course, in semidarkness, so the client wouldn't guess he's being duped. Afterward Yash related that at Lucia's place he discovered a large box with broken watches and alarm clocks that were left after her watchmaker grandfather had passed away. Wolfe took an interest in that news and had a burning desire to sell the treasure.

"But who will you sell a watch to that doesn't work?" We asked.

"To just about anybody," Wolfe said. "Oddly it's enough to break off the second-hand so it doesn't get in our way, then you lift the watch up to the soldier boy's ear and click your teeth. Like this: click-click-click!"

"Well, just look out that it doesn't click you," Yosko started to laugh, and we agreed to keep an eye on this activity of Wolfe's, promising to join in if the business worked well. And what do you think? It worked! And how it did work! It's possible, maybe difficult, for someone to believe, but imagine a person who never had a watch and never heard one ticking. One should say that the Soviets were just wild about watches; true, they had a very unique notion about beauty and reckoned that a watch must be big, the bigger the better, that's why they wore impressive onions, while some even tied up alarm clocks on their wrists by rolling up their sleeves, so others could see what a lost braggart they could be.

One day an extraordinary event happened. Golda rushed over to us gasping and told us that a corpse was lying in their house. My mother just threw up her hands, and my granny immediately poured some kind of herb into boiling water to give frightened Golda something to drink, because she couldn't catch her breath at all and kept waving her scarf near her face. From those fragments of phrases that she screamed out and whispered, we understood just one thing: the body belonged to an NKVD* guy, who on more than one occasion had tried to court Leah, and now he tracked down when she would be alone in the house and tried to force himself on her. But Leah, defending herself, smacked

---

* The Russian initials for the Soviet secret police, The Peoples Commissariat for Internal Affairs.

him with a pan over the head, but the fact that she smacked him not with the bottom, but the side, it cut through his temple. He lay there like a flat cake, an elongated one, with his mug covered in blood and not breathing. Golda and Yosko found him right in that unattractive position after they had returned from the store. Again everyone's gaze was directed my way, allowing me to understand that my role as savior had not yet been consummated, and new achievements and new ordeals await me.

"Well, what then," I sighed. "Go there and wait for me, and I'll run over to Mr. Knoflyk. Maybe this time he'll be able to save us.

At Mr. Knoflyk's funeral establishment a red flag was flapping, and on the sign a fresh inscription could be seen: "Red Kharon."*

"What do you think?" Mr. Knoflyk nodded in the direction of the sign. "That's my *oberih*** protective charm now. More than one soldier boy has peeked in here and asked in Russian: "Where can I find comrade Kharon?" I always answered in the same way: "Comrade Kharon's at a meeting in Moscow." And I'm left in holy peace. And in a few days some Soviet Jewish guy dragged himself over and asked in Russian: "Isn't that Grisha Kharon, who was the director of the Zhytomyr NKVD?" I nodded. Then he says: "Say 'hello' to him. If you have any problems, I'm in the State Supply Office. I deal with all issues."

"But I've come to you again regarding a very delicate matter," I quieted my voice, and Mr. Knoflyk immediately took me to his office and got ready to listen to me. "Golda Milker has got into a new mess, this time because of her daughter. When a certain NKVD guy came to visit her, Leah decided to treat him with an omelet. She took a frying pan in her hands and just as she intended to put it on the stove, the NKVD guy got a burning desire to hug her, but he slipped on a spot of cooking oil and cracked his head on the side of the frying pan. He

---

* Kharon is the Ukrainian and Russian word for Charon/Kharon, the Greek ferryman of Hades.

** The *oberih* in the Ukrainian folkloric tradition is usually a handmade charm made of straw, dried flowers, and other items from nature that is placed in the house to protect the hearth from evil.

was so unlucky that now he's lying belly up, and his spirit is wandering somewhere over Vysoky Zamok.*

"Uf!" Mr. Knoflyk wagged his head. "Now that's a mess! We have to bury him properly. And you're incredibly lucky, because at the moment I have a really comfortable coffin – a deep and wide one. We prepared it for his Grace, who was at his deathbed, and was really obese, so fat, that he wouldn't fit through this door. But he changed his mind about dying and he's kicking, and wolfing down honey nut pastries with marzipan. And the coffin is just sitting there. You know what we'll do? We'll put your guest on the bottom, and on top – Mrs. Topolska. I'd guess he wouldn't mind if he has to lie under a lassie?"

"Of course not! He was quite a guy on the make. He couldn't pass up a single skirt."

"Well, that's super. You just bring him here to me."

"Wait a minute, will Mrs. Topolska's family have a problem with this?"

"What family? She doesn't have a family. She was a single lassie, a spinster, but she had a lot of foresight and didn't forget to set aside money for her funeral. In her will she wrote: "I want to lie comfortably, with lots of room and on a soft bed." All three requests will be honored. But tell me: was that guy of yours in a military uniform?"

"Sure, and with a pistol too."

"Then you have to get a suit for him. Over here in a box is Mr. Tsepa's beautiful suit. When they put it on him, it burst at the seams in the back, and the family decided to buy him another one, though I tried to convince them that for Mr. Tsepa it played no role, because no one in this world now will see his back. But they, do you know what they answered me: and how about in the other world? And I shut my trap. So take it,- and he shoved the package in my hands, but still didn't let go of it because the thought came to him that it would be worth putting makeup on our guest – what if along the way I meet one of his buddies, so Mr. Knoflyk also gave me a red beard, a gray hairpiece, and a box with paints for his kisser.

---

* Vysoky Zamok (meaning "high castle") is the highest point in Lviv, a wooded mountain peak overlooking the city that is a popular spot for local Lvivians and visitors to the city. It once had a castle on top of it in the 13th century.

What can I tell you! The deceased looked better now than he did in life. His former high-cheekboned snout, covered in blood, having become lamblike, suited the image of an old uncle, calmed-down and satisfied with his former life; the black suit suited him, perfectly tailored, and a white rose stuck out of his breast pocket. His black glasses completed the picture, and when "unc" found himself in the wheelbarrow that Yosko and I were pushing straight ahead as we were whistling, all the passersby politely nodded their heads, smiled, and some even took off their hats because "unc" looked like he was alive, and it would be a sin not to give a greeting to such a pleasant type. Even Mr. Knoflyk admired him and smacked his lips with satisfaction. He helped us pull out the corpse from the wheelbarrow and put it in the coffin. Nearby Mrs. Topolska was waiting for her turn on a table. She had some meat on her and was dressed in a dark-blue dress with white lace. One could see that she had prepared it especially for such a solemn moment. Her wax-like fingers were holding a small icon, and her dry, strongly pursed lips resembled ones that had never been kissed. Just as I thought about this when suddenly all our hairs, except Mr. Bouchek's, stood on end, and Mr. Knoflyk clutched at his heart, because our "unc" suddenly came alive and sat up in the coffin. He held onto the sides with his hands and surprisingly looked around everywhere, without comprehending where he had ended up. Then he felt over his face, took off his glasses, looked all around one more time, and muttered:

"Where the heck am I?"

Exchanging glances with Yosko I had already begun looking all over for some kind of good cudgel to send off "unc" back in the very same direction, in which his sinful soul was moving, but somehow the old devil had been turned back, so as to give us even more grief, but Mr. Knoflyk stopped me:

"Wait," and then turned to address "unc": "We found you unconscious on the street. Do you remember who you are and where you live?"

The NKVD guy shook his head and began to search through his pockets, though there was nothing in them.

"Did I have documents on me?" He asked in Russian.

"No," we answered simultaneously. "There wasn't anything. Maybe you got away from the hospital.

"From which hospital?"

"We've got a hospital where they keep people like you who've lost their memory."

"No, I don't remember anything. What's happened – have I died?" He asked in Russian.

Here Mr. Knoflyk delightfully rubbed his hands together and dialed the number of the Kulpark Mental Hospital and informed them that they should come and pick up a crazy guy who had certainly must have scampered off from them.

"We'll come for him right away," they whispered to us.

"Can I lie down a bit more?" The "deceased" asked in Russian and again lay down in the coffin, crossing his arms over his chest. That is how the hospital attendants, who had come from the loony bin, found him. Mr. Knoflyk told them that we picked up this man when he was unconscious, thinking he was dead, but he came to life and now had lost his memory. The doctors bent over the coffin and nodded their heads:

"We know him. That's the dummy Hilko. He escaped from us about five years ago. Well then, get up," they started to make whooping sounds at him.

The NKVD guy sat up again and, dumbstruck, passed his eyes over those present:

"Wha-a-at's my name?" He asked in Russian.

"Don't play dumb, Hilko, 'cause I'll stick you with a needle right now that'll make you remember the time your granny was a young maiden," one of the attendants said. With those words they lifted him up out of the coffin, grabbed him under his arms, quickly dressed him in a straight jacket, and dragged him to a car without any windows. The NKVD guy screamed out something indistinct, but no one was paying attention to him at that point.

"Aha," Mr. Knoflyk concluded. "Our Mrs. Topolska has lost her boyfriend. As in life she was never underneath a guy, and so in death she won't lie on top of him."

———

CONTENTS

The Complete Correspondence of
HRYHORY SKOVORODA

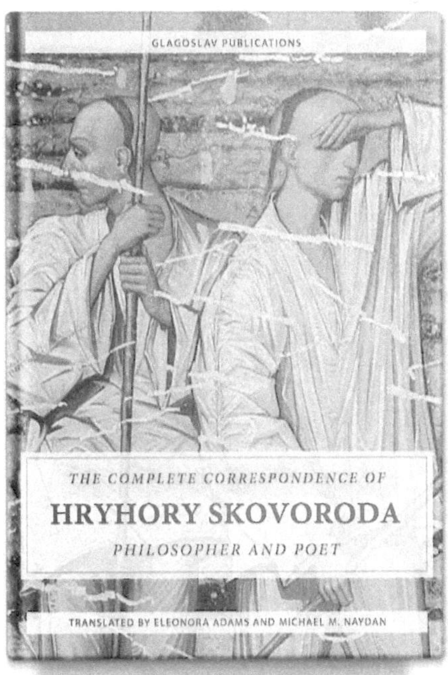

The religious philosopher and poet Hryhory Skovoroda (1722-1794) is described by many as the Ukrainian Socrates and was one of the most learned men of his time. He was a polyglot who knew the Bible virtually by heart, as well as the writings of the Church Fathers and the literature of Greek and Roman antiquity. The eminent literary critic Ivan Dziuba considers Skovoroda the greatest Ukrainian mind ever. And Yuri Andrukhovych, one of the most prominent Ukrainian writers of today, calls him "the first Ukrainian hippie" on account of his itinerant lifestyle and rejection of worldly life. The impact of Skovoroda's life and works has been well documented on major writers in future generations, such as Leo Tolstoy, Andrei Bely and Pavlo Tychyna, to name but a few.

None of Skovoroda's works appeared during his lifetime – they were first published in 1837 in Moscow. The texts of Skovoroda's writings were preserved mostly by Skovoroda's lifelong friend Mykhailo Kovalynsky, to whom he had given the manuscripts. Skovoroda's extant writings consist of a collection of thirty poems entitled *The Garden of Divine Songs* along with other occasional poems, a collection of fables entitled *Kharkiv Fables*, which was published in 1990, and seventeen philosophical treatises. Most of the treatises were composed during the latter part of his life.

Buy it > www.glagoslav.com

Herstories: An Anthology
Of New Ukrainian Women Prose Writers

Women's prose writing has exploded on the literary scene in Ukraine just prior to and following Ukrainian independence in 1991. Over the past two decades scores of fascinating new women authors have emerged. These authors write in a wide variety of styles and genres including short stories, novels, essays, and new journalism. In the collection you will find: realism, magical realism, surrealism, the fantastic, deeply intellectual writing, newly discovered feminist perspectives, philosophical prose, psychological mysteries, confessional prose, and much more.

You'll find an entire gamut of these Ukrainian women writers' experiences that range from deep spirituality to candid depictions of sexuality and interpersonal relations. You'll find tragedy and humor and on occasion humor in the tragedy. You'll find urban prose, edgy, caustic, and intellectual; as well as prose harkening back to village life and profound tragedies from the Soviet past that have left marks of trauma on an entire nation. This is a collection of Ukrainian women's stories, histories that serve to tell her unique stories in English translation. Substantial excerpts from novels and translations of complete shorter works of each author will give the reader deep insight into this burgeoning phenomenon of contemporary Ukrainian women's prose.

Buy it > www.glagoslav.com

Glagoslav Publications Catalogue

- The Time of Women by Elena Chizhova
- Sin by Zakhar Prilepin
- Hardly Ever Otherwise by Maria Matios
- Khatyn by Ales Adamovich
- Christened with Crosses by Eduard Kochergin
- The Vital Needs of the Dead by Igor Sakhnovsky
- A Poet and Bin Laden by Hamid Ismailov
- Kobzar by Taras Shevchenko
- White Shanghai by Elvira Baryakina
- The Stone Bridge by Alexander Terekhov
- King Stakh's Wild Hunt by Uladzimir Karatkevich
- Depeche Mode by Serhii Zhadan
- Herstories, An Anthology of New Ukrainian Women Prose Writers
- The Battle of the Sexes Russian Style by Nadezhda Ptushkina
- A Book Without Photographs by Sergey Shargunov
- Sankya by Zakhar Prilepin
- Wolf Messing - The True Story of Russia`s Greatest Psychic
  by Tatiana Lungin
- Good Stalin by Victor Erofeyev
- Solar Plexus by Rustam Ibragimbekov
- Don't Call me a Victim! by Dina Yafasova
- A History of Belarus by Lubov Bazan
- Children's Fashion of the Russian Empire by Alexander Vasiliev
- Empire of Corruption - The Russian National Pastime
  by Vladimir Soloviev
- Heroes of the 90s - People and Money. The Modern History of Russian
  Capitalism
- Boris Yeltsin - The Decade that Shook the World by Boris Minaev
- A Man Of Change - A study of the political life of Boris Yeltsin
- Gnedich by Maria Rybakova
- Marina Tsvetaeva - The Essential Poetry
- Multiple Personalities by Tatyana Shcherbina
- The Investigator by Margarita Khemlin
- Leo Tolstoy – Flight from paradise by Pavel Basinsky
- Moscow in the 1930 by Natalia Gromova
- Prisoner by Anna Nemzer
- Alpine Ballad by Vasil Bykau
- The Complete Correspondence of Hryhory Skovoroda
- The Garden of Divine Songs and Collected Poetry of Hryhory Skovoroda

  More coming soon...